Other Crooked Lake mysteries by Robert W. Gregg

DEATH COMES ON SILVER WINGS

A CROOKED LAKE MYSTERY

ROBERT W. GREGG

ISBN 978-0-7414-8439-0 Paperback
ISBN 978-0-7414-8440-6 eBook
Library of Congress Control Number: 2013906175

Printed in the United States of America

Published September 2013

INFINITY PUBLISHING

Toll-free (877) BUY BOOK
Local Phone (610) 941-9999
Fax (610) 941-9959
Info@buybooksontheweb.com
www.buybooksontheweb.com

As with my other Crooked Lake mysteries, I owe a debt of gratitude to many others who have helped to make the book possible. I am particularly indebted to Cam Dunlap, a veteran Cessna pilot who graciously shared his knowledge and experience with me; Melissa Brassell, a forensic pathologist whose advice has once more been invaluable; Mark Milner, my cardiologist, who called my attention to a drug called Florinef; David Scull, my attorney, who patiently explained the ins and outs of estate planning to me; Steve Knapp, a photographer who once again has contributed a colorful cover for the book; Brett Steeves, who has magically tucked a falling plane into the photograph on the book's cover; and Kurt Foster, a software engineer who has bailed me out where I lacked computer savvy. If there are errors of fact or logic in the book, they are mine alone.

This book is dedicated to my good friend
and editor par excellence, Lois Gregg

PROLOGUE

Rosalind Seivers waded out into the lake, pushing the pedal boat ahead of her. The water on her feet was delightfully cool, not quite 80 degrees but comfortably above 75. She took three more steps and then swung her legs over the side of the boat. Her feet engaged the pedals and in no time she was beyond the dock and heading for deeper water.

The beds in the cottage were unmade, the breakfast dishes still in the sink, and she had yet to give any thought to lunch. But the spectacular weather virtually demanded that she forget her chores and have some fun. What is more, she had the morning to herself. Len had taken the twins to a miniature golf course, and it was doubtful that they would be back until noon.

On a beautiful day like this, she would inevitably be sharing the lake with others. She could see a Sunfish over near the bluff, and two water skiers were also in sight, one a veritable whirling dervish, the other a novice, straining to remain upright. But for the moment they were far enough away that she thought it safe to remove the top to her bathing suit and pretend that she had the lake to herself. Len would tell her to cover up, but he was twenty miles and more than half an hour away. She dropped the small green and gold bra on the bench beside her, enjoying the thrill that came with this impulsive act of vacation bravado.

It was the third summer in a row that they had rented the old fishing cottage on Rainbow Point, and the first of the three that had rewarded them with near perfect weather. The last two unseasonably chilly and rainy Julys had almost persuaded them to try someplace else, but they had convinced themselves that the law of averages would prevail. And it had. Rosalind stopped pedaling and leaned back, her eyes studying a row of cumulus clouds which seemed to be marching across the bluff in an otherwise clear blue sky.

The sound of an engine caught her attention and she looked around to see if a powerboat was approaching her from the direction of West Branch. There was no one anywhere near the pedal boat, and it was quickly apparent that the sound she was hearing was coming from the sky, not the water. The seaplane was still over a mile away, but it was heading down the lake in her direction and flying at no more than five hundred feet above the lake surface. Probably a small charter that took people for a ride around the lake.

Rosalind watched it approach, imagining what a wonderful view of the lake and the surrounding fields and vineyards she would have if she were its passenger. There came a moment when it occurred to her that she would also be among the attractions visible to anyone on the plane. She picked up her bathing suit top and busied herself covering her breasts.

The small plane was on a path that would take it almost directly over her. It was at almost the exact second that she succeeded in fastening the hook on her bra that she realized that the plane was heading for a landing on the water. She stopped pedaling, worried that the pilot may not have seen her. The plane roared past her, now in what looked like a steep dive. And then it happened, so suddenly and so close to the pedal boat that Rosalind was frozen in disbelieving shock. The plane struck the water and appeared to flip over, its pontoons stripped off by the force of the impact. It took her some time to snap out of it, to process the information that she had been terribly lucky, and that somebody else, perhaps more than one somebody else, would no longer be enjoying this beautiful summer day.

CHAPTER 1

It is doubtful that it will ever be known just exactly how many of Crooked Lake's residents actually saw the crash of the small Cessna. Certainly more than a hundred, probably many more. Kevin Whitman was one of them. He had kissed Carol good-bye, slipped on a pair of bathing trunks, and gone for a leisurely swim. It was while he was toweling off on the dock that he first saw the plane, its sleek silver fuselage reflecting the bright morning sun. Kevin's flying experience had been limited to commercial air liners, but as he watched the plane approach it occurred to him that maybe he should talk with Carol about taking a local charter flight. The idea intrigued him for a few short seconds before the plane suddenly began a sharp descent toward the lake and then plowed into the water at a steep angle not far below Blue Water Point.

Kevin had attended air shows, including one on Crooked Lake, which locals referred to, with some justification, as the cradle of aviation. He didn't know what had happened to the Cessna, but he did know that what he had just witnessed was no aerial stunt. It was a serious accident.

His first thought was to jump into the canoe and paddle out to the site of the crash. Bad idea. Lake residents with power boats would reach the plane well before he did, and they would be in a better position to help, if indeed whoever was in the plane could still be helped. No, what he needed to do was call Carol. Others might also think to call the sheriff, but it was unlikely that that would be their first impulse. He knew nothing about the protocol for handling aircraft accidents, but Carol, as sheriff in this jurisdiction, would surely be involved, and she needed to know that a plane had crashed into the lake and she needed to know it right away.

Kevin sprinted back to the cottage, shedding the towel as he ran and leaving a trail of wet footprints across the deck and into the study.

"Cumberland County Sheriff's Department, Ms. Franks speaking. How may I -"

Kevin interrupted her.

"JoAnne, this is Mr. Whitman and I have to talk to Carol. It's urgent."

"Oh, my goodness, are you all right?"

"Yes, I'm fine," he said, trying to keep his impatience out of his voice. "Please, is she there?"

"Of course. Just a second."

It took almost a minute. Where had Carol gone?

"You okay? JoAnne said you sounded upset." She sounded out of breath.

"There's been an accident on the lake. One of those pontoon planes went down not far south of our cottage."

"You saw it? It wasn't just a bad landing?"

"Definitely not. It crashed and flipped over. I figured you'd want to know."

"How long ago did this happen?" Kevin knew his wife. She was worried. Very worried.

"Minutes, no more than three, maybe four." He was standing by the window, watching as several boats closed the distance to the stricken plane. "Quite a few people must have seen it happen, because there's a small armada on its way to help."

"Can you pinpoint where it went down? I've got to get in touch with Parsons, hope he's got the patrol boat somewhere not too far away."

"It's no more than half a mile south of the cottage, a little closer to the bluff."

"Good. Stay near the phone." Carol hung up.

Kevin went back out onto the deck, the better to observe the attempted rescue. He shared Carol's hope that the patrol boat wasn't way down by Southport or up near Yates Center.

Fortunately, the patrol boat was reasonably close, over on the east branch but not far north of the end of the bluff. Officer Parsons spun the boat around and he and his partner, Officer Damoth, headed full throttle for the Cessna. They weren't the first to reach it. Five boats of assorted makes and sizes were already there, and at least that many more were on the way.

The Cessna was belly up, its pontoon apparatus askew. The pilot and his passengers, if he had any, appeared to be trapped under water. A boater who had dived into the lake, hoping to effect a rescue, popped back to the surface.

"I can't unfasten his seat belt," he announced, gasping for air.

Parsons breathed a small sigh of relief. Apparently only the pilot was on board. He proceeded to take command.

"Everybody stay back," he yelled as he maneuvered the patrol boat closer to the plane. "Okay, Jim, over the side. Quick."

Damoth tore off his shoes, tossed them and his gun into the bottom of the boat, and jumped into the lake. The men in the other boats, who had been engaged in heated speculation about the situation confronting them, fell silent. All eyes were focussed on the Cessna. First Damoth and then the other diver emerged briefly, filled their lungs, and disappeared again.

The attempt to rescue the pilot was doomed from the beginning. Releasing him from his harness had not been easy, and after nearly ten minutes of submersion in the waters of Crooked Lake, it was obvious that he could not be alive. What was not known, or knowable at the time, was whether he had been killed when the plane crashed or had drowned when it flipped over.

Eventually, with the help of other boaters, the pilot's body was brought to the surface. For another ten minutes Parsons and Damoth did their futile best to resuscitate him. They knew it was too late, but they also knew it was what they had to do.

Parsons had recognized the pilot as soon as he was brought to the surface. It was Gil Mobley, who'd been flying around the lake for years. They had not been friends, yet Bill experienced an almost unbearable sadness as he eased Mobley's body into the well of the patrol boat and covered it with his jacket. Damoth was tasked with staying with the Cessna, and an eager young man named Billy Jackson was persuaded to let his boat be used as Damoth's command post.

"I'm coming in," were Parsons' words to the sheriff as he pulled away from the plane and the small flotilla of boats that surrounded it. "The pilot's dead, I'm afraid. It's Gil Mobley. Meet me in West Branch and have an ambulance at the dock."

———

"What now?" Carol directed her question to Officer Grieves in the passenger seat beside her. But she didn't really expect an answer. They were half way from the office in Cumberland to the patrol boat dock, and the sheriff was uncomfortably aware of how little she knew about how to deal with the problem confronting her.

Grieves looked puzzled.

"I suppose we'll be getting the details from Bill," he said.

"I know, but that's not what I mean. Truth of the matter is I don't have a clue just what we're supposed to do. About the accident, that is. The manual doesn't say a thing about plane crashes. A car accident, we know the drill. But a pilot has a heart attack, loses control, the plane hits the water, then what?"

"You think he had a heart attack?"

"I have no idea, but what else could it have been. A seizure of some sort, something that killed him or made it impossible for him to fly the plane. Those little Cessnas don't just fall out of the sky, and I can't imagine an experienced pilot like Mobley deliberately doing something stupid."

"Did you know Mobley?"

"Met him a time or two, but no, I didn't know him. But he had a good reputation, been flying for years."

"Anyway, the ambulance will be there," Grieves said, as if to assure his boss that she'd done all she could.

"Sure, we'll take care of the body." Carol shook her head as she thought about yet another lake tragedy. "But what are we supposed to do with the plane? Tow it to shore? What if it sinks on us? Just whose case is it? There's bound to be more people with an interest in something like this than our little department. I've got a hunch it'll be the feds, like maybe the FAA."

"What's that?" Grieves asked.

"Federal Aviation Agency. I'll have to make a few calls, get Byrnes to make some inquiries, see if he can figure out who's got jurisdiction. One thing's for sure, we can't let that plane just sit out there in the lake. It'll attract boaters, probably swimmers, too. Could be a real hazard, and I don't want anybody else hurt. Bill says Damoth's keeping the crowd at bay, but that won't be easy."

The dock that the sheriff's department patrol boats used was little more than a small beachhead in an otherwise busy commercial waterfront south of West Branch. From the state highway there was nothing to suggest that the forces of law and order in Cumberland County had a privileged position in this network of docks and boats. There was no paved road down to its dock, just a gravel apron, roughly twenty yards wide and perhaps two hundred feet in depth. Today there were four cars and an ambulance parked on it. The ambulance had backed up next to the dock and two men were in the process of maneuvering a loaded stretcher onto it as Carol turned onto the parking apron.

She and Grieves hurried down to the dock, where a small crowd of onlookers had gathered. The patrol boat typically came and went throughout the day, occasioning little excitement. But the appearance of the ambulance made it clear that something unusual was happening, with the result that quite a few people who were otherwise occupied on the West Branch waterfront had taken notice and come to see what the problem was. The problem, of course, was that Officer Parsons had arrived with the victim of the crash of the Cessna. Gil Mobley's body was being transferred from the boat to the ambulance which would take him to the hospital in Yates Center.

"There's no question, I take it," Carol said to Parsons. "He's dead?" Carol knew the answer to her question. Bill Parsons was one of her most senior and experienced officers. She had asked simply because the crash of the plane and the death of its pilot were so unprecedented on Crooked Lake, so unbelievable, that she was still experiencing cognitive dissonance.

Parsons ignored her question, as she had expected him to.

"I hate that damned *Lulu Belle*," he said. "If ever we needed her, it's now. Can't leave Damoth out there on somebody else's boat."

Carol hated the fact that her men insisted on calling one of their two patrol boats *Lulu Belle*. More importantly, she hated it that *Lulu Belle* was in a neighboring marina undergoing work on a balky engine. A chronically balky engine.

"We'll have to make do with the *Daisy Mae*," she said. *Daisy Mae*, a feeble attempt to make their other patrol boat sound more like a pleasure craft than an enforcer of law and order on Crooked Lake.

The process of transferring the victim of the plane crash to the ambulance had just been completed when a midnight blue Mercedes turned sharply onto the parking apron and made an ill-advised and reckless trip down toward the dock where Parsons and the sheriff were talking.

"Where is he?" demanded a tall blond woman as she stepped out of the Mercedes almost as soon as it had come to a complete stop. She was wearing a skin tight pair of jeans, a red blouse, and Foster Grants sun glasses that made it hard to read her face. Forty, forty-five, Carol thought. She didn't think she'd ever seen the woman before.

"I'm sorry, but I don't think I've had the pleasure," she said.

"I want to see him. Where is he?" The woman in the Foster Grants stopped suddenly and focussed her attention on the sheriff. "What did you say?"

"I asked who you are. We don't seem to have met."

"No, I suppose we haven't. I'm Suzanne Mobley. Where is my husband?"

Yes, of course. The pilot's wife. But how can she possibly have heard so soon about the plane crash or that her husband's body would have been brought to West Branch?

"You've heard what happened to the plane?" As she asked it, Carol realized that it was a dumb question.

"Of course. Why do you suppose I'm here?"

"Mrs. Mobley, I'm so very sorry about what happened to your husband."

"Oh, for God's sake, where is he?"

Parsons, aware that the sheriff was at a disadvantage, spoke up.

"He's on the way to the hospital in Yates Center, Mrs. Mobley. They're leaving now." He didn't need to elaborate. The ambulance carrying the pilot's body was pulling onto the state highway as they spoke.

"Why didn't you wait for me?" The question sounded like an accusation.

"My men are doing their best," Carol said, her voice steady. "We had no idea you'd be here."

This was not the time or place for a conversation with the newly widowed woman in the Foster Grants, but Suzanne Mobley cut short any thought that it might be by climbing back into the Mercedes. Slamming the door behind her, she put the car in reverse and, kicking up gravel as she did so, she backed quickly out onto the road and sped away.

"That's one really upset woman," Parsons said.

"It's hardly surprising, Bill. She's just learned that her husband is dead."

"I know, but why so angry?"

"Who knows? People handle grief in all kinds of ways. Look, you're going to have to get back out to the Cessna, and Ken here is going along to relieve Damoth. We've got to keep the curiosity seekers away from that wreck until we find out what in hell to do with it. Let's hope it doesn't take days."

"And that the plane doesn't decide to take a trip to the bottom of the lake."

"If it does, I'm sure the feds or whoever needs to take a good look at it will be able to bring in equipment to haul it back up. Let's try not to assume the worst."

Ten minutes later the small knot of people at the patrol dock had broken up and Carol had started to make the calls that had to be made to put the investigation of the crash of Gil Mobley's Cessna into high gear.

CHAPTER 2

Chambord was supposedly the grandest home on Crooked Lake. Yet, ironically, very few of the lake's residents and visitors had ever seen it. That this was so owed everything to Constance Mobley's obsession with her privacy. The 87 year old matriarch had lived in *Chambord* for nearly five decades, but over that period of years she had ventured out of 'the compound' so rarely that rumors abounded that she had died and that the family, honoring her last wishes, had kept her passing a secret. The truth of the matter was much more prosaic. Constance Mobley was an invalid, confined to her bed and wheelchair where, behind drawn shades, she played solitaire, drank vodka, and rarely saw anyone except her doctor, her long-time personal servant, and her only grandchild, Evelyn Rivers.

The location of *Chambord* was not a secret. It was the lone occupant of a point on the east side of the bluff. The sheriff had driven by it on the East Bluff Road many times, but all she had ever seen of the compound was a forbidding wall of giant evergreens that stretched along the lake side of the road for close to half a mile. Today, however, she would at last have her first look at Crooked Lake's grandest home. She had been told by the woman who answered the phone at Gil Mobley's house that his wife had gone over to 'Mother Mobley's,' and Carol had a question or two she needed to ask her.

Carol had expected to find Suzanne at the hospital, but that turned out not to be the case. For whatever reason, she had apparently changed her mind about seeing her husband's body and had instead decided to visit Gil's mother and share with her the news that her son the pilot was dead. Their meeting at the dock had been so brief and impersonal that it hardly qualified as a conversation. In all probability Carol's involvement in the matter would be short-lived, as the FAA or whoever had jurisdiction took charge of the investigation. But for the time being, responsibility for the case rested with the sheriff, and she was now on her way to *Chambord* to assume that responsibility.

The entrance to the compound was almost as well hidden as was the great house itself. There was no large iron gate, no elaborately carved sign announcing what lay behind the long column of evergreens. There was simply a small gap in the column, small enough that it could easily be missed by anyone driving along the East Bluff Road, yet large enough to admit a car or small delivery truck. Carol took a left turn at the gap in the trees and found herself in a heavily shaded courtyard where a number of cars were parked in front of a large building which looked to be a combination garage and servants' quarters. It was doubtful that any of the cars belonged to Constance Mobley's servants, however. One was a Honda Accord, another a beautifully maintained BMW. The third was the Mercedes in which Suzanne Mobley had arrived at the West Branch dock an hour earlier.

A paved road led off through the woods in the direction of the great house, although the canopy of shade trees made the house itself almost invisible. The road was blocked by a chain, which seemed to account for the fact that the cars were parked by the garage. Whoever was visiting Mother Mobley had had to walk a considerable distance to pay their respects.

Carol left her patrol car behind the BMW and walked among the cars, touching their hoods. As she expected, they were still fairly hot. None of them had been long at *Chambord*. She then set off for the great house, wondering just who the visitors, other than Suzanne Mobley, might be. Perhaps the old lady was having morning tea with a coterie of friends, but Carol doubted it. Much more likely that Suzanne had notified others about her husband's death and they had come rushing over to hear more about it and offer their condolences to the senior Mrs. Mobley. But who were these others? They must necessarily live nearby. There had not been enough time for friends or relatives to gather if they were not already on or near the lake.

As Carol neared the home with the name of a French chateau, it was at once apparent that Constance Mobley had an aversion to sunlight. Not only was the house surrounded by more of the large arborvitae which flanked the road. Blinds shuttered the windows, at least the ones she could see. It was a beautiful morning, but for those inside it might as well have been after sundown. Even if some of the trees had been cut down and shutters opened, the scene which greeted Carol would have been depressing. The house was large, even huge, but it looked more like a utilitarian fortress than a welcoming lakeside home. The stonework had none of the honeyed color which made so many English country houses so attractive, and the windows were disproportionally small for so large a building. The house, Carol decided, was not exactly foreboding. It was simply disappointing, an architectural failure. The lake was barely visible off to her left. She would have liked to walk down to the shore to see whether *Chambord* was more impressive from that vantage point; but her mission was to speak with Suzanne Mobley, not satisfy her curiosity about her mother-in-law's sprawling home. In any event, she would soon have an opportunity to see something of the interior. She doubted whether she'd be pleasantly surprised.

The door was opened by a tall, stoop-shouldered, gray haired man who could have been a young 80 or an old 60.

"Yes, ma'am, what may I do for you?" He gave no evidence that he was surprised to see an officer of the law at the door.

"I'm Sheriff Kelleher," Carol said, "and I need to speak with Mrs. Mobley. Suzanne Mobley. I understand that she's here."

"Yes, she is. There are quite a few Mobleys here."

Was there a hint of a twinkle in the thin man's eyes as he said it?

"I take it that these people are here because of the news about Mr. Mobley."

"That seems to be the case," he said. "If you want to see Ms. Suzanne, she'll be with the others in the parlor. Come with me and I'll show you."

The entrance hall was dark, the wall sconces barely providing sufficient light to avert a collision with an imposing suit of medieval armor just inside the door. Mother Mobley had done her best to announce that she did not welcome visitors. But then, to Carol's surprise, the parlor proved to be brightly lit. It was vast, filled with a surfeit of dark and dated furniture, its walls covered with equally dark paintings and tapestries. It would have been as gloomy as the entrance hall had it not been for at least a dozen floor lamps scattered around the room, all of them discordantly, shockingly modern. The mother of the deceased pilot obviously had no talent as an interior decorator.

"Excuse me, but this is the sheriff," the thin man said. "She is here to speak with Ms. Suzanne."

For a brief moment the occupants of the room seemed to be frozen in place. Six people, all of them staring at this unexpected visitor. Two men had been caught in the act of rising from their chairs. One women was seated alone on a massive couch and another was standing behind it. A third man was leaning against a fireplace mantle some distance away from the others. At the center of this tableau was an old woman in a wheel chair, obviously Constance Mobley.

And then the tableau came to life. The woman on the couch got up. One of the men who had been rising from his chair sat back down. The other positioned himself behind the wheelchair and began pushing it towards Carol. Suzanne Mobley, still wearing the tight jeans and the red blouse, remained on her feet behind the couch. She had dispensed with the Foster Grants.

"I wish I could say that I'm glad to see you again," she said, "but I'm sure you can understand why that's not the case."

"Of course, Mrs. Mobley. This has been a very difficult day for you, and I don't wish to make it any worse. I thought I might see you at the hospital, but I was told that you were here. I promise to stay only a few minutes, ask just a couple of questions."

"Be my guest," Suzanne said. She didn't offer the sheriff a seat, nor did she take one herself. It was obvious that she wanted to hold Carol to her promise: a few minutes, a couple of questions.

"I was surprised to see you at the West Branch dock. You obviously got the bad news very quickly. How did you hear about your husband's accident?"

"Merle told me."

"Merle?"

"Merle Corrigan. He went out to the plane when it crashed, probably thought he could rescue Gil. But it was too late. He thought I'd want to know, so he called me."

"And you called these people and asked them to meet you here at your mother-in-law's?"

"Yes, they needed to know."

Needed to know? Perhaps. But why bring them together when a phone call would have sufficed? And who are they? The only person in the room she recognized was Jeremy Sigler, a well known local doctor.

"Could you introduce these people?"

"If you don't mind, Suzanne, I'll take care of introductions."

It was the family matriarch who extended a bony, arthritic hand. Her eyes were bright, but her voice was weak, the voice of a sick woman.

"I'm sorry, sheriff, that you had to come on such a sad day," she continued, "but fate has decreed it. Even the brave Icarus fell from the sky."

"The foolish Icarus," the man who was pushing her wheelchair said.

"We do not need your sarcasm, Marcus. You will have to excuse my son," Mrs. Mobley said to the sheriff. "I suppose I should say my other son. And that is his wife Carrie. The woman with the unnaturally red hair."

Well, well, what have we here, Carol thought. Almost within a single heart beat the old woman had criticized her son's sarcasm and then resorted to sarcasm herself in introducing her other daughter-in-law.

"You obviously know Gil's wife," Mrs. Mobley said. "She's the one you wanted to to speak with."

"I do, but I'm not here to ask personal questions. Everyone can stay."

That had not been Carol's intention, but there was something about the atmosphere in the room that suggested it might not be a bad idea.

"As you wish. Now please come in. Franklin, pull up a chair for the sheriff."

There were plenty of unoccupied chairs, so it was hardly necessary for the tall, thin man, now identified as Franklin, to pull one up. But he did as instructed, further tightening the small circle in an otherwise spacious room. Carol took the seat.

"Now let me see," Mrs. Mobley continued. "I haven't mentioned Dr. Sigler, but you may already know him. He was kind enough to bring his black bag, just in case I needed medical attention. But as you can see, I'm holding up pretty well."

"I've met the doctor," Carol said. "That leaves the man over by the fireplace."

Everyone turned to look at the man in tan slacks and a sky blue polo shirt who had chosen a corner of the room some distance from the rest of the small company.

"Call me Sheldon if you like. I'm the skunk at the garden party."

"You watch your mouth, Sheldon." For the first time since Carol had arrived, the elder Mrs. Mobley spoke in a voice considerably above a whisper. The effort caused a spasm of coughing that brought both Franklin and Dr. Sigler to her side. She waved them away.

"You can leave me alone. I'm not ready to follow Gilbert into a grave, not yet."

Turning back to the sheriff, she completed introductions.

"That man with a misplaced sense of humor is Sheldon Rivers. I have no idea why he's here. I didn't invite him."

Carol nodded to all of them, leaving her chair to shake hands and look more closely at people she knew not at all. There was not a smile in the room, but then there was nothing to smile about. On the other hand, none of them looked as if they were devastated by what had happened. The word that best described the look on the assembled faces was tense.

The brief conversation she had planned to have with Suzanne Mobley suddenly seemed almost beside the point. She would, of course, need to go over what Merle Corrigan had told Suzanne, and she would have to ask some questions about her husband's recent health history. But the situation had now changed. At least it looked as if it had. Why were all of these people at *Chambord*? Why had Gil Mobley's death generated tension rather than sorrow?

Because she didn't know these people, she had no idea of their personal relationships with each other. Perhaps there was no reason to concern herself with those relationships. What was important was Gil Mobley's tragic accident, and sooner rather than later, she hoped, the whole tragic case would be in the hands of whatever agency investigates airplane crashes. But she couldn't put out of her mind a feeling that something was wrong, something other than that the Cessna had crashed and that a Mobley was dead as a result.

Carol knew herself well enough to know that she would be asking some of the questions that were now bothering her. But she also knew that these questions couldn't be asked that morning in *Chambord's* parlor. Which left her with the reason she had come to *Chambord*.

"I don't need to trouble you for long," she said, not mentioning that in all likelihood some of them might be hearing from her shortly. "I came because I wanted to offer my condolences to you, Mrs. Mobley, and to ask a question or two. I'm so very sorry about your loss."

Suzanne Mobley stared impassively at the sheriff.

"I think you have already answered my first question," Carol continued, "which is how you heard about the accident."

"It's like I said. Merle Corrigan went right out to see if he could help Gil. Like Gil and me, Merle's a pilot. He recognized the Cessna, knew it was ours. He didn't know who was flying because the plane had flipped over. But they brought Gil to the surface, and when they couldn't revive him Merle called me, said they were bringing his body back to West Branch. It's lucky I was home."

Carol knew what Suzanne meant, but lucky wasn't the word she would have chosen.

"It must have been a terrible shock."

"You might say so," Suzanne said. For the first time her voice conveyed a hint of feeling. "He should never have done it. The crazy fool."

"Done what, Mrs. Mobley?"

"Taken the plane up, of course. He did it because I had a headache. A simple stupid headache. I'd promised to go down to Southport and take a friend, Richard Lister, for a ride. Gil, noble Gil, he told me not to worry, he'd do it. And now he's dead. Why Gil? It should have been me."

For a fleeting second, Carol had the feeling that Suzanne meant that she was the one who should have died in the crash. But no, she obviously only meant that she should have piloted the plane. Which led Carol to her other question.

"What do you think happened to your husband?"

"I assume he had a heart attack, or maybe a stroke, just like we were afraid he would. He had no business flying. I've been telling him to stay away from the plane for months. Dr. Sigler, too. But no, Gil always thought he was immortal."

"I take it that your husband had a history of heart trouble. But I'd have thought that he wouldn't be flying unless he was certified as healthy enough to do it."

"Oh, I know. But certification doesn't guarantee that nothing will happen, does it?"

Dr. Sigler interrupted.

"I was Gil's doctor, as well as Mrs. Mobley's. The AME recertified him just over a year ago after his last biennial flight review. So technically he was okay to fly. But Suzanne may be right. I'm not blaming the AME. Stevenson's certainly well qualified. But you'd have to have known Gil. He's a classic type A, a perfect candidate for a stroke or heart attack. I've tried to get him to slow down, take it easy, had him on a regimen of meds that was supposed to help. But it obviously wasn't enough."

"What's an AME?" Carol asked.

"A doc who's licensed to certify that a pilot is fit to fly. Like Perry Stevenson, up in Rochester. But he didn't know Gil like I do."

As she listened to the doctor, it occurred to her that everyone, herself included, was assuming that Gil Mobley's death was the result of a heart attack or stroke which either killed him or incapacitated him with the result that he drowned when the plane crashed. But none of them knew that that had been the case. For the first time she found herself considering the possibility that the crash of the Cessna was due to something other than Mobley's ticker. Engine failure, for example. If so, it wouldn't be her office that would have to make the call. Far more likely that an autopsy would reveal that it was just what everyone believed it was, a fatal coronary.

It was time to go, time to let these people resume their grieving or whatever it was that had generated so much tension.

"I think I'll go along. I'm sorry to have walked in on what should have been a private gathering, but I appreciate your understanding."

"Thank you for your concern," the elderly matriarch said as Carol got up and started for the door. "Franklin, please see the sheriff out."

She had reached the door when the man over by the fireplace spoke up.

"A pleasure to meet you, sheriff. I'm only sorry that you didn't ask the important questions."

CHAPTER 3

By the time Carol got back to the office, Officer Byrnes had pulled together the necessary information regarding jurisdiction in cases like the crash of Gil Mobley's Cessna. It seemed that the National Transportation Safety Board handled aircraft accidents, and that something called FSDO - Byrnes was pleased to tell the sheriff that it was pronounced Fizz-doe - served as the FAA's presence in nearby Rochester. Carol proceeded to spend a considerable amount of time on the phone, reporting the accident and answering a long list of questions to the best of her ability. It was clear that the NTSB would send a team to Crooked Lake in a few days and that the Cumberland County Sheriff's Department's role in the investigation would be preempted by the feds.

Before they arrived on the scene, however, she would have to arrange for the salvage of the Cessna. The NTSB official she had talked with had seemed confident that the plane would stay afloat, but he still tasked her with having it towed to shore and then transported to the nearest local airport. It was an assignment she was pleased to accept. Otherwise, she would have to keep the patrol boat at the scene of the crash and have one or more of her officers tied up keeping the public away from the wreck. It took her about fifteen minutes to locate Barney Davis, who ran a business that was known to handle small salvage jobs. It didn't take her long to persuade him to tackle this one; the fact it would give him a big role in what was sure to be one of the summer's major stories clearly trumped the fact that he had promised to start a project for another client.

Had Carol not spent the better part of an hour at *Chambord* earlier that morning, she would have been elated by the news that what she had begun to think of as the Mobley case was going to be someone else's responsibility. And now it was. There was surely some relatively simple and straightforward explanation for the crash of the Cessna and its pilot's death. The NTSB people who were coming to the lake would have had lots of experience in such matters, and she could think of no reason why their investigation shouldn't be fairly routine and brief. But she was having a difficult time putting out of her mind the strange mood which had been on display at the mansion on Sunrise Point. She knew it was probably her imagination, and that she should chalk it up to the impact of the news that a member of the family had been so suddenly and so cruelly taken from them. But Carol had always trusted her intuition, and in this case that intuition had been reinforced by the last words she had heard before she took her leave: 'I'm only sorry that you didn't ask the important questions.' The speaker had been Sheldon Rivers. Who in hell was Sheldon Rivers? And what were the important questions she hadn't asked?

At the time, she knew - or thought she knew - that it would be a mistake to prolong her presence at *Chambord*. If Constance Mobley was to be believed, and after all it was her home, Rivers was not welcome there. Had she stayed and asked what those questions were, it might only have further stoked his ego. For all she knew, he was just showing off. Nonetheless, Carol was aware that she might be visiting Rivers. Not to mention Marcus Mobley and his red-haired wife Carrie. It was quite possible that the person she most needed to talk with was Mother Mobley herself. Or was it Suzanne, who had insisted that she was the one who should have been piloting the Cessna. Even Dr. Sigler, who might be able to better explain why he and the aviation medical examiner had come to such different conclusions about Gil Mobley's fitness to fly.

She knew where she could find Constance Mobley, Suzanne, and Dr. Sigler. Rivers, Marcus Mobley, and his wife were another story.

"Tommy, it's me," she said when Officer Byrnes answered his phone. "See if you can find where Gil Mobley's brother Marcus and his wife Carrie live. I'm going to want to talk with them. And somebody named Sheldon Rivers. He was at the Mobley mansion this morning. Don't know why, but he's somehow involved with the Mobleys. I'll need his address and phone number, too."

"I thought you were turning this one over to the feds."

"I am. But the way these people were reacting to what happened to Mr. Mobley puzzles me. I know it's none of our business, but I'm curious."

"You want me to call them, set up appointments?"

"No, that's not necessary. I'll probably forget all about it once those NTSB people arrive." Carol doubted that she'd forget all about it, but she also knew that there were more important things to be doing, things that were in her jurisdiction rather than the NTSB's. Then another thought occurred to her.

"While you're at it, how about the address and phone number for another of our lake's Cessna pilots, Merle Corrigan. He's the one who passed the bad news on to Mobley's wife."

"That'd be old 'Wrong Way,' wouldn't it? I don't know about these other people, but Merle's got a house over on the West Bluff Road."

"What's this about old 'Wrong Way'?"

"It's his name, Corrigan. It happened before you and I were born. Some guy named Corrigan took off from New York back in the late '30s and landed in Ireland. Trouble was, his flight plan called for him to fly to California. He claimed his compass malfunctioned, and what with the fog and things he just flew the wrong way. People figured he was dead set on flying to Ireland and simply made the story up, but he became a national hero - 'Wrong Way' Corrigan. They even had a ticker tape parade for him in New York City."

"How do you know all this stuff?"

"My Mom used to kid me that I crammed my brain with lots of useless information, and I guess she was right."

"I'm sure that there's no such thing as useless information. We never know when some odd fact will come in handy, even if we never make it onto *Jeopardy*."

"Thanks, but back to the Mobley accident, should I call Corrigan?"

"Just get me his number, and I'll do it myself. After I've finished this sandwich."

Carol reexamined her priorities while she consumed the remnants of a bearably passable ham and cheese on rye which JoAnne had procured from the nearby Cumberland deli an hour earlier. She decided that she'd defer Rivers and the Marcus Mobleys until later. But Officer Byrnes had promptly produced Merle Corrigan's number along with a note which advised her not to refer to him as 'Wrong Way;' she'd give him a call.

The odds against finding him in so early in the afternoon proved to be wrong.

"Yes? This is Corrigan. What do you want?" The voice was deep and slightly slurred. It was also unpleasant. The man obviously wasn't happy to be disturbed.

"Mr. Corrigan, this is the sheriff. I hope I haven't called at a bad time, but I understand that you're the one who called Suzanne Mobley about what happened to her husband this morning. Do you have a minute?"

"I guess so. What is it you want?" Corrigan's words were still slurred, but he was now more wary than unpleasant.

"I'm trying to put together a picture of just why the plane crashed, and you're a pilot, so I thought you'd be able to help me. You saw the accident?"

"Yeah, I was on my porch, drinking my coffee, when Gil flew by."

"And what did you think happened?"

"Can't be sure, but I'd say he passed out, and in falling forward he put the plane into a nosedive. I'm sure he wasn't trying to set the plane down on the water, not at that angle."

"Any chance it could have been some kind of a mechanical malfunction?"

Carol thought she heard a wry laugh.

"It's not for me to say, is it? Better ask the guys from the NTSB when they get here. You've called them, I assume. But Gil treated his plane like it was his baby. He was a real bear when it comes to maintenance. So I don't think that's why he crashed."

"How about his health?"

"His health? What do you mean?"

"As far as you know, was he in condition to fly?"

"Are you asking me if he'd been on a bender this morning before he took off?"

That possibility hadn't occurred to Carol.

"No, nothing like that. I know that he was certified to fly, but I wonder if you know anything that might raise questions. I don't know anything about your relationship with Mr. Mobley, but I thought maybe being a pilot of a Cessna like he is you'd know whether he was having any health issues."

There was a pause on the line. Corrigan was considering how to answer the sheriff's question.

"Far as I know he was okay. Why, did someone tell you otherwise?"

"I'm just trying to account for why he might have passed out, like you said."

"Look, Gil and I weren't close. We both flew, so of course we knew each other. Not a lot of guys around these parts with our own planes. But we didn't socialize."

"But you did call his wife with the news of the crash."

"So? It seemed like a decent thing to do." The unpleasantness had come back.

"You knew that she also had a pilot's license?"

"Everyone knew. She wasn't shy about telling people. I think she thought she was a better pilot than Gil, and it kind of annoyed him. For all I know, she was right. She's a competitive lady."

Carol found this bit of information - or was it simply guesswork? - interesting. It was certainly irrelevant. But she asked the question anyway.

"I take it you knew Mrs. Mobley fairly well."

"What is that supposed to mean? I know her like I knew Gil. We both liked to fly, we both owned Cessnas, we saw each other around from time to time, traded insider stuff about a common interest. But were we friends? No way."

That Merle Corrigan didn't like the sheriff's questions was obvious. Carol wasn't quite sure herself just why she was asking them.

"I'm sorry to have bothered you, Mr. Corrigan," she said. "You did the right thing in calling Mrs. Mobley. Better to hear it from you than from my office. It's been a sad day."

"That's for sure. Look, I've got to get back to work, okay? You have a good one."

Carol wondered what work it was that Corrigan had to get back to and whether he was up to doing it. She was certain that he'd been drinking - and in the middle of the day. She also doubted that she'd have a good one.

She leaned back in her chair. Why was she involving herself in the crash of Gil Mobley's plane? Before the week was out, according to the official she'd talked to at NTSB, knowledgeable people from that agency would be arriving at the lake to take charge of an investigation into that crash. It was an investigation in which the Cumberland County Sheriff's Department would have at best a marginal role. Had she become so addicted to police work that she had to respond to every unsettling event that roiled the waters of Crooked Lake? Mobley's death was not a police matter, she told herself. It was simply a tragic accident.

Carol made an effort to refocus her attention on other matters, such as some cottagers who'd been annoying their neighbors with a series of very loud late night parties. Kevin might tell her to forget the Mobley case, but he'd be much more interested in it than a brouhaha between neighbors. She found herself clock watching, anxious for the day to end so she could go back to the cottage and share with Kevin a stubborn suspicion that there could be more to the crash of Gil Mobley's Cessna than met the eye.

CHAPTER 4

By dinner time on this warm day in July, it was doubtful that there was anyone on Crooked Lake who didn't know about the crash of Gil Mobley's Cessna. It was, by all odds, the biggest event of the summer, and arguably the biggest event since the flash flood of the previous fall which had claimed the lives of two hikers in the Indian Head Gorge. The lake was alive with rumors, many of them without foundation, about the cause of the accident. And there had been enough observers of subsequent developments to keep the rumor mill humming.

There were the boaters who had rushed to the site of the crash, to be followed by the onlookers at West Branch when Gil Mobley's body was brought to shore. Perhaps the largest crowd of the day was on the beach near *Sherman's Pub and Grub* when Barney Davis's salvage rig arrived with the wreck of the Cessna. Inasmuch as it took considerably longer to load the plane onto a trailer than it had to recover Mobley's body or transfer it to an ambulance, the scene at the *Pub and Grub* probably generated more rumors than anything else that transpired that day.

Not surprisingly, there had been more calls to the Cumberland County Sheriff's Department than usual. Some were made for the purpose of reporting things that Carol already knew. Some sought information which she either did not have or was not about to divulge. A few were products of the rumor mill, and of these two were of much more than passing interest.

JoAnne took a call at 3:20 from a man who declined to give his name. When told that the sheriff would insist on knowing with whom she was speaking, he reluctantly said that he was Edward G. Robinson.

Carol had taken a class on film as an elective in college, and she knew who Edward G. Robinson was: a star of Hollywood's golden age, noted for his gangster roles. There could, of course, be others with that famous name, but somehow Carol doubted that her caller was one of them. Rather than tell JoAnne to say she was unavailable, curiosity persuaded her to take the call.

"Yes, Mr. Robinson, what can I do for you?"

"Well, it happens that I know something about that airplane accident on the lake this morning, and I thought you should know about it."

The voice on the other end of the line was nothing like Robinson's, one of Hollywood's most unmistakable. But then why should it be? The actor had been dead for decades.

"I appreciate your call," Carol replied, trying to strike a tone which was neither excited nor dismissive.

"You understand that I'm not one hundred percent sure about this, but I think I'm right." The man who claimed to be Robinson fell silent.

"Is everything all right, Mr. Robinson?"

"Yes, I'm fine. I'm just not quite sure how to put this."

"That's fine, take your time. Is this something that has to do with the plane or the man who was flying it?"

"That's the problem, sheriff. It's both. I don't think the plane was fit to fly, and I think the pilot knew it."

"How do you know this?"

"Well, like I said, I don't know it. But if I was a betting man - which I'm not - I'd bet that the plane was an accident waiting to happen and that Mr. Mobley was aware that it had problems."

"What do you think those problems were?"

"I have no idea. I don't know much of anything about planes, certainly not these little ones we see around here."

Carol was interested in what she was hearing. The NTSB team would also be interested. But she was irritated that this man who claimed to be Edward G. Robinson was so hard to pin down.

"So you don't know what was wrong with the plane. But I assume that you must have gotten your information from someone. I'd need to know who that someone is."

"Unfortunately, I don't have a name."

Carol was now trying to keep her rising temper under control.

"Okay, no first hand knowledge of the plane's problems, no name of the man who told you they existed. How was it that you heard him discussing Mr. Mobley's plane?"

"Actually, I didn't hear him. The guy who told me about it overheard him one night at the bar out at *The Cedar Post*."

"And his name?" Carol's confidence in Edward G. Robinson was near the vanishing point, and he didn't surprise her.

"Sorry, but I don't know him either. I ran into him another night at *The Post*, and - you know how it is, guys at a bar start talking - and he brought up this business about Mobley's plane."

Carol took a deep breath and posed a follow up question.

"You mentioned that Mr. Mobley knew the plane was having some kind of trouble. You heard that from this same man, the one you were drinking with?"

"Right. Whoever it was that had mentioned the plane seemed to think Mobley knew all about its problems."

"When did you have this conversation at *The Cedar Post?*"

"I stop by there a lot, so I can't be quite sure just when it was, but I'd say about two, maybe three weeks ago."

"Did this man who talked about Mobley and his plane, did he tell you how he knew Mobley?"

"Funny thing," was the reply, "but I don't think he did. I suppose I should have asked him."

"Did he act as if he knew a lot about planes, especially these small ones, the ones with pontoons we see here on the lake?"

"If he did, he didn't say." It was at that point that Edward G. Robinson decided to offer what was, after all, a reasonable excuse for not being able to answer the sheriff's questions. "I know I'm not being as helpful as you'd like, but I didn't know Mobley was going to have this crash, did I?"

"No, of course not." But Carol was still intrigued by the man's story. The NTSB would undoubtedly want to talk with him. "I'm glad you called, Mr. Robinson, and I may want to talk with you again. May I have your phone number?"

There was another pause. If her caller wasn't Edward G. Robinson, he had a problem.

"You know, the more I think about it, the more I'm not sure whether what I heard is true. I thought it was important, but it doesn't make sense that a pilot would keep flying if he believed his plane was in bad shape. I don't want to be accused of spreading rumors."

It's too late for that, Carol said to herself.

"But the people from Washington who'll be investigating Mr. Mobley's crash will be interested," she said, "and I think we should let them be the ones to decide whether the rumor is false.

They'll want to talk with you. So we do need your phone number so they can reach you."

"Look, I made a mistake calling you. I'm not a rumor monger, so let's forget the whole thing."

The phone went dead.

Carol felt frustrated, but soon reconciled herself to the fact that the NTSB team would eventually decide whether the plane had been in flying condition. If it hadn't been, it was much less certain that Mobley's awareness of that fact would ever be known.

The other phone call to pass along a potentially important rumor came just as Carol was clearing her desk preparatory to heading back to the cottage. This time the caller did not hesitate to identify himself, and the name didn't have the dubious ring to it that Edward G. Robinson had.

"Hi, sheriff," a high pitched nasal voice greeted her. "I'm Jim Hacklin. That was a terrible thing, wasn't it, Gil Mobley's death in that accident this morning? I mean, Gil was a neighbor, well, sort of a neighbor, and you don't expect people you know, people you see a lot, to get killed like that. Especially when they die doing what they're good at."

This sounded like an invitation to have a discussion about a good neighbor and a bad accident. What did Hacklin want?

"It was certainly a tragedy, Mr. Hacklin. But what can you tell me about it?" Carol's question reflected the fact that Robinson's call was still on her mind.

"I don't know anything about the accident, except that I still can't believe it happened. But there's been something going on over at the Mobley place, and I - well, maybe I'm out of line, but I just thought it was funny the crash coming like it did right after that ruckus over there."

"What ruckus are you referring to, Mr. Hacklin?"

"I'm afraid you'll just figure I'm a busybody, but I think - no, that's not it, I *know* that something was going wrong in Mr. Mobley's life. Maybe I should say his marriage. It may not have a thing to do with the crash of his plane. But there's been trouble at the Mobleys. It started last weekend and it's been keeping up now for days."

Carol repeated her question.

"What is this ruckus you're telling me about?"

"There's been a lot of yelling, name calling. Things you don't usually hear. They're quiet neighbors, Mr. and Mrs. Mobley. We've lived two houses away from them for several years, and they've never bothered us or anybody else around here as far as I know. But then all this commotion started over the weekend. Gil - that's Mr. Mobley - he's been shouting at his wife, and she's been going after him, too. You don't like to hear things like this, so Jill and I tried to stay inside and ignore it. But it hasn't been easy."

"Do you know what they've been arguing about?"

"We've tried not to listen, but it's been hard not to hear them. It has something to do with Mrs. Mobley's first husband. Mr. Mobley called him all sorts of terrible things. Mrs. Mobley, too. I mean Gil's used language when he yells at her that Jill and I haven't heard in years."

"Why are you telling me this, Mr. Hacklin?" Carol asked.

"What if that plane crashed because Mrs. Mobley fixed it to crash? She was a pilot, like him. She knows planes. What if she hated him enough to kill him?"

Carol was finding it hard to believe what she was hearing. Two unsolicited phone calls in a single afternoon, both of them offering opinions as to the crash that had killed Gil Mobley. Never, in her experience, had the local citizenry been so anxious to help the sheriff's department do its job.

"Did you hear anything that makes you think she might have wanted to kill him? That's a pretty big accusation, Mr. Hacklin."

"I know it is, and I certainly don't bear Suzanne any ill will. But, yes, I heard her, clear as day, telling him he was as good as dead where she was concerned. Anyway, maybe she didn't do something to the plane. Maybe he saw his marriage breaking up and decided to kill himself."

Wonderful, Carol thought, now I have two theories, three if you count Edward G. Robinson's.

"Why did you decide to share this information with me, Mr. Hacklin?"

"Well, of course I wouldn't have if it hadn't been for the plane crash. But Jill's been afraid that their quarrel might lead to violence, and when we heard the news this morning she told me I ought to tell you about what's been going on."

"Have any of the other Mobley neighbors talked about this?"

"No, but that's not surprising. The McIntyres have been on a cruise somewhere, the Mediterranean I think. And down the other way there aren't any cottages for quite a distance beyond the Mobley place. Gil once told me that's why they bought the place, for the privacy."

"Mr. Hacklin, I can tell you that the National Transportation Safety Board is sending somebody up here to investigate the accident. It's what they always do in cases like this. It would be better for you and your wife not to talk about what you've been telling me. I shall pass it on to the investigators, but at this point we do not know that your suspicions are true, and it would be wrong to spread rumors at a time when the Mobley family is coping with their tragedy. I'd appreciate it if you'd let me have your number. I'll give it to the people who will be conducting the investigation, so you can expect a call from them. In fact, you may well see them when they visit Mrs. Mobley."

Carol wrote down the number and made a mental note to have Officer Byrnes see what he could learn about Edward G. Robinson and Jim Hacklin. But the thought uppermost in her mind was the strange tension she had felt in *Chambord* that morning. What she had heard in the phone calls from Robinson and Hacklin may have been nothing more than the product of overwrought imaginations. On the other hand, what if it could explain, in some way not yet clear, why everyone at Constance Mobley's mansion had been so tense.

CHAPTER 5

"God, what a day," Carol announced as she let herself in the kitchen door. "Why don't you pour me a cold one and I'll tell you about it."

Kevin gave her a hug and turned his attention to the refrigerator.

"Sure a swim first wouldn't be a good idea?" he asked.

"Any other day, yes. But I don't think I've got the energy to change into my bathing suit."

"That bad, was it? I kept expecting you to call, let me know what was going on, but you've obviously been saving it for tonight."

Carol shed her holster and jacket and took a seat at the kitchen table. Kevin popped two beers and joined her.

"I don't know about bad, but it's sure been weird. The good thing is that I'll be handing this one over to the NTSB. And I'll bet they have their hands full."

"You mean we won't be having a case to unravel this summer?"

"I knew you'd be disappointed, but I don't think the feds have much confidence in those of us out here in the nation's backwaters."

"Too bad. They just haven't read your résumé. But I take it that airplane disasters automatically become the responsibility of some federal agency."

"They do." Carol took a sip of her beer. "What are we doing in here? Let's sit on the deck."

"You're the one who parked yourself at the kitchen table. I figured that if you were too tired to take a swim, you were too tired to make it all the way out to the deck."

"Well, I've changed my mind. You coming?"

"Of course."

The late afternoon sun lit up the bluff across from the cottage. Most of the boaters had gone home for supper, and the lake was nearly as calm as it had been more than eight hours earlier when the Cessna took its fatal plunge.

"That's where it came down," Kevin said, pointing in the direction of a prominent cottage across the lake and some distance south of their cottage.

"They came and took it away this afternoon. I suppose that was on your orders."

"I was just following NTSB orders. They didn't want it sitting out there in close to two hundred feet of water. All I did was hire it done. You really did have an armchair seat, didn't you?"

"I could have done without it. I assume the pilot is dead."

"You haven't heard?"

"No. Remember, you told me to stay near the phone, but it never rang."

"Too busy. But I assumed that by this time everyone on the lake would know. I can't remember a day when the office took so many calls. But yes, Gil Mobley, the pilot, is dead. You probably saw Parsons taking him back to West Branch."

"I did. The binoculars aren't the best, but I got a pretty good look at what was going on. You couldn't tell whether the man they pulled out of the plane was dead or alive, though. I wasn't optimistic. Do you want to fill me in on your day? There's more beer where this came from."

"I'll fill you in, but let me warn you that it's going to take time. Will supper keep?"

"Chicken salad's in the fridge, and I'll husk the corn while you're talking."

By the time Carol had given Kevin a detailed account of what she had been doing since he had reported the crash of the Cessna, the shore line across the lake was in shadow, although the crest of the bluff was still bathed in sunlight. Not surprisingly, what interested Kevin most was not Carol's report of the pending arrival of the NTSB investigating team or the likelihood that Mobley had suffered a fatal heart attack. It was Carol's account of the strange gathering at *Chambord* and the unusual conversations she had had with Jim Hacklin and Edward G. Robinson. Perhaps the crash of Gil Mobley's plane would not simply be a terrible accident that made him somewhat less interested in booking a charter flight over Crooked Lake.

"You surprise me," she said. "I was sure you'd be interrupting me every minute or two."

"I'm practicing self restraint, like you're always telling me to. But now it's my turn. Just let me pop the corn in the pot and put things on the table. I'd say we've got a cracking good case on our hands."

"I was afraid of this," Carol said as she followed Kevin into the kitchen. "In the first place, you're jumping the gun, and in the second, if - and that's a big if - this turns out to be more than an unfortunate heart attack, *I* may be the one to have a case on my hands. Please bear that in mind, professor."

"Okay, okay, but you'll have to admit that there's something rotten in Denmark."

"Oh, please, let's leave Shakespeare out of this. Besides, this is Crooked Lake."

"But it sounds as if you've heard some pretty strange stuff today. You said it looked like an open and shut case - a plane goes down because the pilot has a heart attack. Now tell me, honestly, do you still think it's an open and shut case?"

"I'm just trying not to attach too much importance to what was going on in the mansion, or to make a big thing out of a couple of bizarre phone calls."

"Come on, you yourself said things looked weird at the mansion. And Edward G. Robinson! If there's an Edward G. Robinson living here on the lake I'll eat my hat."

"I'll make a bargain with you. You stop using lousy cliches like that and I'll concede that Mobley's crash is having some strange consequences."

"Good. Now where should I start?" Kevin asked. "How about what sounds like barely concealed animosity within the Mobley clan?"

"And it's not just the Mobley clan, is it? In the first place, who's this guy Rivers? Of course he could be a relative. I didn't want to sound nosy over at *Chambord*, but I'm sure we'll know who he is by tomorrow. Byrnes is looking into it."

"See? You are curious about these people, who they are, what's going on in their heads."

"Curiosity is one thing. Letting it control your priorities is another. What I should be doing is giving the NTSB a chance to do its thing."

"Agreed. But that doesn't mean we can't indulge our curiosity. At least as an after-dinner parlor game."

"Fair enough," Carol agreed. "What's your take on what was going on over at the elder Mrs. Mobley's hideaway?"

"It's pure guesswork, but all that poorly concealed unpleasantness suggests either a family so dysfunctional that it can't even pull together in the face of death or -"

Kevin paused.

"Or what?"

"Or maybe it's Gil Mobley's death that turned them against each other."

"Why do you think it might do that?" The same thought had occurred to Carol, but she hadn't had time to give it any serious thought.

"I'm not sure, but one thing I'd start thinking about is the state of Constance Mobley's health and what's in her will. She may be strong as an ox, but you say she's an octogenarian in a wheelchair. And her doctor was in attendance. What if the clan had gathered not because of the plane crash, but because word was out that the old lady was at death's door? That just might start people thinking about who's going to get what. And if that's on their minds, the death of one of her heirs could well stir the pot."

"Are you really so cynical about human nature?"

"No," Kevin insisted with a smile. "Normally I believe we're a decent, loving species. Making allowance, of course for the occasional Hitler or Stalin."

"Or for the murderers who seem to live around Crooked Lake."

"You said it, I didn't. But look, do you really believe that the other Mobleys were at the mansion just because they'd heard about the accident? And Rivers. You don't even know if he's part of the family. Nor do you know that either he or Gil's brother and sister-in-law live in the area and showed up because Gil's wife had summoned them."

"While we're talking about what we don't know," Carol said, suddenly more animated, "we have no idea whether there are more Mobleys out there. What if there are other sons or daughters, not to mention grandchildren, who'd surely be adults by now? If, as you're suggesting, the family has gathered around because the family matriarch is dying, why were there so *few* people at *Chambord?"*

"It shouldn't be hard to find out how many Mobleys there are, or where they all live. So let's back off on that one for now and talk about your weird phone calls. I'm suspicious of Edward G. Robinson, which makes me suspicious of his story. It contradicts what that other pilot, Corrigan, told you. You can pass it along to the feds, just in case, but otherwise I wouldn't give it another thought. As for Mobley and his wife having a nasty spat, that's what all couples do now and then. I can't see the missus getting so riled up she decides to kill him by tampering with the plane."

"All couples don't have nasty spats," Carol said defensively. "I hope you aren't contemplating one."

Kevin smiled as he leaned forward to kiss his wife.

"No, we're the exception that proves the rule. But you surely don't think Mrs. Mobley actually went so far as to kill her husband, do you?"

"I'm leaving that one up to the NTSB, too. Anyway, all I know is that, according to this man Hacklin, they were in a rip roaring fight not long before the day of the crash. Which means trouble in Mobley land. So Hacklin's story is more intriguing than Robinson's."

Carol yawned and got up to put her dishes in the sink.

"Tired?"

"The day's catching up with me, I think. Now that we've resolved all the big questions, can I leave the clean up to you?"

"Of course, and I won't even be critical if it turns out that we don't have a case on our hands this summer."

"It's a good thing you feel that way, because I'm sure the boys from Washington will have it all wrapped up in a few days without my help."

They were locked in a goodnight embrace when the phone rang.

Kevin was nearest the phone, so he answered. As they both expected, the call was for the sheriff.

"It's Officer Byrnes," he said, handing her the phone.

Carol closed her eyes and shook her head.

"Tommy, it's after nine. Is this call really necessary?"

Apparently it was, because she listened for a moment, shrugged her shoulders, and sat down at the kitchen table again.

Carol's conversation with her colleague lasted about six minutes, during which time Kevin stood silently in the kitchen doorway, watching for clues which might explain what this was all about.

"You don't have to go out, I hope," Kevin said when she got off the phone.

"No, nothing like that. Matter of fact, Tommy didn't need to call me tonight. But he's as bad as you are."

"Meaning what?"

"He's eager to wade into the Mobley accident. I asked him to get me some information. He did, and he couldn't wait to let me know what he found out."

"Do I have to wait for tomorrow, or can you fill me in now?"

"It's just some who's who and who's where stuff, but if you promise not to start quizzing me, I'll tell you what I learned. First thing is that Sheldon Rivers, the guy who thought I didn't ask the important questions, is Suzanne Mobley's first husband. He lives down in Westchester, but he's currently registered at a motel over in Yates Center. Been there for a couple of weeks. As for the other Mobleys, Marcus and Carrie live in Binghamton. But like Rivers, they're here on the lake - just coincidentally, of course - staying at a B & B down around Southport. And they didn't arrive after they got word about Gil's death. They've also been here for about two weeks."

"The plot thickens, and it sounds as if I may be onto something."

"It also turns out that there aren't lots more Mobleys. Constance's husband passed away thirteen years ago, and Gil and Marcus are their only children. Neither Gil nor Marcus has any offspring, but Suzanne does, a daughter named Evelyn from her marriage with Rivers. She's now in her twenties, single but living with a guy named Landers somewhere in the Syracuse area. It seems she's a fairly regular visitor to *Chambord*, but it doesn't appear that she's been there in at least a month."

It was obvious that Kevin was finding this information more than mildly interesting.

"I think you've got two things to worry about," he began, only to have Carol interrupt.

"Sorry, but there's one other thing. Hacklin lives, as he said, near the Mobleys. But there's no one in this area code named Edward G. Robinson."

"That's not surprising. But about those two things you can worry about. One's the plane crash and the other's whatever's going on with the Mobleys. And what happened to the Cessna may be less important. At least it's out of your hands."

"Come on, Kevin, clean up the dishes and come to bed. What happened to the Cessna *is* important, and it *is* out of my hands. And what's going on with the Mobleys is a private matter and none of my business. I can see that I'm going to regret my visit to *Chambord*."

"*Peut etre*, as they say on the Loire. We'll see. Anyhow, I promised to let you hit the sack. I'll be along *tout de suite*."

"You are impossible," she said as she set off down the hall. "*Bon soir.*"

"Not to quibble, Carol, but I think you mean *bonne nuit.*"

He ducked just in time to avoid the flying shoe.

CHAPTER 6

Carol hadn't known when to expect the NTSB team. 'Soon' was the closest to a date they had given her. As it happened, soon turned out to be the very next day, just over twenty-four hours after Gil Mobley's fatal accident. The team took the form of a well-tanned man in his early fifties with an oddly mismatched bald head and a very large ruddy mustache.

"Sheriff Kelleher?" he asked as he entered her office. "Justin didn't tell me you were a woman. I'm Terry Sutherland, NTSB."

His right hand gripped her's like a vise. Carol wondered if his grip was intended to demonstrate that he inhabited a male world and wanted her to know it.

"Welcome to Crooked Lake, Mr. Sutherland. I'm sorry we've had an accident that requires your presence, but I hope it will turn out to be a routine case."

"In this business, no case is routine. But we shall see."

He took the chair across the desk from Carol and declined her offer of coffee.

"I expected several of you," she said. "The man I spoke with said there would be a team."

"There are three of us, but Mancuso and Hardy are at the motel getting us settled in. No need for all of us to hear your story."

Carol frowned. Hear my story? She had given it to the man named Justin the previous afternoon. It had taken nearly an hour, and it wasn't a story. It was the facts as she knew them at the time.

"Things stand pretty much as I reported them when I called yesterday. As requested, I had a local salvage company move the plane to a small airfield near Yates Center. That's over at the north end of the lake. One of my men is keeping an eye on it, but the manager over there is reliable. You won't have any problem with him. The pilot's body is at the local hospital. I haven't scheduled an autopsy yet. I was told to wait for your team and further instructions."

"Right. But I want to go back over what you reported, make sure I understand exactly what happened, what you did."

And so Carol Kelleher, sheriff of Cumberland County, and Terry Sutherland, NTSB investigating team leader, settled down for a thorough rehash of what she had reported the previous day, plus subsequent developments.

It was only about ten minutes into their discussion that Carol came to the conclusion that Sutherland had a fairly low opinion of her department. He never said so, but his manner, if not his words, suggested that he found it highly unlikely that a small handful of law enforcement officials in a rural backwater like Cumberland County was going to be of much help to his experienced professional team.

"Did anybody actually see the Cessna go down?" he asked.

"I don't have a head count, but considering that this is the height of the tourist season and it was a beautiful day, I'm sure that lots of people saw the crash. Probably hundreds." She thought it unwise to say that it had been her husband who reported the crash of the Cessna.

"So there's nobody who can vouch for how high the plane was flying? The angle at which it hit the water? Or witnessed it flipping over?"

"It's like I told your man Justin. If you're looking for more precise figures, you might contact a man named Merle Corrigan. He's one of those who saw the crash, and he's also a Cessna pilot. But I don't think anyone had a really good view of the plane flipping over. It happened some distance from the nearest shoreline, and the sunlight was pretty bright."

"Corrigan, you say. Who's he?"

"Lives on the lake, flies his own plane. He's been flying around here for years."

"There's no mention of this Corrigan in your report," Sutherland said, glancing up from the papers in his hands.

"No, there wouldn't be. I didn't talk with him until after I'd called the NTSB."

Sutherland didn't say anything, but the look on his face spoke for him. He was finding it frustrating that the sheriff's department had not been more efficient. Frustrating, but not surprising.

"Anything else you'd like to add to what you reported yesterday?"

"As I told you, I did what I was asked to do and had the plane brought in and taken to the airfield. Here's the name and number of the local company that handled it."

She passed Barney Davis's card to Sutherland.

"The airfield's not much more than twenty miles from where we're sitting," she added. "There are a couple of other things you should know, things that aren't in the report because they weren't brought to our attention until after I phoned your agency. We had a number of calls yesterday, mostly from people telling us what we already knew. But two of those calls might be important, although I can't vouch for the authenticity of what I was told."

"Okay, let's hear it."

Carol proceeded to share what she had heard from Robinson and Hacklin and handed Sutherland Hacklin's phone number. But it was Robinson's story about problems with Mobley's Cessna that interested the NTSB team leader most.

"I should like to talk to Robinson. I don't see his number here."

"He didn't give us a number, and I had the impression that he regretted calling me. We've checked, and there doesn't seem to be anybody by that name living around here."

"Probably doesn't have a land line," Sutherland suggested.

"That could be," Carol said, "but I suspect that whoever called wasn't using his own name."

Sutherland sighed, shook his head, and then turned his attention back to the typed report, looking for more things that needed clarification or amplification. Finally, he set the report aside and cleared his throat.

"Sheriff, I'm going to need to see several people. Corrigan's one of them. And I need to talk to Officer Parsons. He seems to be the man who got the pilot out of the plane and tried to revive him. How about you get ahold of both of them and get them over here. How long should that take?"

"I think I can reach Parsons and have him here in half an hour, give or take five minutes. At least I hope so. We're a pretty big county and I don't know exactly where he is at the moment. I don't know about Corrigan. He doesn't work for me, and I don't know anything about his schedule or his plans for the day."

"Well, see what you can do. If necessary, I'll come back later in the day, but make him understand that it's important and the sooner the better. And keep after this guy Robinson."

He must have realized that he was ordering the sheriff about, so he added a 'please.'

Carol was interested in the fact that Sutherland had said nothing about talking with Hacklin or with Gil Mobley's wife, who, after all, was also a pilot who often flew the ill-fated Cessna. But she decided against mentioning it. It was his investigation, and he would eventually do whatever NTSB protocol and his own instincts told him to do. The autopsy was another matter.

"The pilot's body is still at the hospital in Yates Center. Do you want me to arrange an autopsy?"

"I was coming to that," he replied. "What's your procedure around here? I mean is there somebody in the immediate area who does it, or do they farm autopsies out to Rochester or some place else that has the resources to handle cases like this?"

"Since I've been sheriff, I've always called on Dr. Henry Crawford. He lives on the lake, and he's very professional. He's had some difficult cases, but he's never let me down."

Sutherland wrinkled his brow, which had the effect of raising his mustache. Thinking how to say what was on his mind, Carol thought.

"Why do you suppose he settled here?" he asked. It was clear what he was thinking.

Carol translated the question in her mind: in other words, why did he choose to practice in a sleepy God-forsaken place like this. She resisted the urge to say so, and fell back on her well rehearsed answer to such a question.

"He enjoys it here. It's beautiful country, don't you think?"

Sutherland managed a half smile.

"I haven't had a chance to look around. Doubt that I will, for that matter. Anyway, I'll be needing to talk with this Crawford fellow. Why don't you let me have his address and phone number."

"I can call him now, if you like, alert him that you want to talk with him."

"No need. I'll get to him after I round up my partners and we take a look at the plane."

Carol was sure that Sutherland wanted to surprise Crawford, deny him the opportunity to tidy up his office, burnish his résumé.

It took only a short time for JoAnne to announce that Officer Parsons would be back in just over twenty minutes and that Merle Corrigan could get away for a meeting at two o'clock. Sutherland decided to join the sheriff for a cup of coffee and a donut while they waited for Parsons. Carol used the time to ask him questions about the NTSB and how he had come to make it his career, and by the time that Parsons walked in the leader of the investigating team had actually relaxed a bit.

Carol left the two men to their discussion. Bill Parsons would not be put off by Sutherland's style, and he could be relied on to tell him exactly what he had told her for her report to the NTSB. What she intended to do with the next few minutes was to call Doc Crawford. The call wasn't strictly necessary, and Sutherland obviously preferred that she not make it, but she thought a heads up to the pathologist and old family friend was in order. Unfortunately, he was not at home. She left a message that urged him to call her but not to tell Sutherland that she had called.

His interview with Parsons over, Sutherland was anxious to be on his way.

"I'll be back at two to see this other Cessna pilot, but right now I've got to get to the motel and pick up my partners. My instructions to the airfield seem pretty straightforward, and first order of business is to see the plane."

Carol, remembering that there was a roadwork detour en route to the airfield, offered to have one of her men accompany him.

"No thanks. This is our job. I'll let you know if there's something you can do for us. Thanks for your help, sheriff. See you at two."

After Sutherland's departure, Carol cornered Officer Byrnes.

"Can you pull up for me a summary of how these guys are supposed to conduct an investigation like this?"

"Not only can I, I already did." He gave his boss a big smile. "It's what they call an Aviation Investigation Manual. It's long and detailed. Believe me, very detailed. Obviously written by bureaucrats who don't want to leave anything to somebody's imagination. It looks like it's mostly intended for big accidents, not piddling little ones like what we've got here. It talks about what they call GoTo teams with dozens of different kinds of specialists. I'll bet that guy you were talking with is disappointed that he got stuck with a Cessna up here in the boonies."

"I'd like to see that manual, so can you run off a copy for my bedtime reading? I don't want to step on their turf, but I'd like to know what's going on and I have a hunch Mr. Sutherland would rather keep us at arm's length."

"No problem, but let me warn you. If you're having insomnia, the manual's going to put you to sleep real quick."

CHAPTER 7

It was 1:50 when Terry Sutherland reappeared at the Cumberland County Sheriff's Office for his meeting with Merle Corrigan. Carol had half expected him to be accompanied by his colleagues, but they had been left at the Murchison Airfield. This arrangement didn't really surprise her, however. Sutherland obviously wanted to be the one to ask the questions, but he would also be anxious to get the examination of the wreck of the Cessna started.

"Any first impressions on the plane?" she asked because she wished to sound interested in his job.

"Too soon. We don't just look at it, you know. We may have to take it apart, and we'll certainly be checking out all the systems."

"I can appreciate that. I was simply wondering how bad it looks."

"You haven't seen it?" Sutherland sounded surprised.

"It hasn't seemed necessary. We knew you were coming, that it would be your problem, not ours."

The NTSB team leader considered this. He would appreciate the sheriff's deference, but not her apparent lack of curiosity.

"Tell me about Corrigan," he said, changing the subject.

"I've never met him, spoken to him just once, and that was yesterday. All I know is that he's been flying a Cessna similar to the one that crashed. Been doing it for years here on the lake. He just happened to see the Mobley plane go down, and he called the pilot's wife to let her know. That's in my report. By the way, Mrs. Mobley is also a pilot. I didn't put that in my report because I didn't think it mattered."

Carol wasn't quite sure why she had volunteered this information. It was doubtful if it mattered. But if the case were hers, she knew she'd want to talk with Suzanne. Again.

But Sutherland didn't seem interested.

"Well, I have to hope Corrigan's more observant than most. I can't see us tracking down everyone who saw the plane crash."

Carol didn't know how important the questions were that Sutherland wanted to ask of Corrigan, but she could sympathize with his reluctance to start questioning the many lake dwellers who must have witnessed the accident. Or, for starters, identifying them.

"I've cleared the conference room for your meeting with Mr. Corrigan. Here, let me show you." She ushered him into the squad room. There were quite a few seats around the table, but there was no evidence that much effort had gone into cleaning it up. Carol took it upon herself to remove several coffee cups and brush up some sugar which had been spilled on the table.

While she was busying herself with this task, JoAnne appeared to announce that Mr. Corrigan had arrived.

Carol, whose only contact with him had been over the phone, introduced first herself and then Sutherland. When the two men took seats, she followed suit. Corrigan seemed to take it for granted that she would stay for the meeting, but the NTSB team leader obviously didn't see it that way. His face registered surprise, then frustration with just a hint of anger. But he didn't ask her to leave the room; he knew that such a request would have been impolite. It also could have had a chilling effect on the man whom he wished to interrogate.

"Mr. Corrigan," he began, too formally Carol thought, "I understand that you were a witness to the crash of Mr. Mobley's plane yesterday morning."

"That's right. I saw it from the porch of my cottage. It's on the lower bluff road, and Gil's Cessna was about a third of a mile away, coming down the lake from the direction of West Branch."

"I just arrived here this morning, and I don't know where all these places are. What's the lower bluff road?"

Carol intervened to explain Crooked Lake's geography.

"You got a good look at it?" Sutherland asked.

"Absolutely. It's a Cessna 185, just like mine. Recognized it instantly. Besides, Gil's got the only other one on the lake."

Sutherland posed the same questions he had raised with the sheriff, and Corrigan provided answers which seemed to satisfy him.

"What kind of pilot was Mobley?"

Corrigan wasn't quite sure what the NTSB man meant.

"Do you mean was he experienced? Maybe a cowboy?"

"Yeah, all those things."

"If you mean did he try to put her down at such a sharp angle, the answer is no. I knew the plane was in trouble the minute it started to dive toward the lake."

"The sheriff tells me someone reported that Mobley's Cessna wasn't in that good condition and that he knew it. What do you know about that?"

"That it's a damn lie," Corrigan said. He looked at the sheriff. "Who told you that?"

Carol had intended simply to be an observer at this meeting, but she felt it was necessary to tell Corrigan about Robinson's call.

"I wish I knew. Somebody called yesterday afternoon and gave me that story. We think he was using a false name."

"And giving you false information. Who'd he say he was?"

"Edward G. Robinson. That ring a bell?"

"Never heard of him." Corrigan was emphatic. "Gil and I didn't get along all that well, but I know for a fact that he treated his Cessna like it was a member of the family."

Carol found herself thinking of Jim Hacklin's story about the row between Mobley and Suzanne. Had he treated his Cessna like he was alleged to be treating the closest member of his family, his own wife?

"So I'm supposed to assume that the plane was in excellent shape?" Sutherland obviously had his doubts. "Thanks, but I'm from Missouri."

Sutherland didn't pursue Corrigan's statement that he and Mobley didn't get along very well. Carol would have done so, but not now. For all intents and purposes the meeting had come to an end. But Corrigan had a question.

"Have you dealt with seaplane accidents before?" he asked Sutherland.

Carol saw it as an innocent attempt to make conversation, but she suspected that Sutherland would read it as a challenge to his credentials.

"We don't get many like this," he said, dismissing the question.

"Up here on the lakes, it's the only kind of accident that's likely to happen," Corrigan said. "Not that we've had any, at least not that I know of. At least not since way back a hundred years ago when Glenn Curtiss was first experimenting with heavier than air craft here on Crooked Lake. You know about Curtiss?"

"Heard of him," was the laconic answer.

"It's a damn shame the Wright Brothers get all the credit. That Kitty Hawk flight of theirs was done in secret, unlike Curtiss. He and some of his pioneer partners made the first flight in public right here on this lake. 1908. You could look it up. Didn't go much more than 300 feet before it crashed, but Curtiss flew another for over a thousand feet just two months later. Within a couple of years he was developing seaplanes that took off and landed on our lake. Can you believe that?"

"How do you know all this?" Sutherland asked.

"Hell, everybody around here knows all about Curtiss. He put this place on the map. We still have a big fly-in every year, lots of seaplanes, even some of them modeled after those original ones. Gil and I've been involved for years."

"Sounds like fun," Sutherland said, obviously disinterested and anxious to get away from the suddenly voluble Merle Corrigan.

It was twenty to three when Corrigan finally went about his business and Sutherland headed back to the Murchison Airfield. Carol realized that she would do well to bone up a bit on Southport's favorite son, Glenn Curtiss. It was amazing that he had left his mark on the field of aviation a whole century ago. She tried Doc Crawford again, only to find that he was still unavailable. In spite of her resolve to leave Gil Mobley's death to the NTSB, she decided on impulse to call Dr. Sigler. It was really Constance Mobley she wanted to talk with, but if the old lady was as ill as Kevin had suggested she might be, it made sense to sound out her doctor first.

CHAPTER 8

The trip to Sigler's took her over to the east side of the lake and up a steep road to an attractive home with a spectacular view of the lake. She preferred to be on the lake with its great advantage of water for swimming only a few yards away. But she admired the setting of places like Sigler's, especially on days like this. And there had been many days like this so far that summer. She parked the car and walked over to a stone wall, topped with half a dozen large pots filled with geraniums, for a better look down the hillside to the lower end of Crooked Lake. On the far western shore she recognized several cottages whose owners she thought she knew. There were several boats on the water, the sound of their engines muted by distance. It was hard to believe that a seaplane had crashed only a few miles to the north just the day before, claiming the life of one of the lake's best known citizens. In spite of the warm air, Carol shivered.

There was one other car in the small parking area, presumably that of a patient. She went into the wing of the building which bore a sign indicating that it was the office of Dr. Jeremy Sigler, announced herself, and took a seat next to a table containing an assortment of the kind of magazines common to such offices. She looked for something interesting, but not finding it settled for a much thumbed copy of *Redbook*.

Carol had almost completed a hasty perusal of the usual mix of articles on health care, sex advice, and style trends when Dr. Sigler himself opened a door across the room from her and beckoned her to join him in his office.

"Good to see you again, sheriff. May I assume that you are not here because you have a medical problem?"

"Quite true. I usually see Dr. Pritchard. In fact I'm due for my annual physical with her in about six weeks. But as you might imagine, I'm here to talk a bit about Mrs. Mobley. Mrs. Constance Mobley, that is, and I hope I won't be asking you to violate your confidentially policies."

Carol took a seat across from the doctor's desk, behind which was a wall containing several diplomas and photos of a small but attractive family.

"Of course." He smiled, but it was not a warm smile. "That was a terrible thing, Gil Mobley's accident. I had seen him less than two weeks ago. It's hard to believe that I won't be seeing him again."

"I didn't know Mr. Mobley, but I, too, was shocked by his death. We see those seaplanes all the time, but I've never heard of any of them crashing. It has to have been a real tragedy for the family."

"Yes, it is a tragedy. Gil's mother is taking it very badly."

"We never expect to lose a child before we go, do we?"

"Do you have children?" he asked.

"No, I'm afraid not. I guess I was a bit picky, waited too long to get married."

Dr. Sigler merely said something like 'oh,' perhaps sorry he had asked the question.

"I needn't bother you for long, doctor. In fact, the case is in the hands of the National Transportation Safety Board. Their people have already arrived, and they may be wanting to talk with you.

"But I'm concerned about Constance Mobley. I would like to talk with her, but inasmuch as you're her doctor I thought it prudent to consult with you first."

"Your concern is personal, I assume, not professional. She's very upset, as you can imagine. I don't think she's up to dealing with any legal issues that might arise right now due to Gil's death."

"It was a rather awkward meeting we had at her home yesterday. I thought she rose to the occasion admirably, but there was an air of tension in the room, and it seemed appropriate that I talk with her personally, just the two of us."

"Are we just talking about her health?" Dr. Sigler seemed concerned about the parameters of a meeting between his patient and the sheriff.

"Just how would you characterize Mrs. Mobley's health? I suspect that it isn't just about her age and her being in a wheelchair. I have the impression that she may be quite seriously ill."

"I'm sure her family would tell you, so there's no harm in my being candid. She has congestive heart failure, and her condition has indeed become considerably more serious in just the last few weeks. I don't need to go into the specifics, but I can tell you that you need to be very careful not to worry her, or tire her out. I'd keep a meeting brief, express your condolences, try to be uplifting, if you know what I mean."

"I appreciate your advice. As I said, it's possible that the people investigating the crash may insist on talking with her. I'll suggest that they speak with you before they do."

"I can't imagine why they would want to speak with her. She had nothing at all to do with Gil's life, whether or when he flies, things like that."

"I'm not that familiar with the board's investigative procedures, but I'll warn them that Mrs. Mobley is very ill."

Dr. Sigler rose from his seat, the meeting apparently at an end. Carol had other ideas.

"Dr. Sigler, I've commented on the fact that there seemed to be a lot of tension during my brief visit to *Chambord* yesterday. What do you think could explain it?"

He sat back down and picked up a rubber ball from his desk top and started kneading it. Almost immediately he put it back down and smiled across the desk at the sheriff.

"Bad habit," he said, shaking his head. "You speak of tension. I'd call it shock. We all had just heard that Gil was dead. Everyone was trying to come to grips with what had happened, and it wasn't easy."

"Of course people were in shock. But I'm not sure it was that simple. You will recall that both Marcus Mobley and Sheldon Rivers made remarks which annoyed Constance. In spite of her ill health and her grief, she responded sharply to both of them. I can't help wondering whether I had just walked in on a conversation that nobody wanted to continue in my presence."

Sigler ran his tongue across his lip.

"I don't think so. We were just surprised to see you."

"You're telling me that I must be careful not worry the senior Mrs. Mobley. Worrying her didn't seem to deter Marcus or Rivers. I probably shouldn't be talking about this, but I can't get it off my mind."

"I think you're making more out of what you heard there than you need to. Gil's death has been a blow to the family. In my experience, bad news can unhinge people. They usually get over it in time."

It was clear that Dr. Sigler did not intend to enlighten her on Mobley family problems. There was one more question she thought she should ask, even if she already knew the answer.

"As I recall it, Mr. Rivers was never properly introduced. Who is he?"

Sigler's smile was one of the saddest Carol had ever seen.

"He was once Suzanne Mobley's husband," he said quietly, as if concerned that someone in the waiting room might hear him.

"I wonder how it happens he was at *Chambord* yesterday."

"I have absolutely no idea."

It was an unhelpful answer. Carol was also of the opinion that it might be a dishonest answer.

CHAPTER 9

Dr. Henry Crawford had been drifting slowly back into complete retirement for several years. He frequently told himself that he would call it quits - for good this time - if only it weren't for the fact that every so often (actually about once a year) someone was murdered on or around Crooked Lake. Which meant that the daughter of his great and good friend, the late Bill Kelleher, who was now the sheriff of Cumberland County, would call upon him to do an autopsy and thus help her solve those murders. And Henry could not turn her down. He loved Carol, much as he had loved her father, but if truth be told he found the challenge of figuring how and when the victims of these murderers had died to be fascinating. Fascinating enough to compel him to keep his hand in as the resident forensic pathologist.

It was not surprising, therefore, that Henry was pleased to learn that he was needed to perform yet another autopsy. This time the request would come, not from Carol, but from someone named Terry Sutherland of the National Transportation Safety Board. It was clear, however, that it was Carol who had arranged it. She had twice called and left brief non-specific messages. She had been no more successful in reaching him on her third call, but this time she had decided she ought to give him a heads-up. He played back for the second time what she had had to say.

"Hi, Doc. It's Carol, and I know I've already left two messages. But if it's possible, I need to talk with you before a man named Sutherland gets in touch. It's about Gil Mobley. I'm sure you've heard that his plane crashed and that he was killed. The National Transportation Safety Board is here to investigate the crash, and they'll need to autopsy Mobley's body. I told their leader about you and said you could do it. Unfortunately, I don't think that he has much confidence in us yokels. He told me he wondered what a good pathologist was doing up here in the sticks. But I want you to do it, not just because you're good but because there's something about the case that puzzles me and - well, we know each other, we trust each other. So slather on the blarney when you see Sutherland, tell him that nobody does it better. Got it? And don't tell him I called."

Henry was about to place the call to Carol when the doorbell rang.

"Yes, sir, what may I do for you?" he said as he looked through the screen at a bald headed man with one of the largest mustaches he had even seen.

"You're Dr. Crawford?"

"Indeed I am," he acknowledged, a hunch taking shape in his mind that his visitor was the man who needed an autopsy performed on Mobley.

"Good. I'm Terry Sutherland and I represent the National Transportation Safety Board. May I come in?"

"Of course you may." Crawford held the door open and led his visitor into a comfortably furnished, well used den. He felt a surge of relief that he had taken the time to listen to his messages before Sutherland arrived. Otherwise, he would quite naturally have mentioned that the sheriff had told him to expect the agent's visit.

"The National Transportation Safety Board, is it? You're up here from Washington?"

"That's right. We're investigating a plane crash?"

"I heard about that. I've lived here for quite a few years, seen lots of those pontoon planes flying over the lake, but I can't recall them having an accident before this. They've always looked perfectly safe, sort of like motorized dragonflies. It was a terrible thing, losing that Mobley fellow like that."

"Did you know Mobley?"

"No, only by reputation."

"It's my understanding that you're a forensic pathologist. I wouldn't think there'd be a lot of need for that kind of specialty up here."

"Well, people die on Crooked Lake, just like they do in Chicago and LA." Crawford decided to show off a bit. "Couple of years ago they found a dead woman up in an attic. She'd been there so long she'd turned into a skeleton. It turned out to be murder. And there was a young woman who'd been in an unheated cottage cellar over one of our coldest winters. Frozen to death she was, but I did a work up on her, led us right to the guy that did it."

Crawford was aware that he was taking a bit more credit for nabbing killers than he was entitled to, but Carol had told him to slather it on. And if it came to that, she'd back him up.

"Those are murder cases, Dr. Crawford. Mr. Mobley wasn't murdered."

"Which, in my experience, usually makes the case easier. Talk around here is that there was probably something wrong with the plane. But that's why you're here. Some think that Mobley passed out and drowned when they couldn't get him out of the plane soon enough. That's where a pathologist comes in, and I never make assumptions until I've seen the evidence."

Sutherland looked at Crawford and self-consciously rubbed his mustache.

"Are you here, Mr. Sutherland, to ask me if I'm willing to perform an autopsy? Because if you are, the answer is yes. I like to help the authorities solve their problems, and I think my record says that I do a good job of it. What's more, I have some time on my hands right now, and I'm sure you'd like to wrap this up quickly and move on to something bigger than a downed Cessna on Crooked Lake."

Crawford thought he'd left Sutherland without much wiggle room, but he knew nothing about how NTSB worked. He put on a confident smile and did the socially appropriate thing.

"By the way, please excuse my manners. I can get you iced tea or, if you prefer, lemonade."

"Thanks, but my colleagues are going over the plane and I've got to get back. Like you said, that's my responsibility. Why don't you put the autopsy on your schedule. Just get to it as quick as you can and keep me posted."

He pulled a card from his pocket and handed it to Crawford.

"Always glad to be of help. Any time you feel like listening to shop talk about how we catch our murderers, just let me know."

He knew he was laying it on thick. There was definitely something odd about the way Sutherland looked at him as he took his leave. Probably thinks I'm some kind of local character, he thought. The idea amused him.

"Carol, Doc Crawford here," he said when he was put through to the sheriff. "You're speaking to the man who's going to be performing the autopsy on the late Gil Mobley."

"So you've seen Sutherland," she said. "Was it a tough sell?"

"Not really. Like you said, he thinks we're just this side of the end of the world. But when I told him we do murders, just like they do on our New York cop shows, he came around. I think he's anxious to get the job done pronto, and I'm available."

"Glad to hear it. I'll give the hospital the green light. And thanks, Doc. When I couldn't reach you, I worried that you'd gone out of town."

"I rarely go out of town, Carol, not when the bass are biting."

CHAPTER 10

Officer Barrett was sitting in his patrol car on a pull off some six miles between Yates Center and the Watkins junction, eating a candy bar. His assignment, catching speeders, was an easy one, but he was bored. And because it was almost ten o'clock and now thoroughly dark, there was nothing much he could do to relieve his boredom. The traffic was light, as it usually was on this road at this hour. He would be on duty until eleven, and he didn't anticipate ticketing anybody. The sheriff had made it clear that what she called 'slow speeders' should be given a warning, reserving tickets for those who were well above the county limit. In fact, she had often told her staff that she hated tailgaters and chronic lane changers even more than she hated speeders. But tailgaters and chronic lane changers were, of course, usually harder to pull over, their danger to other drivers harder to document.

He yawned and rolled down his window for some fresh air. A pair of headlights suddenly came into view far to the west. It took but seconds for it to register that this car was approaching at a dangerously high speed. The driver was no slow speeder. Barrett guessed that he was going at least 80, probably closer to 90 or above. The sign just a dozen yards back of the pull-off where he was parked informed drivers that the speed limit was 55, which was tops on most of the county's country roads.

He set the candy bar down on the seat beside him, started the car and turned on his headlights and siren. The car that raced by him showed no sign of slowing down, much less stopping. Officer Barrett could remember only one car chase in his years on the force, and it wasn't a pleasant memory. The other driver had gotten away and he had ended up in a ditch, lucky to have come through the episode with nothing worse than a banged up fender and a bit of ribbing back in the squad room.

Nonetheless, he swung out onto the highway and gunned the patrol car, hoping to keep pace with the speeder. It was about four miles down the road that his quarry, which turned out to be a recent model Honda, slowed and eventually came to a rolling stop, half on and half off the road near a small stand of sumac bushes in what looked like the middle of nowhere. The driver had either run out of gas or decided that accepting a ticket was a better fate than losing his license.

Barrett pulled in behind the Honda and, leaving the patrol car, cautiously approached it, his left hand gripping a flashlight, his right hand in the vicinity of his gun. The driver rolled down the window. It was a woman.

Before he could begin the well practiced litany of questions and instructions, she let loose a string of expletives.

"God damn it, what in hell do you think you're doing? I don't like it when you bastards sneak up on us and start blowing their God damn sirens in the middle of the night."

"That's what I'm doing because you were exceeding the speed limit by a good twenty-five miles an hour. I want you -"

"You want me to show my God damn license. Well listen up, mister, this is a straight road without any traffic and you expect me to crawl along like some dumb turtle. This is an outrage."

"I don't make the laws, ma'am, I enforce them, and you were way over the limit. Now, please get out of -"

"Why don't you spend some of your time doing something useful, like raising the God damn speed limit instead of bugging the citizens of this US of A. Do you hear me?"

"I hear you. Now will you please step out of the car and produce your driver's license. Now."

"And what if I don't?" the angry driver said.

"You will," Barrett replied, tightening his grip on his gun. For the first time in many a month, he realized that he was nervous.

But the out of control driver pushed open the car door and stepped out onto the road. She nearly lost her footing in doing so. This woman, Barrett thought, is drunk. Very drunk.

In the dark it wasn't easy to size her up, but she looked to be fiftyish. The thing that struck him first was that she had red hair and was wearing too much makeup. As the flashlight played across her face, he decided that she had very red hair and was wearing way too much makeup.

"Your driver's license, please?"

"You already asked me for it once. Do you think I can't hear? I can even read your lips. Right here in the dark." She fumbled in her purse and finally produced the license.

"Carrie Mobley," Barrett read the name from the license. "You're from Binghamton, I see. What brings you to our neck of the woods?"

"None of your God damn business. All you get is my name, rank, and serial number."

Officer Barrett, who had been brought up to be a God fearing Christian, was finding the woman's choice of language offensive. He knew that what people they stopped did was what counted, not what they said. But he had had about enough of this Carrie Mobley. It was at that moment that he made the connection between her name and that of the man who had been killed in the plane crash the previous day. His first impulse was to ask if she were related to the dead pilot, but he thought better of it. If it were true, there was no need to invite her to offer an excuse for her driving or her language. Better to stick to business.

"It's pretty obvious that you've been drinking. I need to see if you're over the limit. You stay right here."

He walked quickly back to the patrol car for the breathalyzer. If Ms. Mobley had an inclination to run or get back in the car and speed off, she didn't act on it. Instead, she leaned against the car door, clearly almost out of it. Just as her ability to run had deserted her, so did her vulgar mouth go silent. By the time he had tested her and written up the charges for speeding and driving under the influence, it had become obvious that Carrie Marcus was in no condition to drive anywhere. He pulled the Honda farther off the road, locked it up, and helped her into the back seat of the patrol car.

As they drove, he tried a conversational gambit that had occasionally worked.

"You know, Mrs. Mobley, one of the reasons we pull people over is to help keep them alive. There are a lot of deer in this area, and they have a way of jumping out into the road when you least expect it. At the speed you were going, you'd never have been able to stop before you hit one. Several people get killed that way every year around here."

"Oh, shut up and drive," came the words from the back seat.

Officer Barrett drove the rest of the way in silence. It was well after the end of his shift when he walked Carrie Mobley up to the door of the B & B whose name she had been able to remember.

The woman who answered the bell was in her bathrobe.

"I'm sorry, we're -"

She didn't finish her thought, and her facial expression went from business-like to alarmed to relieved in the space of a second or two.

"Mrs. Mobley, are you all right? We've been so worried."

"She's had a difficult hour or so. I think she needs a cup of coffee," Officer Barrett volunteered.

"Just leave me alone," Carrie Mobley mumbled. "I've got to lie down."

She brushed aside the B & B owner's arm and staggered into the house, meeting a worried looking man as he came down the stairs.

"Carrie dear, where on earth have you been? What's this officer doing here?"

"We'll talk about it in the morning," she said, shoving past him on the bottom step and going on upstairs.

Barrett was not anxious to become involved in an account of the evening's unpleasant highlights. But he did owe the man, presumably the drunken woman's husband, a brief explanation.

"She was over on Route 19 and I pulled her over for speeding. She's had quite a bit to drink, and there was no way I could let her drive. The car, a Honda, is parked and locked on the roadside about five miles north of Yates Center. Here are the keys."

The worried man came on over to the officer and extended his hand.

"I'm Marcus Mobley," he said. "I guess I should thank you for bringing her home, but I'm terribly sorry you had to get mixed up in this."

What it was that he had gotten mixed up in, Barrett didn't know.

"It's all in the line of duty, sir. But I think you should remind her when she wakes up in the morning that she has two tickets in her purse. Speeding and DUI."

Marcus Mobley smiled a grim smile.

"I don't know what you know about it, but my brother, Gil Mobley, was killed in an airplane crash yesterday. Carrie has been terribly distraught. She hasn't been herself ever since she got the news. I'm sure that accounts for what happened tonight. She's usually such a careful, law abiding driver."

Not bad, Barrett thought. It was intended as a good defense, and it might even be true. Still, she's now in trouble with the law. It was time to pack it in.

"I'll be filing my report first thing in the morning," he said. "Right now I better let you people take care of things here. Good night, Mr. Mobley, and -"

He hadn't heard the proprietor of the B & B identify herself.

"I'm Phyllis Jordan. Thank you for bringing Mrs. Mobley back. If you need to contact me, you'll find me listed in the directory under *Silver Willows*."

As Officer Barrett headed home, he was wondering why Ms. Jordan thought he might want to contact her. She would have had nothing to do with Mrs. Mobley's wild night on the roads of Cumberland County. Was it possible, however, that she knew something which might help explain the woman's reckless behavior? Whether she did or not, the sheriff would probably want to contact her.

CHAPTER 11

Frank Hardy pulled the rental car around to the motel's front entrance, where he had expected to pick up his colleagues for their trip to the airfield. Neither Sutherland nor Mancuso were anywhere in sight. Tony's fault, he thought. He's probably having one of his friendly get acquainted chats with the attractive waitress who had served them breakfast. But he was surprised that Terry, their team leader, hadn't broken up their little tete-a-tete. Sutherland was all business, never in a mood to kill time when there was work to be done. And there was work to be done today. It was their second full day on the Cessna 185 that had taken an unexpected dive into nearby Crooked Lake. Terry had made it clear over breakfast that he hoped they could wrap up the case in one more day, two at the most. Why wasn't he riding herd on Tony?

He hadn't shut the engine off, and was listening to 'I'm Bad' on a channel that played 'oldies' around the clock. Not that 'I'm Bad' was a real oldie, but what the hell. He liked LL Cool J, liked him a lot better than the previous number, something by a group the disk jockey said were The Four Freshmen. No accounting for taste. What with the radio and the engine, he didn't hear Sutherland.

"Turn that damn thing down, Frank." Terry was leaning into the car on the passenger side. "I asked you where Tony is?"

"I thought he was with you, or maybe talking with our waitress."

"Well, he's not with me, and he left the table a good ten minutes ago. I'll go check the room."

But that turned out not to be necessary.

'Hi, guys," Mancuso said as he came hurrying out of the motel. "Sorry, but I forgot my iPhone, then I couldn't find it."

"I'm sure you're going to need it down at the field," Sutherland said, sarcastically.

"Where'd you find it?" asked Hardy, more sympathetic than their team leader.

Terry and Tony piled into the car and they set off for the Murchison Airfield.

"You'll never guess," Mancuso said in answer to his colleague's question. "It was in my bathrobe pocket."

"Of course," Sutherland said. "Just in case you happened to need it while you were shaving."

"Oh, come on Terry. Don't be an old fogey."

The three men from the NTSB lapsed into silence for the next three miles. It wasn't until they followed a large curve in the road and came within sight of the lake below them that Hardy broke the silence.

"Pretty country, isn't it?"

"I guess so." Mancuso didn't sound as if he shared his colleague's appreciation of the area's natural beauty.

"You guess? What's wrong with it?"

"Well, what's there to see except fields, maybe a barn now and then. I mean, look out your window. What's that stuff growing there? That's almost all I've seen since we got out of town. It was there yesterday, too. Day after day, the same old boring fields."

"It's soy beans, Tony. Soy beans." Sutherland doubted that Mancuso would know a soy bean from a squash. "It's what these people raise for a living. Unless they raise grapes, like a lot of them do."

Silence again, this time for no more than a mile.

"Hey, what's that?" Mancuso was looking at a black carriage up ahead on the right side of the road. As they passed the carriage, he looked back at the horse that was pulling it.

"Did you see that?" he asked in surprise.

"Of course," Sutherland resumed his role as tour guide. "They're Amish. Maybe Mennonites. They don't go in for modern conveniences like cars. It's a religious thing."

"Seems like they're making it awfully hard on themselves."

"They are, but so what? They've gotten used to it, like you've gotten used to your iPhone."

"But that's silly. This iPhone makes life a lot easier for me."

"Until you have to spend valuable time trying to find the damn thing," Sutherland said.

"Jeezus," Hardy erupted. "This is one stupid conversation."

The last two miles to the airfield passed in silence.

Murchison Airfield was small, even by the standards of this region of upstate New York. Sutherland had made inquiries and discovered that it was county property, but that it had been named for a prominent family that had done much to see the region through the depths of the depression and subsequently invested heavily in several enterprises that had kept it prospering since the second world war. The area had fallen on more difficult economic times recently, but the Murchison name had stuck.

Like most airfields intended almost exclusively for general aviation, Murchison lacked facilities one expects to find in places that service commercial flights. There was but one main landing strip, and at the near end of the field there stood what passed for the terminal, although it was barely larger than the typical McDonald's, parking lot excluded. Adjacent to it were two hangars. Both were open. The smaller one held two small business jets, the larger several small prop planes. A few other planes sat on the far edge of the field, anchored by tie downs. The parking area held six cars, but except for a few men in front of the larger hangar, the place looked deserted. A small cluster of buildings some distance down the field belonged to an area flying club, or so Terry Sutherland had been told. But he and his colleagues were interested in the larger hangar, and especially the wreck of the Mobley Cessna. It sat along its western wall, looking considerably less air worthy than the other planes in that hangar.

Hardy parked the rental car and the three NTSB men set off for the hangar for the third time since arriving on Crooked Lake and their second full work day. Sutherland hoped it would be their last.

To their surprise and Sutherland's dismay, a tall, well-dressed woman was examining the plane. She was not just looking at it. She was actually touching it; it even appeared that she was fiddling with the controls.

"Ma'am, please don't do that," Sutherland said, hurrying toward the plane. "I must insist that you step back away from the plane."

"What are you talking about? This is my plane!"

Suzanne Mobley was not about to be told what to do or not to do by this man she had never seen. A man who had no business ordering her about.

"Excuse me, Ms. This plane is my responsibility. I represent the National Transportation Safety Board, and I am investigating an accident. You will please come away from the plane."

"I don't think you understand me. This is *my* plane. My husband was killed when it crashed and I intend to find out why."

They were locked in an unpleasant standoff, and Sutherland was unsure how to bring it to a satisfactory end. Compromise was not part of his repertoire.

A man in the uniform of the Cumberland County Sheriff's Department appeared at that moment, attracted by the raised voices. Officer Grieves had been told to make himself available to the NTSB team, and to help provide security. He had allowed the deceased pilot's wife access to the plane, and he now realized that he might have made a serious mistake.

"Mrs. Mobley," he said, "these men are here to figure out why the plane crashed. I think it's a good idea for you to let them do their job. Why don't you join me for a cup of coffee over at the terminal?"

"I'm not interested in coffee," she said testily. She sounded just like she had when Grieves had arrived at the West Branch dock with the sheriff two days earlier. Unpleasant, demanding.

Terry Sutherland hadn't had a crisis of conscience, but he had come to the realization that the approach he was taking to Mrs. Mobley's presence wasn't going to work.

"Look, I'm so sorry about what happened to your husband," he said, trying to sound sympathetic. "That's why we're here. With a small plane like this, we'd normally just accept a proper report, no need for an on site investigation. But when there are fatalities -" Sutherland paused, trying to find the right words. He couldn't find any.

"Can you tell me what happened?" Her tone of voice told him that she doubted that he could.

"No, I can't. Not yet. Tell you what, why don't you and I go over to the terminal and get some coffee. I'll try to explain what we have to do."

Having coffee with the widow was the last thing he wanted to do, but he'd do it if necessary.

Suzanne had just declined a similar offer from Officer Grieves, but it was possible that she might learn something from the man from the NTSB.

"Okay, but don't try to snow me. I'm a pilot, and I'm sure I've spent a helluva lot more hours in Cessnas than you have."

Sutherland instructed Hardy and Mancuso to go ahead and do their thing, then accompanied Mrs. Mobley through the hangar and over to the small terminal. He had no idea how long or with what effect he could keep her occupied. He realized that this was the part of his job which he liked the least.

CHAPTER 12

Carol and Kevin had made a vow the night before *not* to talk about the Mobley case, choosing instead to take a long canoe ride and limit conversation to planning for a winter trip to the Caribbean. They had made no reservations, and if past were prologue, they would probably not be spending any of the holiday season south of Crooked Lake, much less on a Caribbean island. But they always had fun talking about trips they would like to take. These discussions had led to what they called their 'what if diary,' which now ran to nearly twenty pages and included thoughts abut New Zealand, the Greek islands, and Scandanavia, not to mention a safari or two. So what if the demands of their respective jobs and considerations of cost had so far kept them armchair travelers. They enjoyed plotting, and one of these days, or so they told themselves, they'd actually pack their bags and travel.

In spite of the decision to steer clear of the Mobley case, they did engage in a few minutes of pillow talk about it before falling asleep. But just as Kevin began to revisit the question of just who Edward G. Robinson might really be, Carol turned away, flicked off the light, and said goodnight in a voice which told him she meant it.

It was while she was on her way to Cumberland and the morning squad meeting that she came to a decision: she was *not* going to spend any more time worrying about who Robinson is, or what Rivers meant by the important questions, or whether the family matriarch was at death's door, or any of the other things that she hadn't been able to put out of her mind. If any of these things were important, and they probably weren't, it was up to the NTSB to deal with them. When she climbed out of her car at the office, it was with a sense of relief that she had had the good sense to stop worrying about what was none of her business.

Carol's resolve to have nothing more to do with the Mobleys was tested before the squad meeting even got started.

"Morning, boss." It was Officer Barrett, and he was wearing a big grin. "Guess who I ticketed out on 19 last night?"

"Too early in the day for guessing, Jim. Why don't you tell me."

"Carrie Mobley."

Carol frowned.

"Why were you giving her a ticket?"

"Not one but two. Speeding and DUI. And I mean she was barely able to stand on her feet. She's not one of your slow speeders. I'd guess she was doing 80."

"What did you do with her?"

"She got it together enough to give me the name of a B & B where she was staying, so I took her there. Her husband was worried sick about her. No idea how long she'd been gone, but apparently she hadn't told him or the proprietor where she was going. And speaking of the woman who runs the place, she seemed to think you might want to talk with her. She's down at the *Silver Willows*. Her name's Phyllis Jordan."

Carol was suddenly interested in the artificially red haired woman.

"Did this Jordan woman say why she wanted to speak to me?"

"Well, she didn't put it quite like that. She gave me her name in case we wanted to talk to her. But it sort of sounded like an invitation for you to call her. Like maybe she knows something about why Mrs. Mobley'd been out driving drunk late at night. I thought you might be interested."

And I am, Carol thought. But I shouldn't be. Barrett had probably misinterpreted the *Silver Willows* owner's intention. If the Jordan woman really has something to tell me, she'll call me.

"Thanks for the heads up, Jim," she said to her colleague. "Let's see what the day brings."

What the day brought would further put into question the sheriff's decision to wash her hands of the Mobley case.

After the squad meeting ended and her officers set off on their various assignments, Carol retreated to her office to go through what looked like a lot of unfinished business in her in-basket. Five minutes later, JoAnne announced that Officer Grieves was on the line from Murchison Airfield. So that was why he had not been at the squad meeting. Carol had momentarily forgotten that he was still on duty providing security for the wreck of Gil Mobley's plane. She doubted that the NTSB crew needed him any longer, and assumed that that was the reason he had called.

"Hello, Ken. I think Sutherland can handle things over there. Why don't you come in."

"That's what I called about," he said. "I don't know about the feds. Mrs. Mobley came over this morning. I mean the pilot's wife. She wanted to see the plane, and I didn't see any harm in that. But the NTSB team wasn't there yet, and when they arrived the lead guy started to go ballistic. Told her to get away from the plane. Well, you saw how she was when she drove up to the dock the other day. Same thing this morning. She got mad, told him it was her plane. I tried to get her to let them do their job, but they kept at it until he suggested they go have some coffee. I think things have settled down, but I wondered what you think I should do. Their guy's pissed with me, says I should never have let her near the plane. I hate to be caught in the middle like this."

"Sutherland is a bit of a hard ass, but it really is their case now. Unless he comes to me and asks for our help, I'm going to back off. Why don't you stay there until I can get away, then I'll drive over and have a little chat with him. In the meanwhile, let him handle Mrs. Mobley."

"She's gone now, but I'll be surprised if she doesn't come back. She's not somebody you can push around."

"I know, and I'm glad she's his problem."

Two Mobleys acting up, Carrie and Suzanne. Carol had decided to leave the family alone to work out its own problems. In view of what she had heard from Barrett and Grieves, that sounded like a very good idea.

The rest of the morning went by without incident. To her surprise, she even found it a relief to spend some time crafting her reply to a potentially troubling memo from the county administrator. It was about when her watch and her stomach told her it was time to be thinking about lunch that JoAnne buzzed to say she was wanted on the phone.

"Mrs. Mobley," JoAnne said in an exaggerated whisper.

"Which one?"

"Constance."

Given what she had heard from her officers, it would not have surprised her to know that one of the daughters-in-law was on the phone. But the family matriarch herself? What could she possibly want.

"This should be interesting," she said to JoAnne. "Put her through."

It took awhile before the weak but recognizable voice spoke.

"Hello Sheriff, this us Constance Mobley. Would you be so kind as to join me for tea at four o'clock this afternoon."

It was not a question, nor did it suggest that the day or hour was negotiable. The sheriff was expected to be at *Chambord* in - Carol looked at her watch - three hours and twenty-two minutes. She considered asking what the purpose of this meeting was to be, but thought better of it. She'd find out soon enough. Fortunately, there was nothing on her calendar for the rest of the day, nothing that had to be done, no one that had to be seen. Even Sutherland could wait if necessary.

"Why, of course. I'd love to see you. Four o'clock will be just fine."

She expected further conversation, even something about what was on Mrs. Mobley's mind. At least a few words. It was not to be.

"Good. You've already learned where we park, and Franklin will let you in. Thank you."

The line went dead.

Now it was three Mobleys. While she could imagine what might be on Suzanne's mind, she had no idea what had gotten into Carrie the night before or what Constance wanted to talk to her about today.

What she did know was that she had made a decision, not five hours earlier, to walk away from the Mobleys, leaving them to their own problems or, if necessary, to the NTSB. But now she was committed to listening to the matriarch over tea and, depending on what she learned, revisiting the issues that simmered just beneath the surface two days earlier at the gloomy mansion on the East Bluff Road.

CHAPTER 13

It didn't take long to resolve the problem at the airfield. Sutherland's preference for being completely in charge and Carol's for distancing herself and her staff from the Mobley case led to an easy agreement. She sent Officer Grieves back onto highway patrol, and notified Deputy Sheriff Bridges to scrub all future airfield assignments. How the NTSB team would handle security overnight was not her responsibility.

That matter taken care of, Carol headed back to Yates Center and from there down the East Bluff Road. In spite of the fact that she now wanted nothing more to do with the Cessna tragedy, she wasn't able completely to suppress a nagging curiosity regarding *Chambord*. Whatever Mrs. Mobley wanted to talk to her about, Carol would be able to spend a few minutes wandering around the grounds, getting a better picture of a place which she had initially found depressing.

The drive, while relatively brief, was relaxing, thanks to another beautiful day and the knowledge that she would be disengaging from the problems attending the death of Gil Mobley. The road took her past the small Brae Loch College campus, bringing up memories of Kevin's failed effort to stage an opera there several years earlier. She tried to remember the name of the man who had strangled to death the star of that ill-fated production. Carol prided herself on her ability to recall names, and it surprised her how quickly she had forgotten this one. But just before the turnoff into *Chambord*, it came to her. The memory was bittersweet. There would almost certainly be opera performances in their future, but Kevin would not be conducting any of them.

This time there were no other cars inside the wall of tall evergreens which blocked the view of *Chambord* from the road. Carol stepped around the chain and made her way down the path to the house. On her first visit, she had considered going down to the beach, but hadn't done it. This time she made it her first order of business. It was as she had feared. The mansion's outlook from the lakeside was no more interesting than it was from the back.

Why, she thought, had Constance Mobley, obviously a wealthy woman, not chosen an architect with imagination, with flair, someone who could bring the beautiful world just outside her door into the house. The answer had to be that she hadn't wanted to. And why was that? The simple cottage she shared with Kevin was so much more attractive, so much more welcoming.

Franklin appeared at the door so promptly after Carol's ring that he must have been waiting in the hallway for her arrival.

"Good afternoon, sheriff. Mrs. Mobley is expecting you. Please come this way."

They made their way down the dimly lit hallway, but instead of going into the capacious parlor, he led her off to the right, through a side passage, and into what appeared to be a tearoom. At least it contained a set of elegantly carved chairs, surrounding a low matching table, on which sat a silver teapot, a silver cream and sugar set, and two paper thin china cups and saucers. Mrs. Mobley was seated in her wheelchair at one end of the table.

"Thank you so much for coming, sheriff," she said in her low whispery voice. "Please take a chair, whichever one you prefer. I thought it would be nice for us to take tea in here. I like to show off my bergeres. They're Louis XV. Quite nice, don't you think?"

"Yes, indeed," Carol said. "Lovely." She wasn't sure whether Mrs. Mobley was referring to the chairs, the tea set, or the china.

"I had some trouble finding that particular brocade, but it was worth the wait. Of course it was a long time ago. I'm not sure just when."

Carol nodded appreciatively. She eased into the chair that permitted her to see Mrs. Mobley best in the characteristically dark room.

"You mustn't think I suffer from dementia because I can't recall when I acquired the chairs. I like to think I'm doing very well for my age, although Dr. Sigler worries over me constantly. Perhaps that's what doctors are supposed to do."

She turned toward Franklin, who was hovering behind Carol's chair.

"Let us have tea, Franklin. It's English Breakfast," she said to Carol. "It's probably bad form to serve a breakfast tea in the afternoon, but it is my favorite. I hope you don't mind."

Carol wasn't quite sure what she would or could have said if she did mind.

"It sounds fine," she said.

"I should have invited you over sooner, but I'm afraid I was recovering from the shock of Gil's death."

Franklin offered Carol sugar or cream without interrupting by gesturing toward the silver tray.

"I am so sorry about your loss," Carol said, much as she had on Monday.

"Thank you. I asked you here today to apologize for how rude my company was when you were here last. I like to think that my family learned good manners when they were young. Conrad and I certainly did our best to raise them properly. Of course Sheldon isn't family, strictly speaking. But I don't like to have my guests mistreated. So I hope you will forgive us."

"There's nothing to forgive, Mrs. Mobley. Monday was a stressful day, and I should be the one apologizing for not letting you know I was coming."

"You are too kind. You came because you wanted us to know about the tragedy."

"Well, yes. But, please, there's no need to apologize."

Constance Mobley produced a smile and took a sip of her tea. Carol did likewise. The conversation. brief as it had been, had come to a halt following the exchange of apologies. It took a moment for Carol to realize that the meeting was over. The Mobley matriarch had invited the sheriff to tea simply to apologize for what had transpired at the mansion two days earlier.

But now that she was there, alone with the woman, she was suddenly not at all anxious to leave. In spite of her decision to forget about what was going on in the Mobley family, she felt an overpowering urge to ask questions.

"You haven't been well, I understand," she said, opening the conversational door a crack.

Mrs. Mobley set her cup down and cleared her throat.

"I've seen better days, but haven't we all."

"I think you've been a real trooper through all of this," Carol said. "I hope that the Safety Board people haven't bothered you."

"Who are they?"

"It looks like they've left you alone, and I'm pleased to hear that. It's the people who routinely investigate accidents involving planes. The National Transportation Safety Board."

"I can't see any reason why they should bother me. I don't know anything about Gil's flying habits."

"No, of course not. But I remember that his wife said the other day that he shouldn't have been flying the day of the crash, that it should have been her."

"I have no idea what she was talking about." She looked tired, in spite of he fact that they had been talking for no more than seven or eight minutes. Carol remembered what Dr. Sigler had said. She didn't want to wear Mrs. Mobley out, but she did have an additional question or two.

"I'll be going along, but I wonder if you can clarify something for me. You introduced everyone when I was here, but I still don't know who Sheldon Rivers is."

Carol now knew he had once been married to Suzanne Mobley, but hoped her question would elicit a more detailed explanation of his presence in the mansion.

"He was Suzanne's first husband. It was a bad marriage. Suzanne came to her senses, got a divorce, and married my Gil."

"I see," Carol said, not really sure what it was she was seeing. "But he was here, part of the grieving family. I don't understand."

"Neither do I. But I don't want to talk about Sheldon. I fact, sheriff, I'm terribly tired, and I think I should take a nap. If Dr. Sigler were here, he'd shoo you out the door and put me to bed. I don't want to be rude, like Sheldon, but I really have to ask you to leave. I'm sure you understand."

"Of course. Please forgive me for staying so long. And thanks for the tea. We must find an occasion to get together again."

Constance Mobley did not second that suggestion, but she repeated her apology and motioned for Franklin to see the sheriff out.

When they reached the door, Carol ventured to tell Franklin that she hoped Mrs. Mobley was well; the way she said it implied that she probably wasn't.

"She's not well, but she's tough as she ever was. No, let me amend that. She's tougher." He closed the door quietly after the sheriff.

CHAPTER 14

The road from West Branch to Yates Center was devoid of traffic, as it had been since Suzanne Mobley had turned onto it at 11:30. No cars, and for the last several miles no lights of any kind - nothing to light up the road, nothing to indicate that people lived anywhere in the area. The moon suddenly appeared from behind a cloud. It was but a sickle shaped new moon, but it was bright enough that she was able to see the occasional house, set back from the road, a ghost like testament to the fact that this part of Cumberland County was actually inhabited.

As she neared Yates Center, there were more buildings, but only a few more lights. A sign announced that the speed limit had been reduced to 30, but hers was still the only car on the road. At the first intersection in the heart of the small town she encountered the first traffic light since leaving home. As bad luck would have it, the light was red. She waited, impatiently, wondering why it was not possible for the town fathers to shut it off at night, much as local proprietors seemed to close up their shops at sundown.

The main drag, somewhat dubiously called Main Street, was dark. Storefront after storefront was closed. Some held promise of reopening the following morning, but several had Gone Out of Business or For Rent signs in their windows. At least that was what Suzanne assumed the signs said. It was too dark to be sure. On a corner in front of what looked like a pub, two men stood talking. They were the first human beings she had seen since leaving home. Perhaps the pub had just closed, the last business establishment in Yates Center to do so.

She came to a fork in the road and took the lane to her right, heading toward the east side of the lake. Three blocks ahead the *Three Diamonds Motel,* which was her destination, came into sight on the left side of the road. Unlike its neighbors, it announced its presence with a lighted sign which said that it had a vacancy and that it offered both breakfast and wifi. Suzanne chose not to turn in at the entrance but kept going for another long block. She went down a side street, looking for an inconspicuous parking place.

There were no meters to worry about, and there were only two parked cars in sight. She drove past them to the end of the street and pulled up to the curb.

The walk back to the motel took no more than five or six minutes, during which time Suzanne mentally chastised herself for the umpteenth time for ever having married Gil and agreeing to live on Crooked Lake. Everyone she talked with raved about the lake, the vineyard covered hills that surrounded it, the quaint towns which nestled at the head and foot of it. Suzanne didn't like quaint. She liked bustle, and one had to drive a considerable distance to find anything that remotely resembled bustle. The only thing that enabled her to keep from bloody, screaming boredom was the Cessna. And now it was a wreck, occupying the time of a bunch of federal experts on plane crashes in a shed on a rinky-dinky airfield out among the vineyards and cornfields.

Who would have thought that Gil would die in a crash of the Cessna? What were the odds? But there would be no grieving. She would go through the motions, of course. After a decent interval, she would remarry Sheldon and return to something that could be called civilization. It had been almost ten years since she had decided that she was tired of Sheldon. Gil had come along, and his plane and his love of flying had fascinated her and eventually led to divorce. She had thought of the divorce as amicable, and quickly put it behind her. But Sheldon was bitter, at least for the first few years. And then, while she took up flying, first as a hobby and then as a way of life, he had suddenly come back into her life. Initially tentative, arguing that their daughter Evelyn needed a mother, he had gradually become a suitor. To her surprise, she found that she enjoyed his attention. In time it became Gil that she was tired of. He lacked Sheldon's casual charm and sense of humor. Most importantly, however, he had no interest in moving to somewhere other than Crooked Lake. She had tried to persuade him that there were fields from which he could fly the Cessna near almost any metropolis or medium sized city. But he would have none of it.

Now he was dead. She could not rush into another marriage, especially with the man to whom she had been married before Gil. Mother Mobley, after all, had been much fonder of Gil than she was of Marcus. Therefore, if she played her cards right, she stood to inherit a goodly portion of the old lady's considerable fortune.

Suzanne was prepared to assume the role of grieving daughter-in-law for as long as was necessary. Fortunately, it was a role she shouldn't have to play for all that long. Gil had said as recently as several weeks ago that his mother was seriously ill. Dr. Sigler had told him that she might not survive for more than another three or four months.

As she hurried through the lobby of the motel, staying as far away from the desk and its lonely clerk as she could, she felt like a kid doing something excitingly sneaky. She could not become Mrs. Rivers just yet, but there was no reason why she couldn't share an hour of sexual intimacy with Sheldon.

When he didn't answer her knock on the door of his room for what seemed like an eternity, she fretted that he might have fallen asleep. But in what was actually no more than thirty seconds, Sheldon pulled back the chain and opened the door.

"Suzanne, what are you doing here?" His voice said he was alarmed by her presence at his motel room door in the middle of the night.

"I had to see you, Shell," she said, her voice breathless. She threw her arms around him and backed him into the room. It had not escaped her that he was in his pajamas.

"The door," he said, his voice low, "close the door."

He closed it himself, reaching around her to push it shut and refasten the chain.

Suzanne was intent on hugging him, something that Sheldon didn't seem to reciprocate.

"My God, Suzanne, this is crazy. You can't let people see you here at this hour."

"Nobody's going to see me. Except you, and by the way, you look awfully good to me. Here, let me get rid of this." She walked over to the bed, where she discarded her blouse.

She turned back to him, a lascivious smile on her face.

"Look, no bra," she said as her hands went to the fastener behind her.

"No, Suzanne, please. Not now." He reached out to put a stop to the strip tease being performed in front of him. "These walls are thin, and somebody is sure to see you coming or going."

Suzanne dropped her bra on the floor and stood there, looking at him as if she wasn't sure just who he was.

"Shell, it's me. Suzanne. What's gotten into you? I've been going out of my mind since Gil died. He's gone, do you understand? I don't have to worry that I'm cheating on him anymore. Now it's us."

"But you know that if Mother Mobley finds out what we're doing, she'll cut you out of her will. Just like that. She hates me."

"But she'll never know. I didn't say a word to Gloria where I was going, just that my sinuses were acting up and I was going for a drive to clear my head."

"That's great, but Crooked Lake's like a goldfish bowl. Everyone knows everyone else, gossip's the order of the day. For all you know the next person you see will be the guy that waits on you at the supermarket. I'll bet half of Yates Center recognizes your Mercedes."

"Come here, Shell. Just sit on the bed with me for a minute. Right here." She sat down and patted the bedspread next to her.

Reluctantly he crossed over to the bed and sat down.

"Now let's get real," she said, draping an arm over his shoulder and wiggling herself a few inches closer to him. "You think I'm taking a risk. I don't agree. I'm a pretty smart girl, remember? The only dumb thing I ever did was to dump you to marry Gil. But let's pretend that you're right, coming over here was a mistake. I'm only pretending that you're right, you understand. But now I'm here. Why waste such a great opportunity? After all, it isn't as if we've never gone to bed together in the past year. Remember the time we met over in Cooperstown?"

"I remember, but nobody knows either you or me in Cooperstown. This is Crooked Lake."

"Right, and I'm going to get the hell out of Crooked Lake as soon as I can. But all I want now is an hour of your time. And your body."

Suzanne pushed Sheldon down onto his back on the bed and began to unbutton his pajamas.

He groaned in resignation. She took a deep breath in anticipation.

CHAPER 15

"Want to talk about it?" Marcus asked.

The question elicited no response from his wife. She was engrossed in the menu before her. Or perhaps she was only pretending to be studying the menu. One way or another, no conversation was taking place at the table for two on the waterfront deck of the *Harbor View* restaurant.

It was a warm midsummer's evening, and every table on the broad wooden deck was occupied. A variety of boats filled every slip along the dock, and half a dozen others idled just offshore, waiting for a party to finish dessert and vacate its slip. An attractive, well tanned staff of waitresses, all busily engaged in earning money for the college year ahead, were hustling around the deck, taking orders, serving, clearing tables. One of them appeared at the Mobleys' table.

"Hi. I'm Kirsten, and I'll be taking care of you tonight. Let me tell you about our specials. I can particularly recommend the surf and turf at $35.95, and we have crab cakes with -"

"Let's have something to drink," Marcus interrupted her. "I'd like an Old Fashioned. Does your bartender know how to make one?"

"Oh, I'm sure he does."

"Good. Tell him I'd like it with Scotch. And plenty of bitters."

"That's not an Old Fashioned, it's a Rob Roy," Carrie Mobley corrected her husband. "If you're going to go retro on us, let's get it right."

"Would you please get off my case, Carrie? The young lady wants to take our order, not listen to you criticizing me. Why don't you tell her what you're having?"

"When you bring my husband's Rob Roy, you can let me have whatever's on draft," she said.

The waitress, an uncomfortable observer of this marital one-upmanship, hurried to finish her announcement of the house specials and set off for the bar and the drinks.

"What's eating you?" Marcus said. "We came here to enjoy the evening, not fuss at each other. You haven't said one pleasant word to me since Gil was killed."

"If I may correct you again, I haven't said one pleasant word to you since we left Binghamton. And you know why."

Carrie Mobley resumed her examination of the menu.

Her admission that she had been unpleasant to her husband was not intended as self criticism. She stated it as fact, and had she been completely honest, she could have dated the unpleasant words to a time long before they left their Binghamton home for the trip to Crooked Lake. It was not just that she and Marcus bickered a lot. Bickering is a commonplace in many a married relationship, including some that are basically amicable. But Carrie Mobley's issues with her husband were old and deeply rooted in their personalities. Unfortunately, their relationship, never easy, was now undergoing a new source of stress: Constance Mobley's failing health.

Gil, the older of the two sons, had long been her favorite. That hadn't mattered much to Carrie until the danger that the older woman might not have long to live prompted some serious thinking about her will. It wasn't that Marcus was a poor provider. He probably earned somewhat less than his brother; the fact that Gil and Suzanne owned two Mercedes and an airplane, lived in an elegant five bedroom lakeside home, and had a live-in servant testified to that fact. But she and Marcus also belonged to the comfortable upper echelons of the country's middle class. They lived in a nice gated community, paid off their credit card debts in full each month, and took a cruise every year.

Nonetheless, she was offended by the thought that Gil might receive the lion's share of the elder Mrs. Mobley's considerable estate. She didn't mind Constance's favoritism when it only involved the little things like demonstrations of affection. But millions of dollars were not little things. Perhaps Constance would set favoritism aside when it came to writing her will, but it couldn't be counted on. And so she had urged Marcus to take steps to ingratiate himself with his mother. She had even told him what she thought such steps should be, and had been increasingly upset with him when he didn't appear sufficiently forceful in taking those steps.

Indeed, Carrie realized, Marcus had never been as forceful as she wanted him to be. He had always been too ready to settle, too indecisive when big opportunities beckoned, too cautious when big decisions had to be made. It went back to the early years of their relationship. She was in college and he was in medical school when they met. The prospect of being married to a doctor excited her, and she had even begun to tell her friends that her husband-to-be would shortly be a famous surgeon. And then suddenly he had told her that he wasn't sure he could live with the MD grind. He would have to spend time in an internship, then in residency, then in establishing a practice and paying off the costs of all that before it would be possible to live a normal life. So he quit medical school and became a pharmacist. A pharmacist, for God's sake. They had had their first fights over that decision, and now they were fighting again because he could be letting a handsome inheritance slip through his fingers.

Marcus, too, hoped that he would be receiving a significant inheritance. But he was less worried about it than Carrie was, and he was only too well aware that Carrie was a major reason he was out of favor with his mother. 'Butter her up' was the way his wife had put it, and buttering her up was simply not his style. He had explained that to Carrie every time she brought it up, and she had gotten in the habit of bringing it up on an almost daily basis. What is more, she had started to harp back to the long ago decision to be a pharmacist. He found it even more demeaning than he had at the time, and now it made him angry.

The drinks had come and been consumed with little accompanying conversation. Ten minutes later Kirsten reappeared and stood with her pencil poised to take their order.

"Have you made a decision?" she asked.

"Yes," Marcus said, "I think I'll have the shrimp scampi. And the caesar salad."

"That's decisive," Carrie commented before placing her own order. "I'll have the fettucini alfredo and the garden salad. Leave the dressing on the side, and I'll have another beer."

"Well, now that that's out of the way," Marcus said, "do you want to tell me about the drunk driving episode? You've been avoiding me for two days. *Two whole days!* You're lucky that policeman didn't take your license."

"He had no cause to do that, Marcus. Besides, he was a gentleman. So there's nothing to talk about. Case closed."

"But it'll be on your record, and I don't think the officer bought my effort to give you an excuse. People don't drive like maniacs just because they've lost a brother-in-law. What were you thinking?"

"I wasn't thinking about anything in particular. I wanted some fresh air, and I got some. I don't ask where you're off to when you leave the house, do I?"

"You've been asking me every day for a week when I'm going to tell Mom that she's the sweetest octogenarian in the world. So don't tell me I'm always bugging you."

"We're supposed to be enjoying the night out, remember? So why don't you go and get yourself another Rob Roy while you're waiting for your shrimp scampi."

It was a good idea, much better than staring at each other across the table. Marcus pushed his chair back and headed for the bar.

CHAPTER 16

Unlike Marcus Mobley, who dropped out of medical school to pursue a degree in pharmacy, Jeremy Sigler completed his MD and eventually set up a practice as an internist in Pittsburgh. He chose Pittsburgh because his family had come from the area and for some unaccountable reason he had remained loyal to the Pittsburgh Pirates through many a losing season. He thoroughly enjoyed his practice, and had even finally come to terms with his lifelong handicap, a club foot and a left leg which was nearly two inches shorter than the right. Several surgeries and a specially constructed shoe had overcome his self-consciousness, and then in 2002 he had fallen in love with a younger woman who had recently graduated from Carnegie Mellon University. She had first become his office manager and computer specialist. Although he had been impressed by Leah's skills when he interviewed her, it had only taken a few months for him to realize that she was much more than an asset in his office. The only problem was that she didn't really care for the city, and when she began to talk about moving back to the area of upstate New York where she had grown up, Jeremy was confronted with a life changing dilemma. He resolved it by marrying Leah and looking for a place to start a practice on one of the Finger Lakes. That place turned out to be the town of Southport on Crooked Lake.

Somewhat to his surprise, he quickly fell in love with his new home. His income was less, but so were his expenses, and he and Leah made friends easily and soon became an integral part of the local scene. Among their new friends were a couple named Mobley. Both of the Mobleys were charming and good fun, and somehow managed to be down-to-earth and sophisticated at the same time. What is more, they both were pilots of a small plane, with the result that both he and Leah became frequent fliers around the Finger Lakes. Gil Mobley even became his patient when the doctor who had watched over his health decided to retire.

It was in his fifth year as a Crooked Lake resident that the first cloud appeared in his new life. He and a couple of other friends had gotten into the habit of joining Gil Mobley at his home on the lake for a friendly game of pinochle from time to time. One such game was underway on a winter night when the temperature had dropped below freezing and a light snow had started to fall. The evening had been one of easy camaraderie, sustained by good natured joking and more than a few highballs. The hour was slightly before ten when the phone rang and Gil stepped away from the table to take the call. Jeremy was a conscientious doctor, and he made it a practice to notify patients who might need his services where they could reach him after hours. And so it was that he left the card table, bundled up, and drove off to see an elderly man who lived on the West Bluff Road.

Dr. Sigler stood at the picture window, looking down at the lights of nearby Southport and the cottages near the end of the lake. Leah had put little Diane to bed and gone out to see another young mother who had become a good friend. Jeremy had happily consented to listen for their one year old daughter, but at the moment his mind was on that fateful night several years earlier. He could still picture the patient with the unforgettable name, Ellery Bettenger. It should have been a brief visit, a simple procedure, a hearty goodnight, and a return to his seat at the pinochle table. But it hadn't happened that way. The needle hadn't gone where he had intended, done what it should. Twenty minutes later, Mr. Bettenger was dead.

To his great credit, he had not panicked. He knew that his word as a doctor would be believed. The old man had died because he was old, because he was in poor health, because the rare doctor who made an emergency house call had arrived too late. He had done all that he could. His report on the cause of death was medically detailed and accurate, but it did not, of course, tell the whole story. Jeremy Sigler did not make it back to the pinochle game at Gil Mobley's; he had to see to arrangements at the Bettenger house, and it wasn't until five in the morning that he had finally crawled into bed, exhausted but much soberer than he had been two hours before midnight.

That night's calamity had haunted his waking hours and his dreams for months. He never told Leah. Not surprisingly, he never told anybody. With the passing of time, however, after several changes of the seasons, he had finally been able to live a normal life again. Only one thing had changed: he never took another drink. He swore off beer, wine, highballs, cocktails. It wasn't easy. He told Leah that he did it because he had a doctor's knowledge of his own body, and that continuing to drink would lead him to an early grave. Others noticed. Initially some kidded him about his embrace of abstinence. For awhile some praised him for setting a good example for his patients. But eventually the new Jeremy became the old, familiar Jeremy, the Jeremy who said no thanks. Nobody gave it a thought.

Nobody except Gil Mobley.

It happened during Gil's annual physical. Jeremy remembered exactly what was said, at what point in the examination. Gil was sitting on the end of the examining table, undressed except for his under shorts.

"Do you miss a drink now and then?" Gil had asked.

It was the first time anyone had asked that question in many months.

"No, never." He wasn't about to elaborate.

"It's occurred to me that you went on the wagon all of a sudden. Most guys struggle with it, end up going to AA meetings."

He had been anxious to shift the subject, but for some reason Gil seemed bent on talking about it.

"I know you weren't an alcoholic, Jeremy, but we've known each other for quite a few years and, like me, you always enjoyed the happy hour, the night cap. Why'd you quit?"

"It was good for my health. The doctor knows best, you know."

"But so suddenly. I can't remember seeing you take a drink since that night that Bettenger fellow died."

This had been dangerous conversational territory. He had tried to laugh it off as a coincidence, pretending that he'd been trying to make himself take the step for weeks. Gil wasn't buying it.

"Look, doc, we're good friends. You don't need to bullshit me. You were drunk or close to it when you left the game that night. You didn't botch your mission of mercy, did you?"

It was about as close to an accusation as it could be, and he had considered, very briefly, confessing that Gil was right. But he hadn't done so. Instead, he had said that he was deeply wounded by the fact that his friend could even have thought such a thing.

"Of course. It's just my imagination," Gil had said. "Let's forget I ever mentioned it."

But he hadn't been able to forget it. And he didn't think Gil had either.

They had remained friends. At least they hadn't stopped seeing each other, playing cards once in awhile, exchanging dinners as couples. He had remained Gil's physician. But he had been on his guard whenever they were together, always on the lookout for a sign that Gil didn't trust him. Or worse than that, that Gil thought he had some hold over him.

Indeed, the idea that Gil was feigning friendship while planning to unmask him as a failed doctor, guilty of malpractice, had become almost an obsession. And now Gil was dead.

As he thought about it, Jeremy Sigler realized that he was both very much relieved and very deeply worried.

CHAPTER 17

The Cedar Post customarily draws a crowd around 5:30 on a weekday afternoon, and this Thursday afternoon in July was no exception. The bar was lined with men and a few women who had stopped by for a quick one en route home from their workday occupations. Two of them collected their beer from the bartender and moved over to a table in the far corner where a dark bearded man in jeans and a brightly colored sport shirt was holding court. They pulled up chairs from an adjacent table, and the man with the dark beard greeted them by name and urged his colleagues to make room for the newcomers.

"There's room for everybody," he said in a hearty voice. "Just stay clear of those darts."

'We're through," one of the men who'd been having trouble hitting the dart board said. "Can't seem to get in a groove today."

Everybody laughed.

"What seems to be the word?" one of the men at the table asked.

"Nothing official," dark beard answered. "Those federal guys don't like us hanging around, and they aren't about to tell us anything. I suppose they've been told to put it in their report and get it cleared by the agency first. You know how the government does things."

"Any idea what they'll find?" The questioner obviously assumed that the man with the dark beard was an expert and would be likely to know what the investigation would find.

The man in the dark beard was Merle Corrigan, and the investigation was the one being conducted by the team from the National Transportation Safety Board into the crash of Gil Mobley's Cessna. He was presumed to be the resident expert because he was a pilot and because his plane was similar to Mobley's.

"Well, it's hardly likely it was pilot error, not with Mobley at the controls."

"Maybe the plane was having problems. Like my car, always in the garage for work of some kind or other."

"If it was, I can't imagine Mobley taking it up," Corrigan said. "But somebody told the sheriff it needed work. Guy named Robinson. Any of you know a Robinson?"

They all looked at each other, shook their heads.

"Do you think this is going to screw up the fly-in?" It was a question on many minds around the lake. All the locals, whether they knew anything about flying or not, were aware of the annual event and its importance for local tourism and the lake's reputation in the world of aviation.

"I don't see why it should," Corrigan replied.

"I was just thinking people might start to get nervous about those little planes."

"That's ridiculous, Joe. Do I suddenly look nervous?"

"Well, no, of course not. But what about the tourists, you know, people who don't fly all the time?"

"You should look at the figures. These little planes, like you call 'em, they're a helluva lot safer than the car you drive. I bet you don't start worrying about your car every time you read about somebody gets killed on the highway."

Everyone agreed that Corrigan was right about that.

"It must be a shock to lose a friend like that," the man named Joe said.

Actually it *had* been a shock, but not because Gil Mobley was a friend. They had never gotten along well, especially since they had gotten into a heated argument about an issue that didn't really affect either of them. Come to think of it, Merle thought, the subject really had to do with politics, not aviation.

Back in 1981 the nation's air traffic controllers had gone on strike, and when they refused to return to work within 48 hours, then President Reagan had fired them. This had happened before either Mobley or Corrigan knew each other, owned a plane, or even had a home on Crooked Lake. But the subject came up years later during a dinner at a fly-in, and Mobley and Corrigan quickly realized that they held strong differences of opinion on the matter. It should have been a tempest in a tea pot, but both of them took the matter seriously and any prospect that the two local Cessna pilots would become friends vanished that evening at the fly-in.

When Corrigan was asked about his late friend, it didn't seem either necessary or thoughtful to deny that they had been friends. It didn't matter. Gil Mobley was dead. It was simply common courtesy to show him respect, to mouth the usual platitudes - 'a fellow pilot,' 'a fine man,' 'a credit to our community,' 'a great loss.'

"We'll miss him," he said.

The gathering at *The Cedar Post* gradually broke up, some going on home, some going back to the bar for another beer. Merle Corrigan climbed into his car after promising his friends that he would keep his ears open and pass along anything he heard about the wreck of the Cessna. He doubted that he'd be hearing anything definitive from the NTSB boys. That isn't the way they worked. Besides, he had pretty much made up his own mind as to what had happened, based on what he knew about Mobley and how conscientious he was about the condition of his plane. No, there had been no mechanical malfunction that sent the Cessna plowing into the lake. Something had happened to Mobley. And it had happened suddenly, so there had been no time to make an emergency landing. Corrigan could think of nothing that could have done that other than a heart attack.

As he drove home, the near certainty that Gil Mobley had suffered a fatal heart attack turned his attention to his wife. Libby had always had an extreme case of 'fear of flying.' Some of his friends found it amusing that a guy who owned his own plane and went flying as often as he could would be married to a woman who panicked at the mere thought of boarding a plane. Libby did not find it amusing. Her closest friend was her sister, and unfortunately she lived in Santa Barbara, California. The train connection was inconvenient, not to mention that it took a long time to travel across country and back. Worse than that, Libby dreaded the days when he took his Cessna up. There had been occasions when she had become almost physically ill, leading to lengthy and painful discussions in which she tried to persuade him to sell the plane. Except for that one issue, they had a good marriage, but that one issue was never far beneath the surface.

And now, thanks to Mobley's death, it had resurfaced with a vengeance. He had not wanted to tell Libby about the fatal accident he had observed. But there was no way that she would not hear of it. After all, it was about to become the biggest local news story of the summer. So rather than say nothing, rather than give her reason to believe that he was trying to hide it from her, he had brought the subject up himself.

"Libby, did you hear that Gil Mobley is dead?" he had asked as he walked into the master bedroom where she was making the bed.

"I don't believe it," she had said. "What happened?"

"He crashed his Cessna in the lake. It must have been a heart attack."

"Oh, my God." Normally ruddy of complexion, Libby had turned pale. She had reached out to the headboard for support, and for a brief instant he had thought she was going to faint.

He had helped her into a chair, brought her a cup of coffee, done his best to calm her down by remaining calm himself. It hadn't worked. She had pulled herself together, but instead of asking questions, as he had expected, she had given him an ultimatum.

"Merle, I know the plane means a lot to you, but I just can't live with it any longer. I've tried, you know I have. But now all this flying has killed Mr. Mobley. We can't go on like this."

He had tried to reason with her, explain that it had been a heart attack, not an airplane, that was responsible for this tragic accident. Libby Corrigan was no longer listening.

"I won't pretend that you'll be able to sell the plane overnight. But I want you to promise that you will take steps, right now, this very week, to get rid of it. Do you love me?"

"Of course I do. You know that."

"Then sell the plane." That was the last thing she had said to him about it, and he had avoided bringing it up, hoping that in a few days she would have had second thoughts about her ultimatum.

He felt a knot in his stomach. He had been interviewed by the NTSB because he was a pilot. He had just come from a conversation with friends who turned to him for information because he was a pilot. And now he was going home to a wife who was saying that if he loved her he would cease to be a pilot. He didn't know what he was going to do. Merle Corrigan was miserable.

CHAPTER 18

They had agreed on 10:15, by which time the squad meeting would be over and she would have cleared up a couple of relatively minor routine problems. He had suggested his place, rather than her office, figuring they were less likely to be interrupted there. She had taken her old Ford rather than the official car, the better to guarantee privacy.

"Quick, before my neighbor spreads the alarm," Doc Crawford whispered to her when he met Carol at the back door.

"I'm not used to all this cloak and dagger stuff," she said as she followed him into the kitchen.

"Neither am I." Crawford was wearing a big smile. "But my life is so hum drum these days, I thought I ought to spice it up a bit. Besides, I wanted to make sure Sutherland doesn't know I'm briefing you before I talk to him. He's one of those by-the-book guys who'd chew me out for violating government protocol."

"You think he'd really object to you sharing with me?"

"I don't think it, I know it. He was very specific. But he doesn't know how we operate up here, way outside the Washington beltway."

"But you've chosen to ignore Sutherland, and here I am, all ears."

"Well, I hate to disappoint you, but I'm afraid what happened to Mr. Mobley is pretty much what everyone assumed had happened. He died of a heart attack, due to hypertension. Let's sit down. It won't take long, but you might as well be comfortable."

They stepped into the living room and Carol perched on the couch. Doc offered something to drink, but she declined.

"No thanks. I've already had my morning coffee fix and at least another cup or two beyond that."

"Same here, but I'm doing my good host imitation. Anyway, let me be more precise about Mobley's death, and I hope you'll pardon my medical lingo. The way it will read in my report, give or take a few words with a whole bunch of syllables, is that he had a coronary artery thrombus. A blood clot formed in the coronary artery, which blocked blood flow to the heart muscle. Result death, which was virtually instantaneous. It was almost certainly due to high blood pressure. Now here's the odd part. There's evidence that he was taking a potent synthetic corticosteroid - think fludrocortisone. That would be Florinef or one of its generics. Trouble is, it's a drug that raises blood pressure. Now why was he doing that?"

"Good question. I've heard of people taking pills to lower blood pressure, but not raising it. Have you any record of what meds Mobley was on?"

"No, and that's why my report isn't final. I'm just telling you he had a fatal heart attack, not why he was taking the stuff that caused it. I've got to talk with his doctor."

"This isn't my investigation, Doc, but when I met with his wife and his doctor briefly just after the crash, they both claimed that he'd had heart trouble in the past but had been cleared to fly by whoever does that for the FAA. His doctor - it's Jeremy Sigler, by the way - says he had a type A personality. If I understand what that means, he shouldn't have been taking something that would boost his blood pressure."

"Which means that Sigler wouldn't have prescribed something like a fludrocortisone. Much more likely he'd have put him on something to lower blood pressure. In fact, that might have been a condition for letting him fly. And you can't get something like Florinef without a prescription. This gets curiouser and curiouser."

"It sure does. Now what?"

"Well, like I said, it means a chat with Sigler. And I'd best see Mrs. Mobley and collect all the pills he was taking. I hope she hasn't tossed 'em out."

"I'm sure she hasn't started getting rid of his things this soon. By the way, she's also a pilot, and when I saw her she was blaming herself for letting her husband fly that day. Sort of like she had a premonition that something like this was going to happen."

"You think so?"

"No, that's ridiculous, isn't it," Carol said, shaking her head. "I've been over-thinking this Mobley business. Better let you and Sutherland handle it."

"Well, I'll get right on it. Today, assuming Sigler's available."

"What do you know about him?" Carol asked.

"Not much. He's a lot younger than I am. His wife's even younger. I hear they've got a toddler. But like I said, I barely know him. He gets some credit around here, though, because he's been known to make house calls. Can you believe that? I didn't think anybody had done that since I was a pup."

———

It was nearly four o'clock that afternoon that Doc Crawford finally reached Jeremy Sigler. They had met, but barely knew each other. After all, Crawford had retired before Sigler moved to the lake, and they really were of different generations.

"Dr. Sigler, this is Henry Crawford. We don't really know each other, but we've both had the privilege of providing medical care for our fellow citizens here in Southport and around the lake. I need to talk with you, and wonder if you might have some time in your schedule tomorrow."

"Oh, yes, I remember. Aren't you now a pathologist?"

"Yes, on a part time basis," Crawford said, "and that's what I'm calling about. I've been retained by the people who are investigating that airplane crash we had on Monday, and some things came up during the autopsy that I need some help with."

There was a long pause on the other end of the line. Sigler could be heard clearing his throat.

"I'm afraid I don't understand," he said. "I'm not qualified in your area, Dr. Crawford. What is the problem?"

"Don't worry, I don't need medical advice. I just need to talk with you about Gilbert Mobley's health record. He was your patient, wasn't he?"

"Yes, he was, but I'm not sure whether I can help. What is it you need to know?"

"I need to know what medications you had prescribed for him, and what was your diagnosis that led to those prescriptions."

"Oh."

There was another long pause. Crawford wondered if Sigler was concerned about the privacy of doctor-patient relations. But common sense prevailed over a preoccupation with medical ethics where the patient was deceased and a federal investigation was underway.

"I'm pretty tied up tomorrow, but we could do it over the phone now, if that's all right with you."

"That'll be fine. It's still possible I'd need to see you, but it'll help me get on with my report."

"Okay. It's pretty simple, so it won't take long. I'd prescribed Crestor because his cholesterol level tended to be a bit high. And he was taking Lisinopril for his high blood pressure. He complained about not sleeping soundly enough, and last time we spoke he told me was taking Tylenol PM. But that's over-the-counter. I haven't prescribed anything else for a couple of years. Does that sound like what you've found?"

Crawford answered the question by asking one of his own.

"So there would have been no reason for Mobley to be taking something that could raise his blood pressure?"

"Good gracious no," Sigler said. "That's the last thing in the world you'd do if you were Mobley."

"That's what I figured. Can you tell me where Mr. Mobley filled his prescriptions?"

"I think he used the Lake Pharmacy up in Yates Center. I recall phoning a couple in up there. But usually I wrote one out and gave it to him during an office visit. Do you mind telling me what the problem is?"

"I haven't completed the autopsy," Crawford said, "and I'm waiting for a toxicology report. So I'd rather not speculate. But what you've told me will be a big help."

It was a nervous Jeremy Sigler who said good bye to Dr. Crawford. He realized that his name would appear in the autopsy report as Gil Mobley's physician. And although Crawford hadn't said so, there had been the implication that the autopsy might have discovered something in Mobley's system that had raised his blood pressure. If that were true, it was highly likely that the National Transportation Safety Board would want to talk with him. For the man who still lived with the memory of Ellery Bettenger's death, this would be a singularly unwelcome development.

CHAPTER 19

Carol and Kevin were in the middle of a late dinner when the phone rang. Experience suggested it was for the sheriff, so she took the call. She had guessed right.

"Carol, Doc Crawford here. I've got a favor to ask of you."

"Hi, Doc. Just give me a minute to let Kevin know who's interrupting our dinner."

That done, she was back on the phone.

"I sincerely hope that I don't have to leave the cottage," she said. "I've already shed my uniform and I'm feeling like a normal human being for a change."

"You two can do whatever you had planned for the night, scrabble, mahjong, whatever turns you on."

"Thanks, but we aim a bit higher than that. What's the favor?"

"I talked with Dr. Sigler, got the story on Gil Mobley's medical situation. He was taking meds for his cholesterol and his high blood pressure. But like I told you, everything points to a heart attack as a result of hypertension. I'm sure he had stuff in his system that would raise blood pressure rather than lower it. That makes no sense. I have to talk to the pharmacists that filled his prescriptions. What I'd like you to do is talk to Mobley's wife, see what she knows about what he was taking and bring me his pills. I've never met her, and you have, so maybe she'll be more comfortable talking with you about her husband."

"I doubt it, but yes, I can put her on my to-do list for the morning. And don't worry, I won't say a word about the autopsy results. As far as she's concerned, I'm just helping the NTSB team do what they always do in cases like this."

Needless to say, when Carol rejoined Kevin at the table the conversation shifted to the Mobley case.

"Just when I'd decided I could forget about the Mobleys," she said, "it's now my first order of business tomorrow. Doc wants me to pay Suzanne Mobley a visit."

"What's on his mind?"

"Medications. I'm supposed to get her to talk to me about what her husband was taking. And to collect what's left of his pills."

"Which means Crawford's interested in whether Mobley's meds had something to do with the crash."

"Right. It looks like he'd been taking something which raised his blood pressure, which makes no sense for someone who has a tendency to hypertension."

Kevin put down his fork.

"I've got an idea," he said. "Inasmuch as helping Doc Crawford out doesn't come under the heading of official sheriff's department business, why don't I come along? Just the two of us, moonlighting at the Mobley residence."

"I'll pretend I didn't hear that," Carol said. "We're talking about a grieving widow, not a murder suspect. She doesn't need to have a strange man in her living room while she tries to reconstruct her late husband's final hours."

"I'd only be a fly on the wall."

"The answer is no, Kevin. Do you want me to spell that for you?"

"She who must be obeyed," he said with an exaggerated bow.

"Nice line. It's one you've used before, but I can't remember where it came from. Or did you make it up?"

"I borrowed it from the *Rumpole* series on TV, but it originated in Rider Haggard's famous novel *She*. Not to worry, I never read it either."

———

Carol's first order of business the next day was to see Suzanne Mobley. A phone call elicited the information that she would be at home most of the day, and they settled on 9:30 if the sheriff wouldn't mind that she was still in her bathrobe. Carol didn't like people to see her before she was dressed for the day, and was surprised that Suzanne didn't mind. It occurred to her that in the wake of her husband's death, she may simply have lost interest in such things as personal appearance.

It was immediately apparent when the door on the West Bluff Road opened that Carol was wrong on that score. The woman looked just as stunning as she had when they first met the day of Gil Mobley's death. In fact, the effect was actually heightened by the robe. Gorgeous hardly did it justice. The elegant silk fabric's ivory color contrasted beautifully with Suzanne's well tanned face. Instead of making her look tired and indifferent, it suggested a femme fatal, coaxing the man at her door to come in, perhaps to loosen the silk sash that held her robe together.

"I hope you'll excuse my appearance," she said. "I was up late last night and slept in. To be honest, I've lost almost all track of time since - oh, why is it so hard to say it? It's Gil's death, but you know that. Come on in."

Carol followed her through the foyer and into a cool living room. The shades had been drawn and the air conditioner had been turned up high. The day might turn into a hot one, but there seemed to be no reason for such a cold room at this hour.

"Please have a seat and let me get you a cup of coffee."

"Thanks, but I'll pass," Carol said. "This really needn't take long. How are you coping, Mrs. Mobley?"

"I think the conventional answer to that question is 'I've done better.' Which happens to be true. On the other hand, life goes on, doesn't it?"

"I'm sorry once again to be bothering you at a time like this, but like I said on the phone, all airplane accidents call for an investigation. My office really has no role in this, but I volunteered to help out by asking some questions about your husband's health. The other day you said he shouldn't have been flying. You were presumably referring to his medical condition. Just what was his medical condition?"

"He was okayed to fly only if he regularly took something to lower his blood pressure. I think it was Lisinopril. A lot of good that did him. He should have been grounded. Ask Dr. Sigler."

"Was your husband conscientious about taking this blood pressure medicine?"

Suzanne looked at Carol for a moment without answering the question.

"I think so, but I wouldn't swear to it," she said. "He was the kind of guy who could get careless. I always had to nag him to have his physical, see the dentist, cut down on the fried food. I mean, to look at him he was the picture of health. And that was good enough for Gil."

"I got the impression when I was over at your mother-in-law's that you thought your husband's crash was an accident that had been waiting to happen. Is that a fair interpretation?"

Once again Suzanne hesitated before answering.

"I'm not sure I'd put it that way. After it happened, well, you may be right. But not before hand. I'm sure I sounded melodramatic. All I know is that I was supposed to take Dick Lister up that morning, and because I had a headache I begged off. I guess I was blaming myself for Gil's death, and that of course is ridiculous."

Carol wasn't sure whether to take this modification in Suzanne's story at face value or not. She chose to change the subject.

"I'd appreciate it if you'd let me have the pills that are left, the rest of the prescription."

"There aren't any more. I got rid of them."

Doc Crawford would be very unhappy to hear this. Carol found it hard to believe. Had this woman dealt with the sudden loss of her husband by disposing of things that might remind her of him? And begun to do it so soon after his death?

"You've already started to get rid of your husband's things?"

"Does it sound silly? I suppose it does, but I couldn't bear reminders. It's too painful."

Carol was listening to Suzanne, but she was looking at the bookcase across the room behind where the widow was sitting. There were a number of books on display, but even more space was occupied by framed photographs.

"No, it's not silly. But I can't help noticing those pictures," she said as she got up and walked over to the bookcase.

"Is this your late husband?" she asked, pointing to the largest of several pictures of a handsome middle aged man. In one of them he had his arm around a woman who was unmistakably Suzanne Mobley.

"Yes, that's Gil."

She had disposed of her husband's medications. Carol wondered if his clothes had already been removed from their hangars and given to Good Will or the Salvation Army. It was not necessary to pose the question on her mind. Suzanne was too smart not to realize that the sheriff would be interested in what she had done and what she had not done to ease the pain of her loss.

"By any chance did you just drop the meds in a wastebasket?"

"I flushed them down the toilet."

Why did she do that, Carol wondered. In all likelihood, it was simply because it seemed like a logical and easy way to get rid of something that was no longer of any use. Carol might have done the same thing herself. But what if it were to make sure that evidence of a particular medication had been irrevocably destroyed? These thoughts flashed across her mind in seconds, and almost as quickly she brushed them aside. What is the matter with me? This woman has just lost her husband. She's trying to cope with a dramatic and unanticipated change in her life. And here I am looking for a suspicious motive to explain her actions. Carol was once more forced to concede that she had recently had too much experience with suspicious behavior in murder investigations. And she wasn't even involved in a murder investigation. It was time to go, to leave Suzanne Mobley to her own efforts to find closure.

But she was unable to leave one final question unasked.

"Mrs. Mobley, when you flushed the pills, what did you do with the plastic bottles they came in?"

"I put them in the garbage. It's obvious that you are interested in Gil's meds, sheriff. As I have told you, Gil was taking Lisinopril to lower his blood pressure. That and Crestor to control his cholesterol. I would suggest that you speak with the Lake Pharmacy. As for what was left of his prescriptions, the pills are long gone and the garbage was collected yesterday. I'm sorry that I didn't know that I was expected to keep them."

Suzanne Mobley ushered Carol out of the house without a smile, much less a 'good-bye.'

CHAPTER 20

Evelyn Rivers left the thruway at exit 42 and soon headed south on Preemption Road. Her destination was Crooked Lake, and more specifically the home of Constance Mobley, on the East Bluff Road. She never got there.

The deer vaulted over the ditch to her right and onto the road. Evelyn never saw it coming it until the very last second, by which time there was no way to avoid the impact. Suddenly there it was on the hood and then the windshield. The car careened off the road and into the ditch and beyond it into a thicket of small trees. She was dazed but conscious and aware that she was bleeding. All she could see was a spidery network of cracks in the windshield. The deer had been thrown off the hood, presumably dead. She tried to straighten up in the seatbelt, but the pain she felt from doing so made it impossible.

Evelyn experienced a wave of panic. Then, to her surprise, a man appeared at the driver's side window, motioning her to roll the window down. She had trouble moving her arm and shook her head to signal that she couldn't do it. This effort to communicate brought back the pain. And then she passed out.

It was 4:55 that afternoon when she came to. Her head ached, but it was obvious that she was in a hospital. Several people in green hospital gowns were coming in and out of what was presumably an emergency room. A number of unfamiliar monitoring machines were on either side of the bed, and she appeared to be hooked up to two of them.

She tried to get the attention of one of the green gowned people, and finally a young woman, either a nurse or an orderly, noticed and stepped to her beside.

"Am I all right?" It seemed like a more important question than 'where am I.'

"I'll send Nurse Weldon over. Just a second."

The young woman disappeared behind a curtain. It took more like two minutes than a mere second for Nurse Weldon to arrive.

"Miss Rivers," she said, "I see you're back with us. No, no, please don't try to sit up like that."

The nurse needn't have cautioned her. Her own body told her to lie still, to do only what the hospital people instructed her to do.

"I'm sure you don't know where you are or how you are. You're in a hospital in Geneva, and you're going to be just fine. Not in a few minutes, you understand, but in a matter of days, maybe a week. I'll let Dr. Castleberry give you the details, but suffice it to say that you've had a concussion, a few lacerations around the face, and you broke your left arm."

This was not good news, but Evelyn realized that it could have been worse.

"How did I get here?"

"Another car saw your collision with a deer. He called 911 and stood by until the medics arrived."

"What about my car?"

"I don't know, but they have information at the receiving desk. I'll see if I can get someone to come by and fill you in. I'm sure everything will be okay. Excuse me, but I have to see somebody down the hall. You're in good hands."

It was while Evelyn was gingerly trying to examine her body under the hospital gown that it first occurred to her that Constance would wonder where she was. The clock on the wall opposite her bed read 5:12, nearly three hours after she had told Franklin to expect her.

She finally got the attention of the woman with whom she had first spoken after waking up.

"Where's my cell phone? I need to call somebody."

"All of your things are safe in a locker, Miss Rivers. I'd suggest you wait until Dr. Castleberry comes by."

"But I have to let Grandma know why I'm not there. She'll worry."

"I'm sure the doctor will be around in a few minutes. I know it's hard, but try to be patient."

Evelyn could not bring herself to be patient. She pled her case with two more green gowns before someone located her cell and brought it to her.

It was 5:32 before she found herself talking with Franklin.

"Franklin, it's Evelyn. At last. They didn't want me to call, but I knew you'd be worried. You and Grandma."

"I am worried. I think Grandma fell asleep or she'd be worried, too. You said they didn't want you to call. Who are they?"

"I had an accident on my way over to the lake. It was a deer. It just ran right into my car and I went off the road. I'm in the hospital in Geneva, but I haven't had a chance to talk to the doctor yet. So there's no way I'll be able to make it today, probably not for a few days. Please tell Grandma that I'm going to be okay - it's just a couple of broken bones, nothing serious."

Evelyn knew that her injuries weren't something to be taken lightly, but this was no time to add to Constance Mobley's problems. She'd spoken of her to the nurses and to Franklin as if she were her grandmother, but of course she wasn't. She was the mother of her own mother's second husband. She had called Constance Mobley Grandma for many years for the simple reason that she had in fact been a surrogate grandmother. Evelyn had never cared for her stepfather, nor had she had a close relationship with her own mother. But Constance had been different, a recluse where others were concerned but a warm and nurturing presence in Evelyn's life. Moreover, she obviously thrived on Evelyn's love and affection, and that was why she had been on her way to *Chambord* when the deer had run into her path.

"I'm so very sorry about your accident. Mrs. Mobley will insist on knowing why you didn't come. She may not be well, Evelyn, but her mind is still very sharp. She'll see right through me if I try to treat what happened to you as if it were only a temporary inconvenience. Remember, your Grandma is a tough old bird, if you'll pardon the expression. She can cope with the fact that you didn't make it today because a deer had other ideas."

"Thank you, Franklin. I don't know what either Grandma or I would do without you."

Evelyn reluctantly resigned herself to the fact that she would be out of commission for awhile. She still didn't know where her car was or whether it was drivable. She was in some pain, and she didn't know for how long she'd be in the care of the green gowns. She sank back into an uncomfortable pillow and tried to go to sleep.

Constance Mobley awoke from her nap at 6:15 and immediately rang for Franklin.

"Where is Evelyn?" she asked when he appeared at her door. "She's never late."

"You're quite right. Evelyn is always punctual, but sometimes that just isn't possible. She called during your nap. At the moment, she's in Geneva, and she'll probably be there for a few days. She had one of those collisions with a deer that have become such a nuisance on the highway. Evelyn tells me it isn't that serious, but the doctor says she needs to take it easy. So she will not be able to visit this weekend. She's very upset not to be here with you, but I told her that you'd want her to follow doctor's orders."

Mrs. Mobley closed her eyes for a moment and sighed deeply.

"You didn't tell me where she is, Franklin."

"She is in the hospital. Mostly a precautionary measure, I gather."

"I want you to tell me what's wrong with her. If she's in a hospital, it isn't because she got a scratch or two."

"No, of course not. She seems to have broken a couple of bones, but she says that all of her vital organs are fine. She sounded very much like herself, just frustrated that she can't be here with you. She doesn't want you to worry."

"I'm a congenital worrier, Franklin. And it would appear that I have lots of things to worry about. First Gil, now Evelyn. Why don't you bring me a vodka with a slice of lime. What's for supper?"

"I've got that Hungarian goulash you like simmering in the kitchen and some new green beans ready to steam. When would you like to eat?"

"I'm not hungry. Maybe a little later."

"I'll fetch the vodka," Franklin said and quietly shut the door behind him.

Constance turned to face the picture window. If it weren't for the drawn blinds, she'd be looking at the lake as it reflected the late afternoon sun.

CHAPTER 21

Terry Sutherland was sitting at a corner table in the motel coffee shop, reading the sports page of *USA Today*. In another hour he would be on his way back to Washington, but for the moment he was catching up on the baseball standings, which he had neglected while investigating the crash of Gil Mobley's Cessna. Frank and Tony had checked out the previous afternoon, leaving the team leader to complete the draft of their report, which he had done before retiring the night before.

His eggs, which he had ordered over easy, had been overcooked, while the bacon, which he liked crisp, sat on the plate, greasy and unpalatable. He wished that motels would take down their signs advertising 'breakfast included.' He downed what was left of his now tepid coffee and set off for his room to finish packing.

He was giving the room a final once over to make sure he wasn't leaving anything behind when he spotted a small guest tube of shampoo which he hadn't used. Might as well get the company's money's worth, he thought, and tossed it into his dopp kit. It was 8:20 when he pulled the door shut behind him and headed for the elevator.

It wasn't until the rental car was half way to Cumberland that it occurred to him that the sheriff might not be in her office yet. He should have called her ahead of time, but he hadn't. No matter. If she were away from her desk, he'd send her a brief memorandum, summarizing his findings, later. But he knew that he had been a bit abrupt with her, that he really owed her the courtesy of a personal visit.

Fortunately for his conscience, Carol was in. Unfortunately for his schedule, which entailed dropping off the rental car and making his flight, she was tied up with the morning squad meeting. JoAnne told him she would slip a note to the sheriff, so he took a seat and studied the official looking announcements on the wall. At least the office was neater than the one he usually occupied.

"Mr. Sutherland, it's good to see you," Carol said a short minute later.

"Sorry to barge in like this, but I'm on my way to the airport. We're finished."

Carol didn't think it necessary to tell him that she had a deputy sheriff who was quite capable of running the squad meeting.

"I hope you didn't find anything out of the ordinary," she said, then quickly corrected herself. "Other than the death of the pilot, that is."

"No, it turned out to be fairly simple, although even simple things take a bit of time to confirm. It took awhile to give the aircraft a thorough going over, but it didn't crash because of a system failure. It wasn't the plane, it was the pilot. He had a heart attack. You're pathologist confirmed that. For some reason, he'd been taking a drug that elevated his blood pressure, which means he was doing just the opposite of what the AME required for certification. The spike in blood pressure brought on the heart attack, and that accounts for the crash."

"Strange, isn't it?" Carol said. "Poor Gil Mobley isn't around to tell us why he was taking meds that killed him."

"Yeah. It's certainly counter-intuitive. And your man Crawford couldn't find any record that a pharmacy in this area filled a prescription for him that accounts for the drug that showed up at autopsy. He must have taken something by mistake. Anyway, it really doesn't matter as far as we're concerned. We know what happened to the plane, and that's what we were after. When you come right down to it, who can predict when someone's going to be struck by a heart attack? It's happened to guys who have blood pressure readings of 110 over 60."

True enough, Carol thought, remembering her father's case. Nobody would have said he was a candidate for a heart attack.

"How did you leave it with Dr. Crawford?"

"Leave it? Oh, you mean do we want him to keep looking for why Mobley was taking the wrong drug. He can if he likes, but it won't affect my report. Like I said, chances are it was a simple mistake. Hell, a lot of these generics look pretty much alike."

"So it must have been just plain dumb luck that he had his attack while he was flying. You wouldn't be here if he'd keeled over when he was taking a shower, or cooking a barbecue."

"That's a fact. I'd never have had a chance to meet you or visit your nice little lake. And by the way, the lake is nice, what I've had a chance to see of it."

A belated acknowledgement, Carol thought, that Crooked Lake isn't the boondocks after all.

"I hope you won't be offended if I tell you that I hope we don't meet again," she said with a smile.

Sutherland returned the smile.

"Unless I talk my wife into renting a cottage up here one of these years."

After Sutherland had gone, Carol didn't return to the squad room, but closed the office door and reviewed what she had just heard and considered what it might mean.

She wasn't particularly surprised that the NTSB was essentially closing the book on the Cessna crash. But it hadn't closed the book on Gil Mobley's death. Doc Crawford had shared with Sutherland what he had discovered at the pharmacies and what she had told him about Suzanne's disposal of the meds. That information didn't explain the puzzling fact that Gil had been taking a fludrocortisone, but she could understand why Sutherland had decided that it didn't really matter to his investigation.

Whether it mattered to her was something else, however. And she didn't know whether it should. It didn't surprise her that none of the area pharmacies had filled a prescription for Florinef or one of its generics for Gil Mobley. Which meant that the prescription had been filled somewhere else or that it had been filled for someone else.

Carol could not imagine that Gil himself had chosen to take a medication that would exacerbate his tendency to hypertension. Much more likely that he had taken it by accident, which would suggest that it had been prescribed for someone else. And that someone else could not be just anybody. It would have to be somebody whose life intersected with Gil's, somebody whose medications would be where Gil might accidentally come upon them and carelessly assume they were his.

And who might that person be? People do not store their medications in the homes of friends and acquaintances, much less of strangers. They store them in their own homes or keep them in their own pockets, purses, or brief cases. The more she thought about it, the more she kept coming back to Gil's home. And that led to speculation that the person who was taking Florinef or something like it must be Suzanne Mobley. Or just possibly someone the Mobleys employed, like the woman who had answered the phone on Monday and told her that Suzanne was over at Mom Mobley's. Or - the possibilities began to multiply - Gil's brother or sister-in-law, who were in the area and in all likelihood had spent time in Gil and Suzanne's house. What about Sheldon Rivers? He had been married to Suzanne, and Carol had no idea what his current relationship was with either his former wife or her current husband. Perhaps he had also been in Gil's house since coming to Crooked Lake recently.

Carol suddenly knew what she was going to do. She was going to pay a visit to Dr. Jeremy Sigler. Her first question would be 'why would someone - anyone - be taking Florinef.' The more she thought about it, the more she had trouble imagining that it would be to raise one's blood pressure. Her second question would be whether he had ever prescribed such a drug for Suzanne. And while it was just a shot in the dark, she'd also ask whether he had ever prescribed a drug that would raise blood pressure for anybody on her short but growing list of people who had been close to Gil.

Kevin's casual remark that the Mobley case looked as if something was rotten in the state of Denmark no longer sounded so absurd.

CHAPTER 22

Much as Carol would have preferred to talk with Dr. Sigler in person, she ultimately decided to do it over the phone. She had been spending altogether too much time driving all around Crooked Lake on matters related to Gil Mobley's death, a case in which she wasn't officially involved. Talking to Sigler about Florinef would almost certainly be a waste of her time. But if she were to do it, there was no reason to waste even more of her time by taking a forty-five mile round trip to have that conversation.

JoAnne reported that Dr. Sigler was with a patient and would call her back in half an hour, which gave her time to turn her attention to her in-basket. But she was unable to do so. The nagging feeling that there was more to the Mobley case than would appear in the NTSB report simply would not go away. She leafed through the papers in front of her, but her mind was elsewhere.

"Dr. Sigler, thanks for letting me interrupt your schedule," she said when he finally called back.

"No problem," he replied, but his tone of voice said otherwise. Or was that just her imagination? Why did everything and everybody connected with Gil Mobley do this to her?

"I have a question, well, actually two questions. Medical questions. I assume you are familiar with something called fludrocortisone."

"Of course. Fludrocortisone acetate is a generic for Florinef, and not something one prescribes very often."

"If you or another doctor did prescribe it, what would be the reason? I mean, what would be the patient's problem?"

"Probably Addison's disease. And there are forms of chronic fatigue syndrome that might be helped by Florinef. Why are you asking?"

"I'm not sure," she said, which was true only in the sense that she wasn't sure why she was involving herself in the Mobley case at all. "But what is Addison's disease?"

"In a few words, it occurs when there's an inadequate secretion of hormones from the adrenal cortex. A person suffering from it tends to be anemic and weak. The skin often looks discolored, typically darker. For what it's worth, President Kennedy suffered from Addison's disease."

Carol considered this last bit of intelligence. Interesting, but irrelevant at the moment. She turned to the real purpose for her call.

"Have you ever treated anybody for Addison's disease? Or for what you refer to as chronic fatigue syndrome? Suzanne Mobley, for example?"

"Suzanne?" Sigler was obviously surprised by the question. "I'm not her doctor, so I've never prescribed for her. Not for Addison's or anything else. I think she sees a doctor over in Geneva. Rachel Edelstein, I believe. But from what I see of Mrs. Mobley, and I've seen her quite frequently because her husband was my patient, I'd be surprised to learn that she suffered from Addison's or has any of the symptoms of CFS."

"CFS?"

"Sorry about the shorthand. That's the chronic fatigue syndrome I referred to."

"How about your other patients? Ever treat anybody for one of those things?"

"Chronic fatigue, yes. But medication is a last resort. I've never prescribed Florinef for it. As for Addison's, the answer is unequivocally no. Not here, not in Pittsburgh before I moved to the lake. You'll forgive me for asking again, but why are you interested in Addison's disease?"

Carol assumed that she would be pressed on this, and could see no reason not to level with him.

"I know that Doc Crawford discussed Gil Mobley's health with you, but he'd promised the NTSB team that he wouldn't go into specifics of the autopsy with anyone. But he did share one important finding with me: Gil Mobley had been taking a fludrocortisone. Why would he have been doing that?"

"I have no idea, none whatsoever. I was his doctor, and there was no reason under the sun to put him on fludrocortisone. That would have been dangerous."

"So I understand. And it may have contributed to his death. What I am -"

Sigler interrupted her.

"Excuse me, but a minute ago you were asking me if I ever treated Suzanne Mobley for Addison's disease. I'm sure you meant had I ever written her a prescription for fludrocortisone. But you didn't ask if I had ever written Gil Mobley a prescription for fludrocortisone. Isn't that the more important question?"

"I didn't want to insult you by asking that question, Dr. Sigler. You were treating him for hypertension, and fludrocortisone would only have exacerbated that problem. I am puzzled, as is Doc Crawford, as to why Gil had that drug in his system. It seems to me that the explanation lies in the fact that he mistakenly took someone else's medicine. And the logical person would be his wife or someone else who might have been in his home recently."

"I see," Sigler said, sounding somewhat mollified. "For a moment I wondered if you suspected me of trying to kill my patient."

Now it was Carol who was upset.

"It has never occurred to me, Dr. Sigler, that *anyone* tried to kill Mr. Mobley. I am just trying to understand how he could have taken the wrong medication by mistake."

"Yes, of course, but what if someone arranged for Gil to take the fludrocortisone. Let's say someone switched meds, substituting the fludrocortisone for something which was intended to lower Gil's blood pressure."

"Do you actually believe someone did that?"

"No, of course I don't. But I believe that someone *could* have done it, and for a moment it occurred to me that this conversation had something to do with me. After all, I was Gil's doctor and I do write prescriptions for my patients."

"Please accept my apology, Dr. Sigler. We've just had an innocent misunderstanding."

When they said good-bye, Carol was well aware that she might have unwittingly alienated Jeremy Sigler. She hoped he would get over it. But the longer she thought about it, the more she worried that he might not.

———

"Hi, I'm home," Carol called out as she came in the back door at the end of the day.

No answer. She walked through the cottage and out to the deck. No Kevin.

She started back into the house to look for a note telling her where he'd gone, when she spotted him on his way over from the Brocks' cottage next door.

"I heard you drive up," he said, "but I was being a good neighbor. How was the day?"

A warm kiss delayed Carol's answer to the usual end-of-day question.

"Give me a minute to change and I'll tell you."

Kevin had gotten used to seeing his wife in uniform, but he much preferred her in the slacks and blouse she was wearing when she joined him on the deck.

"Why don't you get me a glass of Chardonnay," she said.

"Coming up."

When they settled into their deck chairs with their wine, Carol screwed her face into what looked to Kevin like a pained expression.

"That bad?" he asked.

"I'm afraid so. Gil Mobley's doctor is upset with me for accusing him of having killed Mobley."

"You did that?" Kevin couldn't believe what he had just heard. At no time in their discussion of the death of the Cessna pilot had it ever been suggested that someone had killed Mobley. What is more, the name of his doctor had scarcely come up in that discussion.

"No, I didn't," Carol said with a wan smile. "But I think Dr. Sigler believes that I intimated as much."

"I think you have some explaining to do."

"I know, and frankly I think Sigler may be onto something."

"You'e telling me that he may actually have killed Mobley?"

"No, no, nothing like that. Let me back up and tell you what's going on. Or what I think is going on."

Carol spent the next several minutes explaining Crawford's discovery of fludrocortisone in Mobley's body and Sigler's explanation of what it would be prescribed for and why prescribing it for Mobley would have been a very bad idea. Her effort to identify others for whom it might have been prescribed had led to the unpleasantness with Sigler, and she walked Kevin through that increasingly difficult exchange.

"And he thinks you were laying the groundwork for an accusation that he had fixed it to substitute this fludrocortisone or whatever it is for Gil Mobley's blood pressure meds?"

"That's what he said. The thought had never occurred to me, so you can imagine how that made me feel. But here's what's interesting, other than that I may have made an enemy of Sigler. What if in a crazy way he's right? What if Mobley's death wasn't an accident? What if somebody deliberately switched his meds, set it up so he'd take this fludrocortisone when he thought he was taking whatever it was that Sigler had prescribed?"

"I'd think that would be pretty hard to do," Kevin said. "Hard and risky."

"Why? All it would take would be for someone who had access to the Mobley house to put the bad pills in the bottle where Gil keeps his good ones. Someone like his wife, who then conveniently tosses out the pills and the bottle after his death."

"But what would guarantee that popping a fludrocortisone tablet would cause a heart attack or a stroke while Gil was piloting the Cessna?"

"It wouldn't," Carol said. "And it wouldn't matter. What if whoever switched the meds wasn't interested in killing Gil while he was flying? Suppose her agenda was just to make sure he dropped dead sometime soon. It could have happened at any time, any place. It was just chance that the drug did its work while he was over Crooked Lake last Monday morning."

Kevin considered Carol's logic.

"I'm not saying I buy it, but I agree that if someone was trying to kill Mobley by switching his meds, he couldn't be sure when the wrong meds would take effect. Or even if they *would* take effect. Oh, and by the way, I notice that you've already chosen Suzanne Mobley as the killer. Isn't that a rather hasty judgment when we don't even know if the meds were switched intentionally?"

"You're right about that," Carol admitted. "I mentioned Suzanne only because she lived with him, and would have been most likely to know where he kept his medications."

"You really would like to turn our lake tragedy into a murder case, wouldn't you?" Kevin asked.

"That's not fair. I'm only suggesting that my little encounter with Sigler got me to thinking. And don't tell me you wouldn't be delighted to learn that I've got another murder on my hands."

"Well, now that you put it that way -"

Carol leaned across and gave Kevin a friendly punch on the shoulder.

"No, I'm not putting it that way. We've had more than our quota of murders, as you well know. So keep your powder dry. All I'm doing is maintaining an open mind about what happened to Gil Mobley. Let's have dinner."

CHAPTER 23

Franklin rolled to the side of the bed and reached over to pick up the alarm clock on the bedside table. The clock face was difficult to read, so he fumbled around until he located his glasses. The clock told him it was 3:46. In spite of the fact that he was barely awake, he realized that that couldn't be right. Even with the shade drawn, there was too much light in the room. But the alarm had been set for 6:30 and it hadn't gone off yet. He looked more closely at the clock. The second hand was not moving. The battery had died in the night.

He slid out of bed and turned on the table lamp. His wrist watch read 8:57. Franklin was now wide awake and aware that he had overslept. No tea had been prepared, no breakfast order taken. He could not recall a time in the seventeen years he had supervised *Chambord* and taken care of Constance Mobley that he had failed to bring her her tea at eight.

For a man in his seventies, he moved with remarkable agility. He would have to forego shaving, something he almost never did. He was already late; he could not afford to be any later. It was ten minutes after nine when he finished dressing and hurried down the stairs, out the door, and off through the woods to the great house. It looked as if it were going to be another good day, but for Eldridge Franklin it was already a bad day. Constance was basically a kind and thoughtful woman, but she was a creature of habit who adhered in almost every aspect of her life to familiar routines. Franklin had failed her today.

There was no way to hurry the tea, but he did not wish to appear at her door without it. When it was ready, he set the pot on the tray with the tea service, lemon, and sugar and moved as quickly as possible down the hall to the elevator and up to Mrs. Mobley's quarters in the southeast corner of the house.

He balanced the tray on one hand, a trick he had learned many years ago, and rapped on the door to announce himself. The matriarch of the Mobley family, who was usually awake before he arrived with her tea, customarily called out for him to come in. This morning she didn't do so.

Franklin knocked again, and then spoke up to let her know that he was at the door.

"Constance," he called out, using her given name as she had insisted he do. "I'm late, but your tea is ready at last."

When she didn't answer, he first thought that perhaps she was in the dressing room or her bath.

"May I bring the tea in?" he asked.

There had been other occasions when she hadn't heard him, probably, he'd thought, because she was in the loo. But this morning, unlike those other times, he was concerned because he was late. So late, in fact, that she might have gone back to sleep. But as he waited for a sound from the bedroom, he decided that that wasn't likely. Constance was a morning person. She was accustomed to napping in the afternoon, but never in the morning.

"Constance, it's Franklin. Are you all right?" Although her hearing was quite good considering her age, he raised his voice this time.

He was now angry with himself for being so late. And he was also worried. He tested the door. Constance never locked it, and he pushed it open an inch or two and called her name again.

This time Eldridge Franklin did not hesitate. He opened the door and hurried into the large room with the old four poster bed. The bed was large, and Constance was small and frail, so he didn't see her among the covers until he was at her bedside.

"Constance."

He set the tray down and reached across to shake her. She didn't respond and Franklin now faced the fact that Constance Mobley was either very ill or dead. He knew that she had been sick for some time, but he had never given much thought to the possibility that she might actually be at death's door. For the first time in a very long time, Franklin was afraid, both for Mrs. Mobley and for himself.

He pulled the blankets away, setting aside any concern for privacy. Bending down, he put his face close to hers. She wasn't breathing and she seemed unnaturally cold. He thought about artificial respiration, but knew it was too late. It was even too late for a call to 911. He was as sure as he could be that the woman whom he had served for much of his later adult life was now dead.

With tears in his eyes, Franklin finally got up from the bed and went to the phone.

Dr. Sigler's receptionist answered the phone.

"This is Eldridge Franklin, calling from Constance Mobley's residence. This is an emergency, and I must speak to Dr. Sigler."

Th receptionist began to explain that Dr. Sigler was unavailable.

"No, please, he must be available. Mrs. Mobley is dead. He must come to the phone."

There was some confusion on the other end of the line, but the doctor did pick up.

"This is something about Mrs. Mobley?" he asked.

"Yes, doctor. I think - no, I'm sure she's dead. I was bringing her her tea, and she -"

"Franklin, did you call 911?" Sigler didn't wait for an answer. "Look, stay with her. I'll be right there."

Franklin knew that it would take Dr. Sigler at least half an hour to get to *Chambord*. If Constance were alive now, and he was sure she wasn't, she couldn't possibly be alive when he arrived. He pulled the blanket over her lifeless body and poured himself a cup of tea. And then he started to sob.

———

It took no time for Sigler to confirm that Constance Mobley was in fact dead. There was nothing he could do, nothing that was within his medical knowledge. Instead he called Suzanne Mobley. Fortunately she was home.

"Suzanne, this is Dr. Sigler. I hate to be the bearer of more bad news, but your mother-in-law has just died. I am at *Chambord* right now, and it appears that Mother Mobley passed away some time during the night. Franklin tried to revive her, but I'm afraid that she'd been dead for several hours. I need to talk with you about funeral plans."

From life to death to arranging a funeral. All within the span of a single summer night.

Suzanne seemed less shocked than resigned.

"What can I say, Jeremy? I guess I'm relieved that Gil didn't live to know he'd lost his mother." She could be heard blowing her nose.

"Do you want to come over?" Sigler asked. "There's nothing you can do here, but you may want to say good-bye, if you know what I mean. And arrangements do need to be made. I suppose you'll want to call your brother-in-law. He's in the area, isn't he?"

"I'll tell Marcus. And I guess I'll want to come over to *Chambord*. How is Franklin doing?"

"Not so well. I've always thought of him as somebody who'd soldier on, no matter what. But I have the feeling that he was more emotionally attached to your mother-in-law than I realized. I wonder what he'll do."

"I can't think about that now. One day at a time. That's what I've been doing for the last week. Life's a real bitch, isn't it?"

On that note, Suzanne rang off and Dr. Sigler busied himself trying to comfort Franklin and attending to the transition from sick patient to deceased patient.

CHAPTER 24

Suzanne didn't want to talk with Marcus. Not today, not any day. But she had no choice. She needed the name and phone number of Constance Mobley's attorney. Gil knew who he was, but Gil was dead and she had impulsively gotten rid of her late husband's files along with his medications. Franklin might know, but she felt uncomfortable calling and asking if he would share that information with her. Which left Marcus.

She was sure that her brother-in-law and his wife had come to Crooked Lake and taken up temporary residence in a local B & B because his mother was ill and failing. He could not have known that Constance would die so quickly, or for that matter that his brother would so unexpectedly lose his life as well. But Marcus and Carrie were transparently interested in ingratiating themselves with his mother, the better to improve his standing in her will. His prospects might even be better now that she had lost her other son, the favored one. But what was the status of Constance's will? Had she written one? If so, had she modified it since Gil's death? It had suddenly become imperative that she know these things, and she wouldn't know them until she talked with Mom Mobley's attorney.

Suzanne didn't have Marcus's cell phone number, so she punched in the number of the *Silver Willows* B & B. The proprietor connected her to his room. Unfortunately, Carrie answered. Suzanne didn't care for Marcus; she liked Carrie even less.

"Carrie, this is Suzanne. How are the two of you doing?"

"We're doing just fine. Is there some reason why we shouldn't be?"

"No, it's just that we haven't been in touch since our gathering at *Chambord* the day Gil was killed. When do you expect Marcus?"

"I really don't know. He had gone out before I got up this morning, and he didn't leave me a note. What's up?"

Suzanne realized that 'nothing' was not only dishonest but that someone else, someone like Franklin or Dr. Sigler, might call with the news that Constance was dead. Which would make it look as if she had deliberately been keeping Carrie in the dark.

"I was the one who gave you the sad news on Monday that Gil had been killed. I'm afraid I have more bad news, particularly for Marcus. His mother passed away last night."

"She's dead?" Carrie Mobley was obviously shocked.

Yes, Suzanne thought, that's what passed away means.

"I just talked with Dr. Sigler. It's too soon to have any of the details, but it appears that she just didn't wake up this morning."

"That's, well, I'd guess you'd call it pretty close to unbelievable. We all knew she wasn't well, but so sudden -"

Suzanne had no intention of saying she was calling about Mom Mobley's attorney. It would only prompt thoughts about their inheritance. It was even likely that Carrie would urge Marcus not to share the attorney's name with Suzanne.

"Anyway, I knew you'd both want to know. It's been a terrible week, wouldn't you say?"

"Oh, yes, terrible is the word for it," Carrie agreed.

Suzanne doubted that Carrie really thought of it as a terrible week. After they'd hung up, she found herself thinking about her own feelings about the week. Mom Mobley's death had taken her by surprise, but it was not all that unexpected. They had never been close, but they respected each other. Moreover, the old lady had had a long life and for much of it had lived in what passed for luxury in this part of the country. And if everything went as it should, Suzanne was almost certainly closer to a sizable inheritance. As for Gil's death, it had made what could have been a difficult divorce unnecessary.

She went to her liquor cabinet, selected a single malt scotch, and poured herself a generous drink. I'm really not a very nice person, she said to herself as she wandered out to the porch. Here I am, toasting the death of my husband and my mother-in-law. I did a nice job of pretending to be in mourning at Gil's funeral, and I'm sure I'll put on a good repeat performance when we lay Constance to rest. But what is that old saying about fooling all of the people some of the time? Something like that.

Suzanne drained her glass and took out her cell again.

"Shell, it's me. I didn't expect to find you at the motel. What are you doing, watching *The Price Is Right*?"

"I'm not that desperate. Fact is I just got back from a run up to Geneva, and I was about to call you. Evelyn's in the hospital up there."

"She is? What's she doing in Geneva?"

"She was on her way down to see Constance and she hit a deer. She's got a concussion and a broken arm. Damn lucky she wasn't banged up even worse."

"How in hell did she know you were in a motel down here?"

"We do talk now and then, strange as it may seem. I called her from Westchester, told her I was coming up this way to see you. I even suggested it might be nice for the three of us to get together, but she begged off. I think it's going to be a tough sell, convincing her to give us another chance."

"Thank goodness she nixed the idea of a family reunion. Not a good idea, not now. When the time's right I promise to do my best to mend my bridges. But I've got something to tell you, bigger than Evelyn and the deer. Constance Mobley died last night."

"You're serious," Rivers said, sounding very doubtful.

"Very serious. Sigler called me from the mansion this morning. Seems like she just went to sleep and never woke up. That's the way I want to go."

"Damn. It'll take me awhile to digest this, but Evelyn'll be all broken up. If I know her, she'll figure her accident was the last straw, coming right after the old lady lost her son. She really loved her, you know. She's told me more than once that she was the grandmother she never had as a little girl."

"I suppose it would be a good idea for me to call her. Do you have a hospital number?"

"No, and I think she'll be out of there tomorrow. We've got to let her know bout Constance. She'll want to come down. What do you think?"

"How's she supposed to get down here? Is her car drivable?"

"Don't know, and I'm not sure she does. The decent thing would be for you or me to go up and bring her down. She could stay with you until after the funeral."

Suzanne thought about this for a few seconds and decided against it.

"Shell, it's been at least a year since I last talked to her. I'm about as welcome as the bubonic plague. If she has to be here, let her stay at the motel with you."

"You realize that that'll put an end to our midnight assignations, don't you?"

"Everyone has to sacrifice from time to time. Besides, you were horrified someone would spot me sneaking into your room. We'll just have to put our lust on hold for a few days."

"Just as well. It seems to me that things are getting a bit dicey around here. You've got to be principal mourner. Forget everything else. I'll take care of Evelyn, you carry the torch for the Mobleys - the irreplaceable Gil and his saintly mother, both taken from us in the prime of life. No, that won't work, not with Constance. You're smart, you'll think of some good lines."

"Okay. So you'll notify Evelyn and I'll put on sackcloth and ashes."

CHAPTER 25

Word of Evelyn Rivers' collision with a deer reached the sheriff in a rather round about way. Another driver had called 911, and an emergency vehicle took Evelyn to the hospital. One member of that team, Jimmy Erwin, was in the hospital again the following morning. Remembering the young woman he had transported the previous day, he inquired about her and was given permission to pay her a brief visit. Their conversation didn't last long, but it lasted long enough for her to mention that she had been on her way to visit her Grandmother Mobley on Crooked Lake when she struck the deer. It wasn't until Jimmy Erwin was eating dinner that evening that he remembered that somebody named Mobley had recently been killed when his plane had crashed into Crooked Lake. This led to Erwin commenting on this coincidence to Officer Damoth of the Cumberland County Sheriff's Department, whom he knew slightly. Damoth, of course, told the sheriff.

Carol had never met Evelyn Rivers. She could think of no good reason why she should call the young woman. Presumably Evelyn had already called Constance Mobley, explaining why she hadn't made it. But her parents were both in the area. Perhaps she should call them. Or at least one of them, and that would be Suzanne. After all, she didn't know the woman's father, her only contact with him having been at *Chambord* following Gil's death.

She didn't know what kind of relationship Evelyn had maintained with her mother since her parents had divorced. She suspected that it had not been a particularly good one, but that was only what she'd inferred from what little Dr. Sigler and Constance Mobley had told her. Nonetheless, she put a call through to Suzanne.

The recently widowed woman sounded out of breath when she answered the phone.

"Mrs. Mobley here. What can I do for you?"

It occurred to Carol that Suzanne had probably had quite a few calls since her husband's death. Did she welcome them, or was she tired of people's solicitude?

"This is Carol Kelleher, the sheriff. I'm sorry to trouble you like this, but I've just heard something that I thought you should know about. Unless, that is, you may have gotten the word already. There has been -"

"I know. I heard about it this morning. It came as an awful shock. I know she hadn't been well, but she was emotionally strong, a real fighter. You saw her on Monday, just as feisty as ever, even after hearing about Gil's tragedy."

"Mrs. Mobley, I'm not sure we're talking about the same thing." Carol was alarmed by what she'd just heard. "Has something happened to Constance Mobley?"

"Isn't that what you're calling about?"

"No, I'm afraid not. I've heard nothing about Constance."

"She died last night. Dr. Sigler called me this morning with the news. I haven't had any time to think about what I have to do."

Carol wanted to hear more about this, but decided she should call Sigler rather than question Suzanne. She didn't want to trouble her with yet another piece of bad news, but it would now be impossible to avoid doing so.

"I'm so sorry to hear about Mrs. Mobley," she said, mentally correcting that to the senior Mrs. Mobley. "Unfortunately, I called because of something else. Your daughter, Evelyn, has been in an accident and is in a hospital in Geneva."

"Yes, I know."

So much for being the bearer of bad news, Carol thought. Suzanne Mobley knows more about what's going on than I do. No point in asking her how she'd gotten this information. Perhaps the young woman had called her mother from the hospital.

"Sheldon told me," Suzanne continued. "Evelyn and I aren't all that close. She's probably still blaming me for the breakup of our marriage after all these years. I'm not sure I can blame her."

"I do hope she'll be all right," Carol said. "Much as I love wildlife, the deer on our roads are a real hazard. But I needn't take more of your time. I appreciate your sharing the bad news regarding Gil's mother. It really has been a bad week for you and the whole Mobley family. You have my sympathy."

The minute the call ended, Carol's thoughts turned away from Evelyn Rivers and to Constance Mobley. Evelyn would be okay, or so Officer Damoth's source had told him. The death of Mother Mobley was another story. She didn't really know her, didn't have any understanding of the Mobley family's relationships. And it was none of her business. But not only was she experiencing a surprising feeling of sadness about the death of the Mobley matriarch; she was also feeling a sense of unease. Too much was going wrong in this Crooked Lake family of whom she had known almost nothing a short week ago.

She called Dr. Sigler.

His receptionist reported that he was not in the office and didn't expect to be back until the following morning, which led to a decision to drive over to *Chambord*. If Sigler wasn't there, Franklin probably would be. The trip gave her a chance to think about what might be the future of the lakeside mansion. She couldn't imagine that any member of the family would want to live there. Too big, too old fashioned, too costly to maintain. Too ugly? She supposed that that would be a matter of taste. In all likelihood it would be razed and before long a cluster of cottages would stand where *Chambord* had stood. It was a near certainty, she thought, that many of the trees on the property would come down. Who would want to live by the lake and barely see it?

When she pulled through the gap in the bank of evergreens that shielded the compound from the road, Dr. Sigler's car was parked just ahead of her in front of the garage. For the third time in a week she followed the path to the great house, where Franklin once again admitted her.

"I'm so sorry about Mrs. Mobley," she said to him. "It doesn't seem possible, does it?" She realized that not only did she know very little about the Mobleys, she knew even less about Franklin. How long had he been with Constance? What kind of relationship did they have? What would he do now that his services were no longer needed at *Chambord*?

"No, ma'am, it doesn't." He sounded just as he had earlier in the week. The perfect servant, even when things were falling apart.

"When I came here earlier this week, I assumed that I would have the opportunity to get to know both Mrs. Mobley and you better. Regrettably, things worked out differently. I came by because I thought Dr. Sigler would be here. Do you suppose I could have a word with him?"

"Of course. He stayed to talk with the ambulance people, and I think he's about to leave. Please follow me."

They went down one of the corridors and took the elevator. The door to the large bedroom was open, and Dr. Sigler was sitting at a desk in a far corner, examining the contents of one of its drawers.

"Dr. Sigler, you have a visitor," Franklin announced.

The doctor recognized the sheriff and rose from his chair to meet her.

"Thank you, Franklin. It's all right."

Carol wondered what was all right, that she should be allowed to stay? In any event, Franklin nodded and withdrew, closing the door silently as he left.

"Hello, sheriff. Such a sad day. Constance has only been gone about half an hour. I mean to the funeral parlor, of course. Actually she's been gone for somewhere between eight and ten hours. At least she died quietly in her sleep."

"I'm not exactly sure why I'm here. I guess it's because I'm still marginally involved in the investigation of Gil Mobley's death." Carol knew that this wasn't quite true, but it was better than admitting to her ongoing curiosity regarding the Mobley case. "Do you know what happened to Mrs. Mobley?"

"She had congestive heart failure, and it was only a matter of time before it killed her. Like I told you the day you came to my office, it was always a bad idea to cause her worry or anxiety. Obviously I cannot swear to it, but I wouldn't be surprised if the combination of losing a son and hearing that a much loved granddaughter had been in an accident was the last straw."

"So you know about what happened to Evelyn?"

"Franklin told me this morning. I suppose it was worse that Evelyn was on her way over here to see Constance. Too much trouble, coming all at once."

"May I ask you a question that really isn't any of my business?"

"I'm not sure what I'm supposed to make of that," Sigler said. The blank look on his face gave Carol no sense of what he was thinking.

"Frankly, I'm not either. But I'll ask the question and leave it to you to decide whether or how to answer it. And I shall not say anything to anybody about what you tell me. Do you have any idea as to the late Mrs. Mobley's plans for the disposition of her estate?"

"That's not a hard question to answer, sheriff, because I haven't the slightest idea what's in her will. She lived a very compartmentalized life. I handled her medical needs, Franklin handled everything that had to do with the house and the compound, and Jeff Minchin advised her on legal and financial matters. I have never discussed her plans with either Franklin or Minchin, nor did I ever talk about them with Constance herself. If I had, I'm quite sure she would have politely told me to be satisfied that I was her doctor. Now may I ask you a question? Why are you interested in her estate?"

"To be perfectly honest, it's simply that I'm curious. And I'm curious because I've been unable to shake off the feeling that something wasn't quite right here at *Chambord* the day Gil was killed. We talked about it when we met at your office on Tuesday - the tension in the air, the sense that everyone was on edge. You thought it was simply that they were still in shock, and I'll grant that that's probably the best explanation. But I haven't been able to get it off my mind, and I find myself wondering if it didn't have something to do with the estate, with Constance's will. After all, her two most likely heirs were Gil and Marcus, and all of a sudden one of them was dead. Could those assembled here that day not only have been in shock over Gil's death, but also anxious about its consequences for the disposition of the estate?"

Sigler stared at Carol without comment for a moment. Then he stepped back and resumed his seat at Mrs. Mobley's desk.

"You may, of course, be right, sheriff. I'm not trained in reading people's motives from their facial expressions or their body language. But I heard nothing at that difficult gathering in the parlor to suggest that the family was preparing to go to war over Mrs. Mobley's will."

"Nor did I, Dr. Sigler. I'm sorry I brought it up. Like I said, I guess I'm just being curious. Perhaps it's due to my chosen profession. Anyway, let me let you get back to what must be a very difficult day for you. I'm sure you must be grieving for a wonderful woman. I'm sorry I never met her before this week."

Carol let herself out. As she descended the staircase to where Franklin would be waiting for her, she was wondering what it was that Jeremy Sigler was looking for in Constance Mobley's desk.

CHAPTER 26

The morning sun had already pushed the temperature into the upper 80s, but Marcus Mobley, cooled by the car's air conditioner, rode along county road 37 high above Crooked Lake in comfort. To his left and right he could see acres and acres of vineyards, while far below him the lake waters sparkled. When he looked off into the distance he could even see the ridges that separated Crooked Lake from other Finger Lakes miles off to the east. It was a beautiful day, and Marcus was enjoying the peace and quiet, such a relief after another round of unpleasantness with Carrie over breakfast at the *Silver Willows* B & B.

If he could only have his way, he would spend the entire day driving over these back roads, stopping only at the occasional roadside stand to pick up a small basket of blueberries. Marcus didn't particularly care for the rural or small town way of life, but there were days when it provided a blessed escape from his wife's incessant nagging.

They had wasted more than two weeks at the lake, trying to improve their inheritance prospects, with nothing to show for it. Carrie had insisted on coming to the lake from the day that Doctor Sigler had called to report that Marcus's mother was failing rapidly. It won't do any good, he had told her over and over again. 'Gil's the golden boy,' he had said, 'and any hope I may have had to regain her love disappeared when I married you.' Not surprisingly, Carrie didn't want to hear this. Every time he brought it up it only prompted another bitter row. Since they had checked into the B & B they had quarreled constantly. It was time to go home.

It was simply not possible to solve his problem by putting miles on the Honda. It was close to 12:30 when he arrived back at *Silver Willows*.

"Where in hell have you been?" Carrie greeted him as he came into their second floor guest room.

"I wasn't feeling too good, thought some fresh air would help."

"Almost three hours of fresh air?"

"At least I didn't get ticketed for speeding and driving drunk." Once more, Carrie and Marcus were engaged in a lively marital spat.

It lasted for ten or twelve minutes, then petered out because it had happened so many times that accusations and counter accusations had been reduced to virtual boilerplate.

"Your sister-in-law called while you were out," Carrie said without elaborating.

"What did she want?"

"I think you'll be interested. Your mother died in her sleep last night."

"Oh, my God," Marcus said. "I knew it was coming, yet I never got a chance to say good-bye."

"I don't need to tell you I told you so. You should have been down there at the mansion every day. Anyway, now it's too late. She's gone, and we don't know a damn thing about her will, even whether she gave you a single penny."

"I did my best no matter what you may think," he said tartly. "In any event, now we can go home."

"I'm not leaving here until we've got a straight answer from her lawyer." This had been another sore point. Jeff Minchin had been very closed mouth about Constance Mobley's will. 'I can't say, not at this time,' he would say, and then 'I'm not at liberty to talk about it' or 'I'm sure your mother would prefer that you speak with her, not with me.' Marcus had known that asking his mother point blank what he stood to gain from her death would be undiplomatic and probably counter productive.

"Are you expecting one of those dramatic Agatha Christie readings of the will?" Marcus was now being sarcastic. "All of us sitting around, glaring at each other, waiting for the other shoe to drop?"

"I don't know how they do it, but I need to know now. She's dead, Marcus. It's too late for her to change her mind, so it's time you stopped being so deferential to that wretched Minchin."

"I have no intention of badgering Minchin."

"You're such a wimp." Carrie practically shouted the word.

"You're the one who's been saying that if Gil were out of the way, we'd be the winners. Well, he's been out of the way for nearly a week. What more could we have done?"

Carrie didn't deign to tell her husband once more what he could have done. She turned on her heel and left the room.

"I'm taking the car," she said over her shoulder. "If you need to go out, call Hertz."

Marcus threw himself down on the bed. He had no intention of napping. He was too mad at Carrie. But he was also mad at himself. In spite of her relentless nagging, he knew she was right. He should have been more aggressive in laying out his case to his mother. He had hoped that Gil's death would work in their favor. They all knew that his mother was unlikely to live much longer. But who would have guessed that she'd be gone in a week. Probably not even Mom Mobley herself, so if the will had to be changed she might well not have gotten around to changing it. Damn the luck.

Carrie Mobley pulled out of the driveway and turned north. Her destination was Yates Center and the law office of Jeffrey Minchin. She had never been there, but Minchin and his role as Constance Mobley's attorney had been on her mind for weeks. One of the first things she had done after they had arrived at Crooked Lake was to look up his address and phone number. It had been her intention to put that information in front of Marcus, giving him less of an excuse for not paying Minchin a visit. If her husband was to be believed, he had actually visited Minchin. But he hadn't stuck up for himself. Well, today, having waited too long to do so, she would stick up for the two of them. She would talk with Constance's attorney and she would find out just what the old woman's will had to say about her younger, unloved son. It might be bad news, but at least she would know. And there might even be some way to contest an unfavorable will.

CHAPTER 27

The day following Constance Mobley's death had been an unusually busy one, and Carol didn't arrive home until almost seven o'clock. She was surprised not to see Kevin's car behind the cottage. But she fully expected to find a note on the kitchen table, telling her that there was some last minute trip he had to take, presumably to pick up something he needed for whatever he was cooking for supper. There was no note on the kitchen table. Indeed, there was no sign that supper was ready. The stove was cold, and she could see nothing in the fridge that looked promising. Carol looked in his study, but could find no note on the desk or in any other logical place.

This was strange, for both of them were very good at honoring a mutual pledge to keep each other apprised of what they were up to. She went next door to ask whether the Brocks knew where Kevin was, only to be told that he'd been gone since mid-afternoon and that he hadn't said anything about his plans. Oh, well, she thought, he'll be back soon enough. Might as well take advantage of the situation and go swimming.

The water was a pleasant 78 degrees, and she found the exercise both invigorating and relaxing. But when she climbed onto the dock and toweled off it was 7:20 and Kevin hadn't returned. It was not until she had shed her bathing suit and was rummaging in the dresser drawer for clean underwear that he made a belated appearance at the bedroom door.

"I see I arrived just in time," he said, admiring the view.

Carol instinctively reached for her towel. It wasn't there.

"Here, let me help," Kevin said, picking the towel up from the carpet and handing it to her.

"I'm not sure whether you're Sir Galahad or Peeping Tom," she said as she recovered her dignity. "Where on earth have you been?"

"Up in the meadows. Go on, get dressed and I'll tell you."

While Carol was putting on her clothes, Kevin uncorked a bottle of Chardonnay and took two glasses of it to the deck. She joined him five minutes later, her hair still damp from the swim.

"Not that I'm in a hurry, but do you have a plan for dinner?" she asked as she settled into her chair.

"Damn. Forgot completely about dinner. We can drink our dinner," he said, raising his glass of wine aloft, "or run out to *The Cedar Post*. Unless, that is, you're prepared to settle for BLTs."

"I'm worn out. Let's make it the BLTs, as long as you do them."

"Of course. Sorry to hear it's been a bad day, though. What happened?"

"It wasn't a bad day. Well, I suppose that depends on whom you ask. It was just a long one, lots of running around."

"Who would I have to ask to be told it was a bad day?"

"I'd like to think it would be one or more of the Mobleys, although I can't be sure how broken up they all are by the news. Anyway, the news is that the Grand Dame herself, Constance Mobley, died last night."

"The pilot's mother?"

"Right. One week after she lost her son."

"She didn't go down in a Cessna, did she?"

"Come on, Kevin, that's sick. She died in her sleep, according to the doctor."

"So it's been a bad week for Mobleys, hasn't it."

"Maybe for more of them than Gil and Constance," Carol said cryptically.

"I don't understand."

"Never mind. My mind is wandering. But you were going to tell me where you've been. What happened to our rule about leaving notes?"

Kevin got up and went into the study and came back with a book, which he set down on the small table between their chairs.

"It's an old excuse, I know, but I just lost track of time. I wanted to read this biography of Caravaggio," he said, referring to the book on the table. "And I thought it'd be fun to go up to that lookout where the Random Harvest Vineyards have put out a couple of benches. You know, nice outlook, good breeze. The book was interesting, and I didn't know what time it was."

"Really? That can't be. Remember that old tune? I don't remember who wrote it, but it went something like 'I didn't know what time it was, then I met you.' So you see, now that you've met me, there's no excuse for not knowing what time it is."

"That's very clever, Carol. I didn't know you knew the Great American Song Book. By the way, Rodgers and Hart wrote it. But you'll have to blame Caravaggio."

"The book's that good, is it?"

"Caravaggio's that good. Even better than Rodgers and Hart."

"I remember the name from an art course I took back in college. But I doubt I'd recognize him if I met him in a museum."

"I have a hunch you would. What got me hooked is that this Renaissance guy was a truly great artist but a nasty human being. Among other things, he was a murderer, and in his lifetime people were horrified that he used prostitutes and hustlers as his models for his great Christian paintings."

"And now you're going to tell me I must find time to read this book?"

"No, I'm going to ask you a question that came to me while *I* was reading it."

"Fine, as long as you don't expect me to answer your question. Remember, you're the professor. I'm just a dumb cop."

"I'll forget you said that. You're a smart cop, and you've caught seven murderers since I met you. Seven. And while I was reading about Caravaggio, I started to think about those seven. Now I know none of your Crooked Lake murderers had anything like Caravaggio's talent, and that's not my point. But most people presumably have both good and bad qualities. Caravaggio did; after all, his art hangs today in the world's finest museums. I was wondering how you feel about your murderers. Did any of them have a good side that makes what they did all the more lamentable?"

"I'm not sure I buy your argument," Carol said. "So what if Caravaggio was talented. Jack the Ripper was good at what he did, too. But I see what you're driving at, and yes, I've felt badly for some of the Crooked Lake killers. Like the one who killed the owner of *Silver Leaf* winery. He was a better man than the guy he killed. Which is what makes him a tragic figure."

"I know I'm talking apples and oranges - great talent and good personal qualities are quite different things. But I like your choice, and why not? If the owner of that winery hadn't ended up dead on my dock we might never have met. Life's full of what ifs, isn't it?"

"And to think at first I thought you might have been the one that killed him."

Not surprisingly, and not for the first time, this led to twenty minutes of reminiscing. It could have gone on longer if Carol hadn't reminded Kevin that he'd promised to make BLTs.

It wasn't until they were cleaning up the kitchen that they got around to the Mobley case again.

"I think you said something about this being a bad week for more than the pilot and his mother," Kevin said. "Who'd you have in mind?"

"I'm not really sure. But remember awhile back I was telling you how tense everyone was at the mansion the day Gil was killed. The mood in that room didn't fit that of a grieving family. And you suggested that maybe the sudden death of one of the old woman's sons had gotten them thinking about how it might affect their inheritance. I didn't give it much thought at the time, but you just may have been onto something. In any event, it would be interesting to know who inherits what under Constance's will."

"Interesting, but not the business of the sheriff of Cumberland County. Is that what you're about to say?"

"I guess so," Carol agreed.

"Don't be too sure. People have been known to do strange things when the issue of who gets what in a will is at stake."

"But nobody has done anything I'd call strange, so why am I concerned?"

"You don't know that nobody has done anything strange," Kevin insisted.

"Like committed murder? Is that what you're thinking? Come on, Kevin, Gil Mobley died of a heart attack and his mother died of congestive heart failure. I have it on good authority in both cases."

"If I were you, I'd keep an open mind."

"If you were me," Carol replied, "you'd try to stop rooting around in something that's none of your business. There's nothing in my job description that says I should collect my pay for worrying about Mobleys."

CHAPTER 28

Sheldon Rivers was one of those people who are confident in their ability to know what to expect from their fellow men. He had rarely been caught off guard by people with whom he did business, much less by those with whom he played poker. This talent - and he did regard it as a talent, one in which he took great pride - had stood him in good stead when he chose to play the stock market, as well as in the myriad small ways which gave him pleasure and contributed to a smug sense of superiority in the human rat race. Women, however, were quite another matter. It had taken him years to get over the fact that he had misjudged Suzanne and then lost her to a Cessna pilot named Gil Mobley. But those bad days were now ending and he was concentrating on what he expected to be a smooth transition to what he thought of as the second coming.

Unfortunately, he was now confronted with another demonstration of the fact that women did not accommodate easily to the life he desired and felt he was entitled to live. The problem was his daughter, Evelyn. He had picked her up at the hospital in Geneva and was driving her to her home near Syracuse. Constance Mobley, whom she thought of as her grandmother, was dead, and Evelyn would be in mourning. Or so he had assumed. But she surprised him.

"If it hadn't been for that damned deer, I would have had a farewell visit with her." Evelyn was sitting in the passenger seat of her father's BMW, staring straight ahead as the car gradually closed the distance between Geneva and Marcellus. Her left arm was in a sling and she wore a bandage on her forehead, the only evidence that she had crashed her car en route to Crooked Lake and *Chambord*.

Rivers took his eyes off the road for a brief moment to take a look at his daughter.

"I know," he said. "It will be hard for awhile, but time heals all things."

"That's such a phony cliche, Sheldon," Evelyn said. "It didn't heal your breakup with Suzanne, did it?"

She had always called him Sheldon, not Daddy or Dad, not even Shell. He suspected that it was her way of announcing that their relationship was a proper one rather than an expression of filial love.

"This is no time to be revisiting my marriage with your mother. We should be thinking about Constance."

"There's nothing to think about, is there? Will I miss her? Of course. But we all knew she was failing, that she could go at any time. So if you're worried that I'm not going down to the mansion to pick out those of her things I'd like for my own, forget it. There'll be enough vultures circling over the place without me, my mother among them. Not to mention that witch Carrie. What I want is to get back to my little bungalow and Joey."

Sheldon was uncomfortable, and it wasn't just because he had to drive his daughter back to Marcellus and the insufferable Joey. There had been something in Evelyn's manner ever since they had left the hospital that made it clear that she was suffering his help in her time of need rather than welcoming it.

Joey Landers, Evelyn's lackluster live-in boy friend, had bestirred himself to make arrangements for the damaged car, but otherwise had made little effort to do anything except wish her a speedy recovery. He had even been happy to let Sheldon drive her home. And why was she going home instead of to the Yates Center motel? Sheldon had assumed that Evelyn would stay on the lake for a few days, attend Constance's funeral, give her concussion the rest the doctor had subscribed, and, he hoped, spend at least an hour or two with Suzanne. But she had quickly vetoed that idea.

"Just take me home," she had said, declining to explain herself. And so here he was, heading away from the lake, trying to understand his uncommunicative daughter.

It was not until they were within ten miles of the bungalow that Evelyn broke a long silent spell with an unexpected question.

"How's your problem coming?"

He wasn't sure which of his problems she was referring to.

"My problem?"

"Your health, Sheldon. You've been solicitous of my head and my arm, so it seemed only appropriate to ask how you're doing."

"Well, thank you. I don't recall ever discussing my health with you."

"If you'd rather not, that's fine."

"No, I appreciate your asking. I've got something called chronic fatigue. It's nothing that's going to suddenly just go away. I'm tired too much of the time. And I've been losing weight. Funny, isn't it, a big guy like me, actually shedding pounds without going on a diet."

"We don't see that much of each other, but you don't look good. When you stand up it looks like you're not very steady on your feet. Like maybe you're dizzy. What's the matter?"

Sheldon laughed.

"Maybe I am dizzy," he said. "Too much on my mind. My doc tells me I should get more sleep."

"And are you getting more sleep?"

The smile disappeared from Sheldon Rivers' face.

"Look, I'm doing okay. My doctor knows his stuff, and he's got me on a regimen of meds that's keeping me going."

"Good. I just thought you didn't look so hot."

Evelyn lapsed into silence again. And then, a minute or two later, asked another question.

"What's up with Suzanne?"

"Why should something be up with your mother? I don't know what you mean."

"Oh, come on, Sheldon. You don't normally drop everything down in Westchester and take a two week vacation on Crooked Lake. You told me you were coming up this way to see Suzanne. So what's going on?"

He wondered whether Evelyn knew about Gil Mobley's death. He hadn't told her, and it was highly unlikely that Suzanne had. Perhaps she had talked with Constance and heard about it from her. Indeed that might be the reason that she had been on her way to visit Constance when she had her accident.

"Nothing's going on. Suzanne and I are on speaking terms, and I hadn't seen her in some time. It was a slack period in the business, so I thought I could see how she was doing."

"And how is she doing?" she asked. "It seems like you've been here long enough to find out."

It didn't sound as if Evelyn had heard about Gil.

"You haven't heard about what happened to your mother's husband?"

"No, what happened to him?"

"He was killed when his plane crashed into the lake last week."

"No kidding?"

No, Sheldon thought, I'm not kidding.

"Your mother is having a hard time coping. I think it would be nice if you could bring yourself to call her."

The moment he said it he knew he'd made a mistake. If Evelyn called Suzanne, it was possible that Suzanne would tell her that she planned to remarry her father. He could imagine what would follow. It wasn't a pretty picture. Eventually, of course, Evelyn would have to know. But not now. He would have to lay the groundwork, not suddenly spring it on her while driving her back to that poor excuse of a boyfriend, Joey.

"I'll consider calling Suzanne when she decides that she has a real, honest to goodness daughter, not someone she accidentally bumps into at *Chambord* every once in a while."

They were pulling into the bungalow driveway when Evelyn decided to ask one final question.

"Why did Gil crash his plane? It was my understanding that he was a pretty good pilot."

"I think the investigating board blamed it on a heart attack."

"Oh. I was wondering if Suzanne had decided to get rid of another husband."

"You're an impertinent child, Evelyn. It's no wonder your mother doesn't want to talk with you. Now get out."

As Sheldon drove back to the lake, his mind was on the mess he was in. He shook his head and amended that thought: The mess they all were in. He wanted Evelyn to love her mother, but she didn't, and he knew it was Suzanne's fault. He wanted to love Evelyn, but she was making it very hard for anyone to love her. Anyone, that is, except Constance, and now she was dead.

It was not a particularly long drive, but it was long enough that he resented every mile of it. He wished he were back in

Westchester, far away from Crooked Lake and the Mobleys. Yes, even Suzanne.

CHAPTER 29

It was over a week earlier that Carol had taken two unsolicited phone calls from people she didn't know who claimed to have information about Gil Mobley. The call from Edward G. Robinson she had dismissed out of hand. She was virtually certain that there was no one of that name living in the Crooked Lake area. Moreover, the man's story that Gil's Cessna was unfit to fly and that he was aware of its condition made no sense. Merle Corrigan, who would have been in a position to know, claimed that Mobley took excellent care of his plane. The other call had come from Jim Hacklin. Unlike Robinson, Hacklin definitely lived on the lake and, more importantly, was a neighbor of the Mobleys. He had spoken of a loud and acrimonious quarrel between Gil and Suzanne, but because the case was the NTSB's, not hers, and because Terry Sutherland hadn't seemed interested, she had forgotten about it.

But on the day after Kevin had tried to interest her in a Renaissance artist named Caravaggio, two more conscientious citizens called her. One of them was Phyllis Jordan, owner of the *Silver Willows* B & B. The other was Gloria Garner, who worked as a maid for Gil and Suzanne Mobley. Unlike Robinson and Hacklin, Carol at least knew who these people were. It was at Jordan's B & B that Marcus and Carrie Mobley were staying. Garner had answered the phone at the Mobley house the day of Gil's plane crash and had let the sheriff know that Suzanne had gone to *Chambord*.

Carol found it interesting that so many strangers had called out of the blue to talk about Gil Mobley's fatal accident. Or, more accurately, to tell her things which the callers thought would interest her in her capacity as Cumberland County's sheriff. That they wrongly assumed she was in charge of the investigation was understandable. That they assumed that their information was somehow important to the investigation was another matter. She attributed it to the fact that gossip was a way of life in this corner of upstate New York, at least for some of its residents.

The first of the two calls came from Phyllis Jordan. When the proprietor of *Silver Willows* introduced herself, Carol at first had trouble placing her. Jordan was quick to help her out.

"Don't worry, sheriff. We don't really know each other. But one night last week one of your officers came to our door with a woman named Carrie Mobley he'd picked up for drunk driving. I know he was just doing his job, but it was a good thing he brought her home because I doubt she could have made it on her own. I told him he could call me at any time if he wanted to talk about Mrs. Mobley. Well, he didn't call. I don't suppose I expected him to. But it's occurred to me that you'd be the person who needed to talk with me, and that's why I'm calling this morning."

Carol was puzzled, inasmuch as she wasn't aware that she needed to talk with Ms. Jordan.

"Yes, I remember now that Officer Barrett mentioned meeting you. Please, what's on your mind?"

"I guess you could say it's about that terrible airplane crash that killed one of the lake's pilots. I thought you might want to know about the woman your officer brought back to the B & B that night. Her name is Carrie Mobley, and she's the sister-in-law of the pilot who was killed."

Was this conversation simply going to be about the fact that a paying guest who had been driving drunk was related to the recently deceased pilot?

"Ms. Jordan, the investigation into the crash of that plane has been conducted by the National Transportation Safety Board. My office has had nothing to do with it."

"I don't know anything about this Safety Board, but I'm calling about the pilot's sister-in-law and something she said."

"What is it that you think I ought to know?" Carol asked.

"Well, I don't like to tell tales about people, especially guests in my B & B. But somebody ought to know about this. If you think I should get in touch with this Safety Board you're talking about, maybe you can let me know how to contact them."

"I think you should tell me. I can pass your information on to the people who've been conducting the investigation."

Carol doubted that she'd be doing so, but she would hear Ms. Jordan out.

"When Mr. and Mrs. Mobley made their reservation at *Silver Willows,* I had no idea who they were. I mean I didn't know they were related to the pilot who was killed. He hadn't been killed yet. Oh, dear, I'm not making much sense, am I? I should go back to the beginning."

Carol chose not to say anything, although she wasn't sure whether she really wanted Ms. Jordan to go back to the beginning.

"These people, Mr. and Mrs. Marcus Mobley, came to my B & B two weeks ago this past Saturday. Normally I'd have been all full up, but the Cavanaughs had to cancel because of some problem - I think it had something to do with her sister's health. It was kinda funny, though, the Mobleys not giving me a checkout date. They said they weren't sure how long they'd be staying. When I told them I had some other reservations, they gave me a story about how his mother was very sick, and couldn't I juggle things a bit. Anyway, Mr. Mobley wrote me a big check and, like he suggested, I did some juggling. Do you think that was a fair thing to do?"

"It's your business, Ms. Jordan," Carol said. "But what is it that you think I ought to know?"

"I'm getting to that. The Mobleys weren't bad guests. I mean they didn't trash things like some people do, and they always complimented me on my breakfasts. I take pride in my scones and muesli, and it's nice to hear people say they appreciate what I put out on the table. But they quarreled. They quarreled a lot. And sometimes they didn't keep their voices down, so it was just about impossible not to hear them. It seemed to me that you or maybe that Safety Board ought to know what they were shouting about to each other."

It must run in the family, Carol thought. Gil and Suzanne, according to Hacklin, now Marcus and Carrie according to Jordan.

"I take it you think what they were quarreling about is important," she said.

"I can't be sure, but it sounded important to me. They went on and on about his mother, about what they were going to get in her will. She couldn't stand it that he wouldn't stick up for himself. But what's important, I think, came after his brother was killed in that plane crash. They still kept right on quarreling about his mother's will, but Mrs. Mobley, she started in talking about her brother-in-law. There was one really bad night. She was arguing that now he was dead, they were in a position to twist the old lady's arm and get what they were entitled to. And that's when he told her - I'm talking about Carrie now - that she was the one who wanted him dead, so she ought to be the one to twist his mother's arm."

"Marcus said that his wife wanted her brother-in-law dead?" Carol asked.

"He sure did."

Carol was now paying close attention to this woman who didn't like to gossip about her guests but was obviously enjoying doing it.

"Please bear with me, Ms. Jordan, I have to be sure I have this right. You heard him saying this sometime after his brother's death?"

"That's right."

"Do you recall exactly when you heard this exchange between the Mobleys?"

"It was the night that your officer brought her back to the B & B because she was drunk. I think that's why she went off in a huff that night. Worried me sick, her husband, too."

"Ms. Jordan, are Mr. and Mrs. Mobley still with you?"

"Oh, yes. I asked them just yesterday if they knew yet when they'd be leaving, and they said they'd let me know."

"About their quarrels. Have they said anything more about the death of Mr. Mobley's brother?"

"Not that I've heard. My guess is that after she came home drunk that night they decided they'd better tone it down or people would hear them."

Carol was surprised that people arguing about wanting someone dead wouldn't have lowered the volume much earlier. Either Phyllis Jordan was accustomed to keeping her ear at the keyholes of her guests' bedrooms or Marcus and Carrie Mobley were so preoccupied with their mutual antipathy that they failed to appreciate how easily they could be overheard.

The more she thought about Ms. Jordan's 'news,' the more she was inclined to discount it as unimportant. 'I wish he were dead' is, after all, not an uncommon expression, something said in anger or frustration with no intention to act on it. And if Marcus Mobley's prospects of inheriting from his mother were presumably greater with Gil dead, saying so could simply be a maladroit statement of the truth.

It was just as Carol was ready to step out to the deli to get something for lunch that JoAnne informed her that Gloria Garner was on the phone. At first the name meant nothing to Carol, but JoAnne said the woman had something to say about the Mobleys, so she took the call.

"Sheriff, I'm Gloria Garner, and I worked for the Mobleys until yesterday. I believe I spoke to you the day that Mr. Gil was killed in that awful accident. You were trying to locate Suzanne."

"Yes, of course, I remember." The voice was that of a young woman, perhaps even a girl not long out of her teens, if that.

"I don't know whether I should be talking to you. Maybe I'm just sticking my nose in something that's none of my business. But I keep thinking about it. I couldn't even sleep good last night."

"Don't worry, Ms. Garner. If what's on your mind isn't important, I'll simply forget it." Carol realized that she'd said very much the same thing to people several times recently. But one of these times what she was hearing might actually be important.

"It's about Suzanne," the Garner woman said. "I've been a live-in housekeeper for the Mobleys for almost two years. It's been a good job, at least most of the time. They pay good. But they don't get along, especially lately. I hated to see them go after each other. And I'd hear stuff I shouldn't have been hearing. Did you know Mr. Gil? Or Suzanne?"

Carol found it interesting that Ms. Garner was referring to him as Mr. Gil and to Suzanne by her first name only.

"I never met Mr. Mobley, and I'd never met Mrs. Mobley until the day of the airplane accident."

"Oh, so you don't really know much about them."

"That's true."

"Well, this is what's hard for me, talking about people behind their backs. But Mr. Gil, he was a real gentleman, always kind to me. In fact, he was the one who hired me back when I didn't know what I was going to do after high school. But Suzanne -"

She paused, trying to think how she should say what she had to say.

"I guess I should just say it. Suzanne didn't like me. Right from the first, she was always getting on me for something, like how I made her bed, or forgetting to put things where they belonged. At first I thought maybe she believed Mr. Gil was interested in me. You know, in a bad way. But he never did anything at all, and she didn't have no cause to be jealous or anything. She's a beautiful woman and I'm, well, I'm not much to look at. Then yesterday she fired me."

"I'm so sorry," Carol said.

"She didn't tell me why, just that she didn't need me now that Mr. Gil was gone. But I think she hates me and with him gone there wasn't no one in the house to stick up for me. But that's not what I called to tell you."

Carol had guessed as much.

"You came to the house the other day, and you talked to Suzanne about Mr. Gil's medicine. I was there, out in the kitchen where I was washing up. I couldn't help but hearing what you and her were saying. You wanted his pills, but they weren't in the house. I could have told you that, 'cause Suzanne had me help her find them. Anyway, like she told you, she'd thrown them away. At first I didn't think nothing about it. It weren't any of my business. But then just yesterday, my last day, Suzanne, she told me she wanted me to clean up the bedrooms real good. She was always getting after me about the beds. She expected I'd vacuum under the beds, but the vacuum cleaner won't fit under there. Anyway, I did the best I could, down on my hands and knees. What I found, other than an old magazine, was two pills."

"Did you throw them out?"

"I figured Suzanne would want me to, but I put them in my apron pocket. And that's where they are now. That's why I'm calling, sheriff. You wanted them, and it looked like Suzanne didn't want you to have them. When she fired me, I decided to call you. Do you still want those pills?"

Carol didn't know whether she should want them or not. But in all likelihood Doc Crawford would want them, unless, that is, Sutherland had convinced him that the case was truly closed.

"Yes, Ms. Garner, I'd very much like to have them. We're still not one hundred percent sure what caused Mr. Mobley's heart attack, and it's possible his medications had something to do with it. If you tell me where you're living now, I'll have one of my officers come by and pick them up."

"No, no, please don't send a policeman to get them. My daddy would think I'd gotten into some kind of trouble, and he's got a terrible temper. I'll come to your place, but I don't know where you live."

"My office is in the Foxhall building in Cumberland."

"Will you be there?"

"I can't be sure. If I'm not, just give them to Ms. Franks. She's my assistant."

Carol was ready to wish Gloria Garner good luck in finding a new job when an important question occurred to her.

"Did Mr. and Mrs. Mobley sleep in the same bed?" Ms. Garner might find the question awkward to answer, but she would surely know.

"Not any more. Like I said, they'd been sort of mad at each other lately, and he moved into one of the spare bedrooms. You mustn't think I pried into their life, sheriff, but it was another bedroom I had to clean."

"And under whose bed did you find the pills, his or hers?"

"It was Suzanne's."

"Do you remember how long ago Mr. Mobley moved into the spare bedroom?"

"I'm not sure, but not more than a month."

"Sorry to keep asking questions. You said you didn't like to hear what they were arguing about, but I'll bet you did. Can you tell me?"

"It wasn't nice."

"No, probably not. When people are angry with each other, they can say some things they might regret. Was it about money?"

"No, not money. They have lots of money. No, I think they just don't love each other any more."

"Were they talking about a divorce?"

"Some, but Mr. Gil, he wouldn't give her a divorce. Over my dead body, that's the way he put it."

"Okay, Gloria - may I call you Gloria? I appreciate it that you called. And I thank you for bringing over the pills you found."

Two little pills which Suzanne Mobley hadn't been able to flush down the toilet. Carol promptly called Doc Crawford.

"I have something I think you'll want to take a look at," she said when he answered his phone.

"Want to give me a hint?"

"Suzanne Mobley didn't get rid of all of her husband's pills, Doc. The maid was doing a thorough house cleaning and found two of them under the bed. I hope to have them in my hands by the end of the day. I'll bring them by on my way home, okay?"

"I'm not going anywhere," he said. "It'll be a welcome twofer, the missing Mobley meds and a chance to see my favorite sheriff."

CHAPTER 30

Suzanne Mobley was in a foul mood when she heard the knock on the back door. She was in a foul mood because Sheldon had announced that there was no reason for him to stick around the lake any longer. She had asked if he didn't regard her as a perfectly good reason, and he had assured her that he did, but not now.

"I've been here for more than two weeks," he'd said, "and I do have a business to take care of. I've done all I can up here, including taking a back of the church pew for Gil's funeral and sending an impressive floral arrangement in memory of Constance."

"Too bad Mom Mobley couldn't see the flowers. I doubt that they would have compensated for that 'skunk at the garden party' remark."

"Come on, Suzanne, let's not do this. I did what I came to do, and when things settle down I'll whisk you away from here and we'll start a new life."

"It's Evelyn, isn't it? She was her usual bitchy self and you're having a guilty conscience."

"You should be the one with a guilty conscience, but like I said, let's not get into an argument."

With Shell gone, Suzanne was not interested in company, but she went to the door anyway.

"Hello, Suzanne. I should have stopped by sooner, but you know how it is. You've probably got a house full of flowers by now, but here's a little something to say how much I'll miss Gil. I'm so sorry."

Merle Corrigan handed her a small bouquet of white roses.

"You're very kind," she said, making an effort to suck it up and be pleasant to the fellow Cessna pilot.

"Mind if I come in? I promise not to stay long."

She didn't wish to talk with Merle, but she had the presence of mind to invite him into the house.

147

"I'm sure everyone you run into wants to know what happened to Gil," she said. It wasn't much of a conversational gambit, but she knew it was probably true and it shifted the burden of making small talk to Merle.

"Yeah. They all think I know all about it, but I don't know anything. So I don't say much, just what a bad break for such a nice guy."

"That's nice, but we both know it isn't true. You and Gil were never friends."

"In a way we were." Corrigan looked around him as if looking for a chair to sit in. Suzanne got the message.

"Come on in," she said, leading him into the living room. "Iced tea?"

"No thanks. I really don't intend to stay. But I have a proposition to make to you."

Suzanne had to make a conscious effort not to look as shocked as she felt. She excused herself, saying she'd be right back, and disappeared into the kitchen to pour herself a stiff shot of vodka. It would have been polite to offer Merle Corrigan one, too, but she had no intention of doing so.

"Sorry about that, but I've got one of those wretched summer colds and I could feel a coughing jag coming on." Trying to make her excuse look convincing, she took a good swig of the vodka. It had the effect of making her cough.

"I've got a problem, Suzanne." Merle began to explain himself. "A real tough one. I'm sure you know that Libby is afraid of flying."

"I do," she answered, now totally confused.

"We're an odd couple, I guess. Me a pilot, Libby someone who wouldn't get on a plane if her life depended on it. Anyway, you won't believe this, but after she heard about Gil's accident she issued an ultimatum. Who do I love more, her or my plane? She as much as told me I have to get rid of the Cessna. It's the plane or her, and she means it."

Suzanne couldn't care less what happened to Merle and Libby Corrigan, but she was having a hard time believing what he had just told her. Shell didn't share her interest in flying, but he'd never suggested that he'd like her to get rid of the plane when they remarried. He wouldn't dare.

"It sounds as if she's put you in a tough spot," Suzanne said. "But I can't believe she'd just walk out if you kept on flying."

"You don't know her. You and Gil, you were different. You both loved flying, did it all the time. Libby not only won't do it, she can't understand why it means so much to me. She thinks if I quit I'll feel like a new man, and you know it doesn't work like that. It's not like quitting smoking. So what am I supposed to do?"

"I don't think you came over to ask my advice, Merle. You said you had a proposition. What is it?"

"Look, I have no idea what shape your Cessna's in. Can it be fixed up so you could keep right on flying?"

"I don't know. It doesn't look all that bad, except for the float rigging. I'll have to have it checked out by somebody who knows his stuff. Are you here to offer to do it?"

"I'm afraid you'd need someone better qualified than I am to do that. But how about you taking my Cessna off my hands. I don't have a figure yet, but I'm going to get it appraised. I thought I'd give you first refusal."

This wasn't the proposition Suzanne had expected.

"You're telling me your wife is really more important than the plane?" That wasn't the way she had meant to put it, but she knew it was probably the truth.

"Hell, Suzanne, put yourself in my place. I love to fly the damn thing, you know that. But what kind of a guy would ditch his spouse so he could keep a big expensive toy."

You're talking to one, Suzanne thought. Except I'm not facing your dilemma.

"I think you need to have it out with Libby," she said. "I can't believe she'd actually do this to you. There's got to be room for compromise. Tell her you'll only fly on Sundays, and only if there's no wind. Make up something. I sure wouldn't sell the plane if I were you."

Corrigan got up and walked over to a large picture window. His view of Crooked Lake was very much like the one he had from his own cottage.

"I appreciate what you're saying, but I've made up my mind. Maybe I can take up golf, I don't know. So, how about it, do you think you'd be interested? It's the same model as yours, it's in good condition, you'd feel right at home. And you wouldn't be reminded every time you took it up that you were sitting in the seat where Gil got killed."

Suzanne hadn't thought of that.

"I'm not sure what I'm going to do with our plane, Merle. But thanks for the offer. Why don't you do some research and give me your asking price. No promises, you understand, but I'll give it some serious thought."

"Thanks. But do me a favor, will you? Whatever you decide, make it my Cessna you take up during the September fly-in."

A surprising request, she thought, and a touching one. Merle Corrigan was trying, in his own way, to patch up the quarrel which had ended his friendship with Gil so many years earlier.

But what was on her mind as she watched him drive away was the realization that she would have to get rid of the plane that was still parked up at Murchison Airfield. Just as Merle wouldn't keep his Cessna because Libby had a powerful if irrational fear of flying, she didn't think she'd keep her Cessna because Gil had taken one final and fatal flight in it.

CHAPTER 31

The Crooked Lake population fluctuates every summer as cottage owners settle in for a much needed break from city life and renters and tourists come and go. Carol Kelleher, sheriff of Cumberland County, had no idea how many people were in residence on any given day or week. But she was acutely aware of just how many people who had a role in what she thought of as *l'affaire Mobley* were in the immediate area. The number was dwindling.

Gil Mobley was dead, and so was his mother, Constance Mobley. Sheldon Rivers, first husband of Suzanne Mobley, had departed for his home in Westchester County. Carol knew this because Deputy Sheriff Sam Bridges had stopped by the motel in Yates Center for a cup of coffee and witnessed a confrontation at the checkout counter between Rivers and his former wife.

"You can't do this, Shell," Suzanne had demanded, trying to wrest his bag from his hand.

"Let's not go through this again," Rivers had replied. "There's nothing more I can do here. When things settle down, I'll be back. Now please let go. People are watching."

Nor was Rivers the only one checking out. Phyllis Jordan, proprietor of the *Silver Willows* B & B, had called the sheriff that same morning.

"I believe you should know that Marcus Mobley left here this morning to go back to Binghamton," she had reported.

Carol didn't regard the information as of any great importance, but did find it interesting that Ms. Jordan did.

"I remember that they never gave you a date when they'd be leaving," Carol said.

"*They* didn't leave. Only he did. Mrs. Mobley has stayed in her room all morning, didn't even show up for breakfast. Same thing yesterday."

Two dead, two on their way back home. And then Franklin, *Chambord's* factotum, called with the news that Evelyn Rivers, whom he had expected to see when she was discharged from the hospital, had instead gone back to her home in Marcellus. Franklin had offered no reason why he thought the sheriff should be informed of this change of plans. But he had thought it strange, and quite unlike Constance's only grandchild.

Let's see, Carol said to herself. Who's left? Suzanne and Carrie. Dr. Sigler. Oh, yes, Franklin of course. Other names popped into her mind, but they weren't family or close to the Mobleys.

Three of these people whom Carol had met at *Chambord* and who were still on the lake were not happy campers. That Suzanne fell into this category was apparent from Bridges' story about her argument with Sheldon Rivers at his motel. She didn't like the fact that her ex-husband was leaving. Carol could think of no obvious explanation for that. Had he found it within himself to be a comfort to Suzanne in the aftermath of Gil's death? What little she had seen of him at *Chambord* suggested otherwise. He had positioned himself apart from the others, looked surly, spoke sarcastically, and chided her for not asking the 'important questions,' whatever that was supposed to mean. But for some reason Suzanne had wanted him to stay, and he had been dismissive of her entreaties.

Carol didn't know whether Carrie Mobley was in a bad mood, but Phyllis Jordan's report seemed to have hinted as much. Something had happened to send Marcus on his way back to Binghamton without his wife. And the fact that she had spent most of the last two days in her room at the B & B, not even taking breakfast, pointed to a marital spat. Of course Marcus might have left simply because his job necessitated it, and Carrie might have remained behind because she wanted to enjoy the lake for a few more days. On the other hand, she had no car, and had apparently made no effort to rent one.

The truth of the matter was that Carrie was frustrated that Constance Mobley's lawyer, Jeff Minchin, would not divulge information about the matriarch's will. Marcus had told her that he wouldn't, but she was convinced that that was only because her husband was such a wimp. Angry with Marcus, she had stomped off for an impromptu meeting with Minchin, convinced that she could get him to open up to her. But he hadn't, and before she left his office she had begun to fear that browbeating him might actually have jeopardized their prospects. Browbeating. That was what Minchin had accused her of doing, and he had obviously resented it. She had remained at the lake and stayed in her room because she was both frustrated and frantic. Her time at the B & B had been divided between watching bad TV and trying to figure out what she might still be able to do to salvage a good inheritance from her late and unmourned mother-in-law.

The third unhappy camper was Dr. Jeremy Sigler, and Carol had no idea that anything was bothering him. Constance Mobley had passed away, of course, and Sigler must be feeling badly about her death. But while he would miss her and the checks she regularly wrote to him, what really was worrying him was another patient he had lost some years before, a man named Ellery Bettenger. It wasn't that he still thought a lot about Bettenger's death, although he occasionally had a momentary pang of conscience. Jeremy Sigler couldn't shake off the fear that Gil Mobley knew that he had been guilty of malpractice in the Bettenger case and was in a position to blackmail him. When Gil died in the plane crash, he had initially assumed that his worries were over. And then it had dawned on him that Gil might have made a record of his suspicions and tucked it away in his safe deposit box.

Would he never be free from this gnawing fear that the one great mistake of his life would yet be revealed? Dr. Sigler wasn't one to be passive when he could do something about a problem. So he took a trip to Gil Mobley's bank and asked to see Gil's safe deposit box. He had no key to the box, and he was not registered as one of the people who was entitled to access. But he had prepared what he thought of as a persuasive case. As the bank surely knew, Mr. Mobley had just died and he, Jeremy Sigler, had been his doctor. He would claim that there were important medical records he needed for a professional report, and that Gil had promised to turn them over to him. Unfortunately, Gil had died before doing so.

Unfortunately for Sigler, the bank would not allow him to open the safe deposit box. He was informed that Mr. Mobley's wife had permission to use the box, and that he should speak with her. The doctor pleaded the urgency of his request, his reluctance to bother the grieving widow, and a number of other reasons why an exception to bank rules should be made in this case. Neither the teller nor the bank manager was prepared to make an exception, however. When Jeremy Sigler left the bank he was even more anxious than when he had arrived. If Gil had left a damning report in his safe deposit box, the person who would be the first to read it would be Suzanne Mobley. Heaven knew what she would do with it.

Of course he didn't know that such a report existed. After all, Gil hadn't known that he would have a fatal heart attack, so why would he have gone to the trouble of accusing his doctor of malpractice and locking the accusation away in the bank. Yet Jeremy couldn't shake the thought that in Gil's safe deposit box lay an envelope with an inscription that read: To Be Opened in the Case of My Death.

CHAPTER 32

It was one of those days when nothing got done, at least nothing of consequence. Carol didn't begrudge a slow day, and had even been known to relish an hour of what could charitably be called day dreaming. But there had been too much day dreaming on this late July afternoon. The stack of papers in her in basket was actually taller than it had been after morning roll call. The yellow pad in front of her had none of her usual notes and doodles. Her coffee cup sat unfinished and cold on the side of the desk. Even Deputy Sheriff Bridges had noticed that she was there in body but not in mind.

"Something wrong?" he asked as he paused at Carol's open door.

"No. I'm fine. Just can't seem to stay focussed. I'm sure you've had those days."

Sam smiled.

"Quite a few. Just yesterday I got to thinking about our anniversary coming up, and I haven't given much thought to a celebration."

"I'd say you were focussed. I mean anniversaries are big events. Of course, I'm no authority, being a two year novice."

"I'll bet your mind's on that Mobley business."

"Probably too much of the time. But actually I was in my anti-Mobley mood, trying not to think about it. I think I was thinking about Caravaggio."

"Caravaggio?"

"Never mind. It's not important. You concentrate on your anniversary."

Sam's interruption snapped Carol out of her mental meandering, so that when Kevin called she was actually alert.

"Hi, it's me, and I'm calling to propose -"

"You're proposing?" Carol interrupted. "I thought we'd been through that a couple of years ago."

"No, no, I'm calling to offer a proposition for tonight. How about we drive over to Ballentyne Falls and have dinner at the *Falls Inn?*"

"You're serious? That's a great idea. I haven't been there in years."

"I know. That's why I called and made a reservation. We owe it to ourselves to do something daring once in awhile. When can you get away?"

"Give me forty-five minutes. All I'm doing is spinning my wheels."

"You'll have to change into something sexy. They don't allow uniforms in their dining room, waitresses excepted."

"No problem."

Carol faced what was left of the afternoon in a much brighter mood. It wasn't their anniversary, but it was beginning to feel like one.

They had a brief debate about what dress would be most appropriate, but they settled on something which Kevin considered her most alluring and which she put on because he did.

The *Falls Inn* occupied a perch at the upper edge of a state park two lakes east of Crooked Lake. It was a moderately long drive, but the scenery was pleasantly bucolic and the traffic was light. By tacit agreement, they talked about nothing serious en route, if one discounts reminiscences of their aborted honeymoon in Umbria two summers earlier.

The dinner was superb, the evening vista from their window table memorable, the trip back to the cottage a pleasant prelude to one of their most satisfying and romantic nights of the summer.

No alarm had been set for the morning, but Carol's inner clock woke her abruptly from sleep at 6:45.

"What are you doing?" Kevin asked. Carol was out of bed but he was half asleep and still struggling to figure out what was going on.

"I have law and order to attend to, right here on Crooked Lake. You're welcome to stay in bed and relive last night."

She disappeared down the hall in the direction of the bathroom, but Kevin was awake enough to remember he had an agenda.

"Wait a minute," he called after her, crawling out from under the covers and into his slippers.

"Sorry, I'd love an encore, but I've got a squad meeting in just over an hour."

"I know, so take your shower and I'll find something for breakfast. But I want to tell you about my dream."

"Okay. I'll need about ten minutes," Carol said and closed the bathroom door. Kevin turned his attention to blueberry pancakes.

"Now what's this about a dream," she said when she joined him at the kitchen table.

"Well, it wasn't a dream so much as a bit of creative thinking in the middle of the night. I've decided that we've been letting too much grass grow where your friends the Mobleys are concerned."

"*We've* been letting too much grass grow. Is this a subtle way of saying that I've been remiss in my duty as sheriff?"

"Now when have I ever said anything like that? No, it just dawned on me that we aren't paying enough attention to the Mobleys."

"Oh come on, Kevin, they're practically all we ever talk about these days."

"I know," he said. "We talk about them a lot, but we don't do anything about them."

"And what is it you propose we do about them?"

"I was thinking of asking them point blank about their meds."

"I thought that was Doc Crawford's responsibility. Or maybe Jeremy Sigler's. He's the one who looked after Gil Mobley and his mother."

"Why don't we pretend it's our responsibility? Okay, your responsibility. The question's the same, where did Gil get the wrong meds? They didn't just materialize from out of nowhere in the medicine cabinet or bedside table. Odds are that somebody had a prescription, filled it, and brought the pills into the Mobley house. There may be other possibilities, but however it happened, you need to know who might have had - what was it, Flora something?"

"Florinef or a generic."

"Okay, Florinef. Let's ask all of them if they've ever taken it, if they've ever filled a prescription for it."

"All of them?"

"All of the Mobleys, the ones who are still alive. Plus that guy Rivers who used to be married to Gil's wife. We know that they've all been here. You actually saw them the day Gil crashed his plane."

"I'm sure there are lots of other people who've been in Gil's home. Sounds like a pretty open ended search to me. Besides, Rivers has already gone home, all the way down to someplace in the metropolitan area. Same with Marcus Mobley, except he's in Binghamton."

Kevin shrugged.

"We've got to start somewhere. Bad break about Rivers and Marcus, but they shouldn't be hard to find. I'm on my summer vacation. I'll do it."

"And just what do you expect is going to happen? That one of them will break down and confess to being careless with his medications?"

"No, of course not, but at least we'll know if any of them was on Florinef. We'll be one giant step closer to knowing where the stuff that did Gil in came from. And just maybe we'll know who switched his meds for him. Voila, our murderer!"

"Why is it that every two or three days you start thinking of Mobley's death as a homicide? There's not one shred of evidence that that's what it was."

"But that's because we've been assuming from the beginning, thanks to those NTSB guys, that this was just a simple case of a heart attack bringing the pilot and the plane down. What if we'd started from the premise that somebody wanted to kill Mobley? After Crawford found that Florinef stuff in him, we'd be looking for someone who had it in his possession and switched it with Mobley's meds. And if that didn't work out, then we'd fall back on his accidental death - Gil had the bad luck to confuse the bad meds with the good ones."

"And why did one of these instant suspects want to kill Mobley?" Carol asked.

"Money, for one thing. With Gil out of the way, Marcus moves to the head of the queue in the old lady's will."

"So what you're saying is that I should pick Marcus or maybe his wife as a murderer and find some evidence to prove it. If it's that simple, why bother to question Suzanne or Rivers at all?"

Kevin drenched another of his pancakes with syrup.

"Money's only one possibility. It's just the obvious one. Otherwise why would everyone have been here on the lake, waiting anxiously for the Grand Dame to die? We know they didn't come running when they heard about what happened to the Cessna. Anyway, murder has many motives. We just don't know what they are yet. Could be sex, some old grudge, who knows. Let's find out."

"If you're going to have dreams like this after we make love," Carol said, "I think I should consider withholding my favors. But right now I have to get to the office."

She pushed away from the table, planted a kiss on the top of Kevin's tousled hair, and went off in search of her gun and her car keys.

"You can't fool me," he said. "You're going to do it. I can tell by that look in your eye. Tracking a killer is a lot more fun than chasing down speeders and breaking up bar brawls."

"If you say so," Carol said as she finished buckling the gun belt. "Don't get carried away and forget to do some shopping. The list's on the fridge."

CHAPTER 33

It had not been her intention, but Carol spent much of that day considering Kevin's dream. She tried to focus on other business, but found it impossible, as Kevin had probably assumed she would. It was a crazy plan, one that was likely to end up both as an embarrassment and a waste of time. But she, too, had found the behavior of the Mobley clan fascinating, and there had, after all, been all of those unsolicited phone calls calling her attention to trouble in the lives of the deceased pilot's family. Some of those calls had almost certainly come from gossips or cranks, but should she discount all of them? And then there was Jeremy Sigler, who hadn't liked her questions about the drug that had aggravated Gil's hypertension. It had been Sigler who first broached the idea that the pilot's death may not have been an accident.

The result of worrying these matters for the better part of the morning, she decided, was going to be several phone calls. She had never followed up with Jim Hacklin, the neighbor of Gil and Suzanne Mobley who had called to report that he had overheard them quarreling. She had taken her cue from Sutherland, who had shown no interest in speaking with Hacklin. But now perhaps it would be a good idea to pay Hacklin a visit, especially in view of the fact that Gloria Garner, the Mobley's former maid, had also heard the couple arguing angrily. In fact, it might make sense to see Ms. Garner as well.

Before she asked JoAnne to arrange meetings with Hacklin and Garner, she added Phyllis Jordan to the list. The proprietor of *Silver Willows* might be able to tell her more about her long staying guests, Marcus and Carrie Mobley. It was even possible that Carrie was still in residence at the B & B. If so, a chat with her might be revealing. There was, of course, a fourth person who had thought it a good idea to tip her off as to problems in Mobleyland. But that would be Edward G. Robinson, and that would be a dead end. Or would it? Whoever had called seemed certain to have used a phony name, yet *someone* had placed that call, and he had had his reason for doing so. Suddenly, discovering who Edward G. Robinson really was took on added importance. Carol would urge Officer Byrnes to give it another try.

But before she had a chance to talk with Byrnes or place calls to Hacklin or Garner or Jordan, JoAnne reported that Carrie Mobley was on the line and claimed to be 'very anxious to speak with the sheriff.'

Carol couldn't imagine what had prompted this call from the red haired woman. She had just been thinking about her, wondering if she might still be at the B & B.

"Mrs. Mobley, how nice to hear from you."

"I'm sure you have an awfully busy schedule, sheriff, but I really need to talk with you. Is there some time today when I could come by your office?"

"I didn't know you were still in the area," Carol said. "I'd heard that you and Mr. Mobley had returned home."

"He did, but I decided to stay here. That's what I need to talk about."

Carol knew that Kevin would be excited by this unanticipated development. To her surprise, she was, too. Even better, Carrie wanted to talk with her in person, not over the phone. She would have JoAnne juggle whatever was on her schedule for the afternoon to make that possible.

"I can make time this afternoon. What would be good for you?"

"Anytime. This is important, so I'm flexible."

"How about a late lunch?" Carol asked, thinking about the advantages of an informal setting for their meeting.

"That's fine, if we can have some privacy. I don't know places around here, so I'll leave it up to you."

"Good. Do you know Cumberland?"

"Is it far?"

"No, but that's where I have my office. Tell you what, it'll be easier if I pick you up. Are you still at that B & B?"

"I rented a car this morning, so if you don't mind, I'd rather come and get you. How do I get there?"

Suddenly, it looked as if this would be an interesting day. An unexpected luncheon meeting with Gil Mobley's sister-in-law. A place where they could speak in private, and to which Carrie would drive. They agreed on 1:30, and she gave Carrie instructions on how to get to the office and had JoAnne reserve a corner table at *The Antlers, a* roadside tavern just across the county line.

"Your guest is here," JoAnne announced at a little after one. The expression on her face was one with which Carol was thoroughly familiar. It said that the person waiting to see the sheriff was strange, perhaps even bizarre.

"Thank you so much, sheriff," Carrie Mobley said as she swept into the office. "I was afraid you wouldn't have the time."

Carol would have recognized her from the copper colored hair, but otherwise she bore little resemblance to the woman she had met at *Chambord*. The clothes she had worn on that occasion made her appear stocky, even slightly overweight. Today she had selected a tailored suit that made her look both trimmer and younger. But the colors were all wrong, and the cartoonish red hair and a surfeit of makeup had the effect of making her look surprisingly like a circus clown.

"Please, there's no problem. I assume you are anxious for us to be on our way. And I'm more than happy to drive."

"Thanks, but I like to drive. It sounds funny, but when Marcus is at the wheel I always feel like I'm trapped." She seemed to regret having said that, and hastened to correct herself. "It's not that he's a bad driver. It's me. I like to be in control."

Something Phyllis Jordan had said about the argument she had overheard at the B & B suggested the same thing.

"That's okay. I get to do a lot of driving on my job. Glad to be a passenger today."

With Carol giving directions and Carrie driving just under the speed limit in deference to her passenger, they arrived at an unprepossessing restaurant in the middle of nowhere. Two large sets of antlers above the entrance made the roadside sign with the name of the place superfluous.

"Not much to look at," Carol said as they climbed out of Carrie's rental Ford, "but they serve pretty decent Italian fare."

Carol had anticipated the paucity of cars and hence the privacy which Carrie had wanted. *The Antlers* was busy during the evening, but was too far from the nearest town to attract a large crowd at the lunch hour.

They took the back corner booth, well away from the handful of other diners. Carol ordered iced tea and cheese ravioli; Carrie opted for a draft beer and spaghetti and meatballs. It soon became obvious that while she had been anxious to have this meeting, Carrie Mobley was unsure just how to proceed.

"So Mr. Mobley has gone back to Binghamton," Carol said, seeking to break the conversational ice.

"I think he was bored, to be honest. There isn't much to do around here, especially if you don't much like swimming and water skiing. Marcus and I aren't much like Suzanne and Gil."

"How then does it happen that you and your husband chose to stay at a B & B on the lake?"

"We'd kind of drifted away from the family, from his brother and his mother. It seemed like a good idea to spend some time with them, to get to know them better. And Marcus was kind of burned out. He needed to get away from his job for awhile."

"I guess we all need a break now and then," Carol said. "What is it that your husband does?"

"He's a pharmacist," Carrie answered. As if that wasn't an adequate explanation of what a pharmacist is, she chose to elaborate. "It's sort of like being a doctor. You have to know everything about how the body works. People think it's just about filling prescriptions, but it's more than that."

Carol tried not to let her face register her interest in this information about Marcus Mobley and his job as a pharmacist. She had asked Officer Byrnes to find where Marcus and Carrie lived, but she had neglected to ask what he did for a living. And it might be important.

"How about you?" she asked Mrs. Mobley. "Do you work outside of the home?"

"Mostly volunteer work. I trained as a librarian, but I quit that not long after college. It wasn't much fun. We couldn't have kids, and sometimes I think I'm in a rut. Have you ever felt that way?"

"As it happens, being sheriff has been a demanding job. But I seem to be the one asking the questions, and you had something you wanted to talk to me about."

"Yes, I do. There's something that's been bothering me, and I don't know how to handle it. But the day you came over to Mom Mobley's place, the day Gil died, we got to talking about you after you left. No one was being catty, it wasn't anything like that, but Sheldon Rivers made some comment about it being strange that you were a woman. You know what I mean, that the sheriff up here is a woman. It was Constance that spoke up and called him a misogynist or something like that. She said you'd been a lawyer over in Albany before you took over as sheriff, and that the country'd be better off if there were more smart women like you running the country."

Carrie paused to see how the sheriff was reacting to what she was telling her. Carol smiled.

"That's very flattering," she said, "but there's nothing all that special about women in law enforcement. Or in law, for that matter."

"Well, anyway I got to thinking about a problem I'm having, and it occurred to me that maybe you could help me. Because you're a lawyer, and, like Constance said, a smart one."

Carol had no idea what it was that Carrie Mobley thought she could help her with. Somehow it had to do with the fact that she was a lawyer. Which was true. And a smart lawyer. At the moment Carol doubted that that was true.

"I'm not sure I can help, but try me."

"It's about inheriting money," Carrie said, easing into whatever was bothering her. "I know that when people die, their money goes to their heirs. But they get to decide who gets what, because there are usually a bunch of heirs. I'm not sure how I ought to put my question, but I assume that the decision has to be fair. I mean, wouldn't it be wrong if somebody fixed it so the money doesn't get distributed fairly? Like what if a person is dying and somebody cons her into giving all her money to him. Do you see what I mean? If something like that happens, is there a way for the people who got cheated to get what's coming to them?"

So this is what this lunch is all about, Carol thought. If Carrie had intended to disguise the 'somebody' and 'the people who got cheated,' she had failed to do so. It was time to be sympathetic but cautious.

"I see what you're driving at, Mrs. Mobley. And I'm sure there are people who could help you to understand issues like the one you're describing. Unfortunately, there are a lot of legal specialties, and estate law is not mine. In fact, I haven't practiced any kind of law in almost eight years. So I'm simply not qualified to answer your question."

"But you must have some knowledge about things like this," Carrie said. She was obviously disappointed by what she was hearing. "Isn't there something in the Constitution about due process of law?"

"Yes, there is, but that's really another matter. Look, let me suggest that you talk to an attorney, one who handles wills and trusts and things like that. I take it you and your husband don't have a lawyer?"

"Most people don't have lawyers, sheriff. If you haven't done anything wrong, why would you need to hire a lawyer?"

"But you're going to have to talk to one to get an answer to your question. If you need to see someone before you go back to Binghamton, I can give you the names of a couple of attorneys who live around the lake. There's a Jeffrey Minchin over in Yates Center, or perhaps -"

"Oh, forget it. These lawyers don't want to talk to you unless you become their client and they can start billing you. I thought you'd be different."

"I am different, Mrs. Mobley. I'm the sheriff of Cumberland County, not a practicing attorney."

"I didn't mean to be rude, sheriff," a more subdued Carrie Mobley said. "I guess I'm just terribly disappointed. Maybe I should just go back home. This has been a miserable three weeks."

Carrie was obviously not referring to Crooked Lake weather, which had been spectacular. Nor did Carol think she was talking about the recent deaths of her brother-in-law and mother-in-law. Much more likely that she was thinking about someone she thought stood in the way of Marcus - or was it Carrie herself? - inheriting from the late Constance Mobley.

It had not been a memorable lunch, but it had been a surprisingly interesting one. Carrie Mobley might have been disappointed, but not the sheriff. She now knew of two people whose professions made it easy for them to secure a medication which would have led to a spike in hypertension. One was Gil Mobley's doctor. The other was Gil Mobley's brother.

CHAPTER 34

Back at the office, Carol turned her attention again to the people who had called her with comments critical of the Mobleys. She decided to begin with Phyllis Jordan, inasmuch as she had just come from lunch with Carrie Mobley and it was Carrie that Jordan had called her about. This time she would meet the woman rather than listen to her over the phone. That proved to be more difficult than she had expected, inasmuch as the B & B owner had left a Brae Loch College student in charge while she went to Rochester on a shopping trip. Unable to make an appointment, she tried Jim Hacklin. It being a weekday, it was not surprising that he was also unavailable. His wife was familiar with the reason for her husband's call to the sheriff, but she thought it was best that he be the one to talk with the sheriff.

"I heard them once or twice," she said, "but he's the one who really got upset by their carrying on. I think you should see Jim. When he gets home, I'll have him call you back."

That left Gloria Garner, and this time Carol was in luck. Which seemed to mean that Gloria was not. Apparently no new job had materialized. Inasmuch as the young woman was adamant that the sheriff not come to her family's house, Carol agreed to meet her later that afternoon in her office.

She wandered down the hall to where Officer Byrnes could normally be found. He was searching for something on his computer, but abandoned that assignment as soon as he saw Carol.

"You look frustrated," he observed.

"Less frustrated than stymied for the moment. Tell me, can you think of any way we can track down our friend Edward G. Robinson?"

"Still interested in him, are we?"

"We might be. But I'd like to know who he is."

"I wish I could think of something. Best I could come up with is what Sherlock Holmes used to do. He'd put a notice in the personals in the paper - you know, bait to draw somebody out. It always worked."

"I didn't know you were a Holmes fan."

"Actually I liked Watson better, but Holmes was really smart."

"I've got a hunch a notice in the personals wouldn't work here. We're not London, and this isn't the 19th century."

"I know, which is why I didn't suggest it. But it would be fun to put something in the *Gazette*. Something like 'Anyone knowing the whereabouts of Edward G. Robinson or next of kin, please leave a message at such and such a phone number.' You could use mine if you like."

"Am I supposed to take this seriously?"

"Not really. But it's the best I can come up with."

"I don't even know if the *Gazette* has a personals page," Carol said. "Or if it does, whether anybody reads it."

"If it has one it's because people read it," Byrnes suggested.

"Why don't you check the paper, then try your hand at a Robinson personal and let me see what you've come up with."

"You'd really do that?"

"When all else fails, try the impossible."

"Aye, aye, sir."

———

Kevin had argued that they should confront the people who were close to Gil Mobley with a pointed question about the drug which had been found in his body and which might have been the cause of his death. Carol thought of it as a risky strategy. While it didn't say so in so many words, such a question could be read as a subtle implication of guilt. But of course that had been Kevin's intention. Raise the subject and watch their reaction. The guilty will give themselves away.

She thought about it for maybe as many as five minutes and then called Suzanne Mobley.

"Hi, Suzanne, it's the sheriff. You doing okay?"

"Depends on what you mean by okay," she said. Carol wondered if a phone call from the sheriff made it less likely that she'd be doing okay.

"I'd like to drop by if it's convenient. Nothing important, it's just that I'd like to stay in touch."

"Well, of course." Suzanne didn't ask why the sheriff needed to stay in touch. "When did you have in mind?"

Carol didn't want to make their meeting sound urgent; nor did she want it to take place at any old time. She tried to fudge the matter.

"I have to be in Yates Center at 2:45. How about it if I stop off on my way? If that doesn't work out, let's shoot for another date."

Happily it did work out, probably more because Suzanne was curious than that it was the only free spot on her calendar.

The air conditioner was going full blast, just as it had been the last time Carol had been in the lake shore house. But Suzanne was much less elegantly attired. Carol thought she might have been doing some house work, now that she had fired Gloria Garner.

"Coffee? I remember that you didn't want any when you were here last. So maybe you'd rather it be iced tea."

"No, I'd enjoy a cup of coffee. I'll take it black, unsweetened if you please."

Once more she was seated facing the photographs on the bookcase. Gil was still there.

When Suzanne returned with the coffee, she offered an apology for her appearance.

"I hadn't expected company, which accounts for this." She plucked at her blouse and lifted a foot to show Carol a shoe that was somewhat run over at the heel. "I decided to be lazy."

Carol did not wish to discuss Suzanne's attire or her daily routines. Better to get straight to the reason for her visit.

"When I was here last, we were talking about Gil's medications, the ones you had tossed out. You mentioned that he was taking something to control his blood pressure. How about Florinef?"

"What's that?" Nothing in the way she asked the question or the look on her face betrayed anxiety. Either she didn't know what the drug was or she had practiced deception until she was good at it.

"Maybe you'd know it as fludrocortisone acetate. Does that ring a bell?"

"No. Should it?"

Carol had gone this far. The next step should not be difficult.

"It's a medication that, among other things, raises one's blood pressure. The autopsy on your late husband indicated that he had been taking it."

"But that's ridiculous. My husband was taking medication to *lower* his blood pressure. Why are we having this discussion?"

"Please, Mrs. Mobley, I'm trying to help the people investigating your husband's death." This was not technically true, but it was better than telling her that she was investigating a possible murder. "When we met at your mother-in-law's, you said that your husband should not have been flying that day. That you were afraid he would have a stroke or a heart attack. Dr. Sigler said much the same thing. And your husband did have a heart attack. Moreover, we know he had been taking a medication that could have induced it. I'm sure you see my problem."

"I can't imagine why Gil would have taken this Florinef or whatever it is. He wasn't stupid, and he certainly wasn't suicidal. Are you sure that the autopsy got it right? I've heard that they can make mistakes."

"I suppose it's possible, but I'm sure it's highly unlikely. Anyway, it would help if you could think whether someone who might have been taking a medication like Florinef has been in your house in recent weeks or months. Meds can get mixed up. All I'm asking is that you do what you can to help us figure out how your husband took a drug that probably killed him."

When Carol left the Mobley lake house, she knew nothing she hadn't known when she arrived. Her first adventure into indirect accusation had gotten her nowhere. She now knew neither that Suzanne Mobley was complicit in her husband's death nor that she had had nothing whatsoever to do with it.

Carol had pulled her punches. She had said nothing about what Gloria Garner had discovered under Suzanne's bed. If the pills turned out to be Gil's prescription, the subject would be moot. If they turned out to be Florinef, she would be paying the pilot's widow another visit.

———

The sheriff's meeting with Suzanne's former live-in maid provided no new information, although it did give her a better picture of Ms. Garner. Over the phone she had said that she wasn't much to look at, but in fact she was a reasonably attractive woman, if a bit overweight. She was clearly uncomfortable in Carol's presence, but that was not surprising. Unfortunately, she hadn't yet found another job, which meant that she was living at home with a difficult father. Whether there was a mother in the house, she didn't say.

Her story about the Mobleys was almost word for word what it had been during their telephone conversation. Carol pressed her about Gil's statement that he'd grant Suzanne a divorce over his dead body, but Gloria insisted that those were his very words. It was obvious that the young woman was hugely relieved to be done with this interview and on her way. Carol hoped that she'd find a job soon.

Ms. Garner had not been gone for twenty minutes when Doc Crawford called.

"I have a bit of news to pass on to you," he said. "About those pills that turned up under the bed at Gil Mobley's."

"Good. They've been on my mind because the maid who found the pills was here in my office just this afternoon. What did you find?"

"My toxicology guru has confirmed that I was right. Two pills, two different medications. One is Lisinopril, which you take for high blood pressure. The other is that generic for Florinef. As I'm sure you know by now, that's what Mobley should definitely not have been taking."

"I'm surprised. I figured they'd be the same."

"If you weren't paying close attention, they would look the same. Both white, same size - but one was lightly scored. Mobley could easily have assumed they were both his own prescription."

"Only if they were in the same bottle, Doc. Or at least an identical bottle. You know, I'm beginning to think that someone may have deliberately switched Gil Mobley's meds."

For the first time since she'd heard about the crash of the Cessna, Carol actually believed that she could have a murder on her hands.

CHAPTER 35

It was a grand night for swimming, and Carol and Kevin made the most of it. While whatever Kevin had planned for dinner simmered on the stove, they parked on the deck, still in their bathing suits but with a glass of Chardonnay in hand.

"That smells good. What is it?" Carol asked.

"It's my own chili, with a caesar salad on the side."

"Chili? We're in the middle of summer."

"I know, but inasmuch as I spend my winters down in the city, you'll never get a taste of my chili unless I do it in the summer. Don't worry, it's good in all seasons. Besides, it'll keep while you tell me about the day's excitement."

"That's good, because there are a few things you've got to hear about. Please don't say you told me so, but I think I'm getting interested in your theory that Gil Mobley was murdered."

"Sounds like a productive day. Whom did you accuse?"

Carol laughed.

"I'm not that reckless, but it was an interesting day nonetheless. Where should I begin? Let's make it your argument that Marcus Mobley stood to gain pride of place in Constance's will with Gil's death."

"Like I said, money is still the root of all evil."

"I don't know whether it's the root of all evil, but Carrie Mobley cornered me today and tried to get me to give her a lesson on the law of inheritance. And she didn't sound like she thought Gil's death has improved Marcus's prospects, and hence hers. I'm reading between the lines, but it seems pretty clear to me that Carrie is worried that with Gil's death it will be Suzanne, not Marcus, who will get the bulk of Constance's estate."

"And she asked you to help her break the will?"

"Not quite, but she's interested in knowing whether that's possible. She didn't mention names, but I suspect she believes that Gil and Suzanne manipulated Constance into favoring them and cutting Marcus and her out of their rightful inheritance."

"I can't believe that she came to the sheriff for help on a matter like that. She must be desperate."

"Thanks, Kevin. She had heard that I was a lawyer and took it for granted that I was a good one. If it were known that this is a murder case - and let me remind you that as of this moment it isn't - she would never have come to me. But as far as she's concerned, the sheriff's department is ticketing drunk drivers, not investigating Gil Mobley's murder. Anyway, I told her that I couldn't help her, that it wasn't my field and that I hadn't been a practicing lawyer for years."

"Otherwise you'd have a conflict of interest on your hands when she and her husband become suspects in Gil's murder." Kevin seemed to find this amusing.

"You should know that I don't offer legal advice to anyone. Well, maybe you in a pinch. In any event, the major development of the day has to do with Suzanne, not Carrie. I took your advice, told her point blank that Florinef had been found in Gil's body, and asked her what she knew about it. She claims she's never heard of it, is sure Gil never took it. I didn't tell her that pills had been found under her bed because we didn't know what they were. Now we come to the really interesting stuff. After I'd talked with Suzanne, Crawford called with his report, and one of the two pills is definitely used to raise blood pressure. So Suzanne may not know what Florinef is, but somehow it found its way under the bed she sleeps in. Probably put there by gremlins."

"Fantastic!" Kevin said, his face wearing a big smile.

"Yes, but what does it prove? That Suzanne was fiddling with the meds and dropped some on the floor? That Gil had somehow gotten the drugs mixed up and *he* dropped a couple on the floor? After all, he was still sleeping with his wife until not long before he died. Or maybe they were being nice to visitors, gave them their bed, and the *visitors* lost the pills during their sleepover."

"I think we're going to have to find out exactly who visited the Mobleys recently," Kevin suggested. "How about Marcus and Carrie? Or Suzanne's former husband? Even Gil's doctor, or that other Cessna pilot? They were all right here on the lake, and it's not unheard of to invite relatives, friends, even ex-spouses, to drop by for a drink. And what if somebody had one too many and passed out on the bed?"

"My head is spinning." Carol said. "Let's take a break and have the chili."

As promised, Kevin's chili was good, and the subject of after dinner conversation on the deck had switched to what they might do over the weekend if things were reasonably quiet on the law and order front.

Unfortunately, the mood was broken by the phone.

"Don't answer it," Kevin said.

"That's a luxury I can't afford," she said as she went to the study.

Kevin watched the sunlight fade on the bluff across the lake for several minutes, then began to worry that Carol had not reappeared. It was a quarter after eight when she resumed her seat on the deck.

"That's a call I didn't expect," she said. "Rachel Edelstein. Dr. Rachel Edelstein, to be precise. She's Suzanne Mobley's gynecologist. In fact, she called because Suzanne asked her to. Suzanne even gave her my home phone number, although I'm not sure how she got it."

"And what did Suzanne want her to tell you? That's she's a wonderful woman, grieving over the death of her husband?"

"Let's not go there, Kevin. Why shouldn't Suzanne be grieving? I would if something happened to you."

"Okay. I suppose I do have my doubts about her, but I'll try to behave."

"You're right, however, about what Dr. Edelstein had to say. She told me that Suzanne has just undergone a terrible trauma, she's depressed, doesn't know what she'll be doing now that Gil is gone. And she claims I've been badgering her about some drug, asking if she's been taking it. Of course the drug is Florinef, and of course Suzanne says she doesn't know what it is, much less that she's been taking it. Which may be true. Anyway, Dr. Edelstein was uncomfortable to be making the call. She didn't want to bother me with one of her patient's problems. She seems to think Suzanne is simply all on edge because of what she's been going through."

"She sounded straightforward? You don't think she's holding anything back?"

"I don't see why she would, but it was just a phone conversation with someone I've never met or heard of."

"Maybe Suzanne is beginning the process of lining up friendly witnesses who can testify to what a devoted wife she is."

"Kevin, if I'm going to play along with your 'Gil was murdered' gambit, you've got to keep an open mind. We don't begin to have evidence that somebody arranged for Gil to start taking Florinef. Even if were true, we haven't a scintilla of evidence that that somebody is Suzanne."

"I love that phrase, 'scintilla of evidence.' I've often wondered just how much it takes to make a scintilla. But you're right. It's just that I'm anxious to put on my sleuth's hat. I'll do my best not to go overboard too fast."

"How about not going overboard at all?"

CHAPTER 36

The following morning Carol was called out of the squad meeting to take a phone call from Jeffrey Minchin. She had met him on a couple of occasions, but knew little about him except that he was an attorney who had lived and practiced in Cumberland County for a quarter of a century and had one of the lowest handicaps on the Crooked Lake Country Club's golf course. That, and that he was Constance Mobley's attorney, which she knew because Jeremy Sigler had told her so.

"Mr. Minchin, good morning."

"Hello, sheriff. From things I've been hearing this week I thought I ought to give you a heads up on Constance Mobley's will. More specifically, it seemed appropriate to let you know that I've filed the will at the court house and that I shall be meeting with Mrs. Mobley's heirs tomorrow at 10 o'clock in the mansion. You are welcome to be there if you think it desirable."

"Thank you, but I'm a bit confused. What is it that you've been hearing that prompted your call? And just what is this meeting tomorrow all about?"

"Sorry, but I was under the impression that you have an interest in the disposition of Mrs. Mobley's estate. I don't presume to know how it is that you're involved, but one of the heirs wanted me to contact you. As for the meeting, well, it's a bit unusual. Mrs. Mobley specifically asked me to read her will to the assembled legatees, not talk to them individually, which is what I usually do. This business of reading the will is really just something that happens in fiction or on television. But she insisted."

Carol was quite sure she knew who had asked Minchin to call her, but decided not to mention a name.

"I don't believe that it's necessary for me to be present tomorrow, but I have gotten to know the family through the investigation into the crash of Gilbert Mobley's plane, so I'll take advantage of your invitation. May I ask if Mrs. Mobley - Mrs. Constance Mobley - changed her will after her son's death?"

"No, and I don't know whether she had any intention of doing so. This may sound like a strange question, sheriff, but is there some problem in the Mobley family that I should know about?"

"None that I know of. As I mentioned, my knowledge of the Mobleys has only to do with Gil's tragic accident. I have helped the National Transportation Safety Board in their investigation. That's how I came to meet Constance Mobley."

"I see." There was just a hint of doubt in Minchin's voice, but he left the matter there. "Well, then, I'll be seeing you at *Chambord* at ten tomorrow."

"Thanks again, and have a good day."

———

Carol made it a point to be one of the last people to arrive at the mansion for the reading of the will. She also made it a point not to wear her uniform or drive an official car. Her presence would obviously come as a surprise, perhaps even a shock, to some of those in attendance, but there was no need to make it look as if she were there in her professional capacity. Kevin had expressed the view that Carrie had arranged for her to be present for the express purpose of putting Suzanne on notice that she and Marcus intended to contest the will. While Carol agreed that it was almost certainly Carrie who had pushed Minchin to invite her, she was less certain just what she hoped to gain by the sheriff's presence.

The huge parlor looked very much as it had on the morning of Gil's death, with one important difference. The blinds had been raised, and it was the sun, not the several ill-assorted lamps, which brightened the room. Some attempt had been made to create what looked like a formal setting. Chairs had been positioned in two semi-circular rows, and a table had been pressed into service as a make shift lectern, where Minchin would presumably hold forth.

It was Franklin who let Carol in, much as he had on earlier occasions.

Carrie was seated in the second row next to Marcus, who had returned to the lake from Binghamton for the occasion. Dr. Sigler was at the far end of that row, leaving three vacant chairs between himself and Marcus and Carrie. Suzanne had taken a chair in front of Sigler and appeared to be engaged in inventorying the contents of her purse. The only person Carol did not know was a young woman at the opposite end of the first row. Unlike the rest of the small company, all of whom were dressed as if in church for a funeral, she wore casual slacks and a canary yellow blouse and had one arm in a sling. Carol assumed that she was Evelyn Rivers.

Franklin quietly took one of the vacant seats in the second row. He was the only person in the room who wasn't staring at the sheriff. Carol had no intention of occupying a ringside seat. Instead, she sat down on a couch some distance behind the assembled legatees. From the couch she could watch and listen to the interaction between Minchin and those who had come to hear how they had fared when Constance drafted her will.

Minchin looked as if he were stalling for time. He was rummaging through a large briefcase, as if searching for the will. Carol doubted that he had forgotten to bring it with him. She also thought it strange that none of the handful of people in front of her were talking with one another while they waited for Minchin to begin the reading of the will. On second thought, it probably wasn't so strange. She had witnessed this same tense atmosphere before, in the same room and with most of the same people.

Minchin coughed to get everyone's attention.

"Ladies and gentlemen," he began. "I'm unaccustomed to this sort of thing, but as I explained when I called you, Mrs. Mobley asked me to pass along information about her will in this way. I'm sorry not to have been more forthcoming when some of you contacted me, but I felt that my first obligation was to adhere to her wishes."

He coughed again.

"Forgive me, I seem to have a summer cold. There is no law governing occasions like this, but folklore suggests that I, in my capacity as the late Mrs. Mobley's attorney, should simply read the will verbatim. That seems to me to be unnecessary. There are passages in the will which convey Mrs. Mobley's wishes in certain contingencies, and I see no reason to read those passages when those contingencies have not arisen."

That should shorten proceedings, Carol thought. She hoped no one would object to Minchin's decision. Unfortunately, Carrie Mobley chose that moment to speak up.

"What are these contingencies you're talking about?"

The attorney looked uncomfortable.

"The obvious one is the death of a legatee, and Mrs. Mobley did make provisions for such cases. But other than Mr. Gilbert Mobley, none of her legatees died before our meeting this morning. In effect, those other contingencies in the will have no effect, so I see no point in reading them."

"But you will be reading what you call a contingency in Gil's case. Is that right?"

"That is correct," Minchin replied.

"Which means that Constance never got around to changing her will after Gil's death?" It was Carrie Mobley again, and it was obvious that she was unhappy.

"That is true." Carol suspected that Jeff Minchin regretted that he had raised the issue of contingencies.

There was a moment of silence, and the lawyer took advantage of it to begin reading the germane provisions of the will.

"I'll mention this first, because it makes clear that Mrs. Mobley wanted to treat *Chambord* differently from the rest of her estate. She stipulated that it should go to Eldridge Franklin, and she attached no strings. Therefore, Mr. Franklin, you may do with the property - the house and the entire compound - as you see fit."

As if Constance had ordered them to do so, everyone else in the room turned in their seats to look at Franklin. Carol wondered whether anyone cared about this particular bequest. She saw the mansion as a white elephant, and a costly one at that. In all likelihood, Franklin would be selling it, probably sooner than later.

"Now let us look at how Mrs. Mobley chose to settle the balance of her estate. I shall begin with that contingency involving her older son. She had planned to leave fifty percent of it to Gilbert, with the stipulation that should he predecease her, that fifty percent would go to Gilbert's wife, Suzanne."

Because she was sitting behind the assembled legatees, Carol was unable to observe Suzanne's reaction. She suspected that Suzanne would be elated with this evidence of her late mother-in-law's continuing affection.

Minchin pressed on, seeking to avoid another interruption.

"Another twenty-five percent of the estate, excluding *Chambord,* goes to Mrs. Mobley's younger son, Marcus."

The words were barely out of his mouth when Carrie Mobley stood up abruptly, knocking her chair over in the process and almost falling down as she tried to regain her balance. It was an embarrassing moment for her, and an alarming moment for Minchin and virtually every one else in the parlor. Carrie proceeded to march off in the direction of the door to the hall, saying nothing as she left the room.

Carol could hear whispered conversations in front of her, but they came to a swift halt as those remaining in the room seemed to sense that this was not the time to speculate on what they had just observed. Minchin looked shaken, but he prudently chose not to comment on Carrie's departure.

"To continue," he continued after an uneasy minute, "the other twenty-five percent of the estate, once more excluding *Chambord*, goes to Mrs. Mobley's granddaughter, Evelyn Rivers. As you can see, it is a simple will, the number of those inheriting quite small."

At that point, he paused, picked up the will from the table and folded the uppermost page back.

"Oh, I should have mentioned this earlier." He was obviously flustered. "Forgive me. There is a stipulation that certain specified pieces of furniture and art here in the mansion have been bequeathed to Dr. Jeremy Sigler. I'm sorry, Mr. Franklin. Shall I read you her list?"

"That will not be necessary, Jeffrey." It was Sigler, rather than Franklin, who spoke up. "I'll have a talk with Franklin when we're through here. Constance will have remembered things I complimented her on, but I will be happy to let Franklin have them if he so desires."

The reading of the will, such as it was, had come to an end. Much as Carol would have liked to hear what was being said by whom and to whom, she chose not to join the legatees. The only person she really wanted to speak with was Evelyn Rivers, and she was confident that she would be able to catch up with her before she reached her car.

Suzanne Mobley broke away from a brief tete-a-tete with Franklin and came back to where Carol was sitting.

"Hello, sheriff. You seem to be the only person here who didn't merit something in Mother Mobley's will."

"Thank goodness. That would have stirred up a hornet's nest, don't you think?"

"Probably, although I doubt that it would have been any more dramatic than Carrie's exit. What brings you here today?"

"I came because Mr. Minchin invited me."

"He did?" Suzanne's surprise was genuine.

"Yes, and your guess is as good as mine as to what he had in mind. Now at least I can say I have actually been present at a reading of a will. It's reputedly a very rare event."

Out of the corner of her eye Carol saw Evelyn leaving.

"It's nice to see you again, Suzanne, but I have to get back to county business. This has been a rare morning off for me."

Carol made her departure quickly, aware that Suzanne Mobley would soon be asking Jeffrey Minchin why he had invited the sheriff to the reading of the will.

CHAPTER 37

Before she saw Evelyn Rivers at the reading of the will, Carol had given little thought to Suzanne's daughter and why she might wish to talk with her. She had heard that Evelyn was close to Constance and that she had recently suffered a concussion and a broken arm from a collision with a deer, but otherwise she was a total stranger. Yet for some reason, Carol had a feeling that she had to make her acquaintance before the young woman left the lake.

She walked purposefully away from the mansion toward the parked cars, Evelyn some thirty yards ahead of her. The young woman was already in her car, the engine running, when Carol came along side and wrapped on the window. Evelyn rolled the window down and turned a puzzled face toward the sheriff.

"Hello, Evelyn. I'm Carol Kelleher, and I'm the sheriff of Cumberland County. I would very much like to talk with you. Might it be possible for us to take a short drive together?"

"Is something the matter?" It was an understandable question, inasmuch as Carol was not in uniform and she had never been introduced at the meeting by either Suzanne or Minchin.

"No, not at all. I have been involved in the investigation into the airplane crash which killed your step-father, and that has given me an opportunity to get to know your mother. It also enabled me to meet your late grandmother, a fine lady I wish I had met sooner. If you can spare a bit of your time, I'd really like to talk with you."

Evelyn turned off the ignition.

"Is there something about my grandmother's will that bothers you? Or is it my mother?"

"There really isn't anything specific, Evelyn. It's just that I've necessarily become a part of your family's life in the last couple of weeks, everyone in the family, that is, except you."

"You know my father, too?"

"Not well. We've been introduced, but haven't really talked." And that's unfortunate, Carol thought, because I've never had a chance to ask him what those important questions are that he claims I didn't asked the day we met.

"What did you have in mind?" Evelyn asked.

"If you aren't in a terrible hurry, perhaps we could go into Southport for an early lunch. Would that be okay?"

"You're talking about just me, aren't you? My mother isn't included?"

"No, it'll be just you and me."

It was agreed that they'd drive separately and meet at the diner in Southport. It shouldn't take more than thirty minutes to get there. Carol hoped Evelyn wouldn't change her mind, but thought that she could count on her curiosity about what she might learn from the sheriff.

Forty minutes later they were seated in a booth in a corner of the diner, orders placed and iced tea on the table.

"I think I've heard that you live up near Syracuse. What is it that you do?"

"I'm not really into a career," Evelyn said. "Good jobs aren't easy to come by right now, but I'm taking night classes so I can become a therapist. Or maybe a trainer. At the moment I'm teaching yoga. I've got a couple of interviews lined up. Grandmother's bequest is going to be a big help. Do you have any idea how much it might be?"

"I'm afraid not. Your mother probably has a pretty good idea, but I've never inquired into the Mobleys' financial situation. Your grandmother obviously thought highly of you, though. You must have been very kind to her."

"I wasn't looking to inherit from her," Evelyn said defensively. "It's just that she was a good friend. We liked to talk, to play games. Sometimes just to sit and read by the fire. We used to play Chinese checkers all the time when I was much younger. You know, don't you, that she wasn't my real grandmother?"

"Yes, she couldn't have been, could she? Were you and your mother and father close?"

Evelyn made a noise in her throat that started as a laugh before she choked it off.

"Hardly close. Frankly, I don't think they ever wanted children. I'm sure I was an accident. Sheldon's okay. But he's self-centered. You talk to him and he's not really listening. He needed a course on fathering, but he never took one. But compared with Suzanne, well -"

She didn't finish her thought, nor did she have to.

"Do you see either of them often?"

"I see Suzanne as little as I can. We'd run into each other once in a while at what she called Mom Mobley's, but I doubt we ever exchanged more than a dozen words. You know, 'how've you been,' that kind of thing. But she didn't care. I suppose in the beginning I blamed her for abandoning Sheldon, but to be honest I didn't lose much."

"Until just the other day, your father has been up here at the lake. I guess you know that. Did he tell you why?"

"Well, it wasn't because of me. I mean if he'd wanted to see me, he'd have stayed in Syracuse. It had to be because of Suzanne."

"So they had maintained an amicable relationship?" Carol asked.

"The divorce was really unpleasant, but it was almost ten years ago. Who knows? She never talked to me about anything, and he never talked to me about her. Just the other day when he drove me back home from the hospital, I asked him why he'd suddenly decided to spend two whole weeks seeing Suzanne. All he would say was that he thought he'd see how she was doing. Go figure."

Carol was intrigued by what she was hearing. Should she pursue the matter further? She was debating the matter with herself when their sandwiches arrived. As the waitress departed, she took the plunge.

"Do you think there is any possibility that your father and Suzanne might be regretting the fact that they split?"

"I can't imagine why they would, but I guess it's not impossible. He didn't remarry, and when you think about it, he and Suzanne had a lot in common. They were both selfish, and I don't think they ever really loved each other. But in some funny way I think they got off on each other, if you know what I mean."

Carol knew what she meant, although she had no idea whether Evelyn was right about her mother and father. After all, her views about her parents' relationship would have been formed when she was in elementary and middle school. How sophisticated about such things would she have been at that age?

Perhaps it was time to let Evelyn take over.

"I hadn't meant to be the one asking all the questions," she said. "I wanted you to join me because I'd like to get to know you. Why don't you tell me about yourself. What if your inheritance is substantial, as I suspect it may be?"

"I haven't had time to think about it. One thing's for sure, though. I'm not going to sit around and do nothing just because I've inherited a lot of money. If I can find the right guy, I expect to start a family. And I'll make sure it's a better one than Sheldon and Suzanne had."

"Without a full time job, it must be hard to make ends meet," Carol said.

"It is, sort of. I've got a small place I share with a guy named Joey. We manage. Sheldon used to send me a check once in awhile. I think he'd help more if it weren't for Joey, and if I was honest with myself I'd have to admit I don't blame him."

"Why is that?"

"In spite of his problems, I think Sheldon wants the best for me, and Joey, well, he's not the best. He loves his acoustic guitar and he's convinced he and a bunch of his friends can make it as a band. But mostly they just fool around."

"Fathers can be quite possessive where their daughters are concerned. But like I said, I don't pretend to know your father. I saw him the day Gil died. I came by the mansion to report what had happened, and he was there. But he just stood off in a corner, didn't say much."

To Carol's surprise, Evelyn gradually relaxed and talked more freely. What had begun as a brief lunch turned into a considerably longer affair. Iced tea glasses were refilled twice, and Evelyn even consented to sherbet for dessert.

They talked about Constance and Franklin. There was even a conversation about Suzanne, with Evelyn sharing episodes in her life with her mother. But most of what they talked about was her father, with whom Evelyn had obviously had a strange, off and on, relationship. Although she didn't profess to know him well enough to be sure about such things, Evelyn believed that he was in financial trouble. She blamed it on his penchant for making ill-conceived investment decisions. She also confessed to being worried about his health. A football player in college and an active outdoorsman, he had, according to his daughter, retreated into a sedentary life. What in her opinion was worse, he seemed to be chronically exhausted and unsteady on his feet. These physical changes seemed to have frustrated Evelyn, the more so since he refused to talk about them.

They even devoted a few minutes to Gil Mobley, but Evelyn admitted that she barely knew him.

"From what I could see, he and Suzanne didn't have much in common except an obsession with airplanes. He was pleasant enough, but we never talked about anything. And why would we, with Suzanne around? They avoided me, and I suppose I avoided them."

Later, as she was on her way back to the office, Carol took stock of what she had learned over lunch with Evelyn Rivers. It added up to much of what she had already assumed, little of which was new. In many ways, Evelyn was like many a young person just beginning to make her way in the adult world. But she was different in the sense that she had just come into what was likely to be a sizable inheritance and that she was estranged from her parents. Except that the latter wasn't entirely true. It might be true of her relationship with Suzanne, but Sheldon was another story. While they weren't close, the young woman had not written her father off. Nor did it sound as if she was ready to. Sheldon Rivers remained a mystery, a self-centered man who had never remarried, someone who might be in financial trouble and who might also be sickly. Carol was sorry that it had not been possible for her to spend more time with him before he packed up and went home to Westchester.

CHAPTER 38

The people who had attended the meeting with Jeffrey Minchin at *Chambord* left with decidedly different feelings about what they had learned. Without a doubt, the person who was most satisfied was Suzanne Mobley. Although she was unaware of just exactly how much she was inheriting from Constance, she had discussed the matter often enough with Gil to be virtually certain that it would be a large amount, easily in the range of seven figures, perhaps even eight. Much of it would presumably be in stocks, and she was confident that, unlike Sheldon, Mother Mobley had handled her investments prudently. What is more, she was also the sole beneficiary of Gil's will. Their marriage may have been on the rocks, but she had visited the safe deposit box and knew that he had not changed his will in the relatively few weeks since they had begun talking about a divorce. Fortunately, he was a chronic procrastinator. Even if he had contemplated altering the will, she was still his wife at the time of his death and she was sure she could have successfully challenged any will that disinherited her.

The prospect of suddenly becoming a multimillionaire was thrilling. Of course she had always assumed that it would only be a matter of time, but now that that time had come, Suzanne was euphoric. Her euphoria was enhanced by the fact that Carrie had been devastated that Gil's death had not thrust Marcus into the role of principal beneficiary. Suzanne had always been sure that that would never happen. She knew Mother Mobley too well. The final piece of good news was that *Chambord* went to Franklin, not to her. She had no interest in the mansion, and while she could have sold it and made a handsome sum from doing so, she was relieved not to have to spend her time and money maintaining the place while trying to find a buyer.

Suzanne had to call Shell, but she was in no hurry to do it. She was still miffed that he had cut short his stay and returned to Pelham, though she had to admit that he was accomplishing nothing by sticking around. Other, that is, than sexually satisfying her in their occasional late night assignations at the motel.

What she decided to do first was to pay a visit to Merle Corrigan. She had been surprised when he told her that he was going to have to sell his Cessna and wanted to give her first refusal. Initially the idea hadn't interested her, but the more she had thought about it, the more convinced she became that she didn't really want to repair the plane that she and Gil had shared and that he had ridden down to his death in the lake. It wasn't that she was superstitious, or that it would perpetuate the memory of what had happened and how and why. Instead it was simply a desire to put Gil behind her. She would be beginning a new phase of her life in Westchester with Shell in the not too distant future. Why not do it with a new plane?

Of course Merle's Cessna was not a new plane. But it was relatively new, and it would have been excellently maintained. There would be no need to shop around for another aircraft. And so she edged the Mercedes through the gap in the evergreen wall and set off in the direction of Merle's cottage on the other arm of Crooked Lake.

Merle, who worked out of his home most of the time, was there, which was fortunate, inasmuch as Suzanne wasn't particularly eager to talk with Libby Corrigan and knew that Libby wouldn't be eager to talk with her.

"Hi, Suzanne," Merle greeted her at the back door. "How've you been managing?"

"Pretty well. I should ask you the same question, in light of what you told me when last we spoke."

"It isn't easy, but we do what we have to do. Libby's relieved that I'm selling the plane."

"That's why I'm here today," she said. "For some reason, I have trouble imagining myself back in our old plane. I'm not ready to make you an offer, but I was wondering whether you'd mind if I took your plane up for a little spin around the lake. Just to see what it feels like, you know."

Merle gave her a rueful smile.

"I'd assume anyone who might be interested in buying her would want a test drive. So sure. You want to take her up now?"

Suzanne hadn't planned on doing it that day, but why not.

"That would suit me fine, if it's okay with you."

"No problem at all. You won't need me along, will you?"

"I'd prefer to be by myself, thanks."

And so it was decided. They went on down to the dock where the familiar Cessna was tethered. Merle was mainly a bystander as Suzanne, an expert at such things, got the plane ready for take off.

"I promise not to be long," she announced as she settled into the cockpit. "Just a short jaunt down to Southport and back."

"Enjoy," he called out as she started the engine and maneuvered away from the dock. She waved back and then the Cessna began to gather speed as it headed north on an almost perfectly calm lake. As she became airborne, Suzanne experienced a familiar sense of elation. She had not flown since Gil's death, fearful that to do so would be seen as disrespectful of her husband. But enough days had now elapsed, and no one would begrudge her this form of therapy.

The plane gradually gained altitude, and once she had climbed above the bluff she banked it to the left and circled back toward Southport. She knew what she was going to do, but she first wanted to spend a few casual minutes savoring the pleasure of once more being aloft and completely in control of her day.

Having buzzed Southport, she headed back up the lake in the direction of the bluff and the spot where Gil had gone down. She wasn't sure just why she wanted to do it, but had made up her mind that she was going to fly directly over the place where he had crashed. For a brief moment she had contemplated approaching the place at what was believed to have been Gil's altitude and then taking a cautious dive toward the water before leveling off. Common sense dissuaded her from doing that, but she was determined to see the accident site from the air.

During the flight she found herself thinking about the fatal heart attack. Why had it happened while Gil was in the plane, over the lake? The explanation, she knew, was that it had been pure luck. Whether good or bad luck depended on one's point of view. Had it happened on the ground, with people nearby, Gil might have survived with the quick thinking of some of those people. There would have been a call to 911, a trip to the hospital, prompt medical attention. But a heart attack which resulted in the plane falling into the lake was another story. Unless the attack was immediately fatal, he would have drowned, or so she'd been told.

In any event he was gone. Now there would never be an argument about a divorce. And wasn't that what she really wanted?

It was impossible to pinpoint the exact spot where the plane had hit the water, but Suzanne knew she was close, probably not more than one hundred feet from it, one way or another. There was nothing below except blue water, no float or other device to memorialize the event. She flew on another two miles, then turned and headed back toward Merle Corrigan's cottage.

When she touched down, she could see Merle, still sitting on a bench at the end of his dock. He had been witness to exactly what she had done, and could not help but be aware of why she had done it. As she came along side the dock, he stood up and came over to meet her and to secure the Cessna.

"How'd it fly?" he asked.

"Couldn't have been better. I felt right at home."

"Good. I thought you would."

Suzanne climbed out of the plane and cautiously stepped onto the dock.

"What are you asking for the plane?"

"You interested?"

"I am."

"Just give me a minute here and we'll go up to the cottage and talk business. If you have time today, that is."

"I believe I have," Suzanne said, thinking of the money from Constance Mobley's estate that would soon be hers. "I know it won't be easy for you, but we'll be doing each other a big favor."

CHAPTER 39

Jeremy Sigler was anxious to get away from *Chambord*, but both Eldridge Franklin and Jeff Minchin wanted to talk and he didn't want to be rude. He didn't want to think about how he and Franklin would divide up the furniture and objets d'art that Constance had willed him. There was plenty of time to have that discussion. And Minchin didn't really have an agenda; he seemed to think it would somehow look wrong to simply zip up his briefcase and hurry away after the reading of the will.

But at least Suzanne Mobley had chosen to leave promptly without talking to him. The fact that she had done so didn't mean that his worries were baseless, but it gave him a bit of breathing room.

In the end he exercised his default excuse - a patient is waiting for me - and hastened out to his car. No patient would be at the clinic. He had seen to that by canceling all of his appointments until later in the afternoon. He needed to take a drive out into the countryside, preferably a long drive. Lunch didn't matter; Jeremy wasn't hungry. What he was was a nervous wreck.

As he left the compound and headed north, away from the lake and the villages which nestled at the end of its two arms, he wished his car were less conspicuous. Why had he felt compelled to drive a Cadillac, a black Cadillac with a license plate that not only announced that it was owned by an MD but that the MD's initials were JVS? Jeremy Vinson Sigler. At the moment he wished he were anonymous instead of the best known physician on Crooked Lake.

For a few minutes he debated whether he should drive all the way up to Rochester. He knew a few people in Rochester, although none of them well. But that would be pointless. He really did have a patient at four. Besides, there was nothing he could do up there that would help him solve the problem that was Suzanne Mobley. If in fact she was a problem.

If she knew that he was guilty of malpractice in the death of Ellery Bettenger, it would be because Gil had told her so. And he didn't even know whether Gil believed it or had only harbored a suspicion that it was true. But he could readily imagine that Gil might have raised the subject with Suzanne or, if he hadn't, that he had made a record of his suspicion and tucked it away where she might eventually see it. In his safe deposit box, for instance. He had tried, unsuccessfully, to gain access to that box with a contrived story about needing certain medical papers.

Jeremy had wrestled with this problem for some time, but his anxiety had grown exponentially since Gil's death. He had tried to avoid Suzanne, but that was proving hard to do. They had been together at *Chambord* twice, and he had encountered her in the pharmacy and at the post office in Southport. Was this strategy of avoidance a mistake? Might it be better to seek her out, tell her the same story he had used at the bank, ask her permission to open the safe deposit box, and collect the non- existent papers?

He debated the matter with himself for another ten or so miles before turning around and heading back to the lake. To approach her in this way would be risky. He knew that. But it was only a matter of time before Suzanne herself would be visiting the bank. Perhaps she had already done so. If he did nothing, he could count on more sleepless nights, or days in which he couldn't concentrate on his job or his family. If he broached the subject with her, at least he would know where he stood.

By the time he reached West Branch he had made up his mind to visit the Mobley cottage. He was actually relieved to see Suzanne's Mercedes parked there.

"Dr. Sigler," she said, obviously surprised to find him at her door. "What brings you here today?"

"I realized that we didn't exchange more than a quick hello at *Chambord*. By the way, it sounds as if you've come into a nice inheritance. Congratulations. I'm sure Gil would have been pleased. Anyway, I wanted to see how you're doing."

"Not bad. I was numb at first. That was to be expected, I suppose. But you can't go on that way. So, all in all, I'd say I'm coping fairly well."

Jeremy stepped into the house he had come to know well over the years. As usual, it was chilly.

"Coffee, Jeremy?" she asked.

"If it's been made, but don't go to any trouble. I'll only be here a few minutes."

"No problem. Black I presume?" He nodded, and Suzanne disappeared into the kitchen. Sigler took a seat on the couch. He was conscious that his heart rate had gone up.

The coffee served, they chatted for a few minutes. But Jeremy was aware that it was a perfunctory conversation. They had never been close, and now they were simply going through the motions. Better to raise the issue that had brought him there and be on his way.

"Suzanne, I have a favor to ask of you. Gil had been participating in a study I was doing for the Pingren Foundation, something to do with the synthesis of fats. He was keeping a record, and I never got the last data before he died. I can't be sure, of course, but I think he was keeping the papers in his safe deposit box. I'd be grateful if you'd give me permission to open the box and see if they're there."

She set her coffee cup down and smiled for the first time since he'd arrived.

"I'm sorry, Jeremy, but there aren't any papers like that in the safe deposit box. I opened it just a couple of days after Gil's death - I had to take out his will. There wasn't anything related to some foundation study."

Jeremy drew a deep breath.

"Perhaps they were in a sealed envelope. The data was personal, and there are privacy issues."

"I didn't see anything like that."

He tried to read her face, but it told him nothing.

"Well, I suppose he could have kept things like that in the house. If I remember correctly, he had a desk in a room back there." He waved a hand toward the hall.

"I think you're out of luck, Jeremy. I was anxious to get rid of things that would remind me that he was gone. Our maid and I went over the place from top to bottom. I hope I didn't throw out something that was important, but we did get rid of a lot of stuff."

"Don't worry, it's not the end of the world," he said, but he didn't mean a word of it. There was no Pingren Foundation study. There might, however, have been a sealed envelope in the safe deposit box. If so, it was doubtful that it was still sealed. Had it contained a damning statement from Gil? If so, Suzanne had already read it.

As Jeremy Sigler drove the rest of the way to his home and office high above Southport, his mind was focussed on just one thing: he had to find out whether Suzanne Mobley knew what had happened the night of that long ago pinochle game. But how would he be able to do that?

CHAPTER 40

Marcus and Carrie Mobley had driven directly back to their Binghamton home after the reading of the will. It had taken them approximately two and a half hours, and they had made the trip without exchanging a word. Marcus had remained silent because he had absolutely nothing to say. His wife had said nothing because she had said it all before. In fact she had said it many times, and she knew that it would simply irritate her husband. She also knew from experience that when Marcus was irritated he vented by driving recklessly. It was a trait the two of them shared.

Once the car had been unloaded at the house on Gloxinia Drive, Carrie headed for the liquor cabinet and poured herself a stiff drink of scotch.

"It's only three o'clock. Isn't it a bit early to start in on that stuff?" Marcus asked.

"Hear ye, hear ye! He can talk!" Carrie said, her voice full of sarcasm.

Marcus chose not to say what was on his mind. Instead, he set off for the den to check his messages.

In spite of their efforts to ignore each other, they both eventually stepped cautiously out of their shells.

"What's for dinner tonight?" he asked, trying to keep his voice in neutral.

"Am I expected to cook? You've been here for several days, while I've been doing more important things over on Crooked Lake. So I should ask you what's for dinner."

"I've been eating out, other than yogurt and things for breakfast."

"Are you proposing that we eat out tonight?"

"No, I'm tired of it." Adopting a more conciliatory tone, he made what he thought of as a peace offering. "I think I'll run down to the market and pick up a couple of steaks to put on the grill. That okay with you?"

"Whatever you say. While you're at it, the cupboard is almost bare. Stop by *Ziegler's* and pick up another bottle of scotch. Black Label, if you please."

Marcus and Carrie both knew that the ice had been broken, but they also both knew that they still hadn't had a conversation about their share of his mother's inheritance. Which meant that the evening promised another round of unpleasantness.

The steaks were good, and Carrie had limited herself to one fewer scotch than was her normal quota for the evening. Had the inheritance issue not been so sensitive and had it not come to a head so recently, the Binghamton Mobleys might have managed to set aside their differences for the evening and talk about other things. Marcus even suggested as much.

"The time has come," he announced, "to talk of many things - of shoes and ships and sealing wax, of cabbages and kings. What do you say?"

"Very clever, Marcus. Should I applaud?" Carrie wasn't amused. "We're in a hole and you want to show off with *Alice in Wonderland*."

"It's from *Through the Looking Glass*, Carrie."

"Did you learn that in medical school?"

"What on earth is the matter with you? I'm trying to help us lighten up, for God's sake. Can't we have a civil conversation?"

"I could if we hadn't just gotten shafted by your mother. Or should I say your sweet-talking sister-in-law. Gil is dead, Suzanne isn't grieving as far as I've noticed, and now she walks off with half of Constance's money. And what do you get? Leftovers."

"Look, I'm not going to pretend I'm ecstatic, but she had a fortune and we're getting a quarter of it. You're going to be able to go on one helluva shopping spree."

"Christ, you're such a pollyanna. Doesn't it bother you that Suzanne gets the last laugh? She knew you came to the lake to get a better deal from Constance. And even with Gil out of the way, it doesn't happen. Suzanne, she's not even related to Constance and she still gets twice as much as you, her own son. You should be furious."

"I tried, Carrie. When Gil died, I thought there was every chance mother would come around. But who'd have figured that she'd die days after Gil did. That she'd never have time to rewrite her will. I knew she didn't have long, but just a few days?"

"That was rotten luck, but where were you? You should have been at her bedside every day, her loving son, worried about her, ready to do anything she asked."

"She'd have seen right through me. I don't dissemble very well. You know that. Besides, you were the one that was all worked up about our inheritance. Not to mention the one who wanted Gil dead. Remember? I wasn't keeping track, but I'll bet you said it a dozen times."

"And what did you do about it?" Carrie asked in an accusatory tone. "You're a pharmacist, after all. They know all about poisons, things like that. You could have taken care of Gil without any trouble instead of waiting for him to crash his plane."

Marcus rolled his eyes.

"You've got to stop reading those goddamn mystery novels. It never works. People who poison people tend to get the chair or, if they're lucky, spend their lives in jail. I never liked my brother, and in spite of what you may think I really love you. But why should I put myself in jeopardy by killing Gil?"

Carrie, accustomed to answering questions with one of her own, said nothing. But she gave her husband a puzzled look.

"Marcus, tell me the truth," she finally said. "You didn't put something in Gil's coffee the morning he died, did you?"

"Why on earth would you think that?"

"Well, you looked kind of funny when you said that thing about my reading habits and poisoning people. So tell me, did you poison him?"

"What is this? You've been telling me for weeks that I never lifted a finger to help us get our share of my mother's money. And now, all of a sudden, you're asking me if I killed my brother."

"But did you?"

Marcus got up from his chair and went over to his wife and leaned over and kissed her on the top of her head.

"The answer is no, Carrie. If I'd spiked his coffee with something fatal, the answer would still be no. Pharmacists don't poison people, but even if they did they'd deny it. It's like the CIA. If you're in it, you never admit it, even to your loved ones."

"I know I can be bitchy sometimes, but you know you can trust me, don't you?"

He was going to say that she was bitchy most of the time, but he bit his tongue.

"No, I can't trust you any more than the guys in the CIA can trust their wives. You'd say something without thinking. You wouldn't mean to, and then it'd be too late."

The usually pugnacious Carrie was now subdued. Unhappy but subdued.

"So all I can do is speculate about whether you helped get Gil out of the way?"

"Speculate all you wish, dear, but frankly I'd urge you to forget it. What difference does it make? Absolutely none. Mother died before she could change her will - *if* she would have changed it, which I doubt. Gil's dead, she's dead, Suzanne gets twice what we get, life goes on."

"But doesn't it make you mad?"

"Maybe. If I thought about it a lot, yes, it probably would. But what's the point?"

"Well, you ought to try getting mad more often," she replied. "It'll make you feel better. Try it on Suzanne."

"I expect to deal with Suzanne by staying as far away from her as possible. You should do the same."

It was more of a truce than a commitment to turn over a new leaf, but Carrie and Marcus managed to spend a largely strife-free evening. They actually settled down to a game of scrabble, marred only by five minutes of conflict over her insistence that there was no such word as 'niqab.'

CHAPTER 41

Sheldon Rivers told his secretary to hold his calls, that he wasn't feeling well and was going home.

"Are you going to be all right?" she asked, sounding worried.

"I'm going to be fine, Annie, but right now I need to get off my feet. No need to tell anyone I'm sick. Just say I had another appointment downtown, that I should be back tomorrow."

"You don't look well."

"Probably not, but these things come and go. I'll be fine."

Sheldon walked unsteadily out of the office, took the elevator down to the parking garage, and drove away from the Craybill Building, heading for his suburban ranch home on Carrington Drive.

As he had said to his loyal secretary, these flareups of his came and went. But they sapped his energy and, more than anything else, frustrated him. Accustomed to vigorous outdoor life, he hated the fact that he was not only slowing down, which was to be expected of a man his age, but that he was in near chronic discomfort.

There had been no reason to stay longer at the lake. Suzanne had wanted him to, but it had become apparent that his presence there was not only serving no useful purpose, it was putting his future agenda at risk. Why do that when everything was going so well? Gil's death made his refusal to agree to a divorce from Suzanne moot. What is more, she would benefit financially from it. And then there was Constance's death. It would prove to be a far greater financial boon than Gil's. Suzanne would be free to marry him and they would soon be living in clover, or whatever passed for clover in Pelham. There was, of course, the remote possibility that with Gil gone, Constance would rethink her obligation to Marcus. But such a scenario was unthinkable. The old lady hadn't liked her younger son and had disliked his rattle brained wife even more. What's more, there probably hadn't been time for her to change her will. No, Sheldon thought, everything was going his way.

At least it was if he kept Suzanne at arms length for awhile. It hadn't been easy, but he was confident that Constance knew nothing of their plans. With the old lady dead, the only thing to fear was that Marcus or his busy body wife would figure out what they were up to and use that information to challenge the old lady's will. It was this problem which decided him to return to Pelham.

But now that he was there, back home in his bachelor quarters on Carrington Drive, he had been forced to face the other problem, his own health. Several months before taking the trip to the lake, he had visited his doctor and complained that he was almost constantly exhausted. After a series of tests, Dr. Murphy had given him a brief discourse on body mechanics and the information that he had low blood pressure and that whenever he stood up blood would tend to pool in his lower legs. One treatment led to another, until eventually Dr. Murphy wrote him a prescription which added a generic of something called Florinef to the drugs which he now took on a daily basis. Sheldon Rivers pulled into the garage and stepped gingerly out of the car. His first steps after rising from a lying or sitting position were always the most difficult, so he braced himself against the car and then the garage wall until he reached the door to the rear of the kitchen. He wanted to lie down, but first things first. The bottle of vodka was on the ledge next to the sink, right where he had left it that morning. He located a glass, added a couple of ice cubes and an inch of vodka before making his way back to the bedroom. He customarily took his pills at night before retiring, but he rationalized that no harm would be done by taking one more now.

Annoyed with himself for having failed to keep his collection of medications together in one place, he first rummaged through the drawer of his bedside stand, then checked the medicine cabinet in the bathroom. They weren't in either place.

"Damn it," he said aloud to the empty room.

Eventually he found them in his dresser drawer, although he was tired from the effort. He removed the cap and shook the plastic bottle into his cupped hand. Two pills tumbled out. The bottle felt empty. He shook it again and realized that it was empty. Strange. He had refilled the prescription just before leaving for the lake. There should still be many pills remaining, perhaps as many as twenty or more. Sheldon studied the information on the small bottle. It indicated that no more refills remained, which meant he would have to get a new prescription from Dr. Murphy. It wasn't hard to do so, but it was a nuisance. He was also puzzled that his supply was so low. He must inadvertently not have put the cap on tightly. The pills would be in the dresser where for some reason he had put them away the night before.

He went back to the dresser and removed his underwear, socks, and pajamas from the top drawer. But there were no pills there.

The low pill count was a problem, but Sheldon's need to take one of the remaining pills right now was of even greater importance. He closed the dresser drawer and proceeded to chase down one of the pills with the glass of vodka. Having done so, he slipped off his shoes, removed the wallet from his back pocket, and lay down on the bed.

He wasn't tired, at least not in the sense that he needed to sleep. What he needed was the relief that came when he was lying on his back. If he could fall asleep, so much the better. It would enable him to shut down his mind and stop worrying about his physical condition and the less than satisfactory shape of his financial balance sheet. It bothered him that he would now be remarrying Suzanne not just to rectify a past mistake but to shore up his financial security. This is what he had wanted to happen, but now that it was happening he felt diminished. Was this what men meant when they spoke of being emasculated? Try as he would, he couldn't get it off his mind. He stopped thinking about the reduced supply of Florinef tablets. All he could think of was Suzanne. Suzanne who was so good in bed, Suzanne who was also about to turn his life into one of limitless leisure. He should be happy. He wasn't.

It was the better part of an hour after he lay down and started to worry about the millionairess he was soon to marry that the bedside phone rang.

"Mr. Rivers speaking," he said. He was unsure whether to be annoyed that his thoughts had been interrupted or pleased that he might be able to put those thoughts out of his mind for awhile.

"Shell, it's me," Suzanne said. "I couldn't remember your schedule, but figured I'd catch you or leave a message. I've got good news."

"Glad to hear it." Sheldon silently added a mental reservation. "Just your luck to find me at home. I miss you. How are things going?"

"Things are going very well. We're going to get half of Mom Mobley's estate. Forget the mansion and the compound. That's how she's rewarding Franklin for his years of service. But otherwise, we get the lion's share. So you can stop worrying that she had second thoughts about Marcus. And you'll probably be pleased to hear that Evelyn gets twenty-five percent. That should keep her out of trouble for a few years."

Sheldon wasn't surprised. This is what he had expected. And he was delighted by news of Evelyn's inheritance. It might even help her to part company with Joey Landers. It was no time, however, to express his own personal concerns that Suzanne's good fortune, not his own financial acumen, would be supporting them.

They talked for awhile about the unusual fact that Constance's attorney had actually read the will. Suzanne took obvious pleasure in reporting Carrie's walkout when she learned that their efforts to ingratiate themselves with Marcus's mother had been a failure. And then the conversation turned to Sheldon's health.

"How are you doing?"

Sheldon was reluctant to dwell on his physical problems. It made him sound old, not a robust man in his late fifties who was anxious to resume a relationship with Suzanne. But he had casually mentioned some time ago that he was chronically tired and that he was taking something for that problem. 'If I follow doctor's orders,' he'd told her off handedly, 'I should be my old self pretty soon.' Suzanne, who was herself in good physical condition, had taken him at his word.

"I'm fine," was his disingenuous answer to her question. "It's just a matter of sticking to Dr. Murphy's regimen."

"Maybe you could hurry things along by taking up yoga," Suzanne suggested. "Sorry, Shell, that's a joke."

"I hope so. Down at the Athletic Club we prefer to lift weights."

Their conversation at an end, Sheldon Rivers' once and future wife told him that she loved him.

"I love you, too," were his last words before hanging up. Nothing was said about the missing Florinef tablets.

CHAPTER 42

Thursday morning began somewhat differently than usual at the Cumberland County Sheriff's Department. Carol had arrived somewhat earlier than was her habit, but so had Deputy Sheriff Bridges. He caught up with her as they left the parking lot.

"Morning, Carol. May I have a few minutes of your time before squad meeting?"

"Of course. What's up?"

"Let's go on in," he said. When they reached Carol's office, Sam quietly closed the door behind him.

"This is going to sound a bit odd," he began as they settled into their chairs.

"Would it sound less odd if we had coffee?" Carol asked.

"I'm not sure, but yes, coffee's a good idea. I'll get it." JoAnne had the pot steaming, and Sam was back with two cups in less than a minute.

He knew that they didn't have a lot of time, so he plunged right into what was on his mind.

"I think you should take a break," he said. "Nothing major, but maybe a long weekend. It's not just me. My sense is that the boys are pretty much of one mind about it. This isn't easy to say, but we're afraid that this business of Gil Mobley's death is getting you down. You've been all wrapped up in it for more than two weeks now, and, well -"

Sam paused, trying to find the right words.

"I take it you think I'm wasting my time," Carol said. She was surprised, and she looked uncomfortable.

"Don't get me wrong. We couldn't have a better sheriff, and you know I'd follow you into hell if it comes to that. But I'm worried about you. Same with the rest of the team. Bill and I got to talking about it last night. You don't say much of anything about it at squad meetings, but it seems like it's on your mind all the time. Like yesterday, you being at the Mobley place when Gil's mother's estate got divvied up. What's that got to do with us? I figured when the NTSB guys tied things up it was all over. But you can't let go."

"And you think I should take a break."

"I can't tell you what to do, Carol. You're my boss. But if I were you, I'd get away for a spell. You stay here, with what's left of the Mobley tribe right down the road, some of 'em calling you every day, and you'll go crazy. Look what happened to that guy on TV. Monk was his name."

Carol laughed.

"Thanks, Sam, but please don't confuse me with Monk. He was a genuine obsessive compulsive, had to have everything in a precise order, salt and pepper shakers just so. That's not my problem."

"Just the same, could you bring yourself to take a long weekend? You and Kevin. I checked, and you haven't had a vacation in fifteen months, if you discount your stay in the hospital last summer."

"If I ever need an analyst, I may give you a call," she said, now more relaxed. "You may be right about my obsession with the Mobley case. It's just -"

"See," Sam interrupted, "there you go. There is no Mobley case. There was when the plane crashed, and you helped the feds clear it up. But that's history. Now there's just a bunch of people who thought they'd inherit more than they did. Let's leave that for the lawyers and marriage counselors."

"I like you, Sam. You know how to speak truth to power. Except that my power is pretty modest. Tell you what I'll do. I'll take your suggestion under advisement, even sleep on it. In the meanwhile, pass the word that I've still got all my marbles and that I'm still Carol Kelleher, not Adrian Monk."

"Thanks. I thought you'd be mad."

"I will be if you don't get out of here and let me start the briefing."

———

"You'll never guess what happened to me this morning," Carol said to Kevin when they took their wine out to the deck that evening.

"No idea, and I'm not a good guesser. You tell me."

"I got a good talking to from Bridges. He told me I was likely to go off the deep end if I didn't agree to take a vacation."

"You let your subordinates talk to you like that?"

"Actually, he had a valid point. He thinks I'm so obsessed with what's going on with the Mobleys that I'm losing touch with reality. The way he sees it - he and the rest of the officers - is that there's no reason to be spending all of my time on what's left of Gil's family."

"Sounds as if he lacks confidence in your judgment. So you told him to stuff it, right?"

"No, I told him I'd think about it, which I've been doing. Funny thing is, you and I've been having that same discussion. Is there more to Gil Mobley's death than an unfortunate heart attack? No, it could happen to anyone. Did someone deliberately see to it that he took the wrong meds? No, it was just an accident. I don't know what I believe, and neither do you. What I do know is that Sam's right - there's no evidence that somebody tried to kill Gil and succeeded, yet I can't put it out of my mind."

"And you think his suggestion that you take a vacation might be a good idea?"

"What do you think?" Carol tossed the question back to Kevin.

"Well, you aren't the vacationing sheriff type. Where do you think you could go and what do you think you could do that would take the Mobleys off your mind? Two days away from the office - two days max - and you'd be chomping at the bit to get back to the office. And then what? You'd be fixated on the Mobley case again. Right?"

"Perhaps, but Sam thought you should come along. How does that sound?"

"It never occurred to me that you were talking about taking off somewhere on your own."

"Sam also spoke about a long weekend, not a real vacation."

"Why do I have the feeling that you've already decided to take Sam up on his suggestion?"

Carol got up, collected the two now empty wine glasses, and headed for the kitchen.

"Now, here's my plan," she said when she returned. "Unless you have some pressing need to do something you haven't told me about. I would like for the two of us to pack one small overnight bag, jump in the Toyota early tomorrow, and drive to Pelham. It's just north of the city. I've made a motel reservation for two nights, which should give us time to enjoy the fresh air of Westchester County."

"I suspected as much," he said. "But Pelham? I can't remember it ever being mentioned in *Travel and Leisure*."

"With good reason. But it happens to be where Sheldon Rivers lives. Do you remember him?"

"Rivers? He's Suzanne Mobley's first husband, right?"

"Very good. You've been paying attention. I'll be taking a weekend vacation, just as Sam suggested. But there's no reason why I can't fit in a little business while we're enjoying ourselves. I made a note of addresses and phone numbers back when I first met everybody at *Chambord*, so I called and made an appointment with him."

"You're really something else, do you know that?" Kevin was obviously impressed. "This means that you won't have to put in for vacation days."

"Oh, yes, I will. As far as Sam's concerned, I'm going to be seeing both Mets - the art museum and the opera house."

"I think you'd better tweak your story a bit. The Metropolitan Opera doesn't have a summer season. Maybe we should do something else."

CHAPTER 43

Carol had driven to the city only once in her life, and that had happened when she was a practicing attorney in Albany nearly a decade earlier. Kevin, on the other hand, had made the trip from the city to Crooked Lake and back by car many times over the years. The result of this disparity in experience was that Kevin got to plan the trip and sit behind the steering wheel when they set off downstate the following morning.

The trip took them through New York's southern tier counties and into the Catskills, and it was not until they reached Liberty that Kevin consented to take a break and turn the wheel over to Carol.

"About time," she complained as they changed places at a rest stop.

"I thought you were enjoying the scenery," Kevin said. "After all, I do this every year. I could do it with my eyes closed."

"All the more reason why I should take over."

The switch accomplished, they headed on for their destination across the Hudson, New York's commuting suburb of Pelham.

"Isn't it about time that we began to think about what we're going to say to your friend Rivers?" Kevin asked. They had spent the drive with barely a mention of the reason they were actually taking this brief vacation. Instead they had worked on a crossword puzzle, listened to several CDs, and wondered aloud about what life might be like in the many small towns through which they passed.

"Excuse me," Carol said. "I thought I'd be the one talking to him."

"I was hoping to get in on the act. After all, you're out of uniform and he doesn't know I'm not in the law enforcement business, so what does is matter if there are two of us to just one of him? I figured it would improve the odds that we'd learn something."

It was a subject they'd visited many times.

"We shall see," Carol said. "But you're right, we ought to plan strategy. Let's talk about what we know."

"It isn't much, is it?"

"Considering that you've never seen the man and I've only seen him once, I'd say we know quite a bit. We know he's Suzanne Mobley's first husband and that Evelyn Rivers is his daughter. Make that their daughter. We know he'd made the trip from Pelham to the lake a couple of weeks before Gil Mobley's death, stayed at a motel in Yates Center, and was among those who attended the gathering at Constance Mobley's mansion the day Gil was killed."

"Yes, but why?" Kevin asked. "Why did he come to the lake? And once he was there, why did he show up at the mansion when Gil was killed?"

"I thought your theory was that everyone was at the lake because word was out that Constance was at death's door. They all hoped to benefit from her will."

"Not everyone. What chance did Rivers have of inheriting any of Constance's wealth? He wasn't part of the family, and from what you've told me Constance loathed him."

"How about Evelyn?" Carol asked. "How about Rivers coming to the lake to put in a good word for his daughter?"

"It makes no sense," Kevin countered. "Evelyn was her own best advocate. Unlike her father, she was close to Constance. You told me so yourself. No, I can't see Rivers coming to the lake to convince the old lady to remember Evelyn in her will."

"But the fact remains that he was at the lake. And I doubt very much that it was because he had a sudden hankering to take a wine tasting tour. Whatever it was that brought him to the lake, it's the fact that he came rushing over to *Chambord* that's most baffling. It certainly wasn't because he wanted to join a wake for the man who'd stolen his wife from him."

"So why then *did* he come rushing over to *Chambord*?"

"There's only one possible explanation," Carol insisted. "Suzanne called and invited him. That's what we've been assuming all along, that she got in touch with everyone and set up the meeting. It makes sense where Marcus and Carrie are concerned. Same with Dr. Sigler. But why Rivers? Like he said that morning, he was the skunk at the garden party."

"That's one of the questions we're going to have to put to him when we see him. But we're not just stumbling around in the dark here. If Suzanne arranged for that gathering at the mansion and included Rivers among the invitees, it means that she had to know that he was in the area. Now how would she have known that?"

"Of course," Carol chimed in. "She knew he was already there because the two of them had planned for him to come to Crooked Lake, and it wasn't because the lake is so beautiful in July."

"Which brings us back to why," Kevin said. "By the way, you're drifting to the right, which means you aren't concentrating on driving. Want me to take over?"

Carol would have to acknowledge that she was paying more attention to this discussion about Sheldon Rivers than she was to the road and the traffic. But they were nearing the Tappan Zee bridge, and she had no intention of trading places with Kevin until they had crossed the Hudson.

"No, I'll be all right. But how's this for a theory as to why Rivers came back to the lake? Let's suppose that he and Suzanne had begun to have second thoughts after all these years. What if they've got an itch to get back together, or at least to talk about it. I know, it's unlikely, but it's not unheard of. And it fits, more or less, with some of the things I've been hearing. Like Suzanne's maid's story."

"What story is that?"

"I never can remember just what you know and what you don't know. But I'm thinking of what the maid overheard when Suzanne and Gil were quarreling. It seems she wanted a divorce, and he said something like 'over my dead body.' I know it doesn't prove anything, but one reason people get divorced is so they can marry other people. Right?"

"Wait a minute," Kevin interrupted. "Suzanne has just been the big winner in the Mother Mobley sweepstakes. If you're right, and Constance had an inkling of what was going on, don't you think she'd have cut Suzanne off without a dime?"

"Only if she knew, and I can't imagine either of them telling her."

"Maybe not, but the chances of word getting around would certainly be greater if Rivers was hanging around the lake. If what you're suggesting is true, I'd think the smart thing for Rivers to do would be to stay down in Pelham until Mother Mobley passed away."

"Logically," Carol said in defense of her theory, "but logic has a way of getting lost when the sex drive kicks in."

"But it's one thing to get careless about what you're up to and quite another to flaunt it. They might have gotten away with it if they were careful not to be seen together in public, but how do you explain Suzanne inviting Rivers over to the big house after Gil is killed. Or him accepting the invitation. That was really dumb."

"It looks that way, but they did get away with it, didn't they? They must have cooked up some cock and bull story that worked because everyone was so traumatized by Gil's sudden death."

Suddenly, as if on cue, Carol and Kevin both fell silent. It was Carol who broke the spell. She laughed.

"Can you believe us? If Sheldon Rivers were in the back seat right now, he'd probably be laughing his head off."

"I should give up on opera and apply for a position in our creative writing department," Kevin said. "We really were on a roll there, weren't we?"

"In another five minutes we'd have had Rivers sabotaging Gil Mobley's Cessna."

"I wouldn't go that far."

"Me either, but I think it's a good thing we had this little brain storming session today. No point making fools of ourselves when Rivers is in the room."

"But let's not assume that our guesswork is all wrong," Kevin said, now in a more reflective mood.

"Fair enough," Carol said, "but it's better to assume nothing when we talk to Rivers. For all we know, whatever he and Suzanne are up to has nothing to do with what's been going on in Mobleyville. Anyway, I'm on vacation, thanks to Bridges, and it just happens that we're going to be in the town where Suzanne's ex-husband lives. Just one of those 'fancy meeting you here' moments."

"Let me remind you that this won't be a chance meeting. You called and made an appointment. So he'll know you're coming and he'll wonder why. What are you going to tell him?"

"Same thing I told him over the phone," she said. "That I've been puzzling ever since that day at *Chambord* over just what he meant when he said I hadn't asked the important questions. And it happens to be true."

CHAPTER 44

Carol and Kevin checked into their motel, and then drove around Pelham for half an hour to get their bearings. Pelham proved to be a small town, although they both commented on the fact that it was considerably larger than any of the communities on Crooked Lake. Kevin's research had identified it as the closest commuting suburb to the city itself, and it looked to be prosperous but not ostentatiously so. They located Rivers' home and calculated that it would take them no more than twenty minutes to make their eleven o'clock appointment the following morning.

The drive had been tiring, less because of the miles they had logged than the fact that a good portion of it had been spent building a case against Sheldon Rivers. The problem was that it still wasn't clear what the purpose of that case might be. They had, however, speculated that Rivers and Suzanne could be contemplating a second marriage, although they had nothing more than their own wild imaginations to support such a development. Rather than revisit that subject, they had had a light supper and watched an old Bill Powell/Myrna Loy movie on TCM. Actually, Kevin had watched it. Carol had dozed off well before the closing credits.

As planned, Carol was wearing slacks and a blouse instead of her uniform. Kevin, for more obvious reasons, was also dressed casually. They arrived punctually at eleven.

"Mr. Rivers," she said, using her warmest, most pleasant voice, "I'm so glad you were willing to see me. I don't believe that I said anything about my husband coming with me, but he was getting restless so I urged him to come along. Kevin, this is Mr. Rivers. Sheldon, am I correct?"

"Yes, I'm Sheldon. I'm not sure I would have recognized you."

"That's understandable. I'm always looking for an excuse to leave my uniform at home."

"Well, come on in. It isn't every day that I have an opportunity to talk with someone in law enforcement about a case."

Carol smiled and shook her head.

"There really isn't any case, Mr. Rivers. Like I told you over the phone, the National Transportation Safety Board handled the investigation of Mr. Mobley's death. I wanted to stop by because I remembered the last thing you said when I left Constance Mobley's home the day we met."

"I know. Anyway, come on in. It isn't too late for coffee is it?"

"I'd love some," Carol said. "Black, no sugar. How about you, Kevin?"

Kevin tried to look as if he found the situation a bit awkward, his role that of a fifth wheel.

"If it won't be any trouble," he said. "Black for me, too."

Rivers led them into what was presumably a living room, and both Carol and Kevin were immediately struck by the inescapable fact that he was having trouble walking. He didn't literally hug the wall, but stayed close to it as if uncertain of his balance. By the time he reached the kitchen door he appeared to be more sure of himself.

"Make yourselves at home. I'll only be a minute."

Carol quickly took in the room. Nothing special, but she found herself comparing it with the room in which she had last seen Rivers. Measured against *Chambord's* parlor, the living room promised to be a relaxing place to read a book or carry on an informal conversation. She chose an old fashioned and over stuffed chair. She hoped it wasn't their host's favorite.

The coffee turned out to be unusually good, much better than what had been available at the motel. Rivers hesitated before taking a seat on a low bench across from the sheriff.

"You'll have to forgive me," he said. "I often find it difficult to get into a comfortable position. If I move about while we talk, don't think I'm anxious for you to be gone."

Whether he's uncomfortable or really anxious for us to be on our way, Carol thought, I'd better get on with the purpose of our visit.

"It's like I told you over the phone, Mr. Rivers. The day we met at Constance Mobley's home, the last thing you said as I was leaving was that I hadn't asked the important questions. That piqued my curiosity. Somehow I can't get it off my mind. So I thought I'd take this opportunity to ask you what were the important questions I hadn't asked."

Rivers smiled and set his coffee cup down on the bookcase.

"I've thought about it since you called to say you'd like to see me. Funny thing is, I can't remember saying anything like that. Maybe I did, but I can't imagine that I had anything specific in mind. You know how it is, strangers making small talk."

Carol doubted that Rivers couldn't remember, or that he had simply been making small talk. There had been something about the way he had made the remark about important questions that suggested he knew exactly what he had in mind. But she was not about to challenge him on it.

"I guess I attached more importance to it than I needed to. Probably because I had no idea who you were. It wasn't until later that I learned that you used to be married to Suzanne Mobley."

"Of course," he said with a smile. "Everyone else was family, not a fugitive from a past life. I suppose you've heard all about me since then."

"Actually, Mr. Rivers, I've heard almost nothing about you since that day, and my source has been your daughter. Evelyn seems to be a fine young woman. Someone who seems to be worried about you."

Rivers was obviously surprised to hear this.

"How did you meet Evelyn?"

"She was present when Constance's attorney explained the will, and we had lunch afterwards."

"Are you at liberty to tell me what she had to say about me?" He sounded both curious and reluctant to ask the question.

"I'm sure she wouldn't mind," Carol said. "She wishes you'd listen more to her. But that's probably what most young people say about their parents. She's clearly more interested in you than she is in her mother. And I know she's concerned about your health. Should she be?"

"I'm not who I used to be, but who is? I've got something the doc calls chronic fatigue syndrome. There's something else, but I can't recall what he called it. There's always a fancy name for what ails us, isn't there?"

"Oh, and there's one other thing," Carol said. "She didn't say so in so many words, but I have the impression that she wonders whether you and Suzanne might get married again."

She considered asking him whether Evelyn might be onto something, but chose not to. Kevin was not so reticent.

"Have you considered it?" he asked, speaking for the first time since having been introduced.

Carol gave her husband a look which said 'don't be rude.' But Rivers gave no evidence of being offended, although he did get up and moved awkwardly to a chair nearer to Kevin.

"I suppose many couples who split have occasional second thoughts. In any event, it's hardly the time, is it, what with Gil just laid to rest."

"I'm still puzzled as to why you were at *Chambord* right after Gil's plane crashed." She might not learn anything else from this trip to Pelham, but Carol was determined to press for an answer to this question.

"Suzanne called and told me I should get over to the mansion."

"I had assumed that, but did she tell you why you should be there?"

"I thought it had to do with inheritance, now that Gil was dead. As it happened, we talked around the issue. No one wanted to look greedy. In any event, it had nothing to do with me. I'm not family, and Constance didn't like me."

"But if you and Suzanne were to remarry, you stood to become quite wealthy, unless Constance were to change her will in favor of Marcus now that Gil was dead."

"I see you've been doing your homework, sheriff. Yes, I suppose that's true. Hypothetically. But I'm not rushing to the altar with Suzanne, and Constance didn't change her will, as I'm sure you know. Why don't you tell me why you are in Pelham, drinking my coffee and asking me all these questions."

"Because, as I've told you, I'm interested in those important questions I didn't ask when I was at the mansion. But I do have one other question, and then we'll be leaving. While you were at the lake, did you spend any time at Suzanne and Gil's house?"

"You must remember, sheriff, that I had been married to Suzanne before Gil came along. He and I were not what you would call friendly. So you won't be surprised to learn that I never

215

darkened their door. I even kept my distance after Gil's death. Satisfied?"

Not surprisingly, the conversation in Sheldon Rivers' rambler petered out shortly thereafter. Carol asked no more questions, and Kevin had the good sense not to intervene again. A clock somewhere in the depths of the house struck the noon hour and after a round of perfunctory good-byes, Carol thanked Rivers for his time and expressed her hope that he and Evelyn would be able to reconcile their differences. It wasn't long before she and Kevin slid into a booth at *Ruby Tuesday's* and launched into a discussion as to whether after lunch they should cut short their vacation or drive up to the Berkshires for the night.

CHAPTER 45

Carrie Mobley had spent almost all of her time at Crooked Lake worrying that Marcus's share of his mother's will was going to be a mere pittance, and haranguing her husband about what he must do to prevent such an injustice. But she had found time to do a bit of shopping in Southport. She hadn't found anything that really interested her, but she had finally purchased one of those gaudy summer flags that the lake people like to install behind their cottages. A multicolored mixture of birds and butterflies and garden flowers, the flag had an uncertain future at the Mobley's Binghamton home. Carrie had not even removed it from the shopping bag which now rested on a work bench in the garage.

But when she stepped out of the car after a trip to the grocers, she decided to break it out and see if there might be a place for it in the garden. It was wrapped in an old newspaper, which fell aside as she unfurled the flag. The newspaper would have been put in the trash can had it not been for the fact that a story about the lake having set a record for consecutive rainless days had caught her eye.

The flag never did get planted that afternoon, but Carrie did take the newspaper into the house with her in order to read the Crooked Lake weather story. One thing led to another, and before discarding this old issue of the *Gazette* she found herself perusing the personals. A plea on behalf a missing dog who answered to the name of Rusty. Best wishes to a grandson who was going off to college, the first in his family. The Scanlons moving to Boca Raton, Florida. Why did people go to the trouble of putting such mundane things into what wasn't much more than a local gossip sheet, she wondered? On the other hand, why did people bother with personal trivia on Facebook?

The last item in the personals column caught her eye because it contained a phone number. 'Anyone knowing the whereabouts of Edward G. Robinson or next of kin, please leave a message at 315 887-8574.' Like the dog, Robinson must have disappeared. She hoped he wasn't one of those people suffering from dementia who simply wanders off when the family isn't paying attention. Carrie set that thought aside and put the *Gazette* in the waste basket under the sink.

It wasn't until 7:45, when she had finished clearing the dinner dishes from the table and was setting out a peach pie for dessert, that she remembered the weather story in Crooked Lake's *Gazette*. She shared the news with Marcus and they spent a few minutes reflecting on the only aspect of their time at the lake which had been enjoyable.

"Even in good weather, people still have their problems, don't they?" Marcus observed.

"Yes, and they have to tell the world about it in the paper," Carrie said. "There, right next to the weather story, there's stuff about a dog called Rusty running away and a man called Edward G. Robinson going missing. Life must be pretty dull over there."

Marcus was suddenly disinterested in the peach pie.

"There's a piece about Edward G. Robinson?"

"Yes, right next to one about somebody named Scanlon. Why, do you know this Robinson person?"

"No, no, it's just -" He let his thought tail off and then got out of his chair.

"Where's the paper you saw this in?"

"It's under the sink," Carrie said. "In the waste basket."

Marcus retrieved the paper and quickly scanned it until he spotted the personals column.

"It gives a number to call, doesn't it."

"Well, yes, I think it did. But so what? Who's Robinson?"

"There isn't any such person," Marcus replied as he resumed his seat at the dinner table.

"I don't understand. You just said you didn't know him. How can you be sure there isn't any such person?"

"Because I made him up!" Marcus almost shouted at his wife.

"You made him up?" Carrie was understandably confused. "Come on, eat your pie."

"This is weird. What's the date on this paper?" Marcus unfolded the paper and spotted the date on the first page. "It's last week's. I never thought they'd try to find me."

"What on earth are you talking about?" Carrie asked.

"You were always on my case to do something to get Gil out of the way. It was a dumb idea, but I tried this Edward G. Robinson stunt. I should have figured it couldn't work."

"Come on, Marcus. You aren't making any sense. What is this Edward G. Robinson stunt?"

"It doesn't matter any more, but I called the sheriff after Gil was killed and gave her a story about his knowing his plane wasn't in condition to fly and then flying it anyway. I thought it would start them thinking he was suicidal, and that that would somehow screw up Suzanne's inheritance prospects."

"So the sheriff thinks you are Edward G. Robinson?"

"Don't be stupid. She has no idea who Robinson is, other than a Hollywood actor, and she's not that dumb. I gave her a crazy story and I'm sure she didn't buy a word of it. So I just hung up on her. I'd never have tried something like that if it wasn't for you hounding me to do something, always 'do something.'"

"I thought you said you wanted to poison Gil."

"Oh, for Chrissake, Carrie, I never said I'd poison him."

"Yes, you did. But you said you'd deny it, like guys in the CIA deny that's what they do."

Marcus was frustrated. He got up from his chair and walked over to the kitchen door and started pounding on it.

"Now listen to me," he said, turning around and facing his wife. "I didn't try to kill Gil. No one knows that I pretended to be somebody named Robinson. Can we just forget this whole business? I don't want you to say anything - do you hear me, *anything* - to anyone about that damned personal in the *Gazette*. It has nothing to do with me. There isn't any Edward G. Robinson, so no one is going to read the personals column and call that number. Do you hear me? Just leave it alone."

"But what if it could still mess up things for Suzanne?"

"It won't. We agreed to cut our losses, remember? All we'd be doing if we talk about this Robinson thing in the *Gazette* is get ourselves in trouble. Big trouble. So we forget we ever saw it. Come on, tell me you never heard of Edward G. Robinson."

"But that's a lie. I know he's an actor."

"Carrie, don't do this to me. You know damned well what I mean. You don't want the sheriff coming down here to Binghamton with a warrant for our arrest, do you? So forget you ever heard of this Robinson guy."

"I'll try."

Christ, he thought as he forced himself not to say what he really wanted to say, how could I ever have made such a horrible mistake. It wasn't his Edward G. Robinson phone call to the sheriff that was on his mind, it was his decision to marry Carrie.

CHAPTER 46

Marcus Mobley was nervous. He had no confidence that his wife, either in an unguarded moment or because she might take a perverse pleasure in it, wouldn't mention his Edward G. Robinson phone call to the sheriff to one of her friends. He couldn't even be absolutely certain that she wouldn't say something which would suggest that her brother-in-law had died because he had been poisoned. This was highly unlikely, but Carrie had a penchant for putting her foot in her mouth and not even being aware she had done it. Why had he never learned to be more circumspect where she was concerned?

As if his conversation with Carrie about pretending to be Robinson weren't bad enough, he found himself facing another problem the next morning. It came in the form of a phone call to his pharmacy. He was in the process of helping a customer when his assistant nudged him and suggested he step back inside for a moment.

"It's a woman who says she's the sheriff of Cumberland County. She wants to speak with you," Miss Silverman said, sotto voce. Her tone of voice was conspiratorial.

Marcus told his assistant to say he'd be with her in a minute and returned to the counter. His mind was no longer on the customer, which meant that he had to ask her to repeat her name and the prescription she was picking up.

What could the sheriff possibly want? He had not seen her since the morning of Gil's death, the morning when she had stopped by *Chambord* to talk with Suzanne. Before he left the lake it had become common knowledge that the people from Washington who were investigating the crash of the Cessna had determined that Gil had died of a heart attack. Everyone seemed to believe that the case was closed. Had something happened, had something been discovered, which suggested otherwise? One thing was obvious: the sheriff had taken the trouble to find out where he lived and that he was a pharmacist by profession.

He took longer with his customer, a Mrs. Helmand, than he needed to, and he realized he was doing so because he was afraid of what the sheriff might tell him. Or worse, might ask him. But it was too late to pretend he was not at the pharmacy, and common sense told him that it was not a good idea to keep the sheriff waiting.

He picked up the phone and went as far from the service counter as he could.

"Sheriff?" He started to say that her call came as a surprise, but decided that it would be better to say nothing and let her do the talking.

"Hello, Mr. Mobley. We've only met the once, and that's because the investigation of your brother's death wasn't my responsibility. Unfortunately, there are a couple of matters that the NTSB left in my hands when they completed their work, and that's why I'm calling. Is there any time in the next two or three days when it would be possible for me to stop by and talk with you?"

"Here?" Marcus blurted out. "You mean in Binghamton? The pharmacy?"

"Yes," Carol said. "It's not that long a drive, and I do need to see you. If the pharmacy isn't convenient, we could meet at your home."

"No, no," he said, trying not to sound as if the very thought of meeting at his home, with his wife about, was out of the question. "I mean, couldn't we talk some place other than here or at the house? I'm in the Bronwin Medical Building, and there's a small luncheonette on the first floor. Can we do it there?"

"Of course. But you haven't suggested a day or time. I'm flexible, but I would hope we could meet tomorrow or the following day. Late morning is preferable, if that's possible."

Marcus hated the prospect of this meeting. On the other hand, he wanted desperately to know why the sheriff needed to see him. So the sooner they met the better.

"I can see you any time between ten and one tomorrow," he said. "Is that okay?"

"That's excellent. Let's make it eleven. I feel quite certain that my GPS will get me to the Bronwin Building with no problem."

"Is there anything I should be doing for the meeting?" It was as close as he thought it wise to come to asking the sheriff what the meeting would be about.

"No, nothing at all. So I look forward to seeing you at eleven. I'm sure we'll recognize each other."

They may have seen each other only once, but Marcus agreed that recognition would not be a problem. For one thing, she'd be in uniform. The very thought made him uncomfortable.

Carol, back in the office in Cumberland, smiled to herself as she considered what must be going through Marcus's mind. Actually, there was nothing mysterious about her meeting with the pharmacist. She needed to talk with him about two things: whether he and Carrie had spent any time in Gil's lake house recently and the fact that the autopsy had revealed the presence of Florinef in Gil's body. And it was important that they discuss these matters face to face rather than over the phone.

She and Kevin had decided to forego a drive up into the Berkshires and had returned directly to the lake after their meeting with Rivers. Ideally, they would have stopped off in Binghamton en route, thereby avoiding a second road trip. But it hadn't worked out that way. Probably better, she thought.

There was no reason to suspect Marcus of having substituted Florinef for Gil's hypertension medication. But unlike Suzanne, he would have had easy access to Florinef thanks to the fact that he was a pharmacist, and that made it at least possible for him to have played a contributing role in Gil's death. Once again she was imagining the Mobley case as a murder. Bridges, whom she hadn't yet told about visiting Sheldon Rivers on her 'vacation,' would be disappointed in her.

———

It had not been difficult to dissuade Kevin from coming along on the drive to Binghamton.

"That's a round trip I could do without," he had said, claiming to prefer working on a paper he was writing for a fall conference in San Francisco.

"Good. You've been talking about that paper for weeks and I haven't seen you doing anything about it."

"Mobleys come first," he said. "But not twice in one week."

That decided, Carol set off down Route 17 for her meeting with Marcus Mobley. Fortunately, Bridges had taken the day off for root canal surgery. She felt sorry for him, but grateful that she would be able to talk to Marcus and be back that same day without having to tell Sam the truth about what she had been doing with her time. That moment of reckoning would come tomorrow. She hoped that she would learn something in Binghamton that would provide justification for these two mid-summer road trips.

The luncheonette was almost empty when she walked in, and she had no trouble spotting Marcus at a corner table. He shook hands and pulled a chair out for her. Carol could not remember the last time a man had done that. Kevin had long ago learned that she didn't need his help.

"This weather is something, isn't it?" Marcus said. It was a statement, not a question, and Carol had to agree. Unless you were a farmer who had to worry about his crops, the upstate region had had its best weather in years, one day of sunshine after another.

"Unbelievable," she said. "I'll bet you wish you were still at the lake."

Marcus was very glad to be back at work, three counties and more than 75 miles away from Crooked Lake. He knew better than to say so.

"Unfortunately, I have a job which requires my presence. I'd already been gone longer than I should have."

"I understand, and I don't propose to keep you away from your job for long. Maybe half an hour. Are you interested in lunch?"

"No, thanks. I brought a yogurt and a thermos of iced tea from home. But have something to drink, if you like."

"Coffee, I think." She waved at a waitress and placed her order.

"I should have looked you up before you left the lake, but this gives me an excuse to get out of the office for the day. I've been trying to account for peoples' comings and goings during those days around the time of your brother's death. You and your wife came to the lake when?"

His answer corresponded with what Mrs. Jordan at the B & B had told her.

"And you left - what was it, seven days ago?"

"That sounds right, but then I had to go back for that awkward reading of the will by Minchin. We didn't stick around, not even overnight."

"How come you didn't stay with your brother and sister-in-law?"

This question obviously surprised Marcus.

"You probably don't know it, but Gil and I were never close. And to be perfectly honest, Carrie and Suzanne didn't get along at all. They had plenty of room, but it never occurred to us to propose staying with them."

"While you were at the lake, did you ever visit them at their home, or go to see Suzanne after Gil was killed?"

Marcus managed a chuckle.

"I'm sure it sounds like the courteous thing to do, especially after what happened to Gil, but we didn't do it. I never saw Gil before he died. Same with Suzanne. Of course I saw her at *Chambord* the day we met you and again the day we all met with Minchin. We didn't go to the lake for some kind of family reunion."

"No, it doesn't sound like a reunion. Why did you choose to spend those days on the lake?"

Marcus knew it wouldn't do to say it was for the swimming or perhaps the fishing.

"My mother was failing, and inasmuch as we hadn't seen her in well over a year, we thought we should make the trip. Sort of a last visit. Of course, we didn't know that she would go so quickly."

"It was a sad day, I'm sure. I didn't know her well, but I feel privileged to have met her."

Marcus's effort to smile in acknowledgement of the compliment was at best halfhearted.

"That's kind of you," he said.

"Have you ever speculated about what happened to your brother?"

Marcus looked at Carol as if he hadn't understood the question.

"I thought those people from the aviation board said it was a heart attack," he said. "Is there a problem with that?"

"I was simply wondering what you thought when you heard he'd crashed."

"I don't know anything about planes. At first I thought there was something wrong with the plane, you know, the kind of thing that sends them looking for the black box. But then everybody was talking about a heart attack. Why, was it something else after all?"

"Your brother had a problem with hypertension, which can lead to a heart attack. But the investigation discovered that he had been taking a medication that raises one's blood pressure. You're a pharmacist, what do you make of that?"

It was obvious that Marcus was uncertain where this was going. He was particularly concerned that the question was being asked because he was a pharmacist.

"What I do is fill prescriptions," he said. "I don't write them."

"Of course. But if the patient had a history of hypertension, what would you think about such a prescription?"

"I don't understand what you're driving at, sheriff," Marcus said. "I don't usually know a patient's medical history. I rely on the doctor who's prescribing for him."

"Okay, and I know you weren't Gil's doctor. But the fact that he had high blood pressure and had ingested something that was guaranteed to raise his blood pressure would raise a flag, wouldn't it?"

"Well, sure. But I can't believe that Dr. Sigler would prescribe a drug like that."

"I'm quite sure he didn't." Carol said. "But I also doubt that your brother consciously took a medication that was dangerous to his health. That would seem to leave two possibilities. Gil took the wrong pills by mistake or someone deliberately switched his meds."

"Are you suggesting that somebody tried to kill Gil?"

"Like I said, that's one possibility. And if that happened, it looks like he succeeded."

"That's terrible," Marcus said. "Do you have any evidence that that's what happened?"

Carol sidestepped the question and addressed the Florinef issue.

"If you as a pharmacist were asked to identify a medication to deal with hypotension, what would it be?"

Her use of the word for low blood pressure would let Marcus know that the sheriff was familiar with the relevant scientific jargon.

"There are more than one," he replied.

"How about Florinef?"

"That's a possibility."

"Have you ever filled a prescription for Florinef or one of its generics?"

"I think you just accused me of trying to kill my brother." Marcus made no attempt to hide his anger.

Deja vu all over again, Carol thought, except this time it was Marcus Mobley and not Jeremy Sigler who had said it. The difference was that she had never intended to accuse Dr. Sigler, whereas she had entertained that thought in Marcus's case.

"I'm not accusing you of anything, Mr. Mobley. I'm only trying to account for the fact that Gil had Florinef in his system when the autopsy was performed." How many times had she said the same thing over the past three weeks?

"In answer to your question, I've been a pharmacist for my whole adult life. I cannot possibly remember how many prescriptions I've filled and when for the myriad of medications on the market. I shall, of course, wrack my brain and try to come up with the information you're seeking. Is there something else?"

"No, I don't think so. I appreciate you taking the time to talk with me. As I said, this wouldn't take long. Please give my regards to your wife."

It wasn't until Carol was back in her car and on her way out of Binghamton, headed for Crooked Lake, that it occurred to her that she hadn't paid for her coffee. It was an oversight she rarely made, and she felt a moment of guilt. But on second thought, it was no big deal The bill could not have been more than $2.50. Marcus could cover it easily.

CHAPTER 47

Merle Corrigan had agreed to be patient regarding his Cessna. He and Suzanne Mobley had agreed on a price, one that he wished were higher, one that she thought was already too high. Nonetheless they had shaken hands in the end, with the understanding that she would produce a check just as soon as she could, certainly by Labor Day at the latest. The matter settled, they had not seen each other for a number of days when Merle surprised her with a call one sultry afternoon.

Would you mind if I dropped by, he had asked, and inasmuch as her life had become one dull, boring day after another, a visit from Merle sounded to her like a welcome change of pace. She had told him to come on over, and it was close to four o'clock when he got there.

"This heat getting to you?" he asked when they settled down in the living room with a couple of beers.

"You talking about my thermostat? I'm sorry. I seem to keep it in the 60s, mostly out of habit. Would you rather go out on the porch?"

Corrigan smiled.

"I'm okay. It's just that I haven't been this cool since back in May. Libby, she has a real aversion to air conditioning. She feels about it like she does about the Cessna."

"I'll bet she's happy about my taking the plane off your hands."

"I'm sure she is, but she keeps telling me it's still out there at the dock. I think she's afraid our deal will fall through. That's not going to happen, is it?"

"Like I told you, probate or whatever they call it will take awhile. But I'm rustling up the cash. No, we're still on."

Merle got up and moved to the couch beside Suzanne. He put his hand over hers, giving it a light squeeze.

"Thanks, Suzanne. I'm not sure what I'd do without you."

She gently removed her hand from his.

"No problem," she said, obviously confused by what had just happened and not sure what to make of it. She expected him to say something which would help explain this unexpected overture to intimacy. He surprised her.

"Were you and Gil happy?" he asked. His hands remained in his lap, but he didn't move back to the chair.

Suzanne started to laugh, then thought better of it.

"Perhaps I should ask you the same question. About you and Libby?"

"I could never leave her. I realized that when she gave me the choice of the Cessna or our marriage. I guess none of us ever knows just how our lives are going to turn out."

"I can agree with that," Suzanne said. "If anybody had told me I'd feel like I do now that Gil's gone, I'd have said they were crazy. But the truth is I don't feel anything. You know I was married before I met Gil, don't you?"

"I'd heard."

"It was a very different life. A city life, a city man, no plane. Hell, I'd never been in a plane, much less flown one. No, that's not quite true. I'd flown up to Boston to see my family, and once to London. But it never occurred to me that one day I'd be a pilot."

"And a good one. Gil knew what he was doing, but you were a natural. I used to wonder if he was maybe jealous of you."

Once again Merle Corrigan had surprised her.

"What makes you think that?"

"Well, I remember that he taught you how to fly, but it was almost no time before you were flying circles around him. Figuratively, of course. I often wished it was us, you and me, during the fly-ins."

Suzanne was flattered, but not sure how to react to this man she had known for some years but not well.

They continued to talk, and by the time they were on their second beer the awkwardness of their conversation had largely dissipated. Most of what they talked about concerned planes and flying, but then Suzanne asked a question which abruptly changed the subject.

"Do you have the same doctor that Gil had? Jeremy Sigler?"

"No. In fact, I'm going to have to find myself a new doctor. Earl Leonard is retiring, or so he tells me. He's been threatening to for several years, but I think he's serious now."

"Do you know Sigler?"

"Barely. Why do you ask?"

"I'm not really sure. He and Gil were friends. After a fashion, that is. But somehow I don't believe that Gil really liked him. I know that sounds funny, but I got the feeling he rubbed Gil the wrong way."

"Maybe Gil didn't like his bedside manner. You know, too gruff."

"No, that's not it. It was more personal. At least I think it was. They used to play pinochle together all the time, but not so much in recent years. I asked because Dr. Sigler came by recently and talked about some study Gil was involved in, a study Sigler was conducting. He wanted to have a look in Gil's safe deposit box to see if some papers related to that study were there. I checked, and there weren't any papers related to any study. Besides, I never heard Gil talk about this study of Sigler's."

"Sounds like you've got yourself a puzzle."

"It's probably my imagination, but it doesn't feel right. I guess I was hoping Sigler was your doctor and you could tell me what you think of him."

"Tell you what I can do," Merle said. "I think I know a few people who go to Sigler. Let me ask around. I won't mention you, just say I'm looking for a new doctor now that Leonard's retiring."

"That would be awfully good of you, Merle. I could do it, I suppose, but I know I wouldn't be comfortable."

Suzanne leaned over and gave Corrigan a quick kiss on the cheek.

"It won't be a problem," he said. "You say that now that Gil's gone you don't feel anything. That must be terribly hard to live with. I don't know what your plans are, but I'd like you to know that you can count on me. Not just about Sigler, but whatever you need. Like you helped me with the Cessna. I know we've never been close, but things are different now. Please let me know if there's anything I can do. Anything, you understand?"

"You're very sweet, Merle." This time she put her arms around him and kissed him full on the mouth. She watched him out the back door and followed the car as it went down the road and out of sight.

Strange man, she thought. He's giving up his plane and it's making him miserable. Libby's not going to be able to make everything right. Neither am I. And then her thoughts turned to Sheldon.

CHAPTER 48

As Carol reflected on what she had learned from her meetings with Sheldon Rivers and Marcus Mobley, the thing that stood out was nothing either of them had said but rather something she had observed. It had not been on her agenda when she left Crooked Lake, but it just might prove to be more important than any question she had raised or any answer she had listened to. It was the obvious problem that Rivers had had when he walked, sat down, or stood up. When she had observed him at *Chambord*, he had remained essentially motionless beside the fireplace across the room. In his home in Pelham he had met them at the door, guided them to his living room, brought them coffee, and seen them to the door when they left. And he had been conspicuously unsteady on his feet and, yes, uncomfortable. It might be the result of an accident or an injury incurred playing tennis, but he had carried no cane and he had not ventured to comment on some recent misadventure. Could it possibly have to do with one of the chronic diseases Dr. Sigler had told her about, a problem which could be treated with Florinef?

Her instinct was to call Dr. Sigler, describe what she had seen, and get his opinion. She debated the matter with herself for a time, mindful of the fact that Sam would probably recommend another vacation if she did so. In the end Carol did what she knew she would do when the idea first occurred to her. She called Sigler.

As usual, Jeremy was willing to take her call even if he was tied up with another patient. They agreed on a meeting time, and Carol soon found herself once again on her way to his aerie high above Crooked Lake.

"So you think you need my medical advice again?" he said as they retreated to his office. "If I weren't such a good citizen, I'd start charging you for consulting services."

Sigler smiled at his own witticism.

"With your help," she said, "I'm able to sound well informed about things I know nothing about. When I write up my report on this case, I'll give credit where credit is due."

"This is about a case?"

"I'm not sure. It's the Mobley business, and I'm involved only because I can't stop worrying about how Gil happened to ingest some stuff that isn't good for someone trying to control hypertension."

"Oh, yes. Back to Addison's disease, is that it?"

"Perhaps. That's what I want to talk about. I had a meeting with Sheldon Rivers. First time since that day we all met at *Chambord*. Seems like a long time ago, doesn't it?"

"I understood that he'd gone home. Somewhere down state."

"He lives just north of the city, and that's where I met him." Carol didn't offer an explanation as to why she had taken the trip to Rivers' home. "We had a perfectly good chat, but what I want to ask you about concerns his physical problem. Or problems."

"He has a physical problem? I wasn't aware of it."

"Neither was I, and I'm no expert. But let me tell you what I saw while I was with Mr. Rivers. Maybe you'll have an idea what the trouble is."

"I make it a point never to offer a diagnosis without examining a patient, but go ahead."

So Carol did her best to describe what she had observed the day she and Kevin had talked with Suzanne's former husband. She mentioned both general impressions and specific instances when Rivers had seemed to be in some kind of trouble. Dr. Sigler listened intently, nodding his head from time to time but refraining from interrupting with questions.

"I know that doesn't sound very professional," she said. "I've never been very good when my doctor asks me to describe symptoms or tell me how much it hurts on a scale of one to ten. I'm sorry to be so imprecise."

"Actually, you've been quite precise, sheriff. And now you're going to ask me if Florinef would be prescribed for what you've described?"

"I was hoping you could tell me."

"Understandably, given the Florinef that was found in Gil's body. Like I said, it's hard to answer that question without personally seeing Rivers. I'm not criticizing your powers of observation, but I'd feel a lot better if I could see him. Or at least talk with him."

The doctor leaned back in his chair, his face registering deep thought.

"I notice that you didn't mention asking Rivers if he was taking Florinef."

"No. Perhaps I should have, but it seemed at the time as if I might be overreacting to his problem. I felt I needed more information first."

"And perhaps I can provide that information," Sigler said. "All right, this is what I would propose. Let me talk with Rivers. After all, we do know each other, and I have no reason to think he wouldn't talk candidly with me. Needless to say, I won't mention your name."

"Won't he assume that you called because I'd told you about his problem.?"

"No. Remember, I saw him that day we all met at *Chambord*. Now that we're talking about him, it occurs to me that he may have been showing some of the same symptoms that day."

"He did?" Carol looked surprised. "I don't remember him moving around much at all."

"And that proves my point, sheriff, although quite frankly I didn't think about it at the time. No, I think he'll be quite willing to talk with me. People who are having physical problems are usually pleased when a doctor takes an interest in their condition."

———

Jeremy Sigler waited impatiently for the last of his patients to leave so that he could turn his full attention to Sheldon Rivers. He had had no idea how Gil Mobley had come to ingest Florinef. But he knew that Suzanne Mobley was the person in the best position to switch Gil's meds, assuming that she could get her hands on a medication like Florinef. And he also was almost certain that Suzanne was itching to dump Gil and remarry Sheldon. Gil had as much as told him so. What would make more sense than that Suzanne had obtained the hypotension meds from Sheldon?

Of course he had no idea whether Rivers was taking Florinef or something like it. What the sheriff had told him was far from conclusive on that point. But it was not out of the question. He knew he had not observed Rivers acting as if he were suffering from something like orthostatic hypotension. He had told the sheriff he had, however, and he'd tell Rivers the same thing. More importantly, he had no idea whether Florinef had ever been prescribed for Suzanne's former husband. But if it had, Rivers had been at the lake and in a position to share those pills with Suzanne. He might have done it inadvertently or he might have done it deliberately. It really didn't matter. Either way, there might now be a chance to gain a hold over Suzanne Mobley, and that was something Jeremy Sigler very much wanted to do.

———

It wasn't until that evening that Dr. Sigler caught up with Rivers at his home.

"Sheldon, this is Jeremy Sigler, up on Crooked Lake. If I'd been better organized, I'd have been in touch before you went back home. How are you doing?"

"Dr. Sigler? I was expecting a call from someone else."

"Not to worry. I'll keep it brief. I asked how you were, because I've been worrying about you ever since we saw each other at Constance's."

"You've been worried? Did I look that bad?"

"I've never known you to look bad, Sheldon, but you didn't look like yourself. Of course it's been awhile since I saw you last, and age has a way of catching up with all of us."

"Well, I'm okay, or so Dr. Murphy tells me. As long as I follow orders. What's on your mind?"

"I wish I could tell you I'm calling to see if there's anything to the rumor I hear about you and Suzanne, but in fact it is your health that's on my mind."

"Me and Suzanne? What rumor is this?" Rivers sounded concerned.

"Forget I said it. You know how people are, somebody loses a spouse, especially when it's an attractive woman, and they start speculating about what comes next. At least that's the way it seems to happen up here - small town stuff."

"Well, I'd appreciate it if you'd scotch rumors like that. Suzanne's been a widow for less than a month. She doesn't need that kind of talk."

"You're right, and I'll do what I can to nip it in the bud. But I really did want to talk about your health. When I saw you the other day at *Chambord* I was reminded of a couple of patients of mine who have what we docs call orthostatic hypotension. Did your doctor - Murphy is it? - did he ever mention it? Or maybe Addison's disease?"

"Addison's I think I would remember. It doesn't sound familiar. The other one, I don't know. All I know is what pills I'm supposed to take."

"That's why I called. I figured if I was right, I could suggest something that would make a new man of you. Of course Murphy's probably already done that. Has he put you on something?"

"Yes, it's got one of those unpronounceable names. But it's a generic for something called Florinef. It's being refilled right now. I almost ran out before I got back home."

"Well, if your Dr. Murphy is already on top of this, there's no need for me to stick my nose in," Sigler said. Then he changed the subject.

"Have you heard about Mom Mobley's will?"

"I have, and it came out about like I thought it would. I didn't really know Franklin, but I had a hunch he'd inherit the property and the mansion. What he'll ever do with it, I don't know. He won't be able to maintain the place, that's for sure. The split between Gil and Marcus, that wasn't surprising from what I'd heard. Of course, it'll be Suzanne, not Gil, that inherits. Such irony. If Suzanne and I had never divorced, we wouldn't be having this discussion. Life is weird."

"And unpredictable. But I was pleased that Constance left so much to your daughter. Evelyn was just about the only close friend she had. I hope this helps her get the start in life I'm sure she deserves."

Rivers laughed.

"Did you ever see that old show, 'The Fantastics?'"

"I don't think so."

"Well, there's this song in it where two guys are comparing vegetables with their children. If they plant radishes and cabbages, they know they'll get radishes and cabbages, but - I think I remember the line - with progeny it's hodge-podgeny. With your kids, you never know how things will turn out."

"That's clever. Never heard it, and my daughter's got a ways to go before she becomes a problem. But it sounds like you've got a point."

Sigler knew that he was now on he right track. Two more minutes of small talk and he turned his attention to a search for doctors named Murphy in Westchester. He was confident that he'd get a confirmation of what was wrong with Sheldon Rivers and what Murphy had prescribed.

CHAPTER 49

Deputy Sheriff Bridges spoke briefly with Carol after the morning briefing the next day and asked if he might have ten minutes before he set off for his daily rounds. It was with mixed feelings that she agreed, and they repaired to her office to 'catch up.'

She was certain that Sam would want to hear how she had enjoyed her vacation. She preferred to focus on his root canal surgery, but knew that she would have to tell him the truth about her trip to Pelham.

"I see you've survived," she said. "I've never had one of those things, but I hear they're rough."

"I guess it depends," Sam replied. "In any event, this one wasn't as bad as my first. I'm a little sore, but I'm told I'll be back to normal in a few days. But take my word for it and don't put something like this on your bucket list."

"I'll do my best to avoid it, and I hope you've had your last one. You're welcome to take more leave if you need it, you know."

"Come on, Carol, I'm an ex-Marine, as you may remember. Enough of that. Tell me about your vacation."

"I've been dreading this, Sam, but you're entitled to the whole truth and nothing but the truth. I did take a vacation, and Kevin even went along. But I didn't do much vacationing. In fact, I don't expect you'll be all that surprised when I tell you what I did."

"I'm not sure I like what I'm hearing."

"You're just going to have to get used to the fact that you work for a sheriff who's got a one track mind. I'm sorry, but I went down to a place called Pelham, New York, and spent an interesting couple of hours with a man named Sheldon Rivers. I'm sure you've heard of him. He used to be married to Suzanne Mobley."

"Why am I not surprised? You're a workaholic, Carol. No, it's worse than that. You're addicted to police work. Are you going to tell me you really are dealing with murder? That you're ready to make an arrest? Otherwise I may have to see if there's such a thing as a restraining order you slap on sheriffs."

"No such luck, and I doubt that a restraining order would stick. But the fact is I don't believe the Mobley case is a figment of my imagination. Did somebody hasten Gil Mobley's death? I think so. Can I prove it? Not yet. Do I have a suspect in mind? I do. In fact I have more than one suspect in mind. Am I ready to make an arrest? No. In our business, we don't make an arrest until we're sure there's been a crime. But bear with me, Sam. There was a crime, and you're going to help me prove it."

"What can I say?"

"Kevin has an expression you should commit to memory: 'She who must be obeyed.'"

"It's that serious, is it?"

"It's that serious. Now may we talk about what you're going to be doing next?"

"I think the root canal surgery is acting up."

"I'm sure your dentist gave you something to cope with pain. If not, I've got some Tylenol in my desk drawer here."

"Okay, let's hear it."

Carol had been giving a lot of thought to what had to be done next. First things first. She had to keep after Jeremy Sigler for a report on his conversation with Sheldon Rivers. She also had to find out if anyone had visited Rivers during his stay at the lake, especially if it turned out that Dr. Murphy had placed him on a regimen of Florinef or something like it. This brought her to a task for Sam.

"I do have something I want you to do. You're familiar with the *Three Diamonds Motel* in Yates Center. You were there the day that Sheldon Rivers checked out and Suzanne Mobley tried to persuade him to stay. Remember? I want you to find out whether Rivers had any night visitors while he was staying at the motel. You may have to turn the staff there upside down and inside out to do it, but we need to know."

"You think this is important?"

"Let's say it may be important, and that's reason enough to ask questions. The way I see it is that somebody - Suzanne Mobley, Marcus Mobley, Sheldon Rivers, Jeremy Sigler, somebody - brought medications that could have played hob with

Gil Mobley's blood pressure into his house. And that raises the obvious question: where did somebody get those medications? Sigler and Marcus, one a doctor and the other a pharmacist, would have had no trouble obtaining them. Rivers is another possibility if he was taking those meds to treat a malady of his own. Which is why I want to know whether Rivers had visitors at the motel. Because if he did, they could have walked out with those meds and taken them to Gil's."

Sam looked puzzled.

"So I'm to find out if Rivers had a visitor, but if you don't know whether he was taking the meds you're worrying about, what's the point?"

"I hope to know what medication Rivers had been taking in a day or two, hopefully today. But I think we need to move fast, so I want you to get started on his visitors at the motel. Just in case."

"Sounds as if you're pretty sure that Rivers is taking the same drug that killed Mobley."

"I'm far from sure, but I'm being proactive. And even if it's the same drug, it doesn't mean it killed Gil. But it raises the possibility that someone thought that it might do the trick. Anyway, unless you're lucky or plan to bribe the motel staff, I'll probably know what Rivers is taking before you have a list of his visitors. So let's get started."

———

Carol called Dr. Sigler, only to learn that he was waiting for a call back from Rivers' doctor.

Temporarily frustrated on that front, Carol tried to reach Gloria Garner. She had never asked her straight out to give her the names of people who had visited the Mobley house over the last month, and she doubted that Gloria would be very helpful. But it was worth a try. The woman who answered the call mumbled something about Gloria having a job interview. Carol left a number for her to call, but did not disclose the fact that it was the sheriff who wanted to speak with her.

Her efforts to focus on other matters were largely unsuccessful until Gloria returned her call after lunch.

"Gloria, it's the sheriff. Are you making progress in getting another job?"

"I'm hopeful. At least I've had three interviews, and I think I'm less scared than I was at first."

"That's good. There's no reason to be scared. You need a job, but they need someone to help them. I hope you get some good offers. But I called because I needed to ask you a question. Another question about the time you worked for the Mobleys. Are you able to talk with me for a few minutes?"

"Right now is okay. I'm the only one at home."

"Good. You lived at the Mobleys when you worked for them, so I imagine you have a pretty good idea whether they had visitors. I don't expect you to remember all the people who came and went over there, much less their names. But I'd appreciate it if you could answer a few questions."

"I'll try," Gloria said. She didn't sound as if she was likely to be of much help.

"First, thinking back for maybe a month or six weeks, do you remember whether they had many callers?"

"That's easy. There'd be days go by and nobody came to the door."

"Did Suzanne Mobley expect you to answer the door or did she do it herself?"

"Most of the time it was me, but there were times when she sort of took charge. That happened when she had a party."

"So they had parties. Let's talk about those. What do you remember about these parties?"

"I only remember two, and that's because she had me get things ready."

"You did the cooking?"

"No, they never gave dinner parties. Oh, there was one once, but it was a long time ago. It was more like they'd serve drinks and I'd be fixing stuff to go with them. Suzanne, she had a funny name she called them."

"Hors d'oeuvres?"

"That's it."

"When did they have these little parties with drinks? Before Gil was killed or afterwards?"

"Like I said, there were two. They were both before he died."

Okay, thought Carol, now comes the hard part.

"Try to remember those parties. Tell me what you can about them."

"Like who was there?"

"Yes, that and anything else that you can remember."

"Well, they were small parties. I don't think there was more than three or four people at either one. The only guest I recognized was Mr. Mobley's doctor."

Carol was disappointed, but not surprised.

"Do you have any idea who those other people could have been?"

"We weren't introduced, and I don't remember any names."

Carol did her best to describe Sheldon Rivers, Marcus Mobley, and his wife Carrie. It didn't help. Carrie of the flaming red hair would have been the most memorable, but Gloria couldn't recall a woman with red hair.

"You mentioned that Mr. Mobley's doctor was there. Do you remember if he was at both of those parties?"

"I'm not sure, but I don't think so. I'm not much help, am I?"

"There's no reason why you should recall things like this, Gloria. If it turns out to be really important, I can always talk to Mrs. Mobley herself. But thank you, and good luck getting one of those jobs."

Once again, Carol felt as if she were spinning her wheels. For a brief moment she considered placing a call to Jim Hacklin, the neighbor of the Mobleys who had overheard them arguing. But she decided against it. It was doubtful that the Hacklins kept track of the Mobleys' visitors, and she wasn't anxious to plant the idea that Suzanne was under police surveillance.

It wasn't until she was clearing her desk and getting ready to head home that Ms. Franks reported that Dr. Sigler was on the phone. She hoped he would have more to report than Gloria Garner had.

"I was hoping it would be you, Dr. Sigler. Have you learned anything?"

Jeremy Sigler had briefly considered saying 'no.' He had his own agenda, and wasn't particularly concerned with the sheriff's interest in Sheldon Rivers. But on reflection he could think of no reason why he shouldn't pass along the information he'd obtained from Dr. Murphy. There had been a number of

Murphys who practiced medicine in the general area of Pelham, but finding the right one hadn't been as hard as he had anticipated. What is more, Rivers' doctor had readily accepted his explanation for the call and had shared the fact that Suzanne Mobley's first husband was experiencing both chronic fatigue syndrome and orthostatic hypotension. Rivers had been right; he was taking a Florinef generic by way of treatment.

So he repeated what Dr. Murphy had told him. And while it didn't prove anything, it meant that the pieces of the puzzle she had been worrying about, off and on ever since Gil Mobley's death, were beginning to come together.

"Many thanks," Carol told him, and meant it. "You've been most helpful. A month ago I'd never heard of Florinef, and now it's become a part of my everyday vocabulary."

CHAPTER 50

Merle Corrigan was still trying to understand what had motivated him to behave as he had at Suzanne Mobley's. He was almost as surprised as she must have been by what he had said and done. It was as if for a few reckless minutes he had become a love-sick adolescent. And that had not been his intent. The problem was that he still wasn't sure what had been his intent. It was too late to undo the damage, and it would only compound the problem if he tried to apologize.

There was only one thing he could now do, and that was to do as he had promised - see if he could help her to understand what Dr. Jeremy Sigler was up to. He had no reason to believe Sigler was behaving strangely, but Suzanne thought so and he had said he would sound out his acquaintances, some of whom were patients of Sigler's. It was an assignment which made him uncomfortable, but he used the excuse that he needed to find a new doctor and was simply seeking counsel. It turned out not to be as difficult as he had imagined. Not, that is, until he raised the subject with Gary Harding.

Merle had already talked with three of his friends, one of whom had been a patient of Sigler's for two years, another who was quite satisfied with a doctor down in Corning, and a third who insisted that he was in good shape and didn't like doctors because 'all they're interested in is finding problems that will sustain their lucrative practice.' Harding came into the picture when Merle accidentally ran into him while cashing a check at his bank in Southport. He took advantage of the situation and persuaded him to have a quick cup of coffee.

"I've got myself a problem, Gary," Merle began after the waitress had set the two coffee cups on the table. "My doctor is closing up shop without much notice, and I don't know where to turn. I thought maybe you'd have some advice. Libby sees that woman over in Geneva, and frankly I can't see myself having her checking on my prostrate."

Harding smiled.

"You might find it stimulating. Sorry, that's a bad joke." He put on a thoughtful face. "I'm not sure I can be much help. I've got a list a yard long. A cardiologist, an orthopedist, a dermatologist, you name it. Jeremy Sigler's supposedly my primary care physician, but I don't see him all that much."

"Sigler's supposed to be pretty good, or so I've heard. You and he get along?"

Harding considered the question, took a sip of his coffee.

"He's good. We used to play pinochle, mostly down at Gil Mobley's, but I hardly see him anymore. Just once a year for a physical, minor things."

"So he'd be your recommendation, is that it?"

"I guess it depends. He's on the wagon, for what it's worth."

"Meaning what?"

"It's none of my business, Merle. I don't have any complaints. I'd suggest you talk to Gil, but of course he's no longer with us."

"Gil Mobley?" Corrigan asked.

"Yeah. Sigler was his doctor, and he spoke highly of him. Said he was good when he was sober, and he did stop drinking. Quit cold turkey."

"Gil told you this?"

"I remember the only time Gil ever poor mouthed Sigler. We had a card game a few years back when Sigler got called away by a patient. Gil called Doc a damn fool, tried to talk him out of going out on such a nasty night. And it was nasty, awful cold and snowing to boot. What made things worse, the man died on him. Poor Doc, he never did come back that night. Doctors must feel awful to lose one of their patients, and we all felt sorry for him. Sigler took it hard, even decided to lay off the booze. Gil and the others, we never talked about it. Too painful, I guess."

Merle had no idea what Suzanne would make of this information. Or was it a lack of information? But he was supposed to be talking with Harding about his need to find a new doctor, not Suzanne Mobley's relationship with Sigler.

"Did Gil ever talk about changing to another doctor?" he asked.

"Not that I ever heard of. Gil had to be in shape to fly, just like you, so I doubt he'd have stuck with Sigler if he thought he was unreliable. Terrible shame about Gil, wasn't it."

Merle agreed that it was indeed a shame. They talked until the coffee was gone, then went their separate ways. His way took him up the lake to Suzanne's. If she were at home, he'd give her a progress report. It wasn't much, and he might need to talk with more of his friends. At least she would know he was doing what he could to help her with her Sigler problem, whatever that was.

Suzanne was at home. In fact, she hadn't yet showered or dressed for the day. Merle had never seen her like this, no makeup, hair unbrushed, still in shorty pajamas, her robe askew. But she didn't sound embarrassed when she invited him in.

"Hi, Merle. Nice to see you. What brings you here at such an early hour?"

It wasn't early, but he didn't think that commenting on the time of day would be appropriate.

"I thought I could give you a heads up on what I've learned about Dr. Sigler. But I can come back when it's more convenient."

"Oh, come on in. I'm having a lazy day. You'll have to excuse my appearance."

She led him through the house and out to a screened porch, where it was comfortably warmer than it was inside.

"Now about Dr. Sigler," she said. "I don't want to make it sound more important than it is. I guess I'm just curious."

Merle had the impression that Suzanne had been more than mildly curious about Sigler. He proceeded to report what Gary Harding had told him. Suzanne listened without comment.

"That's about it," he finally said. "Does it help?"

She smiled.

"I wish I knew. We all know about looking for a needle in a haystack. I think I'm looking in a haystack, but I'm not sure what I'm looking for. Did your source mention the name of Jeremy's patient who died?"

It hadn't occurred to Corrigan to dig that deep for information. Chances are that Harding wouldn't have known the patient's name, but he regretted he hadn't asked.

"Sorry, but no. It was quite awhile ago."

"Anyway, thanks for doing my legwork for me."

When he left, Merle was mildly disappointed, both because he hadn't solved Suzanne puzzle and because she hadn't given him a goodbye kiss. Suzanne, on the other hand, was mildly encouraged. It wasn't that she now knew why Jeremy Sigler was so interested in what he thought might be in the safe deposit box. But something in what Merle had learned from his friend had rung a bell. The sound was faint, but she had heard it. She never did get dressed that day, but she did a lot of thinking. By the time the happy hour rolled around, she thought she knew what Dr. Sigler's problem was.

CHAPTER 51

One didn't simply walk into the *Three Diamonds Motel* and ask the manager or whoever was on the reception desk for a list of a guest's visitors. Not even if the person asking for this information was wearing the uniform of the Cumberland County Sheriff's Department. Deputy Sheriff Bridges had to approach his task with discretion, seeking information in ways that would elicit answers without raising eyebrows. After all, Sheldon Rivers was not known to have committed any crimes, and he was entitled to have visitors as long as they were not ladies of the night who might tarnish the reputation of the village's most respected motel.

Sam began work on his assignment by taking inventory of the people he knew who worked there. Unfortunately, it was a very short list: two people, neither of whom was a friend or someone in a position of authority. One of the two was an old high school classmate, Bill Felton, who had fallen on hard times, not to mention the fact that he had struggled with problems related to diabetes for many years. The motel had retained him in a custodial job thanks to a soft-hearted manager. The second was a young woman, Sarah Corwin, whose parents were close to Sam and his wife. Local scuttlebutt had it that she should have gone off to college and 'made something of herself,' but she had stayed at home and now served as the hostess in the motel's small coffee shop. Neither of them promised to be of much of help to Sam.

But he had to start somewhere, so he picked a slack hour and sat down in the corner of the coffee shop.

"Hi, Sarah, how are things going?" he asked as the young woman he had come to see came over to his table.

"Okay. Nothing special. Can I bring you some coffee?"

"That's the reason I stopped by, that and the possibility I might see you. Doesn't look very busy. Would the boss object if you joined me?"

Sarah laughed.

"Of course not. He encourages me to make small talk with the guests."

"And I bet you're good at it," Sam said.

She was back in a minute with two coffees and took a seat where she could see others coming into the shop.

"How are your parents? I haven't seen them in almost a month," Sam asked.

"They're fine. I think they're concerned that I don't have a boy friend at the moment."

"I thought you were -" Sam didn't finish his thought. "Sorry, it's none of my business."

"You thought I was still seeing Buddy Clark, right? It's okay. It just didn't work out. This really isn't a very good place to start up a relationship. The summer people don't stay around long. Which leaves the locals, most of whom I've known since kindergarten. The kids are too young and most of the businessmen are too old."

"Do you ever consider moving away from here?"

"From the lake?" Sarah made it sound like the last thing in the world she'd consider. "I know what you mean, but I love it here."

"Me, too. And I'll bet you move up the ladder here in no time."

"I'd like to think so, but I kinda screwed things up the other day. Do you feel like giving a girl some advice?"

"I've always been your Uncle Sam, haven't I?"

"This time it may be different," she said. The smile that always came to her face when he used the 'Uncle Sam' line failed to appear this time. Sarah surveyed the lobby, and seeing no one who might need her attention she told him how she had 'screwed up.'

"It happened about two weeks ago. There was this man in the coffee shop for breakfast, and he started talking to me. What was my name, was this just a summer job, things like that. I was busy, but when the breakfast crowd thinned out he was still there. He said he'd like to have another cup of coffee back in his room and he asked if I'd bring it up for him. I don't think I'd ever been asked to do something like that before, but he explained that he had a bad leg and didn't walk so good, so I agreed. He was very polite, gave me a nice tip, but he asked if I could sit with him for awhile. I should have said no, but I thought a few minutes wouldn't do any harm, so I sat down and we talked. I guess I lost track of the time because the front desk called and said I was wanted downstairs. I knew right away that I was in trouble."

"It doesn't sound all that bad to me," Sam said. "Unless this man was coming on to you."

"No, no, it was nothing like that. He was very nice, and he didn't say or do anything improper. He seemed to take an interest in what I was doing, whether I had plans to go to college, that kind of thing. But Mr. Markham, he really chewed me out. I'd no sooner got back downstairs than he had me in his office. What on earth was I doing in that man's room? You're job is in the coffee shop."

"Markham is your boss?"

"He is, and he's usually very good to me. But this time he sounded like Dad used to sound when I violated curfew. He said I was going to get myself into real trouble, and that I should never do something like that again."

Sam thought about this for a moment.

"I'm not sure I'm following you. The manager was upset about what? That you'd left your post in the coffee shop or that you'd gone up to a guest's room?"

"Oh, it was me being in a man's room, mostly. Stupid, that's what he called me, like I was some kid who ought not to trust men."

"That's probably good advice, Sarah."

"Not you, too! I'm 20, you know. I think this guy was just lonely and needed someone to talk to."

Sarah didn't seem to know the man's name, and another several minutes of conversation, while pleasant, was irrelevant to Sam's mission.

He waited for Sarah to disappear into the kitchen before going to the reception desk and from there to Markham's office. The least he could do for Sarah was to let the manager know that she was one smart girl who felt badly that she'd disappointed him.

"Good morning," he said as Markham rose to meet him. "I'm Sam Bridges. You can see I'm with the sheriff's department. I stopped by this morning to say hello to Sarah Corwin. She's the daughter of good friends. She tells me that she made a mistake recently that upset you, and I thought I'd stop by and put in a good word for her."

"That's good of you, but Sarah's going to be all right. She's smart, and I hope to keep her. Motels don't run background checks on our guests, as I'm sure you know. But once in awhile somebody gets it into his head that a motel is a good place to pick up a woman and have a quickie with no one the wiser. I think we had such a guest recently, and I was worried that Sarah might get into trouble with him."

"How did you know this guy might be bad news?"

"Well, for one thing Sarah left word that she was taking coffee up to room 214. That didn't make sense. All the rooms have coffee makers, so why ask her to bring it up from the shop? But we were already keeping an eye on 214. He was single, but he'd had a woman in his room at least twice. One of our night staff spotted her coming in. We checked it out, and found he'd gotten himself an extra card key."

"I can see that you're in a tougher business than I realized."

"It isn't really that bad, but the last thing we want is for word to get around that we tolerate call girls."

Sam smiled.

"For what it's worth, our department's never had any complaints about prostitutes working around the lake. Anyway, I appreciate your concern for Sarah. Like I said, she's a fine girl from a fine family."

Sam was already on his way out of the lobby when it occurred to him that maybe he should ask for the name of the man in 214. He retraced his steps back to Markham's office.

"Sorry to bother you again," he said from the doorway. "Can you give me the name of this man who'd been having women in his room?"

"Oh, he's been gone for over a week now. There's no reason to make an issue of it."

"I understand, but something just occurred to me - something that has nothing to do with your motel. I can assure you that we're not interested in harassing him. All I need is a name."

This wasn't, strictly speaking, an honest answer. But if by some chance the man in 214 had been Sheldon Rivers, there was a possibility that the sheriff would be interested in harassing him, even if Markham wasn't.

It was obvious that the manager was regretting that he'd been so freely discussing the motel's problem with some of its guests and the company they keep.

"We don't normally violate our guests' privacy. Has somebody who's stayed here done something illegal?"

"No, not at all. Actually, what I'm interested in is the woman who visited him. Not Sarah, but the other person."

Come on, Sam said to himself, just give me a name. The last thing he wanted to do was to get involved in an explanation of the so-called Mobley case.

"Well, if it doesn't have anything to do with the *Three Diamonds*, I guess it won't do any harm. The man's name was Sheldon Rivers."

Was Sheldon Rivers, not *is* Sheldon Rivers. A minor detail. By sheer luck, courtesy of Sarah Corwin's natural friendliness, and perhaps her naivete, he had learned that Rivers had had company while staying at the motel. And it had been a woman. Markham hadn't seemed to be interested in whether any men had paid Rivers a visit in his motel room. His concern for the reputation of the *Three Diamonds* lay elsewhere. Sam was confident that Carol would assume that Rivers' visitor had been Suzanne Mobley. He was equally confident that she would be paying Suzanne a visit very soon.

CHAPTER 52

Suzanne Mobley had always prided herself on her memory. It had been her ticket to good grades in school, even when she hadn't really understood much of the subject matter of her courses. It had given her a satisfying feeling of one-upmanship when she could call people by name even when they couldn't recall hers. And now she was confronted with the challenge of dredging up information from her memory bank to flesh out the report Merle Corrigan had given her about Dr. Jeremy Sigler.

It probably wasn't worth worrying about, but she continued to be puzzled by Sigler's interest in something he thought might be in Gil's safe deposit box. Whatever it was, it certainly wasn't in the safe deposit box. But Sigler hadn't been satisfied. Perhaps it was somewhere in the house. Perhaps, she thought, it doesn't exist. And then Merle Corrigan had passed along something he had heard from one of Gil's former pinochle partners.

It wasn't much, and there was only this man Harding's word for it, but he claimed that one of Sigler's patients had died on a night when the doctor had been playing pinochle with them. Harding had been vague, but he remembered that Sigler had been a heavy drinker. Had Gil suspected that Sigler had been drunk the night he lost his patient? That he was guilty of malpractice? He had never said anything like that to her, but then he had rarely shared what transpired at their pinochle games with her.

She had thought long and hard about Harding's story, trying to find a way to link it to Sigler's recent behavior. If there was a link it was presumably because Gil had suspected Jeremy of malpractice and had told him of his suspicions. If Jeremy knew he was guilty, he might well have been fearful that Gil would expose him. Of course Jeremy might know that he was innocent of any wrong doing. But he could still fear that he might be forced into a potentially humiliating defense of his record. Either way, he would worry that Gil might go public. The fact that he hadn't done so did not mean that he wouldn't some day. Even from beyond the grave. Which made it imperative that he find out if Gil had put his suspicions in writing and hidden them away somewhere, like the safe deposit box.

Suzanne had put her mind to the task of remembering whether Gil had ever said something about a pinochle game which Dr. Sigler had to leave early in order to care for a patient. In spite of her good memory, she wasn't optimistic. In addition to the fact that Gil rarely talked about their games, it would have been several years ago when Sigler was both a regular at the card table and perhaps a heavy drinker. But there had been something, an elusive something that she couldn't quite bring into focus. In the end, however, her memory came to her rescue. Harding had said that it had been a bitter cold night. She remembered that on one such night she had poked her head into the card room to ask if the men would like her to put on a pot of coffee. Dr. Sigler's chair had been empty.

I'm going to find out whom Jeremy Sigler went to see that cold night, she thought, even if it takes me a week. But she doubted that it would take more than a day, perhaps as little as an hour. The *Gazette* only publishes once a week, and it always runs obituary notices. She could forget spring, summer and fall, concentrating on winter issues, especially those that had been published during unusually cold weather.

Suzanne had allowed herself to sleep in and otherwise be lazy ever since Shell had gone back to Pelham. On this morning, the third of August, she was out of bed early and ready to head for the *Gazette* offices by 8:30. It was possible that the paper wouldn't open its doors until 10, but she was anxious to get started. If necessary, she would stop at the diner and have another cup of coffee, but she was too excited to sit in her own kitchen and watch the clock.

The person she was told would help her was late, which she found annoying. With considerable effort she restrained her impatience, and by 9:18 she had settled down at an old, much scarred table in a corner of a small room next to several rows of stacks. In front of her was a pile of winter issues of the *Gazette* from 2006. The woman in charge had insisted that she conduct her search one year at a time, and 2006 seemed as likely as any other year. By 9:45 it had become clear that winter had been relatively mild in 2006, with only one real cold spell. No obituary from that week sounded promising, so she was soon busy looking at 2007.

Of course she might have to go back to 2005 or even a year or two before that, and for a brief moment she found herself questioning her decision not to get in touch with Harding. He might be able to recall the name of the patient Sigler had lost that cold winter night and thus save her the trouble of working her way through these old copies of the *Gazette*. But it was one thing for Merle Corrigan to make inquiries about Dr. Sigler, and quite another for her to start asking around about Sigler's patients who had died on him. So she continued her perusal of the old and yellowing papers.

It was shortly after eleven when she came across the first obituary that really caught her attention. It was in a late February issue of 2009, and the report on the weather that week emphasized that temperatures had been running below freezing for almost two weeks. The obit was for an 82 year old man named Ellery Bettenger, and the date of his death was right in the middle of that stretch of sub-freezing days. Suzanne had never heard of Bettenger. It was an unusual name, and she was sure she would have remembered it if Gil had ever brought it up in conversation. But she was willing to bet that she had found her man for the simple reason that the person confirming the death was not a family member but the deceased's doctor. And the doctor's name was Jeremy Sigler.

CHAPTER 53

While Suzanne Mobley had been searching for evidence that Dr. Jeremy Sigler might have been guilty of malpractice, Sigler had been devoting much of his time to the question of whether Suzanne and her first husband, Sheldon Rivers, might have had a hand in the death of Gil Mobley. He hadn't given the idea any thought until recently. But now, worried about what Suzanne could know about his own malfeasance, it had become a major concern. The knowledge that Rivers was taking a Florinef generic turned the issue into an obsession.

Sigler doubted that he'd be able to prove what he wanted to believe, what he had begun to suspect. But the circumstantial case for it was intriguing. It all began with the fact that Suzanne Mobley wanted a divorce. Gil had not dwelled on it, but he had said things in his visits to Sigler that pointed unmistakably in that direction. Ironically, if Suzanne had obtained a divorce before Gil's wealthy but sickly mother died, she would not have been able to share what was almost certain to be the favored son's munificent inheritance. Fortunately for her, Gil had shown no inclination to grant the divorce and she had declined to force the issue while Constance was alive. As things had worked out, Suzanne could have the best of both worlds - a large inheritance *and* a Gil-free life - thanks to the fact that her husband had 'accidentally' died of a heart attack. And how could this have happened? Jeremy Sigler thought he knew.

The critical piece of the puzzle was the Florinef. Suzanne was in excellent health, and Jeremy was a good doctor. He could think of no reason under the sun why she would be taking Florinef, and he trusted his judgment on this. It was equally inconceivable that she would have purchased the drug for the purpose of substituting it for Gil's hypertension pills. No doctor would have written her such a prescription, and he knew the system well enough to be virtually certain that no pharmacist would have filled a prescription she had forged. Which meant that the Florinef tablets Gil had been taking came from somebody for whom they had been prescribed. And the logical person was Rivers.

It was hypothetically possible, of course, that Marcus Mobley, a pharmacist, had supplied his sister-in-law with the pills. Like Suzanne, he had what could be considered a motive for giving his brother a fatal coronary. But try as he would, Jeremy could not picture Marcus in that role. Unlike Gil, he had always seemed weak, indecisive, someone disinclined to do something so risky. Not that Jeremy knew him well, but he thought of himself as an astute judge of character. He recalled a conversation in which he had told the sheriff that he wasn't very good at judging people's motives by their facial expressions or body language, but it was a lie. He knew Marcus Mobley's limits. His wife, of course, was something else, both irresponsible and willful. She might have nagged Marcus to get rid of his brother, but nothing would have come of it other than a strain on their marriage.

Which left Sheldon Rivers. He was taking a Florinef generic. He was at the lake in the weeks immediately prior to Gil Mobley's death. And while Jeremy did not know it for a fact, Rivers might be the reason that Suzanne wanted a divorce. His protracted presence at the lake where his former wife lived had struck Jeremy as strange. The only time he had seen them together had been at *Chambord,* and while they weren't holding hands they certainly weren't looking daggers at each other. It was obvious that Marcus and Carrie were present because Constance was seriously ill and they were interested in the disposition of her considerable assets. But no such motive could be ascribed to Rivers. So why was he there? The scenery? The weather? The fishing? There were other lakes much closer to Westchester, but Suzanne Mobley didn't live on any of them.

The more he thought about it, the more he was inclined to the view that, for whatever reason, Suzanne and Rivers were thinking of giving marriage another try. At the very least they had been in some contact with each other since he had moved into the Yates Center motel, thereby making it possible for Rivers' Florinef to end up in Suzanne's possession. If they were in it together, he could simply have given her the fatal pills. If not, she was resourceful enough to find a way to relieve him of them. She was one smart, tough woman, and if she had wanted to be rid of Gil she would be perfectly capable of discovering a drug that would cause hypertension. What a wonderful coincidence that her former (and future?) husband was now taking just such a drug.

But what was the doctor to do with this conviction that Suzanne, probably with the assistance of Rivers, had switched Gil's meds and caused him to plunge to his death in Crooked Lake? It was not a case that he could take to Sheriff Kelleher. She would listen, but she would not act without what the media referred to as a smoking gun, and there was no smoking gun in the scenario he had conjured up. In all probability the sheriff had already entertained the possibility that Suzanne had something to do with Gil's death. Suzanne and Marcus and, for all he knew, others. Perhaps she even included him among her list of suspects. She had certainly asked him a lot of questions.

Sigler's worst fear was that Suzanne would tell the sheriff or go public with any suspicion that he had been responsible for the death of Ellery Bettenger four years ago. While under the statute of limitations in New York it was too late for a claim to be filed against him, he knew that his reputation would suffer, probably irreparably, if she tried to do so. Therefore, he needed to take action and do it quickly. And the only thing he could do was to confront Suzanne with her guilt, buying her silence in return for his. If he were wrong, he would have done the worst thing possible: he would have put himself entirely at her mercy. But Jeremy Sigler was convinced that he was not wrong. Suzanne Mobley was responsible for her husband's death.

CHAPTER 54

It was the 23rd day in a row without rain, and the 18th during which the temperature had climbed above 90. Carol and Kevin had long since gotten into the habit of taking an early evening swim when her schedule permitted. The cocktail hour had been renamed the cooling off hour, although the water temperature had gradually become warmer under the relentless heat of mid-summer. Kevin complained that the lake was beginning to feel like the hot tub in his club down in the city, but he still joined Carol in the water.

"You're not getting enough sun," he said to her as they settled themselves on the dock to dry off. Carol had removed her top and was lying on her stomach on a colorful red and orange towel.

"Unlike you, I'm in uniform all day. I don't look anemic, do I?"

"Nothing like that. But you're a bit on the pale side compared to that towel."

"That'll be easy to fix. Tomorrow I'll use the towel with the light blue and white stripes."

She started to roll over, but Kevin reminded her that the Brocks were on their porch.

"I know," she said. "I just wanted to show you that a perfect tan isn't everything."

Later that evening they compared notes on what was on the docket for the following day. Kevin vowed not to spend the entire day in the water, but to try to make some progress on the paper he was writing. Carol knew him well enough to know that it wouldn't be until Labor Day was just around the corner that he'd really knuckle down and finish it.

"As for me, I'm going to start asking some questions of Sheldon Rivers and Suzanne Mobley. According to Sam, they were spending some time together at the *Three Diamonds Motel* while he was at the lake. We don't know for sure if it was Suzanne who was visiting Rivers, but it makes a certain amount of sense, and I'm going to ask both of them about it. If it was Suzanne, it would tend to support the theory that they may be thinking of getting back together. Not to mention that it would have made it easy for his Florinef tablets to find their way back to the Mobley house."

"And," Kevin interjected, "easier to pin a switch of meds on the two of them."

"I'm keeping that in mind, although right now I'm mostly interested in getting a better picture of why Rivers chose to take a vacation on Crooked Lake."

_____

Carol was up and out early. As she made the trip to Cumberland, she was enjoying the feeling that she had been vindicated in treating the so-called Mobley case as worthy of her attention. Sam, who had practically insisted that she needed a vacation from her fixation on the Mobleys, seemed to be more sympathetic with that fixation now that he had met with the motel manager. She knew, however, that it might not have been Suzanne paying midnight visits to Rivers. Even if it had been her, it didn't mean that it was in any way relevant to Gil's Mobley's death. She was fairly confident that before the day was over she'd know whether Rivers' visitor had been Suzanne. It would be a welcome bonus if she also had a better feeling as to how the two of them fit into the puzzle of the crash of the Cessna.

The squad meeting over, Carol concentrated on what she found in her inbox for the better part of half an hour. She had no idea as to Sheldon Rivers' schedule, and she did not want to wake him up or catch him at breakfast. As it happened, he, too, had been up and out of the house early. She reached him at his office, and was lucky to find him alone and in a position to talk with her.

"Good morning, sheriff. I'm surprised to hear from you so soon again."

"I'm afraid, Mr. Rivers, that I'm still involved in tidying up the Mobley case. I don't know about you, but I hate phones. Odds are in a few years they'll be completely passe. Anyway, I wanted to talk with you and didn't have the energy to drive all the way down to Pelham. How are you doing?"

"I'm okay. Any reason why I shouldn't be?"

"No, but I remember that you were having a bit of trouble getting around when I was there. I suppose we all are."

"That's kind of you, but we know it isn't true. You seem to get around very well, but then you must be 20 years younger than I am."

Carol laughed, more to lighten the conversation than because what Rivers had said was funny.

"Look, I'm calling about a very specific matter, and I hope you can help me. You stayed on the lake recently for several weeks. The *Three Diamonds Motel* in Yates Center, I believe. Did your former wife ever spend any time with you there?"

Now it was Rivers who laughed.

"Are you worried about my after hours habits?"

"I'm only interested in whether you and Suzanne Mobley got together at the motel occasionally."

"I'm surprised that you think it matters, but let me be as frank with my answer as you have been with your question. Yes, if my memory is better than my ability to navigate from room to room, Suzanne visited me twice. It might have been three times, but I'm only sure of two. You are welcome to speculate as to what we did, but we are consenting adults and I don't believe I'm obligated to enlighten you."

"Thank you," Carol said.

"I'm sure you wonder about our relationship. Now that Suzanne's husband - her second husband - is dead and her mother-in-law's will is on record, it is no longer necessary to deny that we shall probably get married. Again. It was obviously imprudent to meet at her lake cottage. The motel suited us fine, although Suzanne might have been more discreet, as your call makes clear. I suspect that you called me because you inquired of the motel whether I had visitors."

Carol chose not to confirm Rivers' allegation.

"I appreciate your candor, Mr. Rivers."

"Inasmuch as my visitors at the motel seem to be of some importance, I should tell you that another of the Mobleys dropped by while I was there. Just once, but I want the record to be accurate. It was Marcus Mobley. He came to seek my advice, and I'm afraid I wasn't much help. He seemed to believe that his mother didn't care for him as much as she did for Gil, and he thought I might help him out, inasmuch as she didn't like me very much either. I still cannot imagine why he thought I could be of assistance."

Carol found this information of more than passing interest, but chose not to discuss it further.

"Dr. Sigler tells me he talked with you about your problem of getting around and that you're taking something called Florinef. I hope it's helping."

"Hard to say. I think so, but whatever's wrong with me wants to take it's own time responding to treatment. To make matters worse, I managed to run out of pills about the time I got back from the lake, and it was three days before I got a refill. Apparently my problem isn't very tolerant of my carelessness."

It was not until later, a good half an hour after her conversation with Rivers, that she realized just how important what he had just told her might be. Had his carelessness simply been a matter of not refilling his Florinef prescription before going to the lake? Or had something happened to what should have been an adequate supply of the pills while he was at the lake?

Carol was interested in the fact that Rivers had so readily acknowledged Suzanne's visits to the motel. He had also told her that Marcus Mobley had visited him there, an even more unexpected piece of news. But what interested her most was that the information he had shared with her provided the most plausible explanation of how a pill that is used to treat hypotension happened to be under the Mobleys' bed in their lakeside home.

CHAPTER 55

Carol's efforts to follow up her conversation with Sheldon Rivers with calls to Suzanne and Marcus Mobley were frustrated by the fact that neither of them answered their phones, in spite of frequent attempts to reach them. It was not until after eight o'clock that evening that she finally got through to the Mobley residence in Binghamton. It was Carrie who came to the phone.

"Mrs. Mobley, this is Sheriff Kelleher. I was hoping to speak with your husband. Is he there?"

The pleasant voice which had answered the phone became more guarded.

"He's here, but I don't think he can come to the phone right now."

"I can call back, but I really do need to talk with him."

"He just started watching one of his favorite movies, an old Humphrey Bogart film. 'Key West' I think it is. Do you suppose you could try him at, say, ten o'clock?"

"You're sure that wouldn't be too late?"

"Oh, no. He's a night owl. Can I tell him what this is about?"

"That's okay. No need to interrupt the movie."

Frustrated once again, Carol wandered into the study where Kevin was making another stab at producing a coherent argument in his paper as to why most of Richard Strauss' later operas had been a disappointment to critics.

"Still spinning your wheels, I see," he said. "Join the crowd."

"Thank goodness, two is not a crowd. But Suzanne is still unavailable, and Marcus is watching TV."

"He can't even take a break to talk to you?"

"Apparently not. Carrie says he's engrossed in a favorite film, a Bogart classic called 'Key West.'"

Kevin shook his head.

"I think he's just blowing you off."

Then he suddenly turned away from the desk and stared at Carol.

"'Key West?' That's what he told you?"

"That's what Carrie told me. Why?"

"Humphrey Bogart was never in a film called 'Key West.' My knowledge of films is spotty, but I'm a Bogart man. You're sure she didn't say 'Key Largo?'"

"No, it was 'Key West.' Is there a 'Key Largo?'"

"There is, one of several with Bogart and Bacall. I haven't seen it in years, but it's not bad. As I remember it, though, it's really Edward G. Robinson's film, one of his gangster roles."

"Are you thinking what I'm thinking?" Carol asked.

"I am. If it's one of Marcus's favorite movies, it's just possible that Robinson as well as Bogart is one of his favorite actors. Which might explain why somebody named Edward G. Robinson called you with that story about Gil Mobley and his plane."

"And that the somebody might have been Marcus," Carol said. She sounded enthusiastic. Then frustrated. "Damn, I can't remember the voice. No idea whether the guy who pretended to be Robinson sounded like Marcus. Maybe he disguised his voice."

"He wouldn't have had to," Kevin said. "I know a lot of people whose phone voice isn't much like what you hear when you're in the same room. Besides, you were meeting and talking to a lot of people you didn't know back then. How could you have kept their voices apart? Unless, that is, they had an accent or an unusually high pitched voice, something really distinctive."

"Well, I'm calling Marcus in less than two hours. What do you say we ask him straight out if he's been doing phone impersonations?"

"I think I'd do that."

She chose to defer another call to Suzanne until tomorrow, now that her mind was on Marcus Mobley. After waiting impatiently for ten o'clock to roll around, she finally placed the call to Binghamton. 'Key Largo' had ended, and Marcus himself answered the phone.

"I understand I'm wanted by the Crooked Lake authorities," he said. His attempt to be nonchalant was not very convincing.

"I don't think I'd say that, Mr. Mobley, but I do have a couple of questions I'd like to ask. I appreciate your being willing to take my call this late in the evening."

"Not to worry, the night is young. What's on your mind?"

"I had a chance to speak with Sheldon Rivers recently, and we got around to talking about those weeks he spent at the lake. I mentioned in passing that it had to have been lonely, staying by himself in a motel for more than three weeks. But he brushed it aside, said he'd had quite a few visitors in his motel room. He says that you were one of them."

Carol left it at that, giving Marcus a chance to make what he would of Rivers' revelation.

"He said that, did he?" It was a feeble response.

"Yes, he did, and he didn't need any prompting. I didn't ask, he simply volunteered the information. I had assumed that you two barely knew each other, so what persuaded you to pay him a visit?"

"Actually, it's not much of a story. Carrie had gone out and I didn't have anything to do. I'd only just met him that day I saw you at *Chambord*, and I decided to go over to his motel and, you know, sort of get acquainted."

"What was your impression?"

The question puzzled Marcus.

"My impression? Is this about Rivers? You're trying to get people's impressions of him?"

"You didn't know him, and now you do. At least you know him better than you did before that night at the motel."

"Well, I guess I'd say he was polite. Not very talkative. We didn't have much in common, and he wasn't part of the Mobley family."

"Rivers seemed to think you wanted to talk about how best to improve your prospects in your mother's will."

Marcus laughed.

"It probably came up, but what could he do? If you're concerned about us, don't worry. There's no point in going into my family history. You make your bed, you lie in it."

Carol thought she knew just what Marcus meant, but she wasn't about to ask.

"I have one other question. I understand you were watching 'Key Largo' when I called earlier this evening. I've never seen it. Is it a good movie?"

Silence.

"Are you still there?"

"I'm here."

"Good. I believe that one of 'Key Largo's' stars, or should I say bad guys, is Edward G. Robinson."

"Yes, he plays a gangster."

"Unless my memory is playing tricks on me, he also called me a few weeks ago to let me know that Gil Mobley's Cessna was having some problems and that Gil was well aware of it. Does that surprise you?"

"What do you want me to say?"

"You could give me your recommendation as to whether I should check it out on Netflix. Or you could explain why Robinson happened to call me."

"It's a good film. I don't know anything about a phone call."

"Come on, Mr. Mobley, you disappoint me. When somebody makes a phone call and uses a false name, wouldn't you think it a bit unusual that he chooses Edward G. Robinson? Why not Bill Smith or Joe Brown? Let's forget that you chose to pretend that you were Robinson. Why did you give me that phony story about your brother? And it was phony, right?"

"Look, I was trying to be helpful. My brother had crashed and died, and I thought you'd welcome suggestions that could help explain what had happened."

"I always welcome input from concerned citizens if what they tell me might help my investigation. But that wasn't your purpose, was it? Gil Mobley had a reputation as a meticulous pilot who took excellent care of his plane. So why did you make up a cockeyed yarn like that?"

"I'm sorry to have mislead you," Marcus said, trapped and eager to convince the sheriff that there had been no malicious intent. "Nobody knew why the plane had crashed, and I thought my idea might be worth thinking about."

"Or perhaps you thought of it as a useful diversion, a way to steer the investigation away from the possibility that somebody had switched Gil's meds."

"Why would I do something like that?"

"You'd have to tell me. You didn't happen to tamper with your brother's blood pressure medicine, did you?"

"No, I didn't," Marcus said emphatically. "You asked me that same question when we met over here last week."

"Actually, what I asked you was whether you had ever filled a prescription for Florinef. At the time, I didn't realize that you and Edward G. Robinson were the same person."

"I know it was a stupid thing I did, pretending to be someone else. I'm not even sure why I did it. But I swear that I had nothing to do with my brother's death. Absolutely nothing."

"And I'm not accusing you of it. But I think you can understand why I might have my doubts. Most people don't go to the trouble of contacting the police and using a false name to tell a false story."

"So you don't suspect me of trying to kill Gil?"

"Mr. Mobley, let's just say that for the time being I suspect everybody."

CHAPTER 56

When they awoke the next morning, Carol and Kevin knew that something was different the minute they stepped out of bed. It was the first morning in three weeks that the sun was not visible. In fact, after what seemed like endless days of blue skies, a cloud cover blanketed the bluff and stretched all the way down to the southern end of the lake. The days had been so consistently hot and dry that they had gotten out of the habit of following the weather reports on TV.

"Rain, blessed rain," Carol said. "I hope these clouds aren't a false alarm."

"If I believed in the law of averages, I'd say a big storm is inevitable. But there's no such a thing as a law of averages, so I'm withholding my prediction."

"Want to check the weather channel?"

"Why don't you do it while I start the coffee."

To their surprise, the weather report was decidedly undecided. Predictions ranged from 40 per cent chance of rain by late afternoon to something closer to 80 per cent over night. But Carol had no plans to go anywhere or do anything except put in another day at the office, and Kevin had resolved to fight writer's block on his Strauss paper for one more day.

Breakfast behind them, Carol went through the ritual of strapping on her revolver and kissing her husband good-bye. Neither of them had any idea that the next two days were to be the most important of the summer since Gil Mobley's Cessna crashed into Crooked Lake.

Carol still had not been able to reach Suzanne Mobley at her home, but she was prepared to give it another try as soon as the squad meeting was over. She had been thinking about how she'd approach the newly wealthy widow for many of the last 24 hours, but found herself doing the same thing on the drive over to Cumberland. By the time she reached her office she had made a decision to meet Suzanne at the office, rather than at her over air-conditioned lakeside home. That decision had less to do with the temperature of the house than it did with the simple fact that she was tired of the trip. Moreover, there was something about the woman that got on her nerves. Better to deal with her while sitting at her own desk.

As had been the case the day before, her initial attempt to speak with Suzanne was unsuccessful. Fortunately, there was a message which said she'd be back shortly and to leave a message. Carol chose to call back at ten o'clock but not to leave a message. Her second call elicited a breathless answer on the ninth ring.

"Hi, this is Suzanne," she announced. It was obvious that she had rushed to the phone.

"Good morning. This is Sheriff Kelleher." No need to mention that she'd been trying to reach her for two days. It would only stimulate her anxiety, whereas Carol preferred to create the impression that this was a routine call. "I'm sorry to be bothering you again. I'm sure it's becoming annoying. But I'd be very grateful if you could drop by my office sometime this afternoon. Whenever it's convenient."

"Is it urgent?" It looked as if Carol's attempt to treat their meeting as routine might not work.

"No, it's just that I'm supposed to be out of town for a day or two." Carol never ceased to be amazed at how easily she told small lies like that.

"How would 4:15 be?" Suzanne suggested.

"That's great. You know where I am?"

"Over in Cumberland. I've seen it, the place with all the sheriff's department cars."

"Good. See you then."

Suzanne was prompt, even five minutes early. Her Mercedes gave the parking lot a bit of class.

"It's good of you to meet me here," Carol said when Suzanne had settled into the chair across the desk from her.

"No problem. Your place doesn't look like I expected it to."

Carol wasn't sure whether she meant that it was so small or that it was much brighter and cheerier than most of the places where cops worked on TV shows.

"Well, it's functional, and you know how it is when budgets are tight. You'll have to forgive me if I bring up things we've talked about before," Carol said, getting right down to business, "but I can't recall whether I asked whether Marcus and his wife and your first husband ever dropped by your house when they were at the lake."

She was aware that she was resorting to Colombo's shtick, pretending to be absentminded if not even a bit slow-witted. She suspected that Suzanne wouldn't be fooled.

"You may have, but it doesn't matter. Gil and I were never close to Marcus and Carrie. To be honest, we didn't like them. Carrie, she was simply impossible. So, no, they weren't welcome, and I'm sure they had no interest in pretending to be part of the family. Now Sheldon, that was different. Gil didn't hate him, but they weren't close, and that's hardly surprising. But people knew Shell and I had resolved some of our old problems, had become friends again. I'm not sure friends is the right word. Anyway, it would have looked funny if Shell spent time at our place, so he didn't. Mutual agreement, you might say."

"How about at the motel where he was staying? Did you spend any time with him over there?"

This was the critical question. Carol wondered how Suzanne would respond.

"As I'm sure you know, sheriff, Gil stood to get a very good inheritance from Mother Mobley. If I started fooling around with Shell, it could have screwed everything up. So common sense said to leave him alone. It wasn't hard to do. We'd been estranged for quite a few years."

It was not exactly a direct answer.

"I asked because somebody at the *Three Diamonds Motel* said that you were seen at the motel late at night more than once. Perhaps you had other friends staying there."

"That is absolute nonsense," Suzanne said, her demeanor suddenly changed from casual to annoyed. "I have no idea who these people are who told you this, but they're dead wrong. I have never been in that motel, other than to say good-bye to Shell the morning he checked out. They've mistaken someone else for me."

"Of course, that's probably what happened. It seems that the management there had some problems with guests entertaining prostitutes, and they've been extra vigilant recently."

Suzanne leaned forward in her chair, hands gripping the arm rests.

"I'm being mistaken for a prostitute? Who is it that told you this? By god, I'll sue the bastard."

"It wasn't like that. The person who saw you didn't think you were a prostitute. All he said was that someone was paying a visit late at night to a guest named Sheldon Rivers."

What would Suzanne make of this? Would she admit that, yes, she had been Rivers' late night visitor? Or would she again deny it, thereby conceding that the man with whom she was rumored to be contemplating marriage was having assignations with someone else? She chose the second option.

"Well, it wasn't me."

"Suzanne, I almost hate to tell you this, but I have no choice. Sheldon Rivers has confirmed that you came to his room at the *Three Diamonds Motel* on more than one occasion."

If Suzanne was shocked to hear this, she managed to maintain her composure.

"I don't believe you. I'm sure Sheldon never told you any such thing. Why are you trying to make me admit to something I didn't do?"

"If you doubt my word, you can call Mr. Rivers and ask him. The fact is that both he and the manager of the motel have told me you visited the *Three Diamonds* on at least two different nights. Let's just leave it that you disagree with them. I have only one more question, and it has to do with Mr. Rivers' health. Do you know what he was taking for his orthostatic hypotension?"

"His what?" Suzanne's struggle to maintain her composure was becoming increasingly difficult. And obvious.

"Orthostatic hypotension. That's seems to have been his problem. Perhaps I can help you. He was taking Florinef, or a generic version of it. You may recall that we talked about this once before. The autopsy showed that your husband had been taking Florinef, which had the effect of raising his blood pressure. You told me that you didn't know what Florinef was and that the very idea of Gil taking something that would increase his blood pressure was ridiculous. Unfortunately, ridiculous or not, that's what he had been doing. So I think you can understand why I'm interested that Sheldon Rivers was also taking a drug called Florinef. And why I'm interested in the news that you visited him after he moved into the Yates Center motel."

Carol had still not played her ace: the fact that a Florinef pill had been discovered under a bed at the Mobleys' house. Which meant that Suzanne still had a choice. Her decision did not surprise Carol.

"I hope you will not be upset, sheriff, if I tell you that I am both disappointed in you and really angry. I have very recently lost my husband and my mother-in-law. I am trying to put my life back together at a very difficult time. I would have expected that you would demonstrate some sympathy. Instead, you seem determined to pester me with questions and make false accusations. I have better things to do, so this conversation is now over. Have yourself a nice day."

Those were Suzanne Mobley's last words as she walked out of the sheriff's office and into the parking lot. Carol watched from the office window as she climbed into the Mercedes and drove away in a hurry, much as she had done at the West Branch dock the morning her husband's body had been transferred from the patrol boat to an ambulance following the fatal crash of his Cessna.

CHAPTER 57

On most such evenings, with the sky filled with ominous clouds and occasional rumbles of thunder off in the distance, Carol and Kevin would have retreated to the cottage to have their happy hour inside. But the weather on the lake was so unusual after weeks of cloudless skies and nary a drop of rain, that they had set up chairs on the dock and were actually enjoying the promise of an approaching storm.

"I hope the weather guys stop consulting their maps and their gauges and step outside and take a look around. I'm only a music professor, but I'll put my money on a real downpour before midnight."

"I hope so. We sure need it," Carol said. "One way or another, it's actually refreshing to see the lake this choppy. I don't think there's been a decent race down at the yacht club in more than a month."

"Like they say, everybody talks about the weather, but nobody does anything about it. Why don't we talk about something we can do something about? Like the Mobley case."

"You still think we can do something about it?" Carol asked. "For a change, I may agree with you. But before we get ahead of ourselves, am I not right that it was Mark Twain who gave us that line about the weather?"

"Could be," Kevin said. "But I read somewhere that it could be someone else. Or maybe more than one someone else. Tonight it was me. Can we forget the weather? I'm interested that you agree with me. I mean that maybe we can do something about the Mobley case. Does this mean that you had some kind of epiphany today?"

"Not exactly, but I've been getting it from both sides. Sam tells me there is no Mobley case. It's closed. The NTSB told us so. And you keep telling me that somebody helped send Gil Mobley to an early death. Frankly, I've been skeptical, but somewhere along the way I discovered that you're a pretty smart guy, so I've tried to see it your way. Today I came to a tentative conclusion. Tentative, mind you. I think you're right."

"I'll skip over the I told you so line and ask the burning question: who did it?"

"If I'm wrong, you can still give me credit for thinking of Gil's death as a murder. But I think it has to be Suzanne Mobley."

"Bravo! The most likely suspect turns out to be the killer."

"Oh, come on. That makes it sound as if I picked Suzanne because she was an easy choice. I'm nominating her because I've gotten to know these people and because I've been thinking about them - all of them - day and night. Sometimes the most likely suspect is really guilty, you know. Anyway, I'm not saying she really did switch Gil's meds. I'm saying that I *think* she did, based on what I believe has been some pretty damn good police work."

"I never doubted it. And I'm sure you're going to enlighten me as to how you came to this conclusion."

"I will, but only if you will run up to the cottage and refill our glasses."

"At your service," Kevin said and set off for the cottage at a trot.

When he returned, rain was still a threat, not a fact. The sky was darker, the wind had produced white caps on the waves, and the thunder was louder.

"Let's drink to murder," he said as he handed Carol her glass of Chardonnay.

"If you don't mind, I'd rather drink to the fine art of irritating people with tough questions. Ot if you prefer, the even finer art of lie detection."

"Cheers," Kevin said, raising his glass.

"I'll admit I winnowed the field from the very beginning. But I've taken your suggestion that Gil's death was more than just the result of an unlucky heart attack. Somebody did something that made it more likely, and I've assumed that the somebody was one of a small handful of people, all of whom were at *Chambord* the day he died. Of course it could have been someone else, like John Doe or Betty Crocker, but that doesn't make much sense and it was certainly no place to start an investigation. So it had to be Gil's wife Suzanne, his brother Marcus, Marcus's wife Carrie, Suzanne's first husband Sheldon Rivers, or Dr. Jeremy Sigler. I discounted Constance Mobley for obvious reasons, not to mention Franklin - he's about as unlikely a murderer as Santa Claus."

"Besides," Kevin piped up, "it's only in fiction that the butler did it."

"Let's start with motive," Carol said. "And let's start with Marcus and Carrie. They were well aware that Constance wasn't likely to last much longer, that she was worth a fortune, and that, unfortunately, she much preferred her older son, Gil, to Marcus. With Gil out of the way, she might reasonably be expected to leave a more generous inheritance to Marcus. So he had a motive to see to it that Gil *was* out of the way."

Kevin was shaking his head.

"And being a pharmacist, he had access to this drug that's become part of our vocabulary this summer. But so what? For all we know - for all *Marcus* knew, Gil could have taken Florinef for months without a fatal heart attack. People have been known to live relatively long lives with high blood pressure. It was just chance that he died when he did. And as I remember it, it didn't make a smidgen of difference in Marcus's inheritance."

"Fair enough," Carol said, "but we're talking about motive. What other motive is there for the unloved brother than more of his mother's fortune? Plain old sibling rivalry?"

"We don't know the back story well enough to answer that question, but you're right, money was almost certainly his motive."

"At least it was Carrie's," Kevin suggested. "It doesn't take a psychiatrist to see that she was on her husband's case 24/7 to do something about their problem."

"So let's just say that Marcus and Carrie wanted to upgrade their prospects of a better inheritance by getting rid of Gil, leaving aside for the moment which of them might have done it."

"What about Suzanne?"

"Let me amend that to what about Suzanne and Sheldon Rivers," Carol said. "It's pretty clear that she was in a marriage she wanted out of, and that Gil wouldn't grant her a divorce. I think we can agree that Suzanne and Rivers have been considering tying the knot again, something that wasn't possible with Gil in the picture. But if Gil were to drop dead, voila - on to the altar."

"Of course you've got the same problem you have with Marcus and Carrie: not knowing when or even if the Florinef will do its job. I know, you're going to tell me that their motive is still that Gil stood between them. And I can't see any other reason why they'd want him dead."

"Leaving Rivers aside for a moment," Carol said, "might Suzanne have had other reasons for doing away with Gil?"

"I thought you had already selected her as Gil's killer. You ought to know if she had a motive other than Rivers."

"I know. But she's a puzzle, much more complicated than the rest of the tribe. Maybe they just had a violent disagreement over air conditioning."

"What's that supposed to mean?" Kevin had heard nothing about Suzanne's preference for keeping her house at a near refrigerator-like temperature.

"Just ignore me," Carol said. "She did it, and it's probably all about Rivers."

"That leaves Sigler," Kevin said.

"And if you can come up with a reason why he might have wanted Gil dead, I'd love to hear it."

"I can't. I suspect the only reason he merits a place in this discussion is that he's a doctor and, like Marcus and Rivers, would know all about Florinef and how to get his hands on it."

"So we're left with four people," Carol said, "three of them Mobleys plus Sheldon Rivers. Before I tell you why I vote for Suzanne, why don't you tell me what you think."

Kevin got up and took a couple of steps to the end of the dock. The American flag was now standing out at a right angle to the flag pole, flapping vigorously.

"You realize, I suppose, that we haven't had supper." He turned back to face Carol. "Are we waiting for rain to chase us inside?"

"Am I to infer that you aren't ready to share your thoughts on the Mobley murder just yet?"

"No. It's just that we usually have something to eat before night descends on us."

"It's not all that late. Night isn't descending, it's the storm approaching. If you like, I'll go rustle up some food. But let's eat on the deck so we can watch the storm when it hits."

They managed to find assorted left overs in the fridge and soon resumed the discussion of 'who killed Gil Mobley.'

"I asked who's your candidate," Carol said, "and you haven't given me your answer."

"I've been stalling, as you've probably noticed. The truth is, I haven't been interrogating anyone. So all I know is what you've told me - that, and the occasional fugitive thought."

"Let's hear some of those fugitive thoughts."

"I don't want to say 'elementary, my dear Watson,' but I keep feeling the tie breaker is going to be the meds the maid found under Mobley's bed."

"Very good." Carol reached across and clinked his glass. "But how did the Florinef pill find its way to the Mobley bedroom?"

"Somebody - one of your suspects - put it there. It wasn't put under the bed, of course. It must have been dropped accidentally."

"Agreed. But where did it come from?"

"It could have come from Marcus's pharmacy. You told me that Rivers was taking Florinef, so it could have come from his medicine cabinet. And then there's Sigler."

"But that doesn't get us very far. Marcus's pharmacy is in Binghamton and Rivers' medicine cabinet is in Pelham. Let's forget Sigler."

"Okay, so Marcus or Carrie or Rivers smuggled it into Gil and Suzanne's house."

"But that would have required those three people to have been in the house, and yet they all claim, with rather impressive supporting evidence, that they never visited Gil and Suzanne in their home while they were at the lake."

"I know where you're heading," Kevin said, "and I think we're finally on the same page. Your friend Suzanne was the middle man. Excuse me, the middle woman. One of the them gave her the Florinef and she brought it home and arranged for Gil to take it instead of his regular meds."

"That's what I think happened," Carol said, "and I'm sure I know where she got it. Want to guess where?"

"You're having fun putting me through the hoops, aren't you? Okay, I'll play the game. She got it from hubby number one and prospective hubby number three, Sheldon Rivers."

"With a big caveat. I don't think Rivers had anything to do with it. We talked just the other day, and he mentioned in passing that when he got back to Pelham he found that he didn't have nearly as many of the pills as he thought he had. He thought he'd forgotten to refill his prescription. But I'm willing to bet he's wrong. Suzanne's one smart cookie, and I'm sure she had talked with Sheldon, knew what he was taking and why, and probably did some research on the internet. From there on it was easy. I think he came to the lake because she persuaded him to, and once here she snuck into the motel, took him to bed, and left with a bunch of his Florinef tablets. Did he know what she had done? I don't think so, but it doesn't really matter because now she had the means to switch Gil's medication to something potentially fatal. And I'll bet she was shocked when the switch paid dividends so quickly. That it happened when the Cessna crashed, well, that was unfortunate, but all things considered, it was a modest price to pay for her freedom."

"I'm impressed," Kevin said, looking and sounding impressed. "Something must have happened that convinced you Suzanne is the culprit."

"I saw her today, and we had a nice chat until I told her that she'd been seen sneaking into the *Three Diamonds Motel* late at night. She claimed she'd never been there, so I gave her the bad news that Rivers had admitted to having her in his room on a couple of occasions. It must have come as a terrible shock to her. She denied it, but she now knows that she's in real trouble. For one thing, she must believe that, intentionally or not, Rivers has betrayed her. But she also knows that I can make a pretty strong circumstantial case that she switched Gil's meds."

"So what are you going to do?" Kevin asked.

"I want to sleep on it, but unless I get cold feet over night, I'm going to the district attorney tomorrow."

"I think I can help. I'll snuggle up and keep your feet warm. Speaking of which, have you noticed that it's started to rain?"

"No, I've been too busy convicting Suzanne Mobley."

"Me, too, but we're going to get soaked unless we move."

At that moment a bolt of lightning lit up the sky over the bluff and a loud crack of thunder followed.

"Crooked Lake at its unpredictable best," Kevin said as he grabbed his dinner plate and wine glass and hurried into the cottage and out of the rain.

CHAPTER 58

They watched as the rain became more intense, and when they finally went to bed it was drumming on the roof. At first the sound kept them awake, but long before midnight it had lulled them to sleep. When they awoke at seven, it had stopped, the skies were clearing, and the sodden grass was steaming under the early morning sun.

Carol stood at the door to the deck. The lake, after a turbulent night, was now calm. The rose of Sharon bush was just beginning to come into bloom, and a hummingbird hovered next to one of its first blossoms, sampling its nectar and then moving swiftly to another before flitting off in the direction of a neighboring cottage.

"It changes so fast, doesn't it? If the deck weren't still wet, you'd hardly know that we had a storm last night."

Kevin appeared at her side with two cups of coffee.

"Take one," he said. "Do you ever wonder which you like best, the smell of morning coffee or the coffee itself?"

"That's what I'd call a false dilemma."

"Your feet didn't get cold last night, did they?"

"Do you want to know if I'm going to charge Suzanne Mobley or are you fishing for a compliment as my foot warmer?"

"Both."

"Okay," she said, "you play footsie very well. But funny thing is I didn't think about Suzanne last night. I dreamed about Marcus, if you can believe it."

"You're sure it wasn't a nightmare."

"It was the usual dream, not very specific or realistic. But it was definitely Marcus. Maybe I'm supposed to be having second thoughts about dismissing him as his brother's killer."

"I wouldn't waste time thinking about it. Anyone who'd have the dumb idea of pretending to be Edward G. Robinson couldn't pull off something as challenging as switching somebody's meds."

Carol turned and headed back to the kitchen.

"Let's see what we can find for breakfast," she said. "If I'm going to accuse Suzanne of feeding her husband Florinef, I need to do it on a full stomach."

Deciding what to have for breakfast proved to be more difficult than deciding whether to move against Suzanne. She had made up her mind about the more important matter before she fell asleep. But she had trouble making up her mind between waffles and bacon and eggs. Kevin resolved the problem by making French toast.

Later, showered and dressed, Carol came back to the study where he was scanning the headlines on CNN.

"Wish me luck," she said.

"If you're going to put the cuffs on her, don't you think I should be there, too?"

"No, and even if I did, it's too late. You're still in your pjs, and I've got a squad meeting in less than half an hour."

A quick kiss, and she was out the back door.

Taking the decisive step to arrest Suzanne Mobley hadn't been quite as easy as Carol had made it out to be. She was more than a little nervous as she drove over to Cumberland. It wasn't going to be simply a matter of walking in on Suzanne and saying that she was under arrest. There were a number of things that would need to be done first. In some hard to explain way, this was a part of her job with which she was especially uncomfortable. It wasn't so much that she feared that she was wrong, that she was acting precipitously. It was one thing to engage Kevin with flip banter about it. It was quite another to actually take the steps which would hopefully bring a case like this to closure.

It was 8:25 when she mounted the stairs to her office. It was immediately apparent that something out of the ordinary was going on. One or two of her men typically arrived at the very last minute. But here it was, five minutes before the morning meeting, and the chorus of voices coming from the squad room suggested that everyone was already on hand and talking at once. She could even hear JoAnne, trying to make herself heard.

"What's going on?" she said as she entered the squad room.

"It was that call from Mr. Hacklin," JoAnne said. "Not five minutes ago."

"I told him not to go in, said we'd be right over." It was Deputy Sheriff Bridges. "I was hoping you'd be here in a minute or two. Otherwise I'd have gone."

"Excuse me, but what's this all about?" Sam and JoAnne started to answer her at the same time.

"You tell her," Sam said to JoAnne.

"That man Hacklin, he called and said someone had busted out the back window of the Mobley house."

Carol remembered that Hacklin was the neighbor of Gil and Suzanne Mobley who had reported them having a loud and angry argument not long before Gil's fatal crash.

"When did this happen?"

"He didn't know. Sometime last night."

"Mrs. Mobley called and told him about it?"

"No," Bridges interrupted. "The boy delivering the Rochester papers this morning saw that a rear window had been broken out. He didn't know what to do, so he told this neighbor, Hacklin. Hacklin went over, knocked on the door, called her name, but no one answered. He says the car is still there. So he called here. I told him to watch the house but stay out until we got there."

"Let's get a move on. Sam, you come with me. Bill," she said, motioning to Parsons, "get the men started. We'll get back in touch as soon as we know something."

The hub-bub in the squad room started up again as Carol and Bridges pulled out of the parking lot, barely three minutes after she had arrived, and set off in the direction of the lake. The window might have been in bad shape for days; Suzanne might simply be elsewhere in the neighborhood. But the sheriff didn't like the sound of this. She turned on the flashing dome light and proceeded to ignore the speed limit.

CHAPTER 59

The West Buff Road had never been an example of good highway engineering. It was narrow, almost too narrow in places for two cars to pass each other. Nor had it been maintained as well as the major county roads, with the result that it had stretches which were in dire need of patching. Today, in the aftermath of the storm, there were places where the patrol car bounced along through standing water. But the sheriff knew the road well, and she had visited the Mobley house often enough in recent weeks to know exactly when it would come into view on the lake side of the road.

Most of the cottages in the area lay down a steep bank, accessible by a flight of steps. Cars belonging to those owners or renters were parked on the roadside. The Mobley place, on the other hand, occupied a somewhat larger plot of land, and was connected to the road by a paved driveway. Carol slowed to a crawl and followed the driveway as it wound its way down the hill toward the house and the lake. She parked in front of the garage, through whose windows she could see the familiar Mercedes.

When she and Bridges came around the corner of the garage, they saw a man they assumed to be Hacklin, sitting on the back steps of the house.

He quickly came to his feet and held up a hand.

"Be careful or you'll ruin your shoes. The ground's uneven, and the storm last night makes the path a muddy mess. I learned the hard way."

"We're not worried about muddy shoes," Carol said. "I take it you're Mr. Hacklin. I'm Sheriff Kelleher, and this is Deputy Sheriff Bridges. Nice to meet you in person."

"Same here. I want to show you how the intruder got in. Be careful of the mud." He walked them over to a large window beside the back door. "See?"

It was one of those garden windows that provide extra sunlight for plants. And it was a large one, extending nearly a foot beyond the wall and running three or four feet across the back of the house. What was more important, it had been shattered. The glass had been broken, but so had the frame. The entire miniature garden had been knocked askew. No wind or rain storm had created this disorder. Almost certainly somebody had knocked out the window and used the opening to enter the house.

"We'll come back to this later," Carol said. "Have you seen Mrs. Mobley?"

"No. She hasn't come out, and your colleague said I wasn't to go inside."

Sam started to protest, but Carol brushed it aside.

"You've been very helpful, Mr. Hacklin. I'd appreciate it if you'd stay outside here and if anybody comes by, you're to stop them and notify us. We're going inside. Can you do that?"

"Oh, yes," he said, obviously anxious to be a part of a police investigation.

She and Sam went in through the back door, which was unlocked. They found themselves in the kitchen. Off to their right several plants, presumably formerly in the garden window, lay on the counter. Two had fallen to the floor. Carol looked around. Except for the fallen plants, the kitchen was neat and tidy. She could see no mud, no footprints.

"Let's see what's inside."

They moved down a hall and into the living room. If this were a TV cop show, she thought, they would have their pistols out, pointed ahead of them, ready to take out the bad guy lurking around the next corner. But there would be no bad guy in the house. If there had been a bad guy on the premises, he would long since have disappeared.

The living room was very much as Carol remembered it from previous visits. Suzanne was even sitting in the same place she had occupied when she told the sheriff that she had disposed of all of Gil's meds. The only difference was that Suzanne now had a bullet hole in her forehead and a streak of dried blood that ran from there down her face and onto the familiar ivory dressing gown.

"My God, she's been shot!" Sam hurried across the room and knelt down beside her, his fingers on her wrist. "She's dead, and probably has been for hours."

Less than twelve hours earlier, Carol had been telling Kevin that she was sure Suzanne had tampered with Gil's meds and that she planned to arrest her tomorrow. It was now tomorrow, and Suzanne would never have to face the indignity of being arrested. An intruder had broken into her house and shot her. In the course of one night's sleep, the sheriff's agenda had been suddenly and dramatically altered. She still had to nab a killer, but she had no idea who that killer was. Back to square one.

"We knew something was wrong, but I never imagined this," Carol said. "Sam, we've got a lot to do, and we have to do it fast. I want you to tell Mr. Hacklin he's to go on home, and that I'll be wanting to talk with him just as soon as I can. That means today."

"Do we tell him what's happened?"

"We tell him that Mrs. Mobley is dead. But nothing about her being shot. I'd rather he not broadcast the news around the lake, but I'm not sure we can stop him. In any event, don't tell him what happened to her, although I suspect he'll have it figured out before noon. So send him back to his cottage or off to work, whatever he should be doing. And take a good look at that rain soaked path. I wasn't paying close attention when we came in, but I'm pretty sure I saw footprints, and if I'm right we're going to want to take casts."

"I think you're right. Funny though, whoever broke in didn't seem to leave any prints or any mud inside."

"Maybe it hadn't started to rain when he got here. I've got to get one or two of our men out here right away, not to mention an ambulance. When you're finished with Hacklin, give me a hand going through the house. I don't like the looks of this."

Carol went back into the living room and what was left of Suzanne Mobley. There had been no sign of a gun, but she poked around anyway, trying to imagine where the shooter had been standing when he fired. Or sitting. A tall glass, half full, sat on the coffee table not far from Suzanne's body. Carol leaned over and sniffed the glass. It smelled of scotch.

She took out her cell and punched in the office number. JoAnne picked up promptly.

"It's me, JoAnne, and we have a problem out here. Mrs. Mobley is dead, and we need help. Who's there?"

"Officer Barrett is just leaving. Everyone else has checked out."

"Catch up with Jim and tell him to join us, right away. The Mobley cottage location is in my desk book. And tell him we're going to have to set up a crime scene and make some casts of foot prints. He'll know what we need."

A few more words sufficed to mobilize the limited forces of the Cumberland County Sheriff's Department, and she turned her attention to the task of removing Suzanne's body. Sam came in while she was giving orders to someone at the West Branch fire and rescue squad garage.

"Hacklin give you a problem?" she asked as she hung up.

'No, but I think he's as excited as a kid who's just gotten his first two wheeler for Christmas."

"Barrett's on his way over, and we'll be sending the body on its way in about twenty minutes. Why don't you start searching the house for any sign that the guy who did this stole stuff or was looking for something. I'll join you as soon as I give the hospital a heads up."

Sam chose to start with the kitchen and its overturned window plants. Carol's call to the hospital was quick and to the point, but her mind was already focussing on something that had bothered her ever since she had first walked into the living room. The intruder had smashed out a large kitchen window to get into the house, yet it appeared that Suzanne had been having a drink in the living room when she was shot. Why had she not reacted to the sound of breaking glass in the kitchen?

The two of them worked their way systematically through the house, room by room. Suzanne Mobley's home looked as if she had readied it for an inspection by a prospective buyer. In only two rooms was it not immaculate. One, of course, was the kitchen, with its broken window and dislodged potted plants. A broken glass, much like the one on the coffee table, lay in the sink under one of the pots. The other was a bedroom. Its closet door was wide open and a red and black bathrobe had been tossed across the bed. More importantly, an elegantly crafted wooden jewelry box stood open on the dressing table. It was empty, evidence that the intruder was a thief and had found what he came for.

"I don't want the ambulance people to trample on those footprints in the mud," Carol said to Sam when they met back in the living room. "They'll be here shortly. Find something and block off that area around the garage until Barrett gets here. I've got one more thing I have to do."

Actually it was three things. She first rummaged through what appeared to be Suzanne's desk, looking for a calendar or something that might tell her whether she had been expecting company the previous evening. Unfortunately, she found nothing to answer that question. She checked the land line phone on the kitchen wall to see if there had been any messages. There weren't any. Very carefully, she patted down Suzanne's lifeless body, in search of what she wasn't sure. But it seemed to be a good idea to do it before the body was turned over to the rescue squad and the hospital staff. The dressing gown contained two large, deep pockets, one of which was bunched up under Suzanne's right leg. The other more accessible one lay across her lap and contained what looked like a digital recording device. She went to the powder room and collected a couple of tissues with which she lifted it from the dressing gown and placed it in her own jacket pocket.

Less than ten minutes later the ambulance arrived, followed within another five minutes by Officer Barrett. Inevitably, the sudden presence of two police cars and an ambulance in the Mobley driveway attracted the attention of people from the neighboring cottages on the West Bluff Road.

The local ambulance team consisted of three people. A stocky middle-aged man who was obviously the team's leader got right to work, acting as if situations like this were a daily occurrence.

"She's been dead for the better part of ten to twelve hours," he said after a couple of minutes with Suzanne's body. "Good looking lady. What a shame. Anyway, there's nothing more to be done here."

"I've alerted the hospital," Carol said. "I was going to say treat her gently, but I know you will."

For the small crowd that had gathered, the transfer of Suzanne's body to the ambulance provided the text for the grape vine gossip which was sure to follow. From their roadside view from above the cottage, the neighbors could see that the face of the person on the gurney was covered, a sure sign that she was dead.

Barrett was soon busily engaged in mixing plaster of Paris in a water filled pot he had borrowed from the kitchen.

"Let's get a cast of several of these prints, Jim."

"We'll need them, because there's something strange about the prints. Can you come here for a second?"

Carol went over to where Barrett was working.

"You probably noticed it when you got here," he said, "but there's a couple of things about them that don't make sense. Look at the tracks the guy made through the mud. See the ones going toward the broken window? He didn't walk straight to the window, did he? It looks like he came from the door step."

He pointed to the prints which followed the wall of the house from the door step to the kitchen window. Carol realized that while she had noticed the prints when she and Sam had arrived, she had not paid attention to where they were coming from and where they were going.

"But when he left the house," Barrett said, "it looks like he came out through the broken window. His shoe prints tell us he was walking away from the house. Now how do you explain that?"

"I see what you mean. Why would the intruder, who'd already broken the window to get in, come back out that window when he could have simply used the door? The prints going into the house I can understand. He tried the door, found it locked, and then took the shortest route to the kitchen window and a way in."

"There's something else." Jim was obviously pleased that he was doing more than making plaster casts of some of these footprints. "I'm no expert in such things, but don't these look odd to you?"

He squatted down near some of the clearest prints coming from the window toward the paved driveway. Carol saw it immediately. The left and right footprints were different, and the left one made a deeper impression.

"It looks like two different people, doesn't it," Barrett said, "one of them a heavier man with more of a boot-like shoe. But that's not possible. There's two kinds of prints, but one is always the left foot, the other the right foot. So there was just one man walking around out here, but he wasn't wearing the same kind of shoe on both feet."

"Jim, you're a wizard. Whoever broke into Suzanne's house was wearing unmatched shoes, and I'll bet he walked with a limp, so that the left foot came down harder than the right. Thank God for that rain last night."

She felt a familiar surge of adrenalin. Suzanne Mobley would never go to trial for hastening her husband's death, but Carol now had a new case to investigate, and she was in possession of her first good clue to the killer's possible identity.

There was still a lot to do. Talking with neighbors about what they had seen or heard last night. Dusting for fingerprints. Barrett would have to stick around until the casts had dried. The crime scene tape would help deter the curious from compromising the area, but his presence would be an even better deterrent. She would have to set up a rotating schedule for her officers to watch the Mobley home, at least for the next few days.

She was also anxious to get a report on the bullet at the earliest possible moment, which meant she would need to contact Doc Crawford and arrange for an autopsy. She'd do that as soon as she got back to the office.

"Sam, I hate to do this to you, but I'd like to leave you with Jim. I don't know the neighbors other than Hacklin, and I'm going over there right now. But we have to see if anybody else heard or saw anything unusual last night. Be sure to ask them if they saw an unfamiliar car parked by the road. It's doubtful that the guy who did this came on foot. I'll send one of the other men out to relieve you and Jim before three, and I'll make sure he has a camera to take some pictures of the place."

"Just when you think you've seen it all, something like this happens," Sam said. "And here I've been telling you to stop worrying about the Mobleys."

"Crazy world, Sam. I'm off to see Hacklin."

Carol was greeted by Mrs. Hacklin, who ushered her into their living room and quickly disappeared into the kitchen to serve cocoa and cookies.

"I want to thank you for alerting us to the problem at the Mobley house," she said when Hacklin joined her.

"I'm glad to be of help. There's been a lot going on down there, hasn't there?"

"I hope you didn't stay home from work on my account," Carol said.

"It's not a problem. I've got one of those flexible schedules, even work from home sometimes." It wasn't clear whether he was pleased with his working arrangement or worried that it would be misunderstood. "I'm sure you don't want me to start asking questions about Mrs. Mobley, but it's really shocking to lose two of your neighbors like that within a month."

"I'm as shocked as you are. You can expect people from my department to be around for a few days. There's a lot we don't know. I take it that you weren't aware that anything was wrong down there until the boy delivering the paper told you about the broken window."

"That's right. We were having breakfast when he came to the door. The kid obviously didn't know what to do, but he'd seen what had happened to the window and thought someone ought to know."

"He did right," Carol said, "and so did you. I'm not going to take much of your time, but there's one question that I need to ask. Last night, did -"

Mrs. Hacklin came in at that moment with the cocoa and cookies. Carol thanked her and invited her to join them.

"Like I was saying, did either of you hear anything in the night that was unusual?"

"Well, there was that awful thunder storm," Hacklin said. "And all the rain on the roof. This cottage is pretty old, insulation not what it ought to be. We had a hard time getting to sleep, what with all the clatter."

Mrs. Hacklin agreed.

"Jenny was actually frightened, wanted to get into our bed."

"Jenny. She's your daughter?"

"Just seven years old," she said, sounding like a proud mother.

"Neither of you heard anything that might have been a gun shot?" Carol had decided it was better to have an answer to that question than to keep the nature of Suzanne's death a secret for another day.

"Suzanne was killed?" Hacklin asked. It was a question, but he didn't sound surprised.

"She was. It looks like she was shot by an intruder, but we don't know yet, so I'd appreciate it if you didn't spread it around. Did you hear a gun shot?"

"I wish I could say I did. But we're two cottages away, and the thunder was real loud. Sounded like it was right over the cottage."

His wife nodded in agreement.

"Are your neighbors, the ones between you and the Mobleys, still away?"

"I don't think they'll be back until just before Labor Day."

Unless Sam had better luck with other neighbors, it looked as if the Hacklins were in the best position to have heard a gun shot. But they hadn't. The first Crooked Lake storm in almost six weeks had been a mixed blessing. It had almost certainly made it impossible to hear the shot to the head which had killed Suzanne Mobley. But it had also muddied the Mobley's backyard, so that whoever had broken into the house had left distinctive foot prints there.

CHAPTER 60

"Quick, get me something to drink," Carol announced as she walked into the kitchen at ten of seven. "No, let me change that. Give me a kiss."

They hugged so long and so hard that Kevin had to ask for a time out.

"It's been a day and a half, has it?"

"Closer to a week and a half," she said, coming up for air. "But you're going to bring me back to sanity. Right?"

"I aim to please. How about that drink?"

"Good. You bartend and I'll slip into something more comfortable."

They had spoken only once since Carol left for the office in the morning, and that was when she had called to say that all hell had broken loose and that she'd be late for dinner.

"It's about Suzanne Mobley. I'll tell you when I get home," she had said, adding "if I get home."

Kevin had uncorked the wine and poured two glasses when Carol appeared in mufti.

"I haven't eaten all day, but I'm not hungry," she said. "I hope you haven't planned something *haute cuisine*. I could settle for soup and crackers."

"We'll do better than that, but it won't be anything fancy. Come on, let's enjoy the wine. You owe me an explanation of what's been going on."

They retreated to the deck, now dry after the rain except for one shaded corner.

"Did I tell you about Suzanne?" Carol asked.

"You told me that whatever had complicated your day had to do with her, but you left it at that."

"Well, what happened to complicate my day was that Suzanne was shot and killed."

Kevin had imagined several possible developments, but this one had never crossed his mind.

"This isn't some kind of joke, is it?"

"I wish it were. But no, someone broke into her house last night and killed her. I'm sure you can understand why it's been such a long and difficult day."

"I'm not sure what's the right word for this. Unbelievable? Incredible? Looks like Mobleys will soon be extinct. I hope you have the energy to tell me all about it."

"I think I do, and I will. Maybe you'll think of something to make sense of what happened."

So Carol proceeded to tell the story of this most unusual 24 hours. The strange footprint patterns in the mud. The broken kitchen window. Suzanne dead, a bullet hole in her forehead. The missing jewelry. The neighbors who neither saw nor heard anything suspicious. With Kevin raising questions at every new revelation, it took her the better part of an hour to bring him up to date. Or as close to it as was possible at this point in time.

"Now it's your turn to make sense of all this," she said.

"What kind of challenge is that? All I know is what you've just told me."

"Yes, but I have the feeling I'm not seeing the forest because of all the trees. What am I missing?"

"Okay, try this. There's one thing I don't understand. I know that it might have been thundering when your intruder broke in. But the way you describe it, that window really got battered, pots flying around the kitchen and so on. There would have been a helluva lot of noise, and she couldn't have missed it. If you'd been in the house, like Suzanne was, what would you have done?"

"I asked myself the same question. I'd have locked myself in the bedroom, called the cops," Carol said. "And being a cop, I have a gun and I suppose I'd have been ready to use it."

"Right," Kevin nodded. "But it looks like Suzanne just sat there, enjoying a drink, until the intruder came in and shot her. Which makes no sense at all."

"I know. It's been bothering me all day."

"Be right back," Kevin said. He got up and headed for the kitchen for more wine. "I think I know what happened."

"By the way," he added as he refilled their glasses, "it may have to be soup and crackers after all."

"Either that or finish the bottle. But don't keep me in suspense. What's your version of what happened?"

"I may be dead wrong, but I'm betting on something like this. The intruder came to the door, knocked or rang the bell, Suzanne recognized him and let him in, got drinks for them, and they sat in the living room and talked about the weather or how the Yankees are doing. Sorry, I just made that up. Chances are they had an argument and he ended up shooting her. He left by the door, walked down to the kitchen window, and smashed it to make it look as if someone had broken into the house and killed Suzanne. She was already dead, so of course she couldn't take defensive measures. And then the killer walked off across the muddy lawn to wherever he had left his car."

Kevin had a satisfied look on his face. Carol said nothing for what seemed like a minute.

"That's good," she finally said, "except that there was only one glass, which says she must have been drinking alone."

"Maybe not. Remember you said that there was a broken glass in the kitchen sink. Her visitor could have put his there, where it got broken when he smashed in the window."

"You may be wrong," Carol said, sounding thoughtful, "but it could have happened that way. It would explain why the footprints between the driveway and the kitchen window show the intruder walking away from the house."

"I kind of made it all up as I went along, but the pieces seemed to be falling into place, so why not. If I'm right, the killer wasn't a stranger, much less a thief. He was someone Suzanne knew well enough to let him in and offer him a drink. Unfortunately, he had a gun with him. Of course we don't know whether he intended to kill her. Maybe he's simply another one of these people who pack heat because it's a second amendment right, and then they get into an argument and shoot somebody."

"I find myself wishing that this was just a case of breaking and entry gone wrong," Carol said. "If you're right, I'm going to have to dig much deeper into the matter of motive. And just when I thought I'd gotten to the bottom of the Mobley saga."

They had just repaired to the kitchen for soup and crackers when Carol let out what sounded like a stifled scream.

"Are you all right?" Kevin sounded alarmed.

"I'm fine, but I just remembered something I'd somehow put out of my mind since this morning. Stupid of me. I'd tucked it away in my jacket pocket and forgotten all about it. It's been that kind of day."

"You'll forgive me for not having the slightest idea what you're talking about."

"I was in the process of going through Suzanne's house, looking for things, taking stock of what was where. She was there dead on the couch in her dressing gown, and I checked the pockets. One of them had one of those small digital recorders in it. I put it in my jacket and proceeded to forget it when Barrett and I started talking about footprints. Let me take a look."

She disappeared into the bedroom and returned a moment later with the device, still wrapped in tissue paper.

"You expect it will have some message about her plans, like maybe she was expecting someone?"

"I don't know how she used the darned thing. Let's eat and then we'll take a look."

———

"This doesn't look that complicated," Kevin said as he studied the instrument. "It shouldn't be too hard to figure out. Half of my students use them, although this one looks a bit more upscale than the ones I see in class. Just give me a minute."

It only took seconds to fit the USB plug into his computer.

"Ready? Let's see if there's anything here."

There was sound, more like a rustling of leaves, but no voice could be heard until suddenly there was a woman's voice.

'That's better, don't you think?'

'You didn't have to change for my benefit.' It was a man, his voice slightly more distant.

'Would you like something to drink? Scotch is my poison.'

'Just water. No ice.'

Then silence, with the occasional small blip of background noise.

'Here you are.' The woman's voice again. 'Now to what do I owe the pleasure, Jeremy?'

Carol sat forward on her chair and started to say something. Kevin put a finger to his lips.

'My wife is out, so I could tell you I needed company. But that's not true. I'm here on serious business, and it has to do with your late husband. As you well know, Suzanne, I've been a practicing MD for quite a few years, and I like to think my medical intuition is pretty damned good. Anyway, I've been doing a lot of thinking lately, and I think you -'

His next words were lost in a flurry of noise which was probably thunder.

'Ah, we are going to have some rain this summer after all,' he said. 'But as I was saying, you should hear where those thoughts have led me.'

There was another clap of thunder, followed by several seconds of silence before he spoke again.

'You killed Gil, didn't you?'

'Are you out of your mind?' Her voice was much louder than it had been before.

'No, I'm -' More thunder. He had probably denied being out of his mind, followed by something which sounded like putting two and two together. 'You didn't stab your husband with a kitchen knife or anything as trite as that, Suzanne. You simply saw to it that he took -'

Carol and Kevin were sure of what Jeremy Sigler was saying even if the thunder drowned out his words.

'That's ridiculous, absolutely ridiculous.' By that point the thunder had become so constant that much of what was being said was unintelligible. But occasional snatches of the conversation came through, including Suzanne's angry insistence that he couldn't prove any of it and his retort that she shouldn't bet on it.

At one point it became so quiet that they feared the recorder had been shut off. But the silence was broken this time by another rumble of thunder, and then by Suzanne's voice. And this time it came through loud and clear.

'You're a lying fool, Jeremy, but worse than that you've been guilty of malpractice. I didn't kill Gil, but you killed a man named Bettenger several years ago, and I intend to -'

Just what Suzanne intended to do could not be head over the storm, but both Kevin and Carol looked at each other in disbelief. Had Sigler in fact killed a patient, and if he had how had Suzanne learned about it? For that matter, how did Sigler know that Suzanne had switched Gil's meds?

'I will not listen to your baseless insinuations.' Jeremy was as angry as Suzanne had been as they exchanged accusations.

'Yes, you will. And you will apologize for - what are you doing?' There was a note of hysteria in Suzanne's voice. 'No, don't do it. We can discuss this like -'

Even with thunder booming over the house, the sound of the pistol shot was unmistakable.

They listened, but there was no more conversation. Neither Jeremy Sigler nor Suzanne Mobley had anything more to say, Suzanne because she was obviously dead and Jeremy because there was no one there to hear him. The thunder storm continued unabated, and it was almost seven minutes later that the recording picked up the sound of glass breaking somewhere off in the distance.

CHAPTER 61

In the years since Carol Kelleher had succeeded her father as sheriff of Cumberland County, violence had been a frequent visitor to normally tranquil Crooked Lake. There were those who had been heard to speculate that this surfeit of violence might be due to the fact that their sheriff lacked the tough, no nonsense persona a man could bring to the job. Carol herself paid no attention to such talk, nor did the overwhelming majority of the locals. After all, the perpetrators of this violence had all, in one way or another, paid for their crimes. None of them still walked the streets of Southport or Yates Center. To a person, they were all dead or serving time in jail, and the sheriff enjoyed the respect of the lake community for having brought them to justice. But Carol was not only respected, she was widely regarded with affection, a local girl who had made good and who had never lost the common touch.

Carol was well aware of all of this, but when she finally crawled into bed on the day after Dr. Jeremy Sigler had shot and killed Suzanne Mobley, she was worried that the respect and affection she enjoyed might now have been put at risk one time too many. Her worries were compounded by the fact that while she was confident that she was right about Suzanne's guilt in her husband's death, she had had no inkling of the trouble that had been brewing between Suzanne and Sigler. Kevin had fallen asleep fairly quickly, but Carol had spent a restless two hours wrestling with one nagging question. How could I have missed it?

The uneasy feeling that had kept her awake the night before was back with a vengeance when the alarm went off the next morning. There's no reason to feel this way, she told herself as she got up and set about making coffee. Forget it that she had been unaware that Suzanne and the doctor had sought to frame each other, him for malpractice, her for murder. All that mattered now was that Sigler had shot and killed her out of fear that she would expose him. The recording made that crystal clear. It would be impossible for him to deny it.

But Carol also knew that it might not be that easy to obtain a conviction. Suzanne had obviously not told Jeremy that she was recording their conversation, and New York was a one party consent state, meaning that she had no legal obligation to do so. But. Carol had practiced law long enough to know that there is always a 'but.' There might well be exceptions to the rule, especially in situations like this where the recorded conversation could have dire consequences. Dr. Sigler would almost certainly seek to suppress the recording. And if he did, the case against him would be much less compelling. Unless, that is, his fingerprints could be found on something like the jewelry box, or the footprints in the muddy yard turned out to be his.

Carol showered and dressed and wondered if she should wake Kevin up. It wasn't necessary. He appeared at the kitchen door, looking very sleepy, as she was flipping the eggs, over easy.

"Want me to make some for you?" she said.

"I think I'll go back to bed, but I had to give you a good luck kiss for your showdown with Sigler."

"I may need it." She let him know that she was anxious. "This one should be easy, but I have a funny feeling it won't be. Strange, isn't it? Without his help I might still not know what Florinef is, and here I am, about to hang a murder charge on him."

"You'll do just fine. And he's not entitled to a break just because he killed a killer."

A kiss and two eggs and toast later, Carol was on her way to the office and Kevin had gone back to sleep.

Everyone except Officer Damoth was on hand when the morning meeting started, and he was keeping watch at the crime scene at the Mobley house. If Carol was anxious, none of the rest of them were. There were five casts of footprints on the big table and an air of expectation in the room.

"I hope today's the last day we'll be discussing Mobleys, but I'm not ready to bet on it," Carol said. "I want to take stock of everything we know and what we think we know about what's happened over the last 36 hours. And then I have a little something to add, something to spice up our morning."

"We're getting a pay raise?" It was Officer Barrett. His colleagues laughed.

Carol smiled and shook her head.

The meeting revisited what had they had learned the day before, with special attention to the strange footprints and the theft of Suzanne's jewelry. Bridges reported on what they had learned from checking for fingerprints, which was very little. Apparently no one had replaced Gloria Garner since her firing, with the result that almost every surface was covered with prints. It was obviously too soon to know whose, other than Suzanne's, they were, but it was doubtful that they would be helpful in identifying the intruder. None of the neighbors had seen or heard anything unusual, and no strange car had been sighted. The excitement which had pervaded the room at the beginning of the meeting had largely dissipated by nine o'clock.

"Now it's my turn," Carol announced. She proceeded to share the news that she had discovered a recording device in Suzanne's dressing gown.

"I hate to admit this, because it may destroy your confidence in me. But in yesterday's confusion, I completely forgot that I'd pocketed it."

"I'll bet you've listened to it though," Officer Byrnes said, eliciting a chuckle from his colleagues. "And I'll bet you saved it for the end of the meeting on purpose."

"I confess. I considered calling you all in for a special meeting last night, but it was already past your bed times so I decided to save it for this morning. Tommy, why don't you connect this in to your computer and we'll listen to it."

It was immediately obvious that something important was afoot. The men eagerly crowded around Byrnes' desk, and it was only a matter of a few minutes before the conversation between Suzanne and Sigler began. Not everything was audible, due to the thunder and, as Tommy explained, the fact that the recorder had been in the pocket of her dressing gown, not out in the open.

As had been the case the night before, however, there was no missing the fact that the two people conversing were antagonists, each in a position to destroy the other. Nor could anyone in the room doubt that a gun had been fired, and that it was Sigler who had fired it.

"Wait," Carol said, silencing her colleagues. "Just listen."

They did, and were rewarded by the sound of breaking glass and crashing pots in the Mobley kitchen.

"That's it," Carol said as she started back to the squad room. "The recorder runs on for quite awhile, but you won't hear any more noise except thunder."

"That would seem to do it," Parsons said as they took their seats again. "The intruder was Dr. Sigler."

"Yes and no," Carol said. "I think it's too soon to throw away these casts that Jim made for us yesterday."

She went on to explain her uncertainty as to whether the recording would be allowed in court.

"So what do we do now?" Sam asked.

"I would like for the two of us to go over to Sigler's. I don't want to tell him we're coming. We can sit in his waiting room if we have to, but I'm determined to talk to him today."

"Are we arresting him?"

"That may depend on how he reacts. But one thing's for certain. He'll be shocked to hear that we have a record of his conversation with Suzanne night before last. If he'd known she was taping him, he would never have left the recorder there. So we have him at a disadvantage."

"Do you think he'll deny it?" It was Parsons.

"That'll be hard to do, wouldn't you say? Especially if we offer to play it for him, which I intend to do."

"Boy, I'd love to see this," Barrett said. "How about all of us going along. We could sort of surround the place, just in case he decides to make a run for it."

"No dice, Jim. Sam and I can manage it. The doctor's a smart man. My guess is he'll be cautious, not say anything incriminating. In other words, he'll fudge the issue as best he can. Anyway, I'm ready to go. You ready, Sam?"

"Just let me use the men's and we're off."

———

When they turned into the doctor's parking lot, there were three cars there. Sam was paying close attention to them.

"Do you know what he drives?"

"I'm pretty sure it's a Cadillac. Black, as I remember it."

"I don't see a caddy. Maybe he's not keeping office hours today."

"More likely it's in the garage. You were hoping to see it with mud on the tires, is that it?"

"Am I that obvious?" Sam laughed. "Nobody around the Mobley place saw the intruder's car, but maybe that's because the rain kept them inside in front of their TVs. Just thought I might get a peek at his tires."

"Hopefully we won't need to examine the car. I'm nervous. How about you?"

"No reason," Sam said. "I doubt he wears his gun while he's doing EKGs."

There were two other people in the waiting room. Carol informed the receptionist that she didn't have an appointment but that she was sure Dr. Sigler would see her. The receptionist looked doubtful.

But when the doctor opened the door to the inner sanctum he came directly over to the sheriff, a smile on his face, and invited her to come on in.

"That's not necessary, Jeremy. Take care of your patients. I promise that we'll keep."

"Well, okay if you say so." He turned to the women who were waiting to see him and motioned to the one with a walker to follow him.

It was nearly forty minutes after they had arrived that Sigler put his head out of the office door and waved them in.

"Good to see you, sheriff. And your colleague, he's -?"

"This is my deputy, Sam Bridges. We appreciate you fitting us in."

"No problem," Sigler said, shaking Bridges' hand. "This has been a slow day. I suspect neither of you is here for medical reasons, so what may I do for you?"

They took seats, Sam across the desk from the doctor, Carol off to the side where she thought she might be able to see Sigler's feet when he swiveled his chair in her direction. Whether his shoes didn't match might be important depending on how he reacted to what she was about to ask him.

"We have a couple of questions, but first I wonder if you have heard about Suzanne Mobley."

"Yes," Sigler said, "wasn't that terrible. Ken Rasmussen called me yesterday. He's been a neighbor of the Mobleys for years. He said she'd been shot by somebody who'd broken in. What a waste of a young woman's life."

"I know," Carol agreed. "First her husband, then her. With Gil's mother gone, too, it's almost as if there was a curse on the family."

Carol didn't believe in any such nonsense, but it seemed like a good conversational gambit.

"I presume you're in charge of the investigation. Any idea what her killer was after?"

"We know he lifted her jewelry. But frankly, we don't think that was what he was after."

"Oh?"

"No, he wasn't a thief. We think she knew something that sealed her fate. We're working on what that may have been."

"That's interesting," Sigler said but left it at that.

The time had come to bear down.

"Incidentally, where were you the night before last?"

The sheriff's question got his attention.

"Where was I?" Her question had been a simple one, not hard to understand. Jeremy Sigler was buying time to think about the sheriff's agenda.

"That's what I'm asking you. We know that Suzanne had a visitor, and we're simply trying to figure whom it might have been. It wasn't a neighbor, and we're sure it wasn't Sheldon Rivers, although that possibility had occurred to me. Suzanne wasn't a social butterfly. Any suggestions?"

Sam looked hard at his boss. She already knew the answer to her question. Was she really going to try to tease the doctor into a confession?

"I'm afraid not. I never knew her as well as her husband."

"I just thought I'd ask. But about my other question. Where were you that night?"

Sigler started to say something, paused, then finally made up his mind.

"A few of us used to play pinochle when Gil was alive. We'd talked about getting together again, and I misunderstood the day we'd agreed on. When I got there, the place was dark. I felt like a fool."

It was not a convincing story, and he knew it.

"It happens to all of us," Carol said. "But for the record, perhaps you can tell us who was going to host this pinochle game."

"Joe Curran. You wouldn't know him. This all sounds familiar, sheriff. Several weeks ago you practically accused me of having killed Gil Mobley. Now, unless I'm mistaken, you're trying to set me up as Suzanne's killer. I don't get it. Just what's your problem?"

"My problem, Jeremy, is that I happen to know that you paid Suzanne a visit the night she was killed."

The color drained out of the doctor's face. She had expected him to be angry. Instead, he looked like a frightened rabbit.

"Where did you get that idea?" he asked, struggling to compose himself.

"I got it from what you yourself said."

"I never said *anything* about being at Suzanne's. What are you talking about?"

"I'm talking about the fact that Suzanne made a recording of the conversation you and she had the night she was killed. Not a phone conversation, Jeremy. A face to face conversation in her living room."

"I don't believe you," Sigler said.

"I can understand that you might not. So I'd like to play that recording for you. Officer Bridges has listened to it. So have I. You deserve an opportunity to hear it, too. We'd like you to accompany us back to Cumberland so you can hear it for yourself. Tell you what, why don't you drive your own car. Sam will go with you. That way, if it turns out to be somebody else we're hearing, I'll apologize and you can come right on back to your office. It will all have been a big mistake."

Sam stole a surreptitious glance at Carol. She's setting it up so I can see what shape his tires are in, he thought, smiling to himself.

Sigler also looked at Carol, but he wasn't smiling to himself. After all, he could hardly refuse to listen to the recording.

CHAPTER 62

Carol had never fancied herself as the Sherlock Holmes of the Finger Lakes. If any of her friends or neighbors, much less any the officers who worked with her, had suggested such a thing, she would have been embarrassed and dismissed the very suggestion as nonsense. For some reason, however, on the evening of the 10th of August she found herself wondering what it would have been like to have a Dr. Watson on hand to chronicle the murder case which had come to its shocking conclusion that very day.

If Kevin had been a professor of literature instead of music, he might have been tempted to tackle the assignment, and if he had, she would, of course, have been the first to discourage the idea. Her reason would have been two-fold. In the first place, there was nothing particularly remarkable about the way she worked. Holmes succeeded, as Watson tells it, because he was a master of the art of deduction. Or was it induction? What she did was simply hard, dogged police work, digging into the nooks and crannies of a case until it became clear who had 'dunnit.' In the second place, what she had come to think of as the Mobley case had not been resolved because of diligent police work. It had come to an end because Dr. Jeremy Sigler had broken down and confessed to the murder of Suzanne Mobley, thereby rendering moot her own efforts to bring Suzanne to justice for the murder of her husband.

The scene which had transpired in the offices of the Cumberland County Sheriff's Department was not preordained. Sigler could have listened to the recording of his conversation with Suzanne and then denied that it had been brought to an end by a gun shot. Perhaps it had just been a particularly violent crack of thunder. He could have claimed to have left Suzanne alive and nursing her drink on the couch, only for her to be surprised later by an intruder bent on theft. He might have claimed that what had been said between the two of them was at best inconclusive. As a last resort he could have claimed that the recording was inadmissible in court.

Instead, after hearing the recording, Sigler had done something which Carol had not expected. He had frankly and almost casually admitted to shooting Suzanne. He had even claimed credit for having rid the area of a clever murderer who stood to get away with it unless he, an experienced physician, had figured out that she had deliberately switched her husband's medications. He had gone on to criticize her every move, including the 'devious act' of changing out of a bulky woolen bathrobe so that she could hide the digital recorder where it could better capture their conversation - in a flimsy dressing gown.

It had been quite a show, right up to the end, when the doctor had said he would gladly go to prison for the death of an unscrupulous, manipulative woman. All he asked was that her crazy and vindictive story that he had once been guilty of malpractice be suppressed. Just why he thought this request would be honored by the defenders of law and order in Cumberland County was not clear. What was clear was that Dr. Jeremy Sigler was much more anxious to protect his medical reputation than he was to avoid a conviction which would send him to prison.

"Sounds like he knew the game was up," Kevin said, "and he thought he might as well get credit for accomplishing what you incompetent law enforcement types couldn't."

They were sitting on the deck, rehashing the day's drama and enjoying a bottle of Crooked Lake's best Chardonnay.

"It was amazing to watch," Carol said. "It was as if he suddenly decided that the best defense was to cast himself in the hero's role. I think he knew it was all over the minute he saw Barrett's plaster casts of footprints on the squad room table. He didn't say so then, but it's my guess that that's when he realized that his biggest mistake was forgetting that his footprints in the mud would be a dead giveaway."

"And you didn't know he had a handicap that required him to wear unmatched shoes."

"Not until today," Carol agreed. "But when you think about it, why would someone dress that way? I can see someone carelessly putting on unmatched socks, but shoes? No way. Unless, that is, there's a reason why he had to. So Sam and I paid special attention to Sigler's shoes today, and to how he walked. And there's no question about it, he's our man. After he admitted shooting Suzanne, I asked him about it, and he confessed that he'd had a birth defect. Club foot, a shorter leg, necessitating one specially built up shoe. He'd lived with it for so long he hardly gave it a thought. In any event, it didn't really matter once he'd heard the recording."

"Does it bother you that he's taking the credit for identifying Gil Mobley's killer?"

"Hardly," Carol said with a laugh. "I'm not all that surprised that he suspected Suzanne. After all, he's the one who found out that Sheldon Rivers' supply of Florinef tablets shrank mysteriously while he was at the lake. But we had the better case, because we knew what he didn't, that one of those tablets was found under the Mobleys' bed. I chose not to tell him. Let him think he's smarter than I am."

"What do you think of Suzanne's accusation about Sigler being guilty of malpractice?"

"I don't know what I should think about it, but I have the feeling that there's something to it. Why else would Sigler kill her? He certainly didn't do it because she had killed Gil. If he was really convinced that she had, why not simply help me build my case instead of killing her? I'm reasonably certain he killed her because of her accusation that he was guilty of malpractice. And because he killed her, I suspect that there's truth to the accusation. How she knew, I don't know. Maybe it will all come out eventually, because I can't believe that Sigler's efforts to squelch her malpractice charge will succeed. If I were prosecuting him for murder, I'd sure want to play that recording in court. Once it's on the record, the malpractice charge is fair game."

"Damned if this doesn't remind me of Hitchcock's *Psycho*. We think it's going to be all about Janet Leigh stealing the money. That's act one. Then we get to act two and it's all about Tony Perkins stabbing her to death in the shower. Not that Sigler is Perkins, of course. But all of sudden it isn't Suzanne's crime we're talking about, it's Sigler's."

"I'm not sure your analogy is the one I'd use," Carol said, "but you've got a point. My case against Suzanne is now moot, and I won't be the one to prosecute Sigler. They'll ask me to testify, but it'll be a brand new ball game. All I've been doing for weeks is worrying about Mobleys, about who if anyone had a helping hand in Gil Mobley's heart attack. Now that's suddenly irrelevant. It's all about Jeremy Sigler."

"Do you wish you'd be getting to prosecute him?"

"No way. Remember *Law and Order*? 'In the criminal justice system, the people are represented by two separate but equally important groups: the police who investigate crimes and the district attorneys who prosecute the offenders. These are their stories.'"

"Nice memory, Carol."

"It's not a matter of memory. If you've heard that line several hundred times, it's burned into your brain. Anyway, there really is a division of labor. I'm the investigator, and I'm glad someone else is going to have to prosecute Dr. Sigler."

"And so our summer of Mobleys is over, is it?" Kevin said.

Carol took another sip of her wine.

"Notice how much cooler it is after that storm?" she asked. "Sunny but no oppressive heat."

Kevin looked across at her.

"You're changing the subject. Does that mean that the Mobley case is still alive?"

"It depends on what you mean by 'still alive.' There are a few loose ends, don't you think?"

"Only if you're determined to go after Rivers as a co-conspirator to finish off Gil Mobley."

"I suppose I could go that route," Carol said, "but I don't plan to. In the first place, he's several hundred miles away and I'm not ready to start commuting to Pelham. But I don't think he knew what Suzanne was up to. If he had been, I can't imagine he'd have been so willing to admit she was paying him visits in the motel after dark. Of course I'll put a call through to him, let him know that she's dead. It'll be interesting how he responds. So it's still possible that I'll want to keep that part of the case open. But not very likely."

"You'll have to be calling Marcus and Carrie, too, I assume."

"I'll do that, but I can't imagine that they'll be particularly upset. Shocked, but I doubt they'll go into mourning."

"What about the elderly Mrs. Mobley's will? With both Gil and Suzanne gone, where does the money go?"

"I don't know, and if the truth be known I don't much care. Officially, Suzanne inherited when Gil died. I have no idea whether she has a will or who gets her money now that she's dead.

Probably Evelyn. After all, she is Suzanne's daughter. I doubt it will be Marcus, although I'll bet Carrie will be demanding that he hire an attorney to see if there isn't some way to reopen the whole issue."

"Do you plan to notify the National Transportation Safety Board?" Kevin asked.

"Interesting thought. I'd temporarily forgotten all about Sutherland. He won't be concerned with Sigler. And inasmuch as we never got to put Suzanne on trial for trying to get rid of Gil, she remains officially innocent of any responsibility for the crash of the Cessna. I never figured on the NTSB jumping back into the case even if we'd proved Suzanne had switched Gil's meds. That he had his heart attack when he was flying the plane was just a matter of chance. But I probably should send Sutherland an FYI."

It was at that point that something else occurred to Carol.

"By the way, there's a rumor going around that another Cessna pilot named Corrigan was going to sell his plane to Suzanne. It looks like that plan is dead on arrival. But I'll bet there'll be Cessnas in the air when the September fly-in takes place. Gil and Suzanne may be gone, but tradition lives on."

"So now we can resume normal living. You can go back to ticketing our lake neighbors for petty misdemeanors. I can actually concentrate on that paper I'm writing instead of the latest Mobley rumor."

"Here's to normal living," Carol said, raising her glass.

Kevin was suddenly on his feet.

"How about starting right now, before supper? Let's take the canoe out. It's been several weeks, and that's a crime in itself."

"Best idea I've heard in ages," she said. "Only one caveat: I get to paddle stern this time."

"Always glad to let our sheriff have the last word."

Kevin grabbed the paddles and followed Carol down to the beach.

CPSIA information can be obtained
at www.ICGtesting.com
Printed in the USA
BVOW06s2152220517
484891BV00015B/103/P